WHISPER
IN THE
NIGHT

BOOKS BY D.K. HOOD

Don't Tell a Soul
Bring Me Flowers
Follow Me Home
The Crying Season
Where Angels Fear

D.K. HOOD

WHISPER IN THE NIGHT

bookouture

Published by Bookouture in 2019

An imprint of StoryFire Ltd.

Carmelite House
50 Victoria Embankment
London EC4Y 0DZ

www.bookouture.com

ISBN: 978-1-78681-547-7
eBook ISBN: 978-1-78681-546-0

For my wonderful husband,
who makes every day a new adventure.

PROLOGUE

Sunday Night

"Daddy, there's a man in my room." Fear closed Lindy Rosen's throat and her voice came out in a croak.

The soft chuckling from the gloom sent shivers down her spine. The figure floated toward her, cloaked in shadows like the Grim Reaper. She dragged leaden legs from the bed and, tripping over blankets, staggered to the door. The sinister figure by her window terrified her. Grasping the doorknob with trembling fingers, she threw open the door and fell into the dark passage, forcing out a cry. "Daddy, help me!"

Heart pounding, she stumbled along the hallway and fumbled for the light switch. "Daddy! He's really here this time, I heard him." She waved frantically behind her. "He's laughing at me."

"Calm down, you'll wake your sisters." Josh Rosen slipped from her parents' bedroom and blinked into the light. "It's just a nightmare, Lindy. No one can get inside, they'd trigger the alarm." He squeezed her shoulder and walked into her room, turning on the light. "Come and see. Look – no one is here and no one can stand outside your window, it's too high up." He gave the room a quick scan then yawned. "If this keeps up I'm going to get you counseling. It's not normal to be having recurring dreams all the time."

Horrified he'd refused to believe her, she gripped his arm. "He was there this time. I heard him."

"I used to dream about snakes eating me alive when I was a kid, so I know it seems real enough." Her father rubbed his eyes. "Get back into bed and I'll get the light. I've an early start in the morning."

With reluctance, Lindy climbed back into bed, peering all around, expecting someone to appear out of the wall like magic. She'd turn fifteen in two weeks and wanted her parents to treat her like an adult. Waking her father over the past five nights hadn't made her the most popular person in the house. She sighed. "Okay, I'm sorry to disturb you again. Night."

"Night. Think of something nice. It will help." Her father closed the door behind him.

As the room fell into darkness, Lindy pulled the blankets up to her neck and screwed her eyes shut. She forced her mind to concentrate on planning her birthday party. Sleep came so close she could almost grasp it. The warm bed surrounded her and she burrowed into the soft pillows, drifting into sleep. *It was just a stupid dream.*

Rustling close by woke her and the hairs rose on the back of her neck at the sound of soft chuckling. Shaking with terror, she opened her eyes wide and peeped over the blankets at the window, where the shadow of the man usually lurked. The moon shone through the drapes, spilling across her rug and landing on her backpack overflowing with schoolbooks. The room was empty. She must have been dreaming again. With a long sigh, she closed her eyes.

A heavy weight landed on her, pinning her beneath the blankets. Air rushed from her lungs and she stared into a horrific ski mask, unable to move. She took a breath to scream but a smelly cloth clamped over her nose and mouth so hard it hurt her teeth. Arms trapped, she tried to buck but couldn't get the weight of him off her. Her mouth filled with something horrid and the strange flavor coated her tongue, burning her lungs as she fought for one tiny breath of air.

The backs of her eyes hurt and the faceless man holding her down seemed to melt into ripples. The laughter had stopped but now the man hummed the lullaby 'Rock-a-bye Baby'. Head throbbing in time to the pulse in her eyes, she gasped in more of the foul odor. Using her last ounce of strength, she tried to fight him but her heavy limbs refused to move and her head filled with cotton. The sensation of floating away crept over her, as if sleep was calling her. She forced open her eyes but the man was a fuzzy blur, then the room faded away to black. *Daddy, help me.*

CHAPTER ONE

Monday

It was a few minutes before lunch, when Sheriff Jenna Alton slid from her cruiser and looked up into a cloudless blue sky. From her position, she could see the vast pine forest, fresh from the recent melt, spreading out in endless miles of various shades of green, and higher still a magnificent eagle circled high above the black mountain peaks. She inhaled the crisp clean air and smiled. Life was good in Black Rock Falls as sheriff and she didn't regret leaving her old life as DEA Agent Avril Parker way behind. Her past life had become an unpleasant memory and her new identity close to ideal.

A big black unmarked SUV slid into the space beside her and she glanced at her second-in-command, Deputy David Kane, an off-the-grid Special Forces agent and profiler, like her living a new life under a different name. The powers that be had placed them and Kane's controller, ME Shane Wolfe, together in the same backwoods town to watch each other's backs. Jenna leaned against her vehicle, surrounded by the picturesque town she had grown to love, and smiled. "It's been so wonderfully quiet since Christmas it makes me happy to be here."

"Shh." Kane grinned at her over the hood of his vehicle. "You're tempting fate." He shut his door, and then headed up the steps to the sheriff's department.

With reluctance, Jenna pushed away from her cruiser and followed him inside. She gave the receptionist, Magnolia (Maggie) Brewster, a smile and taken two steps toward her office door when Maggie held up a hand to stop her, then continued speaking into the phone. She leaned on the counter. "Is something wrong, Maggie?"

"I'll put you straight through to the sheriff, Mr. Rosen." Maggie covered the mouthpiece and her worried brown eyes moved to Jenna. "Mr. Rosen's daughter's gone missing."

"Okay, I'll take the call in my office." Jenna waved at Kane to get his attention, and then pointed to her door. "Grab Rowley."

Jenna had hired Jake Rowley as a rookie when she first arrived in Black Rock Falls. In the last couple of years, he had proven to be skilled and trustworthy. Not having a family herself, she valued the close-knit relationship she enjoyed with him, Kane, and Wolfe and his three daughters.

Seated behind her desk, she took a deep breath, opened her notebook and found a pen that worked before lifting the receiver and placing the phone on speaker. "Mr. Rosen, this is Sheriff Alton."

"My daughter Lindy wasn't in her room this morning and the front door was wide open. We've searched everywhere and can't find her."

"What time was this?"

"Seven." He gave a distraught sob. *"It's my fault; she said someone was in her room last night. I didn't believe her. I figure someone kidnapped her."*

Jenna took down notes. "How old is your daughter?"

"Fourteen."

A too-familiar rush of dread hit Jenna. She took a breath and forced herself to concentrate. There was nothing worse than hearing a child had gone missing. "What time did she wake you and did you go check her room?"

"Of course I did. She's been having the same dream for a week but there's never anyone there. It was late, around midnight, I guess, I'm not sure."

"Have you checked to make sure she isn't at a friend's house?" Jenna exchanged a glance with Kane. "Did she have any reason to want to run away?"

"No, she has no reason to run away. Look, Sheriff, someone's taken her. We've called everyone and searched the ranch and she isn't here or with any of her friends. I'm certain someone has abducted her. Lindy wouldn't leave home without her cellphone. It's never out of her hand. Her bed is a mess and the blankets are in a trail to the door, like someone dragged her out of bed. She's only wearing her PJs and all her clothes are here. It was freezing last night and we're miles from her friends." He took a breath. *"You have to listen to me. We can't wait and see if she turns up, you have to do something now."*

The man was frantic and speaking fast to get his point across. Jenna frowned. "Okay, we'll start a search immediately. Give me your contact information and a description of Lindy so I can get the ball rolling. What was she wearing?"

"Bright pink PJs with white bunnies on them."

She made notes. "If you could email me a recent photograph of her, I'll organize an AMBER Alert and search and rescue immediately. Don't touch anything in her room. We'll be right there to see if there's any evidence of a break-in." She gave him the sheriff's department email address and her cellphone number.

"I'll send her photograph right away."

She disconnected and turned her attention to Rowley. "I'm leaving you in charge while I go with Kane to the Rosens' residence. Take down what I need you to do."

"Fire away, ma'am." Rowley had his notebook open and pen raised.

Nerves rattled with the urgency required for a missing child, Jenna took a deep breath. If someone had abducted Lindy from her home as her father thought, then every second she delayed in searching was crucial. "Right now this is a missing girl, who's likely a victim of a crime. Set up an AMBER Alert and a BOLO, then send out a media release. Contact search and rescue – they'll be able to cover more ground. Register Lindy Rosen on the National Crime Information Center's Missing Persons File. As soon as this story hits the media, you'll have a flood of volunteers; call in Webber to assist you in organizing a ground search of a two-mile radius of her home. See if you can get a couple of forest wardens to assist." She waited for him to stop writing. "Any questions?"

"Nope." Rowley stood and hurried from the room.

Sorting priorities in her mind, Jenna picked up the phone. "Maggie, call the Blackwater and Louan sheriff's departments and inform them we need assistance on a missing child case – we'll need roadblocks set up north and south of the highway. Rowley has all the details."

A missing child needed all the resources she could muster. She ran a hand through her hair, going down a mental list of things she needed to do. The first twenty-four hours were crucial. She called Wolfe to explain. "If it's a kidnapping as Mr. Rosen suggests, we'll need a phone tap or at least a phone to record calls and someone to stay with the parents. I'll need Webber and I'll pull in some deputies from Blackwater."

"I'll supply everything you need for the phone tap. Send me the coordinates and I'll meet you at the Rosens' to do a forensic sweep." She could hear Wolfe throwing things into a bag. *"Make sure the parents don't touch anything."*

"Already done." Jenna chewed on her bottom lip. "I'll call in Walters to handle the phone tap." Her semi-retired kindly deputy would be a good choice to remain with the family and monitor the calls. He'd also keep a record of everyone moving in and out of the house. "We're leaving now." She disconnected and frowned at Kane. "Remind me never to tempt fate again."

*

On the drive to the Rosens' ranch, Jenna received an update from Rowley. In the short time since they'd left the sheriff's department, the local media's broadcast of the missing girl had volunteers flocking into town to help search.

They took the sweeping driveway to the Rosens' ranch-style house and Jenna scrutinized the surroundings. The house was part of Glacial Heights, a new spacious residential area on the outskirts of town opposite Stanton Forest. The houses, surrounded by landscaped gardens of over ten acres or more, were set far apart. The new development on this side of town was popular with the influx of people moving to Black Rock Falls. Mayor Petersham had cashed in on the flood of tourists following the town's serial killer notoriety and announced contracts in his last budget for a ski resort, a whitewater rapids retreat, mountain bike adventures and a stack of new residential building projects.

Jenna glanced at Kane. "It's hard to believe the upmarket side of town has spread this far north in such a short time." She shook her head. "I wonder if the Rosens have security."

"I can't see any signs of a CCTV set-up on the perimeter and the gate is open." Kane slowed his vehicle and scanned the area. "Not that surveillance would help. The expanse of trees surrounding the house would conceal an intruder moving in and out of the property."

Jenna peered ahead. "The tire tracks overlap in the driveway as well. They must've had quite a few visitors recently. They'll all make our list of suspects."

"If the front door was open and the alarm deactivated, I'd say Lindy knew her kidnapper." Kane pulled the truck to a halt and slid from the vehicle, then opened the back door and unclipped his bloodhound, Duke, from his harness. "Duke might be able to track her."

Jenna bent to pat Duke on the head. "I'm sure he will."

She glanced down the long driveway as a white van turned through the gate. "Ah good, Wolfe is here. I figured another set of eyes would help and Rowley told me he's bringing Atohi Blackhawk with him as well."

Jenna had known Atohi Blackhawk for some time. The Native American often came down from the res to work for Wolfe as a tracker and his knowledge of the local area was outstanding.

"How did he drag him down from the res so fast?" Kane slowed and parked on a gravel area close to the house.

"Sheer luck. Atohi pulled up as Wolfe was heading to his van. He'd heard about Lindy on his car radio and offered to help." Jenna slid from the passenger seat. She had only just reached the steps when a man rushed out the door. She took in the man's haggard appearance. "Mr. Rosen?" When the man nodded, she squeezed his arm. "We're here to help find Lindy. May we speak inside?"

"Have you got any news?" Rosen turned his grief-stricken expression to the vehicles in his driveway.

Jenna moved up the steps, keeping a comforting hand on Rosen's arm. "Not yet but we're here to help. This is Deputy Kane and our medical examiner, Shane Wolfe. Atohi Blackhawk has offered to take a look around too and see if he can pick up a trail where Lindy might have gone."

"Medical examiner?" Mr. Rosen's Adam's apple moved up and down as he swallowed. "Do you think my Lindy is dead?"

"There's no evidence to make me believe so." Wolfe stepped forward and offered his hand. "I'm here to hunt down forensic clues to help us find Lindy, Mr. Rosen. We'll work together as a first response team."

Jenna guided Mr. Rosen through the door. "We're doing everything possible to find your daughter, Mr. Rosen. The search and rescue team are out scouring the area and we've alerted the media; if there's a sighting of Lindy, we'll know. The townsfolk in Black Rock Falls are very cooperative and have already formed a search party. I've a very capable deputy running a command post from my office." She straightened. "Is there any place we can talk while my deputies take a look at Lindy's room?"

"Yes, yes of course." Rosen led the way inside the house. "My wife and daughters are in the kitchen." He turned to look at Kane and Wolfe. "Her room is upstairs, first door on the right."

Jenna kept her voice calm and followed Rosen down a hallway. "How many daughters do you have?"

"Three: Lindy, April and June." Rosen shrugged. "I wanted to call Lindy Julia, as in July, but my wife objected. She was bullied at school by a Julia."

The smell of fresh coffee wafted out the kitchen, tainted by the odor of burned toast. Three people sat at the table, all had wet cheeks and red eyes from crying. The two little girls appeared lost and confused and Mrs. Rosen stared into space as if in shock. "Would you like me to call a doctor?"

"No, we'll be fine." Rosen squeezed his wife's shoulder and Mrs. Rosen seemed to snap to attention.

Jenna sat down at the kitchen table and introduced herself, then spoke to them as a group. "Mrs. Rosen, your husband mentioned Lindy was having nightmares. Can you explain when this started?"

"About a week ago." Mrs. Rosen dabbed at her eyes with tissues. "Is this relevant?"

With her mind filled with the implications of what could be happening to Lindy, Jenna forced her demeanor to remain calm and in control. She took out her pen and notebook. Often people became less hysterical if they believed she was taking note of every word they uttered. "Yes, especially as she told you someone was in her room a number of times before she vanished."

"It was the same dream every time." Mrs. Rosen peered at her through red-rimmed eyes. "She woke my husband insisting she saw a man in her room. First she said the man was looking through her window, and then hiding in the shadows."

"Of course, I searched the room and looked under her bed the first four times." Mr. Rosen scrubbed his face as if trying to erase the memory. "The window is ten feet from the ground and there is no access, unless the man has wings. Last night, I didn't look under the bed. I turned on the light, glanced around, then went back to bed." He rubbed his eyes. "We have an alarm system. No one could have gotten inside."

"The lights outside come on and we have CCTV cameras for the immediate area if the alarm is activated." Mrs. Rosen lifted her tear-streaked face. "Wherever she is, she knows the person who took her. She must have deactivated the alarm before she left the house and she would never do that for a stranger." She dabbed at her eyes with a tissue. "I've called everyone we know, and she's vanished."

Jenna took down notes. It would be unusual for a girl to run out into the night in her PJs and without footwear in spring. "Does she have a boyfriend with a vehicle?"

"She knows a number of boys from school with cars but nobody special as far as we're aware." Mrs. Rosen sniffed. "I asked her friends but unless they're keeping secrets, she has no one special."

"Okay, I'll need a list of her close friends and their details." Jenna pushed her notebook toward her and kept a reassuring tone. "They might talk to me."

Jenna turned in her seat as Kane entered the kitchen. "Do you have anything for me?"

"There is a sign of a struggle. The blankets on the bed are disturbed, as if kicked off then dragged toward the door. This isn't something that would normally occur so we have to assume someone was inside the home and dragged Lindy outside." He looked at the Rosens. "Did you hear anything at all last night?"

"No, not a thing, we went right back to sleep." Mrs. Rosen sobbed into her hands. "Oh, Lord, I'd hoped she'd wandered off in her sleep but now I'm sure someone has kidnapped her."

Worry gripped Jenna's gut as she looked up at Kane. "It sure looks like an abduction."

"I've given Blackhawk an article of Lindy's clothing and he's taking Duke to see if he picks up a trail." Kane's attention moved to the parents. "When was Lindy last outside?"

"The girls haven't played outside for some time, it's been too cold." Mrs. Rosen wiped her eyes. "I take them to play basketball in town after school, so they get plenty of exercise."

"That's good – it will make her easy to track." Kane straightened. "We'll need your daughter's diary, in case she mentions anyone in particular, her laptop and cellphone. Wolfe found a few hairs on her bed but there's no sign of anyone gaining entry to her room via the window. The front door locks are intact with no sign of tampering, no footprints outside the house in the garden beds below her window." He rubbed his chin. "If I hadn't seen the bed, I'd figure Lindy opened the front door and left willingly."

Jenna nodded. "I'll follow up with her friends. We might get some valuable info."

"She wouldn't run into the dark in her PJs and she wouldn't leave home without her cellphone, even if she knew the person." Rosen slammed his fist onto the table, making the empty cups rattle. He glared at Jenna. "Think about it, Sheriff! She had nightmares of a man in her room. Do you honestly believe a terrified girl would run out the house in the middle of the night or open the door to let him in?" He glared at her. "No way. She'd never do such a thing."

"No, I don't. As it happens, I agree with Kane but I'm following procedure, Mr. Rosen. I'll call her friends. I understand how upsetting this is for you, but you can rest assured we're doing everything possible to find Lindy." Jenna sighed and looked at Lindy's distraught parents. "We'll be setting up a recording device in case anyone calls with a ransom demand." She patted Mrs. Rosen on the hand. "I'm leaving Duke Walters here with you; he knows what to do if anyone calls. Plain-clothes deputies will be dropping by to relieve him. They'll introduce themselves as 'doctor' – it's a code word for police in these matters. We don't want to alert a kidnapper we're here. I don't want you to make contact with the perpetrator if anyone calls – leave everything to the deputies. Please make sure the landline is free so we can monitor all incoming calls and just use your cellphone. It's unlikely her abductor will have your cellphone number."

She noticed Wolfe standing in the doorway.

"I'll need samples of Mr. and Mrs. Rosen's DNA to match against the samples from Lindy's room, and fingerprints of the family. Was anyone else in Lindy's room over the last couple of weeks?" Wolfe placed his bag on the table and pulled out two DNA kits, then his compassionate gray eyes fixed on the couple.

"Yes, the handyman, Sean Packer, he's here today. We've had the man from the security company, Charlie Anderson, come by as well." Mr. Rosen's hand shook as he pushed it through his hair. "Did you find anything?"

"We found no signs of a break-in but the bed shows signs of a struggle. We have to assume someone abducted her but how they entered the house is a mystery." Wolfe looked at the Rosens. "Could Lindy have invited someone up to her room last night?"

"And leave the front door wide open?" Mrs. Rosen looked incredulous. "No way. Lindy always asks if she wants one of her friends to sleep over, and they wouldn't arrive in the middle of the night."

"Sure. I don't mean to upset you, Mrs. Rosen, but we need to ask these questions." Wolfe passed Mrs. Rosen his notebook. "Could you please give me a list of cleaning products you may have used in her room over the last few days? I've taken her bedlinen to do more tests in the lab."

"Cleaning products?" Mrs. Rosen's expression blanked. "In the laundry, you mean?"

"Anything you may have used in her room or in the laundry." Wolfe handed her his notebook then pulled on fresh latex gloves before opening the DNA kit. "Mr. Rosen, I'll need to swab the inside of your mouth."

After Wolfe had collected the samples and scanned the family's fingerprints, Jenna looked at the strained expressions on the couple's faces. "Wolfe's very thorough. If someone was in Lindy's room, he'll find evidence."

"Have you had any other recent visitors we need to eliminate?" Wolfe glanced at the list Mrs. Rosen had handed him. "Any other tradespeople, family or friends?"

"A few since we came here. I'll give you a list. We employed a painter and a pest control service." Mr. Rosen stared into space for some moments. "We use a gardening service. The Green Thumb Landscaping Service. They send three or four men each week."

Jenna indicated to her notebook. "If you could give me the details, we'll pay them a visit this morning."

"I noticed the handyman waiting in the hallway. I'll go get a DNA sample and his prints." Wolfe picked up his bag and hustled out the kitchen.

"Do you have a monitoring company for your security system?" Kane shuffled his feet. "I noticed you have floodlights, and you mentioned the CCTV is connected to the security system. Do you have a backup copy of the CCTV footage?"

"Not here, no, but we're hooked in to Silent Alarms. Its office is out of Black Rock Falls. If the alarm is tripped they call to make sure we're okay and the cameras come on automatically." Mr. Rosen's expression was bleak. "No one triggered the alarm or they would've called me. They're very reliable. The girls have set it off a few times and the response was immediate. I already called them to check the CCTV footage from last night and there's nothing. They're sending someone out to make sure nobody tampered with the system."

"Are you sure you set the alarm last night?" Kane shrugged. "It's an easy thing to forget."

"I was standing right next to him when he set the alarm." Mrs. Rosen lifted her chin. "It was before I set the table for dinner around six."

Jenna looked at the young girls, maybe five and eight years old, and exchanged a look with Kane. The girls had remained silent as if in shock. "Do your daughters know the code to disarm the alarm?"

"No, only Lindy." Mr. Rosen balled his fists. "All these questions. Shouldn't you be out searching for my daughter?"

Jenna cleared her throat. "I know you're upset, Mr. Rosen, but from the moment you called me we've had people out searching. With everyone out searching the streets, someone has to look in the obvious places, and to do that we need as much information as possible." She waited for Rosen to write the list, and then stood. "Use your cellphone to call your friends in case she shows up. I'll leave now and go speak to the people on this list. We'll never give up. You have my word. I'll call you the moment we hear anything."

As Jenna reached Kane's truck, she noticed Blackhawk moving purposely toward her from the trees with Duke at his heels. She looked at him expectantly. "Please tell me you found something."

"Duke picked up her scent from the family's vehicle and back to the porch." Blackhawk frowned. "I figure she was carried from the house."

"There's no forced entry, so how did he deactivate the alarm and sensors?" Kane stared down at Duke. "It doesn't make sense; someone opened the door from the inside." He took the evidence bag carrying a pair of socks taken from Lindy's laundry basket from Blackhawk. "I'll take Duke inside and work back to the front door." He whistled the dog and headed back inside the house.

"Duke wouldn't have missed a fresh trail." Blackhawk turned to Jenna. "Have the people here left home this morning?" His intelligent eyes scanned Jenna's face. "If not, someone else drove out the driveway, leaving a muddy trail. I followed it back and they parked the vehicle behind those trees. One part of the wheel hit the dirt. It turned on the driveway then drove out, leaving a print on the blacktop. It's damp, so within the last six hours maybe."

Jenna waited for Wolfe to finish loading the evidence into his van, then explained what Blackhawk had found. "I'll leave you to do your thing and go chase down Lindy's friends. I'm afraid I commandeered Webber to assist Rowley with the search."

"That's fine. Emily is on vacation for spring break, so she'll assist me." Wolfe frowned. "Right now, we need to make sense of this and the tire track could be crucial. I'll keep you informed."

"Thanks." Jenna went to leave and then turned back. "How is Emily? It must be great to have her home from college."

"It's nice to have my three daughters back together and with her studying forensic science, her help in the lab is invaluable. She's moving back home next fall. Black Rock Falls College now offers full degree courses for both forensic science and law. She can intern with me as well." He glanced past her, and then indicated down the driveway with his chin. "We have a visitor."

A white pickup pulled in behind Wolfe's vehicle and a stocky man stepped out, wearing coveralls and carrying a tool bag. Jenna held up a hand to prevent him walking to the house. "Just a minute, this is a crime scene."

"Yeah, I can see that, Sheriff." The man's intelligent tawny eyes had smile wrinkles around them as he offered his hand. "I'm Charlie Anderson. The boss sent me out to run some tests on the alarm system."

Jenna nodded. "I see." She turned to Wolfe. "Is this necessary or will you be doing an examination of the system?"

"I'll go along with him and get the results." Wolfe frowned. "It could be faulty. If Lindy walked out the front door, the motion sensors should have turned on the floodlights."

"Not necessarily." Charlie stared up at the house. "It depends which set-up they have – some turn off all the sensors once the system is shut down. Others prefer the floodlights and cameras are on a separate circuit, so folks can go outside without triggering the alarm." He dipped into his pocket and pulled out his cellphone. After taking an age to scroll through an app, he held up the screen to show Jenna and Wolfe. "Mr. Rosen had the remote model with both options. I'll explain."

Wishing he would get on with it, Jenna huffed out a sigh. "Plain English and the abridged version please, I've a lost child to find."

"Sure." Charlie cleared his throat. "The Rosens have a remote in their vehicles so when they arrive home at night they can turn off the alarm but activate the floodlights. Or they can turn them off in daylight." He met Jenna's gaze. "My boss wants me to inspect the system and outside sensors for faults, so I'll need access."

Jenna turned to Wolfe. "Is he okay to go?"

"I've checked all possible access points to the house, so outside won't be a problem." Wolfe turned to Charlie. "Don't enter the house without me, and as you've worked inside the house I'll need your DNA and fingerprints to exclude you as a suspect."

"Sure, but I'll need to check the system first. The entire set-up won't take me more'n a half-hour, then I'll be on my way." Charlie looked at Jenna. "Is that okay, Sheriff?"

"I'm on it." Wolfe shrugged. "The tire track isn't going anywhere." He waved the man toward the house. "Let's go."

Jenna heaved a sigh of relief. "Thanks, Wolfe."

She looked up at the house as Kane appeared at the door with Duke at his side. Kane issued commands and Duke walked to the Rosens' car, then went back inside and sat down. It was obvious Lindy's scent trail had stopped inside and she hadn't left the house. She looked up at Kane. "You don't think she's still inside, do you?"

"Nope." Kane pulled his woolen cap down over his ears. "We searched the house from top to bottom. They don't have a cellar but I pulled down the steps to the attic and looked up there as well. Duke reacted inside her room and the hallway. It must have been the strongest scent from his reaction; like Blackhawk said, he found nothing past the vehicle or he would've reacted."

"Okay. There's not much more we can do here." Jenna shrugged. "Let's go."

They headed back to Kane's truck. She climbed inside and leaned back in the seat. "This is a mystery. Any ideas?"

"We don't have any evidence of an abduction as yet but my gut tells me she didn't run away." Kane waved a hand to encompass the property. "This place would be dark and creepy at night. I can't see a kid who's been scared stupid by a nightmare running out here alone in the middle of the night without turning on the floodlights."

"Me either." A cold shiver skittered up Jenna's spine. She stared into the trees surrounding the house and sighed. "Where are you, Lindy?"

CHAPTER TWO

Sheer terror gripped Lindy as she gasped in breaths of mold-smelling air. It was her greatest nightmare: trapped in the dark and unable to breathe. Her head ached so bad and she wanted to rub the throbbing pain in her temples but she couldn't move an inch. A cold breeze like the tendrils of ivy brushed around her legs raising goosebumps but the smelly air in the room wasn't freezing. Under her thighs, the smooth curve of a wooden chair pressed against her. The tight ropes binding her chest and ankles cut deep into her flesh. Her arms looped the back of the chair and its square corners dug into her biceps. An awful taste coated her tongue and a smell like rotting tomatoes sent waves of nausea rolling through her stomach.

It was an effort to hold up her head and her eyelids seemed so heavy. She hovered between awake and asleep, unable to grasp consciousness. How long had she been here? It seemed like days had dragged by. She was so thirsty and needed to pee. *I have to wake up and escape.*

Forcing her eyes wide, she tried to peer into the damp darkness. A tiny beam of light like a crack in a curtain glistened with dancing dust motes and illuminated a cobweb-covered beam. She clung to that tiny glimmer of light and struggled. The ropes rubbed her skin raw and nothing she tried gave her an inch of slack. Panic came in a rush and she rocked back and forth, gasping in the putrid, stale air. The chair creaked but was too solid for her to topple over or break. Exhausted, she flopped forward and sobbed. Tears blurred her vision and wet her cheeks. An unfamiliar noise came from close by. A motor was running and moments later a blast of stale warm air poured over her. Above her, a single dust-covered bulb attached to a long cord flickered into life.

The darkness had suffocated her but now her heart pounded with fear as she scanned the room in the dim light. The door was way across the other side of the room and there was no way she could get to it. A large plastic sheet, like the ones she'd seen inside the house when the men repainted the family room, spread out under her feet. To her right was a line of bunk beds, covered in a thick coating of dust; to her left a table and chairs. Piles of blankets sat on shelves alongside jars of brown preserves that looked like the specimens in the science lab at school. Dust-laden cobwebs hung like lace curtains from the beams above her head and the rustling sound of vermin came from the shadows.

Then she heard the footsteps.

CHAPTER THREE

On the way back to the office, Jenna went down the list of Lindy's close friends. All were aware she'd gone missing and were surprisingly helpful, but none of them knew of anyone she'd leave with in the middle of the night. She glanced at Kane. "We lucked out there. No boyfriend or anyone remotely close to Lindy, no crushes other than an ex-football player who works at the school but, her best friend told me, all the girls like him and he's never paid any special attention to her."

"Hmm." Kane flicked her a glance. "Maybe we'll need to find out who he is and pay him a visit."

When they arrived at the office, Jenna made out Deputy Rowley surrounded by a crowd of people. He was handing out grid maps of the areas surrounding the Rosens' ranch and giving the searchers stickers to display on their jackets. She waited for him to finish speaking, and then went to his side. "It looks like you have everything organized."

"Yeah, search and rescue have a chopper in the air and we've a couple of park wardens leading groups of volunteers in both directions along the perimeter of Stanton Forest. Webber is out with another group door-knocking Glacial Heights, Maggie is manning the phones and Blackhawk is on his way." He waved a hand toward a group of reporters. "They're doing a live feed and asking for people to call in if they've seen Lindy, to check around their yards and volunteer to help." His worried gaze scanned her face. "So far we've not had a single report of anyone seeing Lindy, not even the usual hoax calls."

"That's not good." Jenna ran the list of men Rosen had given her through her mind; any one of them could have seen Rosen set the alarm. "I want to move fast on this case. I'll leave you to handle the search and we'll hunt down the tradespeople who worked on the Rosens' ranch over the last couple of weeks. I'll do background checks on the way." She sighed. "Keep me in the loop via cellphone. I don't want info leaking to the press via a police scanner."

"Roger that." Rowley turned and headed back to the crowd of people.

Jenna glanced up at Kane. "Okay, who do we visit first?"

The next moment her cellphone chimed a message. "This may be a lead." She moved away from the line of townsfolk and led the way back to Kane's truck.

Jenna leaned against the door of Kane's truck and opened the message. Confused, she stared at the message with a video file attached.

Have you ever been afraid, Sheriff?
You should be.
I am the spider and I've caught a sweet fly in my web.
Now the game begins.
You have six hours.
Tick tock, tick tock.

A storm of mixed emotions rolled over Jenna. She swallowed hard. "Is this someone's idea of a sick joke?" She held up the screen to Kane.

"Nope, that sure looks like a threat to me." Kane frowned.

Jenna's heart thumped in her chest as she stared at the cellphone. She had six hours to find Lindy and if she didn't reach her in time – then what? If this lunatic had involved her in some crazy game and she lost, would Lindy pay the penalty with her life?

CHAPTER FOUR

Trying to formulate a plan to find Lindy was Jenna's first course of action. She passed her cellphone to Kane, unable to look at the message a moment longer.

"There's an attachment. Let's see what he's sent you." Kane gave her the phone.

Unease slid over Jenna as she opened the file and shielded the screen to view the display. As the video file played, she stared at it in horror. "Oh, dear Lord, it's Lindy."

In a dark dingy room, Lindy sat tied to a chair. The young girl's head hung down. Ropes bound her but Jenna noticed a slight movement of her head. "I think she's alive. Someone is holding her prisoner. Holy shit, this place could be anywhere." She glanced at her watch. It was nine-thirty.

"Show me." Kane took her cellphone and replayed the video. "Dammit, it's a private number, probably a burner. If we take it to Wolfe, he'll check it out and be able to enhance the video. He might find something in the background to link to the kidnapper. What the hell does he mean by, 'you have six hours'? Is he giving us a time limit to find her?" He handed her back the phone. "And if we don't?"

"I don't know but it sure doesn't sound good. I don't like playing games with kids' lives." She stared at the TV crew. "I'll make an announcement only the kidnapper will understand. I'll say we're open to negotiation for Lindy's safe return."

"Yeah, if we get a dialogue going we'll know what kind of a person we're dealing with." Kane followed her to the TV crew. "Make sure you keep using her name. To him she's a commodity and her life's worth nothing."

Jenna explained to the reporters what she needed and made the statement live to air. She walked away from the persistent questions and went to Kane's side. "I hope I've gotten the message across."

"You did great." Kane led the way to his truck.

"We'll know if he calls again. Come on, we need to get this video to Wolfe; the clock is ticking." Heart racing, Jenna pulled open the door to Kane's truck. "I'll call Wolfe. I gather he still has his tech gear at home?"

"As far as I know." Kane slid behind the wheel.

Jenna nodded. "Do you still have some of Lindy's clothing for a scent for Duke to follow?"

"Yeah, in an evidence bag in the back." Kane patted Duke on the head. "He'll find her if we get close to her location."

Panic rose in Jenna's throat. Lindy could be anywhere in the vastness of Black Rock Falls. In spring, the air temperature was cold to freezing. Patches of snow still lay in the forest and covered the mountains. Intricate patterns of frost swirled over the windows each morning. The kidnapper had taken Lindy hours ago; she was alive but dressed in PJs and with nothing on her feet, she could die of exposure. "Drive."

"From what I can see, the kidnapper's holding Lindy in a disused cellar or old building." Kane started the engine and turned onto the busy main street. "When you're chasing down the people who visited the Rosens' home, find out if they own any old properties."

"There are hundreds of possibilities in town and in the forest. I'll call Wolfe, then Maggie. I'll ask her to make up a list of any possible places and we'll search them first." Jenna listened impatiently for

Wolfe to pick up then brought him up to date. "How long will it take you to finish up? We need info on this video yesterday."

"I'm on my way."

Mind reeling, Jenna turned to Kane. "Give me something, Kane. I've never dealt with this kind of crazy before; if he doesn't call back, how do we negotiate with him?"

"We can't. His message only gave us a time limit to find her. You've offered negotiation and we'll have to wait and see if he responds." A nerve in Kane's cheek twitched. "My first instinct would be to divert the volunteers to the old buildings as well but that might cause a problem. We don't know what game he's playing." He rubbed the back of his neck. "Right now Lindy's alive, and if a search party stumble over his hiding place he might panic and kill her. It's a catch-22 situation. I suggest you make it clear the teams must approach all suspicious places with caution."

Worry for Lindy's safety cramped Jenna's stomach. The image of the poor girl flashed through her mind in a constant rerun. "The kidnapper would've already seen the search and rescue chopper in the air, so it's a bit late to worry about that now. I'll send Rowley and Webber out with them. They'll be able to reach more properties in the shortest time."

"As long as they have a place to land." Kane took a backroad and accelerated, bypassing downtown and heading for Wolfe's house. "We'll need more information to pinpoint the location. It's almost noon now. I hope Wolfe finds something we can use."

"It would sure make life easier." Jenna scrolled through her list of contacts on her cellphone. "I'll tell Maggie to feed the list of suspect properties to the search parties as she finds them – it will save time – then I'll call the FBI and see if they can send assistance, but we'd be lucky to get one field officer at such short notice." She made the calls, then sucked in a deep breath and contacted Mr.

Rosen. "Mr. Rosen, this is Jenna Alton. I'm afraid to tell you we've received a video of Lindy from her kidnapper. She's alive and we're doing everything possible to discover her location."

"Oh my God." Rosen cleared his throat. *"Did he make any demands?"*

"Not yet." She glanced at Kane. "I'll contact you the moment we know anything." She disconnected. "You know, this case seems familiar to me in an odd way. I worked a case involving a drug dealer. He'd send images of himself in a Halloween mask selling drugs outside cop stations, schools and churches. It was as if he wanted us to catch him, and then one day it all stopped. We never discovered his identity."

"Classic narcissistic tendencies. He wanted to make sure he received all the attention so he made a game of catch-me-if-you-can with the cops. He would've loved being mentioned in the media, it fed his ego." Kane pulled up outside Wolfe's home. "Likely he overdosed on his product."

Jenna sighed. "Maybe, or escalated into something else."

"Possible." Kane turned in his seat. "Ah, here's Wolfe. If there's anything on that video, he'll find it."

Huddled around Wolfe's desk, Jenna and Kane watched Wolfe manipulate the film. His equipment came straight from the FBI and was the latest design with all the bells and whistles. Jenna listened intently to Wolfe's narration.

"There's not much to see. The camera is on a tripod angled down to give the narrowest of images. With only one small dim light source the background becomes pixilated." Wolfe zoomed in on the floor. "Plastic sheeting on the floor and the chair is straight-back wooden, like one found in most homes. It's reasonably old, maybe twenty or more years."

Jenna peered at Lindy. "Can you see if she's injured?"

"There's no apparent bloodstains on her clothes and her face appears untouched. From what I can see, her lips aren't blue. The ligature marks on her ankles and arms indicate the ropes around her are very tight but, where her arms are bare, she doesn't have goosebumps." Wolfe glanced at her. "So we're looking for an occupied house or one with heating."

"Can you isolate the background sound?" Kane leaned forward. "I thought I could hear machinery."

Moments later, the humming sound of a motor came through the speakers. Jenna listened intently. "Generator?"

"I don't think so." Wolfe's brow wrinkled into a frown. "More like an air conditioner used to heat the cellar and change the air, so this place is used frequently."

"Maybe not." Kane pointed at the screen. "Look at the rungs on the bottom of the chair. If someone had sat on the chair recently, there wouldn't be dust on them." He moved his attention to Jenna. "Most kids would put their feet on the rungs, this makes me believe she was unconscious when he placed in the chair and tied her up."

Jenna reached for her cellphone and called Rowley. She could hardly hear him with the noise of the chopper. "We believe the building where the cellar is located is occupied."

"It's hard to hear you, ma'am."

"I'll text you." Jenna thumbed in a message and waited for him to respond. Once his reply came through she looked at Kane. "They're doing a grid search north of Stanton Forest and working back to the Rosens' property. The wardens are working through the forest checking cabins heading north and they have two rangers on horseback heading south. Blackhawk and a team are heading west." She scrolled through the file Maggie had sent to her earlier. "We'll head south into the grasslands, I have a list."

"Roger that." Kane pushed to his feet. "Come on, Duke, let's get that nose of yours working."

Jenna stood and turned to Wolfe. "I'll leave you to it. If you find one shred of evidence to narrow this search, call me."

"I always do, Jenna. I'll keep the track on your phone as well but I doubt he'll use the same burner twice. Finding him via the calls will be impossible but I'll keep trying." Wolfe frowned. "I suggest you put out a media report saying you want people to call in if they live in an older home with a root cellar and you're sending out deputies to check each one." He shrugged. "You'd eliminate a whole bunch – no way would the kidnapper be calling from his hideout."

As usual, Wolfe's cool-headed way of looking at situations gave her an advantage. "Sure, I'll call it in now." She put through the call and updated her team with the new situation, then hurried to Kane's truck.

She climbed inside and explained. "I figure calls will start coming in real fast." She glanced at her watch. It was close to two. "We'll head south and wait for Maggie to update the list."

"Roger that, where to?" Kane started the engine, and then frowned. "I think Emily wants a word with you."

Jenna buzzed down her window and smiled as Emily, Wolfe's eldest daughter, ran toward them. "Do you need to speak with me?"

"Yeah." Emily handed a Thermos and a brown paper sack to her. "Turkey on rye and coffee. I figured, like my dad, you all won't have eaten since breakfast."

Jenna gladly took the offering. Kane's stomach had been rumbling for the last hour. "Thank you so much. We'll see you later."

"Thanks, Emily." Kane smiled at her. "Don't forget to feed your dad."

"As if." Emily gave them a wave and headed back to the house.

Jenna's cellphone beeped a message. It was from Maggie. She scrolled through. "No list of possible residences yet but the mail-truck driver called the hotline with a lead. He noticed a pickup on Goldmine Road heading toward the old brickworks around two this morning. Apparently, there is an old manager's house out there. It was rented by a recluse who died three months ago and likely has a root cellar." She added the coordinates to the GPS. "Okay, let's go."

CHAPTER FIVE

He cracked open a bottle of beer and took a long drink as he watched the live news coverage of Lindy Rosen's kidnapping. He grinned at the sheriff's pleas for negotiation. "Huh? As if I'd be so stupid. The idea is for you to find me. Tick tock, Sheriff, tick tock."

The cops were running around like ants after honey and moving in different directions with no clue to where he'd hidden the girl. They'd nothing to go on, no description of his truck, not one fingerprint, zip, nada, and why? Because he was a master of deception. Having the talent of being able to merge into the community without a hint of anyone discovering his secrets made him special, like a super-villain in a comic book.

He liked that he blended in, he was ordinary; it made the game of deception so much sweeter but messing with the sheriff's mind was the bonus. Sending her the clip of Lindy all trussed up was only part of his plan to outwit the sheriff and her bunch of deputies. He'd watched them strut through town like they were superior, but he was the special one. Not many had a mind like his, or the smarts to keep one step ahead of law enforcement. This wasn't his first kidnap. It was too easy and in Black Rock Falls, he wanted to up the ante. He needed a challenge, a buzz of excitement to add to the thrill, and with Sheriff Alton batting a thousand since taking office against the other so-called serial killers she might supply what he craved. Hey, any fool could kidnap and murder but he'd twenty-seven notches on his belt and wanted to make his score at least thirty by summer.

He sipped his beer, and then replayed the video of Lindy. When she'd woken, he'd seen fear in her eyes and loved the way her bottom lip trembled. They were all different – some cried and begged and others spat and screamed at him. Others were quiet, as if they'd accepted their fate. He grimaced. The passive women gave him little pleasure and he preferred the ones with attitude. Hell, Lindy had been terrified of him in her bedroom and the frightened ones always promised a good fight.

Excitement fluttered in his stomach. The lead-up to the kidnapping had been exciting, walking into a house and taking his prize divine – but the kill… He moaned in ecstasy, sucked in a deep breath and let it out in a low whistle. The kill he savored.

CHAPTER SIX

Sinister shadows bathed Stanton Forest by the time Kane drove onto the on-ramp to the highway. He glanced down at the GPS and flicked on lights and sirens. Until they got within a mile of Goldmine Road, he needed to haul ass. He hit the gas, enjoying the way the engine roared into action, the front lifting with the power and the tires gripping the highway as they accelerated to eighty then cruised at a hundred mph.

As they left Stanton Forest way behind, grasslands stretched out in an endless expanse of fresh bright green. On this side of town, the grass would turn yellow, left untouched by cattle. Too many old mineshafts littered the lowlands to risk grazing animals. Industry had taken over and various industrial plants dotted the countryside like clumps of mushrooms. He glanced at Jenna. All business as usual, she seemed unusually quiet. "You okay?"

"I guess." Jenna moved around in her seat. "It's because this case stirs up a heap of old memories I'd rather forget." She cleared her throat. "I know first-hand how it feels to be trapped in a confined space, tied up and ready to die by the hand of a lunatic."

Aware of her frightening experience – when two men she'd trusted kidnapped her with the intent of raping and murdering her – and the PTSD that followed, Kane squeezed her hand. "Yeah, but we made it in time to save you and we didn't have a deadline. You're doing everything possible to find Lindy."

"I'm frightened we're not going to find her in time." Jenna let out a long sigh. "I feel like we're being played."

Kane switched off his siren but kept the blue and red lights flashing to warn other motorists. "It's possible. This guy is different to most kidnappers. He hasn't made any demands."

"How many types are there?" Jenna turned to look at him. "And where does he belong?"

He flashed past an eighteen-wheeler as the GPS announced Goldmine Road was four miles ahead on the right. "There are so many types it's hard to place him in a category. Most who follow his pattern want something – money usually – or why send the video?"

"So if not money, what does he want?"

Kane glanced at her. "I've no idea. Usually, when they abduct a victim the last thing they want is contact with law enforcement, so I figure we can rule out someone who wants a child sex slave or a quick kill. He's made no demands but has made contact for a reason." He sighed. "If he doesn't make any requests within the time limit, we'll have to think outside of the box." He shot her a look. "Perhaps he's using the kidnapping to get to you."

"I don't think I've upset anyone lately." Jenna's mouth turned down. "But then being sheriff is a good enough excuse for some." She straightened in her seat and gave him a determined look. "Okay, we go in using stealth and I'll inform the other teams to do the same." She called Maggie to ask her to contact everyone with her new orders. After disconnecting, she turned to him. "Don't be a hero. The grasslands have the same laws as the mountains; you'd be surprised how many people have gotten themselves killed walking onto people's property unannounced."

Kane smiled at her. "With you to watch my back, not a chance."

He slowed to take the corner and turned off the lights. The GPS informed them the address was 500 yards on the left. Kane slowed to a crawl and peered through a line of trees, searching for any telltale signs of inhabitation, but no smoke came from the chimney and vegetation grew right up to the front porch. As they approached the gate, Kane looked at Jenna. "It looks deserted; this would be the perfect place."

"Yeah, but I didn't see a truck." Jenna picked up the radio mic and called in their position. "Let's take a look."

Kane scanned the immediate area, searching for tire marks or disturbed brush, but found nothing notable. He kept to the tree side of the driveway, using the shadows as cover, then stopped behind a clump of trees about twenty yards from the main house and turned to Jenna. "There could be another way in here; there are dirt roads all over this area and he could be hiding his vehicle in the barn."

"I noticed a few tracks along the highway heading this way." She jumped out the truck and pulled her weapon. "We'll check the barn for a vehicle first, although he could've left her here and be holed up anywhere."

"No doubt watching the search on TV." Kane grimaced. "Having media coverage telegraphing our every move doesn't help." He followed her from the truck with Duke close on his heels.

"Take a few seconds to listen." Jenna stopped under a tall pine. "We heard the distinct sound of a motor running on the video."

"It'll be hard to hear anything now the wind is picking up." Kane moved to her side, sliding his Glock from the holster, and they crept closer using the tree line for cover, then stopped a few yards from the house to listen. A crisp fresh breeze brushed his face, stirring the long grass and bringing with it the unique smell of wilderness. The scent of fresh pine and wildflowers filled the air with no odor of inhabitation. High above a golden eagle circled then dived down to pluck a small critter from the ground before soaring into the air but no sound of a motor broke the silence.

"I can't hear anything." Jenna gave him an enquiring look. "You?"

"Nope." He shrugged. "That means nothing. He could turn off the air conditioning but I'm not sure this place has power. It must be over a hundred years old." He stared back at the road. "There are power lines but they don't come to this site."

"There are industrial machinery plants in this area, and potteries. I'd say they've had power here for a long time." Jenna slid into the shadows of the trees. "I hear there're plans to set up wind farms in the grasslands on this side of town. It would be a lucrative investment in land useless for cattle grazing." She stopped walking and pushed a lock of raven hair behind one ear. "There's the barn, we can slip around back and use it for cover."

"Roger that." Kane followed close behind.

He admired how Jenna took the lead, moving forward into danger boots and all. She'd good reason to use him as a shield; many times in the past she'd become the target of a deranged lunatic. He had to admit he'd willingly take a bullet for her and, after coming close to death recently, she'd proved to be of the same mind when it came to his safety. Ahead, long shadows extended from the trees to the barn and without making a sound, Jenna dashed across the open space. With her back flat against the wall of the barn, she waved him forward. He did a visual scan of the house and blended into the bushes to get a better look. Darkness bathed the front porch but he could make out movement at the front door.

With every muscle on alert, he held up a hand to Jenna and indicated he'd seen something. She followed protocol and slipped into the shadows. He pulled out his binoculars and scoped the house and front porch. The door stood slightly ajar then moved again before closing. No one appeared at the windows, not one sound came from the house. He waited a beat, then took a deep breath and sprinted to her side.

"What did you see?" Jenna's eyes looked huge in the dim light as she peered up at him.

He lowered his voice to just above a whisper. "The front door opened a few inches then closed. I didn't see anything else, no face at the window, nothing. It could have been the wind."

"I hope the place isn't haunted but since I've lived in Black Rock Falls I guess anything is possible." Jenna shuddered. "I can deal with the living and the dead but ghosts are a whole different ballgame."

"Ghosts, huh? Nah, if they existed they'd be hounding me for sure." Kane pulled the evidence bag from his pocket. "I'll see if Duke can pick up a scent." He called the bloodhound to his side and pressed the pair of Lindy's socks to his nose. "Seek."

When Duke sniffed around, then came back and sat at Kane's feet, he looked at Jenna and shook his head. "Nothing. She's not been here."

"Maybe the kidnapper carried her from his vehicle to the house." Jenna stared down at Duke. "Or Duke's scared of ghosts." She patted the dog on the head. "Trust me. I don't want to go inside that creepy place either."

Kane hadn't seen this side of Jenna before and if not for the urgent need to find Lindy, he'd take time to discuss her fears. "There's a side door just ahead." He glanced at his watch. "Three hours to deadline, we need to move along."

Jenna gave him a curt nod and moved swiftly along the side of the barn, hardly making a sound. He followed close behind, ears straining for any sound of movement inside, but heard nothing. They reached the door and squatted down, one on each side. "See if it will open. I'll cover you."

"Roger that." Jenna turned the doorknob and the old wooden door creaked open, making enough noise to alert the entire neighborhood. "Shit."

Kane turkey-peeked around the door. Inside, a thick coating of dust covered the floor and rats scattered away from the light, disappearing into dark holes. It was empty apart from a dilapidated saddle hanging over the gate to a stall. No one had been inside for a very long time. "I'd say it's just the rats and us." He straightened and holstered his weapon.

"No root cellar here either." Jenna stood and peered inside. "We'll do a quick recon of the house. It might have one in the pantry." She indicated to the barn doors. "I guess we can get to the house through there."

A sense of foreboding washed over Kane. His gut instinct never let him down and walking onto the porch after seeing the door open and close could be suicide. He touched Jenna's arm. "Not so fast. It could be a trap. I figure it would be safer to go around back." He turned to Duke. "Stay."

"Sure." Jenna walked back out the door, and then sprinted along the side of the barn. She stopped and looked back at him and pointed to her ear, then placed a finger to her lips.

Kane fell into combat mode. He pulled his weapon and dashed to her side, taking in his surroundings in one quick scan. He stared at her pale face and listened. Faint strains of music carried on the breeze and every hair on his body stood to attention.

CHAPTER SEVEN

A shiver ran down Jenna's spine as she peered around the corner at the old ranch house. The weather had long ago stripped the paint from the log building and moss covered what remained of the wooden shingles. Untidy birds' nests and sprigs of green plants filled the gutters as if nature was claiming the old house back. Shutters covered most of the windows but as they edged their way along the wall of the barn, the back of the house came into view. A window stood open and its torn lace curtains flapped in the wind. Music, very soft, seemed to hover on the breeze. She pressed her back against the wall and turned to Kane. "There's an open window. The music seems to be coming from there."

"Could be someone taking advantage of the adverse possession law." Kane raised an eyebrow. "Although, it sure doesn't look like someone is making improvements but it would be a perfect place to hide Lindy." He peered at the house. "Something doesn't feel right."

"I know what you mean, this place is spooky." Jenna met his gaze. "If it wasn't for Lindy I wouldn't go near it."

Torn between hammering on the door and erring on the side of caution, Jenna eased away from the barn and aimed her Glock at the back door. "Sheriff's department. Show yourselves or we're coming in."

They waited.

Nothing.

Jenna called out again, louder this time, but the only thing coming from the house was the music. She turned to Kane. "What do you think?"

"I can't see any tripwires." Kane moved the binoculars from side to side. "Put a few rounds at the bottom of the steps. If there's a pressure plate, that's where it will be."

Jenna aimed and sent four shots into the ground, sending up a cloud of dust. The sound of her weapon firing echoed around the buildings, announcing their presence, and the wind whipped the dust into dancing spirals. She called out again, and then moved with caution across the open yard to the back stoop. The dried remains of a rambling rose bush wrapped around the handrail and pulled at her clothes as she placed each foot with care on the rotting step treads. The eerie music set her nerves on edge and sounded so ghostly she had to push through her fear of the unknown to make it onto the porch and wave Kane forward. They took positions either side of the door, and heart pounding, she reached for the doorknob. It turned and swung open with a grind of rusty hinges. She waited a beat then turkey-peeked around the door. Relieved no one had set up a shotgun to kill an intruder, she scanned the small mudroom. Her gaze moved over a grime-encrusted sink to an old kerosene lantern hanging on a rusty hook. Cobwebs filled every corner of the small room but another door blocked her view into the kitchen. "Sheriff's department."

Nothing, no creak of floorboards, only the lilting scratchy sound of an old melody that she found strangely familiar and the flapping of curtains against the window frame. She looked at Kane's professional façade and his eyes blazed a warning. Her heart picked up and raced. "Let's take a look."

Jenna sucked in a deep breath and grasped the knob. It turned but the door didn't move. She rammed it hard with her shoulder. "It's stuck."

"Give me a try." Kane moved into the small room, grabbed the handle and slammed his shoulder into the door. It whined and moved a few inches. "I figure something's blocking it."

"I'll take a look through the window." Jenna turned, holstered her weapon and sprinted around to the open window. "Come on, time's running out."

"I'll have to lift you." Kane stamped down the bushes under the window, and then bent down. "Get on my shoulders."

Jenna walked her hands up the rough log wall and peeked in the window. "There's a chair pushed under the doorknob." She pulled open the window and gripped the weathered frame. "Can you push me up?"

"Sure." Kane's palms slid under her feet. "One, two, three."

Hoisted up, Jenna wiggled through the window and crawled over a filthy counter, then dropped to the floor. She had the chair removed and door open as Kane thundered up the steps. The music stopped, and then a few seconds later started again. She pulled out her weapon. "Sheriff's department, come out. I know you're in here."

Only the scratchy sound of music came again. She looked at Kane. "Let's clear the rooms. I figure someone's playing games with us."

"Roger that." Kane shadowed her across the room and they cleared the pantry. "No sign of a root cellar entrance in there."

They checked the two bedrooms and found nothing but old furniture and dust mixed with a good layer of rat droppings.

Jenna slid along the passageway to the family room – and stopped dead. The hairs on the back of her neck stood up and she blinked in disbelief. "T-tell me I'm not s-seeing that." Horrified, she pointed her Glock toward a rocking chair, creaking back and forth. Beside it on a table was an old electric gramophone playing a record.

"I'm seeing it too." Kane moved beside her and the chair stopped rocking. He moved to one side of the doorway and it squeaked back into action. "Okay." He moved to one side again. "The breeze from the kitchen window is moving the chair. The hall is acting like a wind tunnel."

Jenna swallowed hard. "So how is the record playing? There's no power to the house."

"I'll take a look." Kane walked across the room, his boots clattering on the bare floorboards, and examined the wiring. "There's a battery pack with cord running up through the ceiling. I'd say there's a small solar power unit somewhere on the roof. The record player is set to repeat, so it keeps on playing." He shrugged. "No ghosts."

Trying to ignore her pounding heart, Jenna walked over to the front door and pulled it open. "This has been a complete waste of time. Lindy has never been here. I'll call this in. Grab Duke and we'll get back on the road." She glanced at her watch. "Two and a half hours before deadline and we have zip."

The sun was heading for the horizon and a promise of a cold night blasted Jenna as she stepped from another old barn and brushed the dust from her clothes. The teams had searched the properties of every possible place. All the ranch owners had willingly allowed them to enter their properties without a search warrant, which was both encouraging and worrying at the same time. If Lindy's kidnapper did have a place off the grid, he'd be confident and likely act nonchalant, knowing they couldn't discover him. The frightening aspect was that none of the search parties had found a trace of Lindy. Worry for the young girl pushed Jenna to keep going without a break. She straightened and dragged weary legs back to Kane's truck. He'd given Duke a drink of water and glanced up at her as she leaned against the hood and grimaced. "We've looked at four places on this side of town and the team have moved their search to cover as many known buildings as possible. It's like looking for a needle in a haystack."

Her cellphone signaled a message and she peered at the screen. Waves of horror smashed over her at the displayed text.

Too late.

CHAPTER EIGHT

Confused and dismayed, Jenna stared at the screen of her cellphone. "It says we're too late." She looked at Kane. "There should be an hour left."

The cellphone beeped again and an image appeared. With shaking hands, she held out the phone for Kane to see the picture of an ashen-faced Lindy, sitting on a moss-covered wooden bench outside an old dilapidated building. "Oh, my God, it's Lindy." She handed Kane the phone and rubbed both hands over her face. "And we still don't know where she is."

"I recognize this place." Kane frowned over the screen. "I drove past it with Rowley one day. I'm sure it's an old schoolhouse some ways from the Triple Z Bar."

"I'll call Rowley and get the chopper over there." Jenna ran around the hood and jumped into the seat. "There's a chance she could still be alive."

"I don't think so." Kane had enlarged the picture and was shaking his head. His eyes held a tragic expression "There's something tied around her neck and her lips are blue." He slid behind the wheel and handed back her phone. "It's too late, Jenna, and if you want a modicum of dignity for her, call Wolfe to meet us there incognito. If the chopper heads out that way, the media will be crawling all over the place before we get there and we'll need to preserve as much evidence as possible."

All the energy seemed to seep out of Jenna as she stared at the forlorn figure sitting on the lichen-covered bench. She'd failed to find Lindy in time. Kane was right – the girl deserved some dignity. She fought to push out words over the lump in her throat and not scream out in anguish. "Okay, I'll call him. We'll need coordinates. Get going, I'll get the location." She sighed at his obvious reluctance to leave. "What are you waiting for? She's out there all alone and the crows could be eating her."

"Jenna." Kane pulled her against his broad chest and stroked her hair. "You're not to blame. We did everything humanly possible to find her."

Unable to hold back a sob, she inhaled his comforting open-air scent. She could always rely on Kane to calm her shattered nerves. Brushing back tears, she straightened and regained her composure. Being exhausted was no excuse to fall to pieces. She had to find this SOB and bring him to justice. The stark reality of the circumstances around Lindy's kidnapping slammed into her. The kidnapper was playing a game with her and, this time, he'd won. She looked up at Kane. "He's going to do this again, isn't he?"

"Yeah, he is." Kane removed his arm from around her shoulders and started the engine. "But next time we'll be ready for him."

As Kane slowed to turn onto the road leading to the old schoolhouse, he glanced at Jenna. Not many crimes got under Jenna's skin but she'd switched off her compassion and fallen into her professional, almost robotic mode. Her calls had been concise and to the point. She'd instructed Rowley to make sure the media circus was way over the other side of town by landing the chopper at the next old property on their list and remaining there. Wolfe had slipped out of town taking the backroads and would be arriving at the crime scene soon. They'd decided to avoid using the two-way as the media and many others owned scanners. When Jenna's cellphone chimed, he glanced at her. "Wolfe?"

"Yeah." Jenna placed her phone on speaker. "What have you got for me, Wolfe?"

"I'm on scene. I've checked the victim for life signs and taken photos of the scene. I'd take a look around the building but as it's just Emily and me, I figured I'll wait for backup. What's your ETA?"

Kane glanced at the GPS. "Five minutes, maybe less." He slammed his foot on the gas and his truck accelerated. "This perp is playing games. Don't take chances and wait by your vehicle."

"How close are you to the building?" Jenna shot Kane a worried look.

"Right now, we're on the road out front. I drove past to scan the area for a vehicle." Wolfe cleared his throat. *"It's a ramshackle building, no vehicles."* He took a deep breath. *"I can hear you coming."*

"Roger that." Jenna chewed on her bottom lip. "Be on alert, we don't know what kind of crazy we're dealing with." She disconnected and looked at Kane. "Is this another stage of his game?"

Kane accelerated and soon caught sight of the ME's van parked beside the remnants of an old barn. He could make out the small figure of Lindy on the bench some distance away from an old red-brick building with only the skeletal remnants of a roof. "Maybe. Sick people can display many facets of insanity. Not many fit neatly into one box." He pulled in behind the old barn and parked behind Wolfe's van. "One thing for sure – to crave this much attention, he's done this before."

"This place was on Rowley's list." Jenna slid from the seat and pulled out her cellphone to call him. She explained their discovery. "Didn't you check the old schoolhouse down a dirt road about a mile past the Triple Z Bar?"

Kane climbed out the vehicle and opened the back door to release Duke from the seat. He could barely hear Rowley through the speakers on Jenna's phone with the chopper in the background.

"Yes, ma'am, first place we checked and it was clear."

"Roger that." Jenna glanced at Kane. "I need to keep this out of the media. Pull the search teams out of Stanton Forest and move west. Keep away from us. We'll need to notify the parents before the media discover we've located Lindy's body."

"Leave it to me, ma'am."

"Thanks." Jenna disconnected and made her way to Wolfe's side. "What have you got for me, Wolfe?"

Kane did a visual recon of the scene and all the usual mistakes a frenzied killer made were missing. No tire tracks were visible, but the killer or Rowley's search party could've disturbed the new spring growth on the grasses and shrubs surrounding the area. He noticed how Duke stayed close to his heels, stopped frequently, then whined and walked around in circles. One thing for sure, something wasn't right. "What is it, boy?"

He scanned the area, taking in every shadow, but could see no movement. Duke's heightened senses had picked up something and he respected the warning. He moved swiftly to Jenna's side. "Stay alert. Duke has picked up something unusual."

"Okay." She wore a mask of professionalism but he detected the expression of deep sorrow in her eyes when she turned to him. "You're right; Wolfe believes the kidnapper strangled her."

"I hate being right when it comes to kids suffering." Kane stared down at the tragic form of Lindy Rosen, so young with all her life in front of her, propped up on an old bench like a bag of garbage.

He pushed down the rush of anger. The instinct to hunt down and kill the animals who hurt kids rested deep in his subconscious. He swallowed hard and looked at Wolfe, remembering his friend's creed – to learn the story of how victims died, to always treat them as a person and bring their killer to justice. "Did she suffer?"

"I'm afraid so. Slow asphyxiation." Wolfe gave him a direct stare. "I'm making an assumption from the ligature marks around her neck and the pinpoint hemorrhages, petechiae, in the skin and conjunctiva of both eyes, but these are non-specific. I'll give you an exact cause of death once I've performed an autopsy."

"At least he didn't cut her." Jenna wiped the back of her hand over her mouth. "I don't see any signs of a struggle."

"None evident." Wolfe lifted each of Lindy's hands and examined them before Emily slipped a plastic bag over each one. "Her nails aren't broken, the marks on her wrists are consistent with the image we received, and she has no defense wounds. I'll know more in the next twenty-four hours and after I examine the larynx, including the hyoid bone. If I can prove strangulation, I believe it was committed from behind and she had no chance to fight back." He sighed. "The time of death isn't conclusive. We're assuming he killed her in the last hour but from her body temperature, I figure she died as long as six hours ago."

"I'll need to inform her parents." Jenna sighed. "How long do you need to get her ready for them?"

"I'll make her presentable and they can see her this evening. I'll require them to formally identify her and I'll need a day for any other marks on her skin to become visible." Wolfe gave her a long look. "I did a recon of the immediate area to see if I could find any evidence but the area is too clean for him to have killed her here."

"Why do you figure the bench is way out here so far away from the schoolhouse?" Jenna stared at the ground. "Did the killer move it?"

"It hasn't been moved." Wolfe crouched and peered under the bench. "It's been here for a long time."

Kane stared at the old bench. "It would be logical to place the bench under the tree."

"Apparently, apart from the barn there was a one-room school building. I read about it on the internet, it's over a hundred years old." She turned to look at him. "Now it will go down in history as the place we found Lindy's body."

"That's the least of our worries; we need to know where he had her holed up before he moved her here." Wolfe frowned. "Are you sure he didn't use the actual schoolhouse?"

"Rowley said they searched it early this morning." Jenna stared at the old building. "If your time of death is correct, the killer probably moved her here before he sent the video." She shrugged. "We'll take another look. Do you need help to finish up here?"

"Kane, if you help me lift her into the body bag on the gurney, we'll take her back to the lab." Wolfe frowned. "I'd like to get her on ice as soon as possible."

"Sure." Kane pushed down his anger at seeing someone so young discarded like last night's pizza box, pulled on latex gloves and went to work.

They loaded the body into the van and Kane walked back to Jenna and Emily. Wolfe's daughter had a determined expression on her face. "Did you know Lindy?"

"No, but I sure want to discover what happened to her." Emily indicated with her chin toward the old schoolhouse. "Do you figure it's possible the killer held her in there for any length of time?"

"No, that's not the place. It's part of a stupid game this killer is playing with us." Jenna shook her head in disgust. "Rowley searched it with Webber this morning. If there'd been one speck of dust out of place, he'd have reported it."

"You'll look again, won't you, Jenna?" Emily straightened. "We could search it again now."

"I'll go take a look with Kane and if I find anything, I'll call Wolfe." Jenna squeezed the girl's arm in a comforting gesture. "You can leave this bit to us, Emily. Go help your dad."

"Okay." Emily trudged off toward the van.

"I guess we'd better take a look at the old schoolhouse." Jenna let out a weary sigh. "Not that I figure this SOB has left a single clue for us to find." She looked up at him. "Let's get it over with, and then we can hunt down suspects."

"Wait a bit." An ice-cold finger stroked Kane's spine as if in warning. "Duke's acting strange. He smells something."

"He's been hunting down Lindy's scent all day. Maybe he's telling you he found her and now he wants to go home." Jenna jogged away from him through the long grass toward the building. "You coming?"

Kane hustled after her, scanning the area. Without warning, Duke howled, turned tail and ran back to the truck then crawled beneath it. Confused, he stared after him then back at Jenna. To his horror, not three yards out front of the open door to the building, a shaft of afternoon sunlight glistened on a tripwire. Heart racing, Kane took off at a run toward her; she was less than ten yards from death. "Stop, it's a trap!"

CHAPTER NINE

So they haven't found her yet. Excitement sent beads of sweat running between his shoulder blades. On a buzz, he found it hard to sit still and watch his dream of recognition playing out on TV. At first, his brain refused to accept the newsreader's tense story, and when he realized the man was speaking about him, his heart raced so fast, he'd gasped in deep breaths. The media already had a name for him – he grinned into the darkness – they'd named him Shadow Man. He sounded like a comic book character. Hell, maybe they'd create a comic strip about him. The dramatic way the newsreader had described the fruitless effort by the hordes of people searching the forest made him laugh aloud. Did the sheriff in her blah, blah, blah, speech believe he'd obey her command? She had to be delusional if she believed him to be the same type of killer usually roaming Black Rock Falls.

He was unique, one of a kind, and when he'd finished killing in this town, he'd move on and start again – but then he'd adopt a different persona again. He prided himself on being versatile; not having a predictable MO was a gift he had in spades. Most profilers were on an ego trip, believing they'd come close to a fit but, in fact, the BS these so-called experts spewed about him was baloney.

The game with Sheriff Alton had taken his adventure to a new height. She'd be his first female sheriff to dance with and if she was as smart as people seemed to believe, she should have given him a decent challenge. Sadly, she wasn't fast enough to beat his generous timeframe. Now he'd see if she could figure her way out of his latest maze. If she escaped this time, he'd need to be patient to gain the ultimate prize. The wait would make killing her so much sweeter. Soon his win would be all over the news and he'd already planned the next round of entertainment.

The thrill of watching young teenage girls strolling along the sidewalk in town, chatting together or walking alone, heads bowed, staring at their cellphones, stirred him into action. The recent murders in Black Rock Falls hadn't instilled one ounce of caution in them and they continued to stroll around without a care in the world. He rubbed his hands together, itching to pluck one off the street or from their family's oh-so-safe home. He'd formed so many ideas to confuse the cops and there were so many girls in town – he could take his time and choose just the right one. They were such easy prey but first he would bask in his newfound fame on the news. *Then it will be game on, Sheriff Alton.*

CHAPTER TEN

Running headlong into danger was what Kane had trained to do. It was second nature to put his body on the line, but his usual fearless calm abandoned him. Jenna was in mortal danger. She turned to look at him with a confused expression and time went into slow motion. Lungs bursting, he flung himself toward her and as her foot brushed the tripwire, he scooped her up and dived headlong down a small embankment. His feet hadn't touched the ground when a fire-bolt of white light lit up the pasture and the concussive force from an earsplitting explosion picked them up in a whoosh of hot air and tossed them across the grassland like autumn leaves.

Kane wrapped his arms around Jenna as they flew on the cloud of heat, through the branches of a tree, then fell crashing to the ground. On impact, pain shot through his left shoulder and he slid across the rough ground on his back. He lost hold of her as they bounced and tumbled through the long grass. The fall had forced the air from his lungs and he gasped for a breath. Missiles of twisted metal, bricks and wood rained down on him. Disorientated and blinded by the clouds of dust, he reached out like a blind man searching the ground as debris peppered his back like hail. "Jenna, Jenna!"

A massive block of broken bricks crashed down inches from his head and a wave of panic for her safety hit him as he caught sight of her boot in the grass. Ears ringing, he dragged himself toward her. She lay sprawled out, face down and pale as a ghost. He crawled over her inert body and covered her, protecting her from the projectiles dropping all around them. She wasn't moving – not even a slight flutter of eyelids. *Dear God, no.* He spat dirt from his mouth and bent close to her ear. "Jenna, can you hear me?"

Nothing.

Another explosion shook the ground, turning the sky red again, and a wave of heat lashed out at them in a dragon's roar. His nostrils filled with the smell of burning hair. Massive chunks of cement and wood rained down on them, cutting into the ground like a hot knife through butter. He covered his head as a huge block of cement with the remnants of letters carved into it landed a few inches from his face. Pieces of splintered wood stabbed the dirt all around him, piercing his jeans, then a blanket of dark gray smoke poured over them and seemed to crawl away across the meadow, undulating like a serpent. An eerie silence descended and, apart from the loud ringing in his ears, it was as if the world had stopped.

Sure that the debris was no longer falling from the sky, he coughed and pushed to his knees and then used his sleeve to wipe his streaming eyes. He stared down at Jenna. She lay face down in the grass, motionless, head on one side. Scratches and bruises covered her face. *Please God, let her be alive.* Easing two fingers under her collar, he felt for a pulse and, finding a strong beat, gasped back a flood of emotion. He used his shirt to wipe her face, then pulled twigs and grass from her singed hair. Her eyelids twitched and she tried to push him away. Worried she might have spinal injuries, he bent down close to her ear. "There was an explosion, lie still and let me check you out."

He saw her lips move and her eyes opened, but he couldn't make out what she was saying for the buzzing in his head. He shook his head and Jenna pointed to her ears and mouthed, "I can't hear you. I'm okay."

Relief flooded over him and he nodded. "Me too, I think." Then he pointed to his legs and winced.

Jenna held up a dirty hand in a waiting gesture, and then crawled to his side and her eyes widened. She shook her head. "You're not okay." She pushed him down onto his side. "Splinters."

Kane blinked at her. She was yelling at him but he could hardly hear her through the buzzing in his ears. He raised his voice. "It's nothing."

"Don't move." Jenna pushed him hard on the shoulder. "I'll call for help." She pulled out her cellphone. "I'll send Wolfe a message. I can't hear a darn thing." She staggered to her feet and peered around. "There's fires breaking out all over. I'll get Wolfe to call the fire department."

Kane tugged on her jeans to get her attention. "Tell him to get a bomb squad out here as well."

"Okay." She sat down beside him and sent the text. Dirt streaked her face like camouflage paint and the explosion had scorched her hair light brown in patches. Long scratches over one cheek looked like red cat's whiskers. She glanced at him. "Head okay?"

He touched his head, feeling for injuries and finding nothing more than a few scratches, he was glad he'd pulled his thick woolen cap over his ears. "Yeah, I'm good." He checked his weapon and cellphone. "Phone made it too. Those new covers we found are worth their weight in gold."

"What?" Jenna pointed to her ears. "I still can't hear you. You'll have to yell."

The next moment Duke came bounding through the grass covered in soot and grime. The dog launched himself at Kane, and then walked around in circles barking. Not long after, Wolfe came running through the tall grass, face pale and eyes examining them like a hawk. Kane looked up at him and touched his ears. "We can't hear a thing. Is Emily okay?"

Wolfe gave him a curt nod, then placed his bag on the grass. He pulled out his cellphone and made a call, then wrote a message and held it out to them to read.

I've called the fire department and told them it was a bomb. They'll extinguish the wild fires but they'll have to wait for the bomb squad to arrive from Helena. There's a chopper on the way. As Jenna doesn't want the media involved yet, they'll say it is a training exercise. You're not in any danger here, so sit still and let me take a look at you.

Kane nodded and the movement made him nauseous. "Sure, but Jenna first."

Wolfe bent to examine Jenna's eyes and ears, then turned to Kane and repeated the tests. Apparently, they had no permanent injuries but Kane had to push down his pride and allow Wolfe to cut off his jeans to remove the splinters. He'd suffered injuries in the field many a time but having Jenna hold his hand and fuss over him was a new experience. By the time Wolfe had finished, his hearing had returned apart from a strange humming.

"Here." Wolfe pulled a foil survival blanket out of his backpack. "Wrap this around you and I'll help you back to the road. I want you to lie down on a gurney in my van."

Kane shook his head. Lying beside Lindy's corpse was not going to happen. "Thanks but I'm fine."

"Maybe not so fine when the local anesthetic wears off, but the penicillin shot will cover any infection." Wolfe shook his head. "It's just as well I keep a field med kid with me, with you getting injured all the time."

"I've one in my vehicle too." Kane sucked in a deep breath and glanced at Wolfe. "Did my truck make it?"

"Yeah." Emily came through the trees and Duke ran to greet her. "Apart from a good coating of dust, I think it's okay. The old barn protected it from damage."

Kane breathed a sigh of relief. "Thank you, God."

"You know Duke led us here. We turned back when we heard the explosion and Duke was going ballistic, running around in circles barking. So we followed him." She dropped a backpack on the ground. "Dad insisted I wait back there in case he found you in pieces but I could hear you yelling at each other."

"He tried to warn us." He whistled to Duke. "Come here, boy."

Duke ran over to him and did his happy dance. Kane rubbed the dog's ears. "I'm sure glad you're okay." He touched Jenna's arm. "Can you hear me yet, Jenna?"

"Just." She sipped a bottle of water Wolfe had provided. "We have to get cleaned up and go and inform Lindy's parents before the press gets wind of what's happened here."

"You're not going anywhere but the ER. I'll go speak to them and then I'll put out a press release. We'll say we found Lindy's body but that no cause of death has been established." Wolfe's expression was grave. "I figure you'll want to keep the fact she was murdered out of the press for a few days?"

"I would appreciate that, Wolfe, thanks." Jenna leaned back on her hands. "I'm fine. I don't need to see the paramedics."

"I must insist you go to the ER. You could have concussion and Kane needs his shoulder X-rayed. You'll be no good to anyone in this condition." Wolfe patted Jenna on the arm. "Leave everything to me, I'll arrange for the parents' viewing as well and call you later."

"I can't thank you enough, Wolfe." Jenna turned to Kane. "So our killer is not only a murdering SOB – now we have a lunatic planting IEDs." She squeezed his hand. "Thanks for saving my life."

Kane squeezed back. "I guess we should take more notice of Duke, not that I had any idea he was familiar with improvised explosive devices, but he could have picked up the scent of C-4. I'm guessing that's what the killer used."

"Have you figured out a profile for him yet?" Jenna allowed Emily to dab antiseptic on the angry red scratches on her face.

Kane nodded and rubbed his shoulder. "We're lucky to be alive but this killer has made a big mistake. Before he planted a bomb, I found it difficult to profile him and could've gone a few different ways, but not now. This killer is a psychopath and showing advanced narcissistic tendencies. He enjoys killing and has gotten away with it. Problem is, he wants to be famous and craves recognition." He pushed to his feet and winced at the pain in his legs. "So, one, he's not a local, and two, we're looking for a man between thirty and forty, Caucasian, who's worked in a variety of jobs and gained knowledge on the way." He held out a hand and pulled Jenna to her feet. "He'll likely be hiding in plain sight because he is playing 'a catch me if you can' game."

"Yeah?" Jenna gave him a determined look. "Well in the past, I figure he's been dealing with a few backwoods sheriff's departments." Her mouth turned down. "Now he's playing against my team and I don't intend to let him win." She snorted. "I'm going to enjoy taking him down."

CHAPTER ELEVEN

Tuesday

Bruised and battered, Jenna made her way into Aunt Betty's Café. She'd trimmed away some of the singed hair and showered, but the smell of the explosion seemed to have set up permanent residence in her nose. A street sweeper drove down Main Street and the local council workers moved around in organized chaos, cleaning up the mess left behind by the swarms of people and media involved in the search for Lindy. The response had been overwhelming, followed by an outpouring of assistance of food and hot drinks for the teams, supplied by the Black Rock Falls Women's Association. The search had delayed the preparation for the Spring Festival the following weekend, but she assumed the bunting and advertising would be up before the end of the day. *Life goes on.*

Jenna limped up to the counter and placed a large order with Susie Hartwig. She'd called a meeting in her office at ten. Murder investigations involved a lot of tedious grunt work and as they worked long hours for days on end, she made a habit of providing food for her deputies. She leaned casually against the wall and noticed the inquisitive looks from the other customers. The explosion had caused more than a few scratches to her face and in fact, she looked as if she'd lost a fight. She wondered if they'd gotten a look at Kane yet – if so they'd figure they'd both been in a brawl.

The time immediately following the explosion was still a blur – she remembered heading to Kane's vehicle then vomiting and Emily had ended up driving them to the ER. She'd left after a couple of hours but due to his previous head injury, the doctors insisted Kane remained overnight. When she'd returned at six this morning with his clean uniform, she discovered he'd spent half the night running background checks on a list of possible suspects. At the meeting, they'd discuss his findings.

She glanced out the café window to where Kane had parked his sparkling-clean truck. It was hard to believe the dust-coated vehicle they'd found after the explosion was the same SUV. After dropping them at the hospital, Emily had taken the truck home and with help from her sisters, Julie and Anna, had set about putting it and Duke right. She wished she had taken a photograph of Kane's grin when he set eyes on "the beast" and a very clean Duke when they left the ER.

She collected the bags from Susie, slipped out the door and went to the truck. "The town gossips are going to be busy today." She handed Kane the food and climbed into the passenger seat. "You should have seen the strange looks they gave me, like I was a zombie or something."

"And it's not even close to Halloween." Kane grinned at her. "Just as well I stayed here." He started the engine. "Wolfe called. He'll be at the meeting as well. I've sent the case file to everyone so we're all on the same page."

"Wolfe is a rock." Jenna sighed. "While we were stuck in the ER last night, he informed Lindy's parents, arranged and supervised the viewing and gave a press conference."

"That's Wolfe." Kane's mouth twitched at the corner. "He's gotten me out of so many situations, most of them I'd one chance of surviving and he found me that one chance. He's always been someone I can rely on when everything goes to hell."

"Yeah, there's a special bond between you. You're like brothers." Jenna leaned back in the seat. "I asked Agent Josh Martin to sit in as well. He arrived yesterday from the FBI Child Abduction Rapid Deployment Team and worked alongside Rowley. We're lucky to get him – they only deploy the response team if a child abductee is under twelve years old. He's going to give us a run-down of similar cases in the state."

"I *know* him." Kane's brow furrowed into a frown. "I worked with him in my other life on a case before he joined CARD."

Worried, Jenna turned to him. "Will he recognize you?"

"Nope. I don't recognize me." Kane pulled his vehicle into his space outside the sheriff's department. "He's never met Wolfe either... although, Josh might recognize my voice."

"They made a lot of changes to me too." She glanced at him. "I like my look apart from one thing; I'm really a blonde. I've a few scars around my eyes but I'd never know you'd had plastic surgery. What did they do?"

"Hmm." Kane gave her a long searching look and ignored her question. "Blonde... really?" He grabbed the bags from the back seat and handed them to her. "I'll grab Duke and meet you inside."

She figured the few things Kane mentioned about his past life would be all he'd ever tell her. She slid out the truck and made her way to the office. "Morning, Magnolia." She smiled at the receptionist and noticed Wolfe's teenage daughter, Julie, looking at her with an apprehensive expression. "Did you want to speak to me, Julie?"

"She sure does." Maggie beamed at her. "This child spent the entire day yesterday manning the phones. I couldn't have managed without her."

Jenna caught sight of Kane walking up behind her with Duke at his heels. She glanced at Julie. "That was very kind of you."

"It was very exciting." Julie smiled. "I wanted to ask you if I could do an internship here at the sheriff's department."

Jenna smiled. "Yes, as long as it's okay with your dad, we'd love to have you. Bring me the paperwork to sign." She turned to Kane. "I'll need some time to add all our potential suspects to the whiteboard. I'm not sure when Agent Martin is arriving."

"I'll brew some coffee and make sure everyone is up to speed." Kane's stiff gait told her the wounds from the splinters were hurting like hell.

CHAPTER TWELVE

As she entered all the information onto the whiteboard, Jenna grunted and stretched out the ache in her back. She had so many bruises on her body she looked like a statue carved out of blue marble. She made a mental note to tell Kane how much she appreciated the hot tub he'd installed in her gym last year. After making one more notation on the whiteboard, she turned to see him at the door to her office, carrying two jugs of fresh coffee. Rowley followed close behind with the fixings and Walters brought up the rear with the cups. "Has Wolfe or Agent Martin arrived yet?"

"They're outside, ma'am." Rowley placed the fixings on the desk beside the cups and copious amounts of food Jenna had purchased from Aunt Betty's Café. "I'll go get them." He headed out the door.

When the men walked into the room, Jenna smiled at Agent Martin. "Nice to see you. Thanks for coming." She poured a cup of coffee and waited for the men to take their seats. Anxious to get her deputies out interviewing potential suspects, she remained standing at the whiteboard. "Listen up. I have a list of the main persons of interest we have so far. Our investigations to date suggest all these men had the opportunity to interact with Lindy Rosen in the weeks before her death." She pointed to the whiteboard. "Paul Kittredge, thirty-eight, is one of ten men employed by the Green Thumb Landscaping Service. He's of interest because he worked close to the house for a full week prior to Lindy's disappearance and after a background check we discovered he pleaded guilty to a case involving the sexual abuse of a child in his care. The judge in the case gave him a six-year deferred sentence and after he completed the time, he changed his plea to not guilty and the district judge dismissed the case."

"That's the strangest thing I ever heard." Wolfe rubbed his chin. "So he pleaded guilty and now he walks free?"

"Montana laws are complex." Agent Martin's mouth twitched at the corners in a half-smile. "No doubt it was the result of a plea bargain and the law does offer the chance to change a plea in this situation."

Jenna tapped her pen on the table. "Did you chase down any info on any of the other men working for Green Thumb?"

"The owner gave me a list of the men who worked at the Rosens' ranch. The company landscaped the entire block of land over a period of about three months before winter. There were a few gardeners working the same week as Kittredge but he's the only one with priors." Kane reached for a packet of sandwiches. "It seems Lindy was surrounded by potential suspects."

Jenna sipped her coffee. "Yeah, but we'll concentrate on the shortlist for now." She pointed to her second notation. "Local handyman, Sean Packer, thirty-five. This man had access to the house over a period of four weeks and is still finishing up a few small jobs. His background check revealed he was dishonorably discharged from the army." She looked at Kane. "What else can you give me on him, Kane?"

"He's married, has knowledge of explosives from his time in the service and had plenty of time to befriend Lindy and discover the security code." Kane leaned his wide shoulders back in the chair, making it moan. "He fits the profile; in fact everyone on the list fits the profile to one degree or another."

"Moving on." Jenna glanced at Wolfe. "You've spoken to Charles Anderson, the technician who ran the check on the security system.

He's on Mr. Rosen's list as a person who worked at the house. What are your impressions?"

"I don't really have an impression of him. I observed him testing the system and he's proficient at his job." Wolfe's expression gave nothing away. "I'd be interested to know if you found anything on him because he's currently holding art classes on Saturdays at the local hall." He met Jenna's gaze. "Julie goes there with a few of her school friends but it's a mixed class with adults as well. I'd have thought he'd have to undergo a background check before being allowed to interact with teenagers."

"He would and I didn't find any priors on him." Kane sipped his beverage. "He came under my scrutiny because of his work in and around the Rosens' house. He's one of eight technicians working for the security company, so he'd know the system inside and out. I'd say Rosen mentioned him because he had free access to the house and likely interacted with his girls." He sighed. "He's had a varied career. I know about him volunteering to teach at the community art school but he also worked out of Colorado in the mines some years ago, so it's not too far-fetched to believe he has some knowledge of explosives." He shrugged. "That's reason enough for him to be on our list."

"May I butt in here?" Agent Josh Martin raised one black eyebrow in question. "Don't assume any suspect requires hands-on knowledge of explosives. These days everything they need is freely available on the internet."

The men in the room fell into a discussion about the pros and cons of the internet. Agitated, Jenna cleared her throat. "Can we move along? I want these people interviewed today. One of them could be planning another kidnapping."

She pushed a hand through her hair. "The next two on my list came through our crime hotline and although Kane hasn't unearthed any dirt on them, I believe they should be considered as potential suspects. Noah McLeod, forty, is one of the janitors at the high school. The woman who called in worked there for a time and found him to be a bit too familiar with the students. We received a similar anonymous complaint about one of the groundskeepers, Mason Lancaster, the youngest of our potential suspects at twenty-eight." She sat down behind her desk. "Does anyone else have any other pertinent information?"

The room was silent.

"Good." Jenna sat down and looked at Wolfe. "When can we expect the results of the post on Lindy Rosen?"

"I should be through by five. I'll email you the report." Wolfe's gaze narrowed. "Unless you need Webber? If so, I'll need a deputy present for the autopsy."

Jenna glanced at Deputy Webber. She had all but lost him as a deputy since he started working alongside Wolfe. "No, that's fine. The autopsy is crucial, we'll handle the interviews." She glanced down at her notes. "Rowley, you and Walters can take McLeod and Lancaster. Both men work at the high school. I'll head out to the Rosens' ranch with Kane to speak to Kittredge and Packer. We'll track down Anderson via his place of employment and speak with him as well." She glanced at Agent Martin. "Do you have a preference?"

"I'd be interested in attending the autopsy." Martin glanced at Wolfe. "The evidence is all in the post. I'll be heading back to base directly after but I'll be able to come back if you need me."

Jenna nodded. "Thanks, I appreciate your help." She glanced at her deputies. "Okay, you have all the information you need. Let's get this show on the road."

CHAPTER THIRTEEN

Relieved Josh Martin hadn't recognized him, Kane filled a couple of to-go cups with coffee, grabbed a paper sack of sandwiches from Jenna's desk and tucked them under one arm. He took in her bruised and battered appearance. She'd not complained once since the explosion but it was obvious the injuries she'd sustained were causing her more pain than she cared to admit. "Do you want me to drive?"

"Nah, you'd better ride shotgun and relax your sore butt." Jenna smiled at him and pulled a cap over her singed hair, then thrust her arms into her jacket. "We'll take my cruiser, as we're interviewing these men at their place of work." She gave him a worried stare. "Did the doc give you anything for the pain? Those puncture wounds must be painful."

Kane smiled at her then ran a finger gently down the scratches on her cheek. "Ditto. You look as if you've been fighting down at the Triple Z." He sighed. "I guess me landing on you didn't help much either?"

"You protected me from the blast and the splinters." Jenna leaned into him. "I've a few bumps and bruises but you took the mother lode of the falling debris. When I saw that pile of bricks an inch away from your head… it made me sick to my stomach." She shook her head slowly. "I'm not taking any meds right now. I'll need all my senses to solve this darn murder case. You ready to leave?"

Kane gave her two to-go cups in a cardboard holder. "Yeah, I'll grab a Thermos of coffee. Okay to take those chocolate chip cookies with us?"

"Sure." Jenna picked up the bag. "Anything to stop your stomach growling." She smiled at him.

Kane grinned at her, whistled for Duke and headed out the office.

"As luck would have it, Anderson is working in the same area as the Rosens' ranch." Kane dropped his cellphone into his pocket and added the coordinates to the GPS in Jenna's cruiser. "Silent Alarms is a full-service company."

Jenna turned her cruiser into Stanton Road and accelerated. "I know they took over the old bank building on the edge of town. Maybe they needed the extra security if they run the business twenty-four seven."

"Yeah, they offer a top-of-the-range system and around-the-clock surveillance – at a price." Kane leaned back in his seat and yawned. "It's not a company I'd recommend."

"How so?"

Kane rubbed his chin. "They have too many levels of security. In one package, they offer a panic button. So rather than call 911 if they fear for their lives, the homeowner must rely on a security guard to protect them." He cleared his throat. "Some of the options, the motion sensors and lights, are good, so is the storing of any triggered CCTV footage to the cloud, but I figure the nanny-cam option should be something only available to parents, as in they set it up themselves and run it through their cellphones. Having a company collecting that data, for me, is a little disturbing."

"I can't see why." Jenna turned into the road leading to the Rosens' ranch. "If I had a baby at home, I can't watch twenty-four seven so I'd be ecstatic to know someone else was watching on my behalf."

Kane snorted. "If I had a baby at home, I'd be there caring for them myself." He glanced at her and grinned. "I'd be more than happy to be a stay-at-home dad. Sit around watching football all day and changing a few diapers. How hard can it be?"

"You wouldn't last a day." Jenna's eyes flashed as she glanced at him. "You were all tuckered out watching Wolfe's girls for a couple of hours, and a baby is full-time. Trust me, there aren't enough hours in the day to get things done."

Kane held up both his hands in surrender and chuckled. "Okay, okay, I believe you." His eyes danced with mischief. "I'd still rather work my tail off than have a nanny for my kid. I was an army brat and my dad never had too much time for me growing up. Later we were best buddies but by then it was too late."

"Ah, that makes a lot of sense." Jenna turned into the Rosens' ranch and headed along the driveway to the house. "Did Mrs. Rosen say where Kittredge and Packer are working today?"

The awkward conversation filtered back into his mind. Speaking to a distraught woman planning her daughter's funeral had been difficult, but at least she was civil when he explained they were chasing down leads on Lindy's killer. Mr. Rosen was unavailable. His anger had come close to stroke level after identifying his daughter at the morgue and the local doctor had sedated him. "Yeah, Packer's inside the house and Kittredge is working on the grounds somewhere. There're four gardeners here today."

"We tread lightly around the Rosens." Jenna pulled to a halt beside a pickup parked outside the house. "Make sure we speak to the people of interest way away from any family members."

Kane slid from the car. "Sure." He opened the back door and allowed Duke to jump onto the ground. He moved to Jenna's side. "We'll see if Duke picks up anything when we speak to the men. I have Lindy's PJ top in an evidence bag in the back of your cruiser; we'll give him the scent before we speak to them."

"Won't he be confused?" Jenna frowned. "If there're two scents on her clothes, how will he know which one to follow?"

Not able to figure the mind or workings of a dog's sense of smell, Kane shrugged. "I have no idea, but I figured it's worth a try. Right now, we have zip. Wolfe couldn't find as much as one foreign hair on her clothes."

"Okay, so we'll have to rely on good old police work to find this killer. I'll question Packer and you watch his body language and see what you can get from him." Jenna headed toward the steps, and then turned. "Wait here, I'll ask Packer to come outside for a word."

Kane hustled back to Jenna's cruiser and opened the back door. He was out of sight of the Rosens' front door and offered Duke a sniff of the clothes. "Seek."

Duke walked a few feet in every direction, then came back and sat at his feet. Kane patted his head. "Keep that smell in mind when we talk to these men." He leaned against Jenna's vehicle and watched the front door.

Mrs. Rosen appeared looking distraught, red-eyed and ashen. She looked horrified at Jenna's appearance but after Jenna offered an explanation, she stepped to one side to admit her. A few moments later, Jenna was ushering a man from the house. Kane took out his notebook and pen and waited for them to join him by the cruiser. Packer was of medium height, Caucasian with light brown hair and a muscular body. He wore surprisingly clean coveralls and a tool belt around his waist. He was what he would consider quite ordinary in appearance, quite bland-looking with no outstanding features, scars or tattoos he could see.

"Mr. Packer, this is Deputy Kane. You're not under any obligation to speak with us but we are interviewing anyone who came in contact with Lindy before the kidnapping." Jenna spoke in a low, direct tone. "We need to have some idea of who was coming and going over the last couple of weeks."

"Sure, but is this gonna take long?" Packer glanced at his watch. "I usually take a break around now and need to head into town."

"We won't keep you long." She lifted her chin. "How long have you been working at the Rosens'?"

"I've been working here for some time now." Packer rubbed the end of his nose. "Mrs. Rosen wants most of the fixtures and fittin's changed. So, I've been changin' doorknobs, kitchen cupboard door handles, those sort of things."

"Do you have any interaction with the children?" Jenna tilted her head. "Mrs. Rosen mentioned you put shelves up in Lindy's room a week ago."

"Yeah, I've spoken to all of them." Packer narrowed his gaze. "They live in the house – it's hard not to speak to them when they're runnin' past me every few minutes."

"Did you hear Lindy mention anything before her disappearance, about a boyfriend, or her nightmares?"

"I know about the nightmares. They spoke about them all the time." Packer rubbed his chin. "That's why Lindy wanted shelves in her room. Her father wanted another wardrobe but she was frightened someone might hide inside."

"When did you last see Lindy?" Jenna folded her arms across her chest and leaned casually against the cruiser.

"Day before she went missin'. I didn't speak with her; I was workin' in her parents' bathroom." Packer frowned. "Terrible thing that happened to her."

"Was it?" Jenna straightened and moved a step closer. "We don't know exactly what happened to her. Do you *know* what happened to Lindy?"

"I know she was kidnapped and murdered." Packer took a step backward. "It's all over the news and I heard the family talkin' about it."

"Where were you the night she disappeared?" Jenna stared at him.

"At home. Where else would I be?" Packer's face filled with concern. "I don't need a lawyer, do I?"

"These are just routine questions, Mr. Packer." Jenna frowned at him. "The same as we're asking everyone. I don't intend to arrest you. Can anyone verify you were at home?"

"My wife, Aileen."

"I'll be sure to speak with her." Jenna glanced at Kane. "Do you remember seeing anyone hanging around the house before Lindy went missing? Anyone we haven't accounted for — we know about the gardening service, but did you happen to see anyone else?"

"Yeah, the security company had men crawlin' all over." Packer shrugged. "All that security didn't do squat, did it?"

Kane wrote down the name of Packer's wife. He wasn't convinced he was telling the truth. The body language of the man, the way he folded his arms in a defensive manner, and covered his mouth as if to hide something, was a concern. When Jenna looked at him, he straightened.

"Do you have any questions for Mr. Packer?"

"Yeah, I do." Kane cleared his throat and moved his attention back to Packer. "You spent some time in the army. Did they instruct you in the use of explosives and if so what did that entail?"

"Explosives?" Packer shook his head. "Nope, I don't know about explosives. I'm a handyman, jack of all trades maybe, but blowin' up things isn't one of them."

"Okay." Kane whistled Duke and Jenna called the dog to her side.

"Thank you for your help, Mr. Packer. This is Duke; he came from the animal shelter."

"Nice to meet you, Duke." Packer offered his knuckle to the dog.

Kane waited in anticipation as Duke sniffed the man's hand, then walked around in circles and flopped onto the manicured grass. He'd hoped Duke would give him a positive result but he still wouldn't discount this man. The killer hadn't left any DNA trace evidence but could've been wearing coveralls and gloves when he kidnapped Lindy. In his years of experience, he'd found most people became nervous when questioned by law enforcement, yet up to the point where Jenna had asked him to account for his whereabouts Packer had acted as if they were asking him about his favorite restaurant rather than a brutal murder. Most importantly, he'd caught him out in a lie. His background information on Mr. Packer clearly stated his experience in the use of explosives.

CHAPTER FOURTEEN

It was spring break and people filled the streets, enjoying the warmer days. The council had arranged a variety of local attractions in the park. He glanced up to see an escaped balloon drifting by on the wind. What he liked most about the western towns were the festivals; each contained a smorgasbord of delights and Black Rock Falls was no different. Kids of all ages on vacation from school swarmed all over town waving cotton candy or licking ice creams purchased from the street vendors. Mixing with them as they dashed from one store to the other or stopped to buy something from one of the many stalls lining the sidewalk made him feel like a kid in a candy store. So many to choose from, and all so vulnerable. He usually liked to pick out one and follow them, perhaps get close enough to smell their hair and listen to their mindless chatter. Not today, though. Today he had something more important to do.

He stepped inside Aunt Betty's Café and, rather than order something to go then hurry back to work, he took a seat by the window and glanced at his watch. He had half an hour before anyone would miss him and sneaking around without anyone seeing him was one of his talents. He ordered his meal and leaned back in the wooden chair to admire a group of teenage girls walking past giggling and bumping into each other, taking selfies and acting the fool. He lifted the menu to cover his smile. There was the chosen one. Her long pale neck would be perfect to strangle. He bit back a moan, imagining the marks he'd leave behind.

He found something satisfying in the way they looked at him when he choked them. He enjoyed their terrified expressions so much, and he'd never killed them the first time but tightened the cord enough to make them black out. When they woke, alone and scared in the dark, they would be almost grateful to see him again. He would admire the deep red lines on their pristine flesh left from where he had tied them – but best of all, their voices would've gotten all husky. He would wait patiently for them to stop wailing and start to bargain with him.

In the end, he would kill them just to shut them up.

CHAPTER FIFTEEN

Deputy Jake Rowley leaned against his cruiser to wait for old Duke Walters to finish up at Aunt Betty's Café. He'd have left at once but Walters refused to go without grabbing a bite of lunch. He went through his notes one last time as he waited for Walters to join him. He had a great deal of respect for the semi-retired deputy and when the sheriff placed him in a more senior position, it seemed surreal. Walters had been a deputy in Black Rock Falls for a long time and seen at least four sheriffs come and go.

A cool wind filled his open jacket, flapping it about like eagle's wings. He glanced up at the sky, expecting to see rain or perhaps snow clouds drifting toward town, but the sky was blue from town over the green tips of the pines in Stanton Forest to the snowcapped mountain peaks beyond. He zipped his jacket and pulled his woolen cap down over his ears. Spring might be here but the cold weather would hang around for some time yet.

Walters gave him a friendly wave and pushed his Stetson down over his gray hair before weaving his way through the people on the sidewalk on the way to the cruiser. Rowley opened his door and slipped behind the wheel. He had pride in his new cruiser and winced when Walters filled the console with bags of food alongside his two to-go cups of coffee. "I'm sure we'll have time to stop again if you're hungry."

"I'd say from the amount of food the sheriff provided, she expects us to keep going, but I'm too old for that now." Walters fastened his seatbelt. "This type of killer don't stop at one. I've seen his kind before; he ain't looking for no ransom – he enjoys what he does."

"Kane has the same opinion." Rowley started the engine and backed out onto the road. "We'll head straight to the custodian's office at the high school and see if he knows exactly where McLeod and Lancaster are working today."

"The janitor won't be working all day." Walters shrugged. "Most times it's early morning and late afternoon but maybe it's different when the kids are on vacation."

Rowley moved slowly through the traffic and numerous jaywalkers then drove out of the main street and onto Stanton Road. The high school and college sat within a mile of each other opposite Stanton Forest. In less than ten minutes, he drove through the high school gates. He slid into a space in a practically empty parking lot reserved for the teachers. The moment he opened the door a cold alpine breeze smacked him in the face. The crisp clean air had the scent of pine and melting snow with the hint of wood-burning fires. He inhaled. One thing he loved about Black Rock Falls was the scenery. No matter where he stood, all around him magnificent vistas spread out in every direction. He waited for Walters and led the way to the custodian's office. "It hasn't changed since I went here."

"That wasn't that long ago." Walters grinned at him. "For me it was a lifetime and I went to school on the other side of town – they demolished it some ten years ago and built the firehouse."

It was strange, how the smell of a place evoked memories. The school had its own distinctive smell, a mixture of cleaning materials and dirty socks. Rowley made his way to the custodian's office and knocked on the door. A deep voice instructed him to enter and he turned the doorknob and peered around the door. A man in his fifties got to his feet, an expression of alarm on his face.

"Is there a problem, Deputy?"

Rowley held up a hand in a calming gesture. "No, everything is fine. We're chasing down a few leads in a case. Do you know if Mason Lancaster and Noah McLeod are working today?"

"Yeah, they're here and should be back from lunch by now." The man shuffled papers on his desk. "Have they done something wrong?"

Rowley took in the man's agitated demeanor and smiled. No doubt, the custodian was up to something but he didn't have time to find out what. "Nope, it's just routine questions. Nothing for you to worry about." He turned to the map of the school hanging on the wall. "Can you point out where we can find them?"

"Of course." The custodian sat down at his desk and tapped the keys on his computer. "McLeod is waxing the floor of the basketball court and Lancaster is out with his men laying turf on the football field." He pushed to his feet. "Do you want me to take you to them?"

"I know my way around." Rowley waved at the map. "It's much the same as when I was here. Thank you for your time." He headed out the door with Walters close behind.

They found McLeod busy using a polishing machine in the basketball court. He worked alone with the earbuds jammed into his ears, swinging the noisy machine from side to side. Rowley walked in front of him and waved his hands to get his attention. All color drained from McLeod's face and he gaped at him wide-eyed and pulled out the earbuds.

"Noah McLeod?"

"Yeah." He stopped the machine and looked from one deputy to another. "Dang, she called the cops on me, didn't she?"

Interesting. Rowley shot Walters a knowing glance. "Why don't you explain what happened?"

"She's been giving me the eye for weeks, you know, hanging around after school to speak to me." McLeod's cheeks flamed. "She invited me to a party last Saturday night, we kissed, is all, and she changed her mind. I backed right off. I wouldn't hurt her, I love her."

"Love her, huh?" Rowley took out his notebook and flipped through the pages. "How do you spell her last name? I didn't get her to spell it out for me."

"Jocelyn S-M-Y-T-H-E." McLeod looked at his feet. "This will cost me my job."

"Unfortunately you're gaining a reputation for being a little too familiar with the students. It's a crime for a man of forty to make out with a girl of fifteen, and don't give me the excuse you didn't know how old she is. You knew darn well she was underage." Rowley straightened to his full six-two and looked down at the smaller man. "It was only a matter of time before someone made a formal complaint." He took a beat, watching the man's reaction. "So you went to the party on Saturday night and you lucked out, so what did you get up to on Sunday night?"

"I stayed home, had a few drinks and watched TV." McLeod cleared his throat. "I guess you'll want someone to verify that, right? No can do. My wife left me and took the kids over a year ago. I live alone."

Walters stepped forward and his eyes flashed with anger. "I gather you've met Lindy Rosen?"

"Yeah, she's one of the group that hangs around Mason." McLeod snorted. "She's not interested in me, she prefers the ex-football jock type and Mason was a star before he injured his knee." He chuckled. "It must be good to be him."

Unease prickled the back of Rowley's neck. He was looking straight into the eyes of a typical pedophile and wondered how many young lives the man had destroyed. They all "loved" kids and used it as an excuse. He pushed down the anger percolating inside and gave McLeod his best "Don't mess with me" expression. "I'll speak to the sheriff but if you want her to go easy on you, I suggest you don't leave town. If you do Sheriff Alton will have the FBI on your tail before you can blink."

Resisting the urge to punch the disgusting SOB in the mouth, he turned on his heel and left the building. He could hear Walters puffing along behind him and slowed his step.

"Don't go soft on him." Walters jerked on his arm. "The sheriff will want to follow up on that asshole."

Rowley stared at him in disbelief. "Go soft on him? Jesus, man, I've seen things monsters like him do to kids. It took all my strength not to tear him apart with my bare hands." He sucked in a deep breath. "Seems to me, if what he said about Mason Lancaster is true, we could have two potential murder suspects working with kids at a high school."

CHAPTER SIXTEEN

Julie Wolfe walked back to the sheriff's department, her arms loaded with bags from Aunt Betty's Café. She had a deal to think about during her first day as an intern working beside Magnolia Brewster. She liked her; Maggie and her southern charm and big brown eyes brought back a flood of memories of the housekeeper who lived with her family in Texas. It had been hard leaving the only home she'd ever known to start over in Black Rock Falls, but moving had eased the constant reminder of watching her mother waste away. The illness had taken her from an active mom who played basketball with them to a shadow of the person she once knew. Her father had left the marines and remained home, refusing to allow anyone else to nurse her. She remembered the worry in his eyes and the way he'd stayed positive and made her mom fight using every known medical treatment he could find but nothing had worked. She pushed down the tears threatening to spill and concentrated on what Maggie had discussed with her earlier.

A man had taken Lindy Rosen from her home and murdered her right here in Black Rock Falls. She recalled Lindy had suffered nightmares like so many of the girls at school. Not being in the clique of popular girls, Julie had only overheard a few stories but earlier, as she waited for her order in Aunt Betty's Café, she'd listened with interest to a conversation at a nearby table. She walked into the sheriff's department and stowed the bags in the refrigerator in the small kitchenette, then went back to the front counter carrying two bags of sandwiches and drinks for her and Maggie.

The office was quiet and apart from answering the phone, there was really nothing much for her to do. She handed Maggie the food and drink and sat down beside her. "I overheard some girls from school talking in Aunt Betty's about what happened to Lindy. I figured it might be important."

"Well don't keep it to yourself, child." Maggie blinked her large chocolate eyes at her. "Tell me."

Julie's face grew hot. She hated the thought of gossiping but it might stop another girl being hurt. She looked at Maggie's encouraging smile and swallowed hard, then, thinking better of it, shook her head. "It doesn't matter, it's probably nothing."

"Now listen here." Maggie turned in her seat to stare at her. "This here is the sheriff's office; it's where we try to prevent crimes like what happened to young Lindy Rosen. If people didn't call in with things they'd seen or heard, the entire office would grind to a standstill." She patted Julie's hand. "Look around, there's no one here apart from us girls and sure as heck I won't tell anyone outside those you love and trust with the information."

What Maggie said made sense and Julie took a sip of her drink to ease her suddenly dry throat and looked at her. "It's about the nightmares. I know, Lindy was having them almost every night but she's not the only girl at school with the same problem." She placed an elbow on the table and leaned her cheek against one hand. "It's like everyone is having them." She frowned. "Well… I guess not *everyone* but before the man kidnapped Lindy, a few of the girls were talking about seeing a man in their rooms at night."

"Okay, and what did you hear them say at Aunt Betty's Café?" Maggie leaned forward, her face filled with expectation.

"They all had different dreams but seeing someone in their room was the same." Julie tried to unravel everything she'd heard. "Let me see. One of the girls said Lindy had nightmares about a man hiding in the shadows. She was sure he was there, then when she awoke and her father turned on the light he vanished."

"That information was on the news last night, so what else did they say?" Maggie opened the plastic wrap on her sandwiches and nibbled on a ham on rye.

"They all said they'd seen people in their rooms." Julie ran the faces of the girls through her mind, trying to recall details. "Mandy, Amanda Braxton, said she often dreams too but she wakes up and sees her dead grandma in her room at the end of the bed just looking at her. Sometimes her grandma hums nursery rhymes. She said it's happened a few times and last time she pinched herself to see if she was awake – and she was."

"Her *dead* grandma?" Maggie's brown eyes widened. "Anyone else see anything strange?"

"Yeah, there was a lot of talk about bad dreams but they were all talking at once. The others seemed to be dreaming about the man on the news, the Shadow Man." Julie straightened. "One of the girls said just about everyone in her class at school – I guess she meant the girls – had seen him in their rooms but he vanishes like smoke."

"I figure the girls at your school have very vivid imaginations but I'll make sure to tell the sheriff." Maggie made a few notes in a book on the counter, and then smiled at her. "Don't you go worryin' over them girls finding out it was you who told the sheriff. She hears secrets all the time and keeps them locked up in here." Maggie tapped her head. "Now eat your food, we have work to do. I'll show you how to inventory supplies."

CHAPTER SEVENTEEN

Jenna glanced at her watch, made a note in her book and climbed into the cruiser. She waited for Kane to join her and tossed him a packet of sandwiches. "Let's eat now and discuss what you picked up about Mr. Packer, then we'll go find Paul Kittredge. Mrs. Rosen said they go into town for lunch, but if he's back by now he's somewhere on the ranch working with a group of gardeners."

"Sure." He opened a to-go cup of coffee and sipped. "Coffee's still hot."

Jenna stared into the bag of takeout, found her bagel with cream cheese and sighed. Since Lindy Rosen went missing, she'd skipped too many meals, and after finding the young girl murdered her appetite had taken a downward slide. "So what have you got for me, Kane?"

"He's a possible suspect for a number of reasons – close proximity to Lindy, seen as a trusted person by the family, has likely set up a friendship of sorts with the girls. All this could be innocent or he could be grooming them to trust him. He seems very relaxed and that's unusual, although I've seen similar behavior in criminals who're convinced there's no evidence to link them to a crime. It wouldn't mean squat if Wolfe finds his DNA in Lindy's room. He admitted to working there recently. One thing that bothers me: he lied about his experience using explosives." Kane sipped his coffee. "Why would he lie unless he has something to hide?" He bit into his sandwich and chewed. "No one outside our team knows the connection between the explosion at the old schoolhouse and the location of Lindy's body." A frown crossed his face. "That alone makes me suspicious of him. If we add it to the other things we know about him, it makes him a possible suspect."

Jenna pondered his words for a few moments, and then sighed. "It baffles me how a killer can return to the scene of the crime and act as if nothing's happened. Packer arrived this morning and carried on business as usual but from previous experience, a few have fooled us in the past. I guess you'll be able to give me more than one example of a killer who acts perfectly normal after a vicious crime?"

"A crime of passion would be different. They're usually remorseful, shaky, upset by what they did and can't face looking at the body of their victim, but psychopathic behavior follows a pattern of sorts once it's triggered." Kane met her gaze. "It's no good trying to rationalize the mind of one because they don't think like we do and they can't be placed in a box with a label saying they are this or that type."

Jenna nibbled on her bagel. "Yeah, they're usually the opposite of the dirty old men our moms used as an example."

"The problem is many have other psychological trails or crossover behavior, we never know what has triggered them or what's going on in their minds." Kane shrugged. "They could be anyone you meet in the street, there's no particular type, but the one thing they've in common is their lack of empathy, remorse and guilt, so witnessing the aftermath of what they've done means nothing to them emotionally but hearing people talking about the crime might heighten their enjoyment of the kill."

"So why is he playing this game with us?" Jenna turned in her seat to face him. "What perverted pleasure is he getting out of seeing us run around?"

"Two reasons, I figure." Kane glanced out the window at the house then slowly back at her. "He's got away with the same crime countless times before and he needs to kill but wants the added thrill of being chased, so he gives us a clue, then escapes before we find his victim." He took out another sandwich and waved it at her. "Or deep down he wants to be caught. Maybe he's tired of running."

Jenna snorted. "You missed out the bit where he tried to kill us as well."

"I figure he was testing us to discover if we had combat skills but one thing's for sure, this is the lull before the storm. He's already planning his next kill."

Jenna turned as a truck with GREEN THUMB LANDSCAPING SERVICE painted on the side lumbered past and carried on along the curved driveway. She put down her coffee and started the engine of her cruiser. "I figure Paul Kittredge will be in that truck."

She followed some distance behind. The truck stopped beside a stack of rolled turf and four men poured out. By the time she'd pulled up the men had set to work laying turf. They all stopped at once and looked in her direction. She climbed out and shut her door, then headed along a pathway to speak to them. Behind her Kane's boots crunched on the gravel and she could see the men's eyes flicking from her to Kane then back. None of them looked too pleased to see them. She straightened and marched up to them. "We're looking for Paul Kittredge."

"That would be me, ma'am." A man with scraggy dark hair hanging down from under a cowboy hat turned and smiled at her.

Jenna wrinkled her nose as the smell of unwashed male and fertilizer oozed out of him in a fog of stink. Kittredge stood about five-ten with a rugged hawk-like appearance and piercing amber eyes. His dirty clothes clung to him and his bare arms were glossy with sweat and dusted with soil. She offered him a small smile and drew him out of earshot of the other men, who went back to work as if doing so would hide them from scrutiny. "I'm Sheriff Alton and this is Deputy Kane. As you're probably aware, Lindy Rosen was found dead yesterday and we're hunting down anyone who came in contact with her over the last couple of weeks." She pulled out her notebook and glanced at her notes. "I gather you're in charge of the Rosens' landscaping project?"

"Yeah, I'm the landscaper; these guys are come-and-go laborers."

"Did any of them work with you last week?" Jenna glanced at the men. "They legal?"

"It's not my business to question my boss on who he hires." Kittredge shrugged. "I get whoever the boss sends with me, depending on what work we're doing." He glanced over at the men. "Nope, can't say if any of them were here last week. Maybe you should ask them – if you speak Spanish."

"And you do, I gather?"

"Enough to get them working." Kittredge glanced toward the ranch house. "Shame about Lindy, she was a nice kid."

Jenna noticed his mouth twitch up at one corner into an almost-smile and bile rose at the back of her throat. She didn't need to be an expert in body language to translate his reaction. Cold seeped into her and Duke was acting strangely. The dog walked around Kittredge, and then whined, before sitting at Kane's feet. Not a clear indication of recognizing a scent but enough to get Kane's attention. When he cleared his throat, she gave him a slight nod; it was obvious he wanted to question Kittredge too.

"When was the last time you saw Lindy?" Kane hooked one thumb in the belt of his jeans and took a casual stance. To anyone other than Jenna, he looked bored.

"Late Saturday." Kittredge pulled off one gardening glove and scratched the stubble on his cheek. "She wanted to plant a climbing rose for her mom beside the trellis under her parents' bedroom. I dug the hole for her and the girls helped me plant it."

"Do you usually work on Saturdays?" Kane's gaze narrowed. "When I contacted your boss he said this job was Monday to Friday because the family liked some privacy at the weekend."

"True enough but Mrs. Rosen wanted the front garden planted and we ran out of time on Friday and came back Saturday to finish up. I stayed back to help the girls." Kittredge gave Kane a cold stare. "If kids asked you to help them to do something special as a surprise for their mom, would you refuse?"

"You shouldn't be allowed to work anywhere near kids, especially with priors involving child abuse." Kane's voice had dropped to just above a whisper and his expression changed from casual to deadly in a split second. "You need to keep well away from them."

"Well now, that charge was dismissed, which means, Deputy Kane, by speaking about it in public so my workers can hear means you're contravening my civil rights. The fine sheriff here is a witness that you've slandered my reputation."

"Not when you pleaded guilty and you're listed on the state sex offenders' database." Kane had moved closer. "I guess it slipped your mind to tell your boss, huh?"

"The charge was dismissed." Kittredge fisted his hands. "The boss knows and I ain't offended since. I'm not restricted from working near kids – read the court documents."

"Oh yeah, I know how you slid under the radar." Kane's expression was dangerous. "Problem is, you're slap bang in the middle of mine."

In an effort to defuse the situation, Jenna exchanged a meaningful stare with Kane, and then turned her attention back to Kittredge. "What time on Saturday did you last see Lindy?"

"Around four." Kittredge removed his hat and smoothed down greasy hair. "They went inside and I went home. I didn't know she'd gone missing 'til Monday."

Jenna met the man's cold gaze. "Can you account for your movements on Sunday night between the hours of ten and seven?"

"Spent the weekend at the Triple Z, woke up in some woman's bed Monday morning. I don't recall her name." Kittredge gave Jenna a satisfied smirk. "Ask around. I'm sure she'll remember me."

Seething with anger over his arrogance, Jenna made a few notes to cool down, and then lifted her chin. "Do you remember what this woman looked like?"

"Nope." Kittredge pushed his hat back on his head. "I like to drink at the weekends and my memory gets a little fuzzy."

"I see." Jenna wanted to move out of his circle of stink but stood her ground. "So any number of people will vouch for you at the Triple Z?" She glanced back at Kane. "We'll head over there now and speak to the owner. I'm sure he'll remember you taking a room for the weekend."

"He sure will, I live there." Kittredge gave her a lazy smile. "I'm what you call a permanent guest. Speak to old Bob, he'll tell you I was in my regular seat at the bar all weekend."

Unconvinced, Jenna made a note in her book, and then lifted her gaze. "That's all for now, Mr. Kittredge. Thank you for your cooperation." She made her way back to the car, not waiting for him to reply.

"Did you see the way Duke reacted to him? Oh, he is so on the suspect list." Kane grimaced. "What a jerk. Are we planning on checking out the Triple Z now or are we hunting down Charles Anderson?"

Jenna pulled open the door to her cruiser. "The Triple Z as it's not far from here, so Kittredge would have been in the vicinity Sunday night. I figure as Anderson is working way over the other side of town that he'll likely be heading home before we get there. We'll catch up with him on our way home." She waited for Kane to load Duke in the back then climb in the passenger seat before starting the engine. "I'm not convinced Kittredge is telling the truth and if he lives at the Triple Z, he was in close proximity to the old schoolhouse as well. I'll send Rowley and Walters to hunt down his mysterious bed partner in the morning. Right now I want to get back to the office and see what information they have on the other two persons of interest."

CHAPTER EIGHTEEN

"I've gotta go and meet my mom outside the library in ten minutes." Amanda Braxton rolled her eyes at the message on her cellphone, then glanced at her best friend, Lucy, and shrugged. "I wonder what really happened to Lindy."

"On the news this morning they said she walked out of her house in the night and was found dead." Lucy licked sugar from her fingers. "They didn't say where they found her, like it's a secret or something. You'd figure they'd tell everyone what really happened to her."

Amanda sipped her milkshake until the straw gurgled on the bottom of the glass. "She's been telling everyone about seeing a man in her room." She pushed the empty container away. "Maybe she wasn't dreaming after all. I know I saw my grandma's ghost standing at the foot of my bed. It's been happening over the last few nights, I'm sure I wasn't dreaming."

"If I saw a dead person standing at the bottom of my bed I'd figure I'd gone psycho – sure as heck I'd be out the door running for help." Lucy's eyes went round with fear. "Do you figure Lindy thought the man in her room was a ghost too?"

Amanda glanced at her phone to check the time. "I don't know. In her nightmare there was a man hiding in the shadows of her room. He was in the corner near the window, but when she ran to get her dad, no one was there. I guess it could've been a ghost."

"So what's your grandma's ghost look like? Is she all creepy with skin hanging off like a zombie?"

"Nah, she looks like the photo of her in the family room – you've seen it, she's wearing a pink dress." Amanda sighed. "She looks nice, not like when she was sick in hospital."

"Does she say anything?'

"Nope, she just stands there looking at me and smiling." Amanda sighed. "She used to tell me wonderful fairy stories about how they dance in the moonlight inside toadstool circles."

"They what?" Lucy almost spat her drink over the table and giggled. "I guess she insisted the Tooth Fairy exists as well?"

"Yes, and I believed her when I was six, not now though." Amanda leaned forward and lowered her voice. "Lindy told me she thought someone was watching her too."

"How creepy." Lucy shuddered dramatically. "Where? In her room?"

"Yeah, and sometimes on the way home from school she heard footsteps behind her but when she turned around no one was there." Amanda glanced behind her and then turned her attention back to Lucy. "Like they followed her from the bus stop or had been hiding in the bushes along her driveway. You know it's long like ours and it takes time to walk from the highway to the house."

"Did she see anyone?"

"Nope." Amanda pushed to her feet. "I gotta go. My mom will get mad if I keep her waiting." She grabbed her phone and a takeout bag. "You sure your mom won't let you come for a sleepover? I'm sure I can convince my brother to take us riding in the morning."

"I'm sure and anyhow, I don't really want to see your grandma's ghost."

Annoyed by her best friend's attitude, Amanda shook her head. "Okay then, I'll call you later."

"Yeah, we'll need to make plans for the Spring Festival dance. You going with Matt?"

"If Mom will let me. He's nice. We talked about going fishing one weekend."

"Fishing, huh? More like skinny-dipping." Lucy giggled. "Tell Luke I said hello."

"Sure." Amanda left the café and made her way along Main Street, peering into every shadow. Lindy hadn't been alone in thinking someone was watching her. The same thing had happened to her and her neck prickled at the memory. Last week on the walk from the highway to her home, she'd heard rustling in the bushes. At first, she'd figured a bear had wandered onto their ranch and she'd pulled out the can of bear spray she carried in her bag, but bears gave off an unmistakable stink and she'd smell it. She'd looked all around but found no trace of bears, no scat or marks on the trees. The only animals she'd found had been a few squirrels bounding from tree to tree and yet it was as if someone was there, hiding in the trees, watching her.

She pushed past a group of boys hanging outside the computer store, relieved that the town was busy and she didn't have to walk alone. If what she had heard was true, Lindy had been crazy to open the front door to a stranger in the middle of the night. She should've told her parents if she'd figured someone was following her after school.

Her mom was waiting outside the library in her red SUV. Amanda climbed inside and smiled at her. "I brought you some cookies."

"Thanks." Her mom started the engine. "If I'd known you'd be at Aunt Betty's Café I'd have dropped by to collect you."

Amanda gaped at her. "In front of my friends? They'll figure I can't go anywhere without my mommy."

"Sure, I understand." Her mother gave her a knowing look. "Believe it or not I was a teenager once myself."

"You know Lindy, the girl that died?" Amanda decided to bite the bullet and tell her mother her worries. "She told me she had nightmares about a man in her room and thought someone was following her along her driveway after school. I dream about Grandma and I had the same feeling on our driveway too. I look around but there's no one there."

"You've an overactive imagination triggered by what Lindy said to you before she went missing." Her mother smiled at her. "Dreaming about Grandma watching over you is hardly a nightmare and I often feel the same when I'm in the wooded parts of our ranch. The wind in the trees and the animals make strange sounds and the trees cast long shadows. It makes it creepy even in the daytime." She smiled at her. "Don't worry, you're normal."

Amanda heaved a sigh of relief. Normal she could handle.

CHAPTER NINETEEN

As Rowley led the way onto the football field, his gaze set on a tall athletic man, who stood out among the other workers laying artificial turf. From the janitor's description, he had to be Mason Lancaster. He strode toward him with Walters close behind and took in the man. Undeniably handsome, with bronzed muscular arms, but years of working outdoors had wrinkled the skin around his eyes. As they approached, a worried expression crossed Lancaster's face and he stepped away from the other men.

Rowley pulled out his notebook and kept his expression bland. "Mason Lancaster?"

"Yeah, what can I do for you, deputies?" Lancaster waved a gloved hand toward the other men. "We're kinda busy here."

"I won't take too much of your time." Rowley led him some distance away from the other curious men. "I need to ask you a few routine questions."

"In relation to what?" Lancaster pulled out a bandana, wiped the sweat from his face, and then removed his hat before turning to catch the cold breeze blowing from the mountains.

All the advice Kane had given him about body language and attitude poured into Rowley's mind. He assessed the man standing before him. Lancaster appeared relaxed now but he'd seen a different expression when they arrived. "We're investigating the Lindy Rosen case and speaking to anyone who may have been in contact with her in the days leading up to her death."

"Lindy, yeah, I knew her." Lancaster gave him a direct look and shrugged. "As well as I know any of the students that hang around me like butterflies all semester." He shook his head. "Terrible thing her being murdered like that, she was a pretty little thing."

Murdered? A cold chill trickled down Rowley's spine. Could he be looking into the eyes of a killer? "Ah, we don't have a cause of death. Do *you* know what happened to her?"

"Me? Heck no." Lancaster replaced his hat. "I assumed when a girl goes missing then she's found dead, someone murdered her – wouldn't you?"

Rowley straightened. "Nope, I'd wait for the ME's findings. She could have been sleepwalking, tripped over a log and banged her head for all I know." He eyeballed him. "When did you last see Lindy?"

"Hmm, not sure, some of the girls came by at lunchtime before spring break to say goodbye." Lancaster stared into the distance and smiled as if to himself. "The guys call them my fan club."

"Yeah? Many of them come by alone?" Rowley cleared his throat. "Have you dated any of them?"

"Nah, they're just kids." Lancaster snorted. "It's been the same since I injured my knee. The older women see me as a liability, figure I can't make the big bucks any longer, but the kids, they see me as a football star and a celebrity."

"I guess they would." Rowley frowned. "Have you seen any strangers hanging around the school, or hereabouts?"

"People are coming and going all the time." Lancaster glanced at his crew, who were standing around gawking at them. "Will this take much longer?"

"No, I have a couple more questions." Rowley made a few notes. "Can you account for your whereabouts on Sunday night?"

"Sunday? Yeah, I was with one of my girlfriends, Angela Pike. She's one of the teachers here, lives out on Pine, number seven."

Pine Road ran parallel to Stanton Road and was around one mile from the Rosens' ranch. The time Lancaster was at his girlfriend's home was critical. Rowley noted her name and address, and then lifted his attention back to Lancaster. "What time?"

"We had dinner at the Cattleman's Hotel, left there around nine, I guess." Lancaster's forehead creased into a frown. "I spent the night with her but left early to get ready for work. She'll be home now if you're planning on checking out my story."

Rowley closed his notebook. "Okay, that's all for now, thank you for your cooperation." He turned and walked away with Walters.

"I figure we need to hunt down Angela Pike and see what she has to say." Walters looked grim-faced. "He was in the area at the time Lindy went missing."

Rowley made his way back to his cruiser. "Yeah, he ticks a few of the boxes. In the area and he knew Lindy. She likely would've trusted him. We'll go see if Miss Pike is at home." He pulled open the car door, slid behind the wheel and then picked up the radio mic. "I'll call in and let the sheriff know where we're heading."

He listened with interest as the sheriff gave him the details of the Kittredge interview. "He doesn't remember her name? What a sleaze."

"How close are you to the Triple Z?"

Rowley cleared his throat. "Not far. We could swing past there, and then go see Angela Pike on Pine."

"Yeah, it would save you driving out there in the morning. And I'll text you the address of Sean Packer. I want you to speak to his wife and get a statement from her confirming her husband was at home on Sunday night. He lives closer to town, so you can swing by there on the way back to the office."

"Roger that." Rowley disconnected and turned to Walters. "Looks like we're heading out to the Triple Z, to find a mystery woman who sleeps around." He scratched his cheek and stared into nothing, thinking. "I can't see any woman offering up that kind of information. Any ideas?"

"Yeah, I figure I'll leave the questioning to you." Walters snorted a laugh. "Oh boy, this is gonna be fun."

CHAPTER TWENTY

Jenna was having one of those days that seemed to drag on forever and was virtually running on caffeine. She eyed the steaming cup of coffee on her desk with apprehension. Although exhausted in mind and body, the explosion had left her feeling as if a truck had run her over and she doubted she'd sleep again tonight. At times like these, she wondered why she'd gone into law enforcement in the first place, then she glanced up at the crime scene photos of Lindy Rosen and felt ashamed. The girl's eyes held a plea for help. She took a long drink of her coffee. "Whatever it takes, Lindy, I'll bring your killer to justice."

She picked up her phone and called Wolfe. He'd promised the autopsy report by five and he never let her down. "When can I expect your report on Lindy Rosen?"

"If you drop by in the morning, I'll have a preliminary report."

Jenna drummed her fingernails on the desk. "It's taking longer than usual. Any problems?"

"I've run into a few complications." Wolfe sighed. He sounded tired as well. *"First up, the Rosens didn't want me to perform a post. I had to explain that in homicide cases, it was up to my discretion and I didn't need their permission. I figure the idea of someone messing with their child was too much to bear."*

"I can't imagine anything worse than losing a child." Jenna glanced back at the image of Lindy. "I'm sure you explained the process."

"I did and Emily was very helpful. She sat Mrs. Rosen down, gave her a drink and explained she would be there with Lindy during the

examination. It made it a bit easier on her." Wolfe cleared his throat. *"The autopsy isn't why I'm waiting to report my findings – yes, it was a homicide, but you already know that. I wanted to check my readings and make sure the majority of forensic tests are completed before I make my assessment."*

Jenna frowned. "That's unusual, what's causing a problem?"

"Time of death." Wolfe sounded distracted. *"The facts presented to me don't add up to the timeline we have of what we believe happened to her. I'll go through everything again and explain in the morning in detail. Right this moment, nothing is making sense."*

"Okay, we'll drop by at nine, will that give you time?"

"Sure, I'll see you tomorrow."

Jenna disconnected and leaned back in her chair. Wolfe usually gave time of death by calculating the temperature of the body, so something else had happened to make him mistrust his findings. A knock on the door brought her out of her thoughts. "Yes, come in."

"Rowley and Walters are back." Kane indicated behind him with his thumb. "Do you want them in here to give their report now?"

Jenna glanced at the clock on the wall. It was past five. "Yeah, it's late and we still have to go speak to Anderson. It's been a long day and I'm dead on my feet."

"Do you want me to order Chinese for say six-thirty? We'll pick it up on the way home." Kane rubbed his belly in an unconscious move. "Save worrying about dinner."

"Yeah, I'm too sore to cook and too exhausted to eat but Chinese would be nice for a change." Jenna smiled at him. "Then get back in here. I'll wait for you."

"Roger that." Kane hustled out the door.

A few moments later, Rowley and Walters came to her door. "Sit down; Kane will be here in a moment. I've added all our potential suspects' interview data to the files. Make sure you upload your information before you leave tonight. Rowley, you'll be in charge first thing in the morning, I'm attending the autopsy report with Kane."

"Before we start, something has come up that needs your attention." Rowley pulled out his notes. "It came about when we spoke to Noah McLeod. He admitted to involvement with one of the students." Rowley went on to explain what had happened.

Jenna listened in astonishment. "So McLeod figured you were there because of a complaint against him?"

"Sure thing. He almost messed his pants when he saw us coming." Walter chuckled. "Don't think he'll be leaving town anytime soon – Rowley put the fear of God into him."

Jenna frowned. "How so?"

"I told him you'd have the FBI on his tail if he left town." Rowley cracked a smile.

"Did I miss anything?" Kane walked into the room with Duke on his heels, closed the door behind him and took a seat.

Jenna explained, and then looked at Rowley. "Get him in here first thing in the morning for questioning. Walters, go see the parents of Jocelyn Smythe and explain the situation, speak with the girl if possible, get a statement, then I'll turn it over to the DA. He'll likely want to charge him."

"Where was McLeod when Lindy Rosen went missing?" Kane turned to look at Rowley. "He might be our man."

"He doesn't have anyone to verify his whereabouts on Sunday night. He lives alone, said he stayed home and watched TV." Rowley leafed through his notes. "He admitted knowing Lindy Rosen but said she was chasing after Mason Lancaster, the ex-football player."

Jenna nodded. "Then we'll need to interview him about that as well when you bring him in. Ask him what was on TV on Sunday night; he should remember what he watched."

"Yes, ma'am." Rowley made a few notes.

They discussed the interviews with all the potential suspects, finishing with Rowley's talk with Mason Lancaster. Jenna leaned forward on her desk. "So did his girlfriend corroborate his story?"

"Yes and no." Rowley glanced up from his notes. "She said the last time she recalls seeing him was around eleven. She fell asleep soon after, then woke up and found him gone. That was a little after one. She noticed the time because he usually leaves around six if he has to go to work the next morning. I asked her if he'd called her today and she said her mother had just left and she turns off her cellphone during her visit so if he did call, he didn't leave a message." He frowned. "We dropped by the Cattleman's Hotel and they went through the credit card receipts and found he'd paid for their meal around nine, so that part of his story is true."

"So he was in the area, knows Lindy and mentioned her attraction to him. He believes he has an alibi. I wonder if he tried to call his girlfriend to corroborate his story? If so, I bet a dollar to a dime he didn't figure on her cellphone being off when he called." Jenna pushed to her feet, went to the whiteboard and added Mason Lancaster's name. "I think we have a suspect." She turned to look at Rowley again. "Did you find the mysterious lady at the Triple Z?"

"Nope but we found Bob and he said Kittredge is in the bar every night and picks up women regular. He doesn't recall which woman or any particular night, said the days all roll into one."

"Okay." Jenna wrote down the names of the four men they'd interviewed and made notes beside each name. "I figure our killer is one of these men."

Lancaster (Groundskeeper at high school): In the area at the time of Lindy Rosen's disappearance, knows her, has no alibi.

Kittredge (Green Thumb Landscaping Service working at the Rosens'): Lives at the Triple Z, knows Lindy, has no alibi at this time. Sex offender.

Sean Packer (Handyman working at the Rosens): Had contact with Lindy, lied about his knowledge of explosives.

Noah McLeod (Janitor at high school): Also has contact with Lindy, admitted sex offender.

Jenna turned back to look at her deputies. "We have one more person of interest to interview and I'll be heading out to speak with him when we've wrapped up here. Charles Anderson. He's a technician working with a company by the name of Silent Alarms. He installed the alarm system at the Rosens', had access to the home, and had contact with the family, so he comes under our scrutiny."

"Didn't Kane mention he came up clean?" Rowley glanced down at his notes. "He'd have been background checked to work for a security company."

Jenna gave him a long look. "You'd be surprised how many killers have no priors. That's why over half of them are never caught. Anyone who met Lindy is a person of interest until proved otherwise. These five men are the tip of the iceberg. On the way home tonight, I want you to head out to the Triple Z with Walters and see if anyone remembers seeing Kittredge there Sunday evening and see if you can find the woman he spent the night with." Exhausted, she sucked in a deep breath. "First thing in the morning, I want background checks on everyone who worked on the Rosens' ranch over the last month. You'll need to contact the Green Thumb Landscaping Service and Silent Alarms because they would've used a number of men over that time."

"Yes, ma'am." Rowley made notes.

Jenna dropped into her chair and waved them away. "Okay, when you're done, go home and get some sleep."

CHAPTER TWENTY-ONE

Kane waited for Jenna to shrug into her coat. She looked pale and her eyes were huge in her thin face. Knowing how concussion could sneak up on a person, he moved closer and cupped her chin in one hand. "You doing okay?"

"Says the man with a butt full of splinters and torn ligaments in his shoulder." Jenna smiled at him. "You don't look so good either. Are you in pain?"

Kane smiled at her and brushed the red marks on her cheek. "I'm hurting all over but I figure we're pretty lucky to have survived the explosion with a couple of scratches." He eyed her critically. "These are superficial, they won't scar."

"That's good." She looked up at him. "Let's get this interview over with, and then it's Chinese, watching TV then hitting the hot tub." She sighed. "We'll be working around the clock until we solve this murder and I'll need to grab a couple of hours' rest while I can."

"Yeah, a good sleep will help." Reluctantly, Kane dropped his hand. The hot tub would have been his choice too. He turned to head out the door and she touched his arm. He turned and looked back at her. "I'll grab my coat."

"Have you changed your mind about coming over tonight?" Jenna gave him a puzzled look, pulled on her knitted cap and met his gaze. "My sofa is way more comfortable than yours and we can eat in front of the TV." She pointed to his dog. "Duke can come too."

Kane let out a long sigh and smiled. "I'd like that."

*

Anderson lived three miles from the Rosens' ranch, in a small house walking distance from Stanton Forest. The same white pickup they'd seen at the Rosens' sat in the driveway. Kane pulled up behind it and climbed from his truck. He leaned over the back seat and rubbed the dog's ears. "Stay here, Duke, we won't be long."

He waited for Jenna and they headed to the front door. When Anderson opened the door, he gave them a horrified stare.

"What happened to you?" Anderson looked from one to the other. "Been in a car wreck?"

"Something like that." Jenna offered him a smile. "May we have a word with you, Mr. Anderson? We're speaking with everyone who came in contact with Lindy Rosen before she went missing."

"Sure, you want to step inside? It's getting cold." Anderson stood to one side and opened the door wide. He was still in his coveralls. "I've just gotten home but I've had time to light a fire in the family room." He waved them through a door.

Kane did a visual scan of the house. It had a lived-in appearance, old overstuffed furniture and a musty smell of stale lavender as if his grandma lived with him. He glanced down the hallway into a seventies-style avocado and teak kitchen. The house had paintings on every wall in an overindulgence of art, each of landscapes of places he didn't recognize. He'd an appreciation of art. He walked closer to examine a study of a clearing in a forest. It was precise right down to the wildflowers and butterflies.

His quick sweep of the interior hadn't picked up any sign of a security alarm. The house seemed out of sync with a man working in a high-tech profession. "Lived here long?"

"Nah, I inherited it from a distant cousin last summer. I was living down in Colorado, working for the mines." Anderson shrugged.

"When I discovered she'd left me this house, I decided to move here. I had the qualifications to get a tech job with the security company and take a casual job with the council. I run community art classes once a week at night. The security job isn't as hard as working shifts in the mines and it pays well enough."

"Are these your pictures?" Jenna peered at the framed landscapes. "They're very good. Do you sell them?"

"No, they're scenes from places I've been, memories I want to keep." Anderson straightened a frame, and then looked back at Jenna. "Now, you mentioned Lindy Rosen. Have you any suspects yet?"

"Suspects?" Jenna's brow creased into a frown. She flicked a glance at Kane then shook her head. "We don't have a cause of death yet. For all we know she was sleepwalking and died of exposure."

"I can't imagine how she walked right out the house without tripping an alarm or a CCTV camera." Anderson rubbed his chin. "I was in the crew that set up the system. It needs a code to disable it and that's not something I'd imagine she could've done in her sleep."

Kane watched the man's reactions closely. Although his body language was outwardly calm, asking about suspects was a red flag. He shrugged. "Not necessarily. I've heard of cases where people unlock six deadbolts in their sleep. If Lindy had memorized the code, she could've used it in her sleep. This is why we aren't ruling out sleepwalking."

"I see, so how far did she get?" Anderson directed his question to Jenna. "On the TV I heard you were searching all over Black Rock Falls. Surely if you believed she'd just walked out the door, she couldn't have gotten too far."

"It's normal procedure. We'd no idea what happened to her so we covered every possibility." Jenna had ignored him and her face became a mask of professionalism. She'd obviously had enough of his questions and turned the interview back around. "When did you last see Lindy?"

"When I installed the floodlights." Anderson leaned casually against the doorframe. "That was a few weeks ago, I guess. I could check my work sheets to give you the dates I worked there if you like?"

"We already have them from your employer." Jenna lifted her chin. "Did you speak to her?"

"I did." Anderson stared into space for a few moments as if thinking. "She asked me why I had installed a floodlight right outside her bedroom window."

"And why did you?" Jenna pulled out her notebook and jotted down some notes. "Wouldn't that disturb her at night if the sensor lights came on and shone into her room?"

"I guess, but it was on the design approved by Mr. Rosen." Anderson shrugged. "They're outside all the bedroom windows. Lindy's bedroom has a rose trellis. Maybe her father figured someone might climb up it to break into the house."

After Kane had examined Lindy's bedroom, he'd noted the alarms fitted to her bedroom windows. It would have been near impossible for anyone to break into the house without tripping one of the alarms or the CCTV cameras. "So, you don't believe anyone broke into the house and kidnapped her?"

"If the system was activated, not a chance." Anderson shuffled his feet. "I checked it out and everything is working fine. I had the ME watching me as well, and asking questions. Maybe you should speak with him."

"So in your professional opinion, the system was either not activated or Lindy switched it off and walked out the door?" Jenna made more notes, and then lifted her gaze. "Run me through what happens if someone walks onto their property and trips the alarm."

"The motion sensors would activate the cameras and the floodlights simultaneously; a silent alarm sounds in the family room and the parents' bedroom. It's a flashing light." Anderson cleared his throat. "The alarm is raised at head office. Technicians there view the footage and take the appropriate action. First, they call the owner in case they've accidentally tripped the alarm. If not, and we see someone sneaking around or attempting to break in, we call 911."

"Where were you on Sunday night through Monday morning?" Jenna glanced at her notes. "Between the hours of midnight and seven?"

"At work. I do the graveyard shift on Sunday and Wednesday nights, twelve till six, and then I'm on call for any emergencies from around midday, sometimes earlier. But most Mondays and Thursdays, they give the work to the other guys. It's a fair trade; none of them want to work every night."

"Okay, one more question and we'll be on our way." Jenna closed her notebook and slid it and her pen inside her jacket pocket. "Did Lindy attend your art classes?"

"Yeah, for a couple of weeks." Anderson frowned. "It's a community class and anyone can attend as long as I have room. I get the usual crowd, and then a few different people drift in and out."

"Did you notice if she was friendly toward anyone in particular?" Jenna exchanged a look with Kane.

Kane narrowed his gaze. "What the sheriff means is, did she have any guys hanging around her, anyone who may have lured her from the house?"

"I have my hands full during the class; I don't take any notice of what they're doing outside their artwork." Anderson walked to the front door. "If that's all, it's been a long day and I'm still in my coveralls."

Kane waited to see if Jenna had any more questions, then followed her out the door. "Thank you for your time."

He caught up with her. "I'm not too sure about him, two things bother me. He asked about suspects before we released cause of death, and he made a comment about our injuries as well. Most strangers don't ask personal questions when dealing with law enforcement. He seemed way too friendly to me. What do you think?"

"It seems to me everyone we've spoken to is a possible suspect but all we have is circumstantial evidence – not one of them has a motive." She climbed into the truck.

Kane slid behind the wheel and started the engine. "Only if you're looking at this murder as a crime of passion, but psychopaths don't need a motive to kill. They may have a trigger that sets them off on a killing spree but I get the feeling this kill was well planned." He headed back to town. "I don't believe for one minute Lindy just walked out the house and happened to bump into a killer."

"So we're looking at this from the wrong angle?" Jenna turned in her seat and looked at him. "Lindy knew her killer and went with him willingly." She snorted in disgust. "We've dealt with enough pedophiles to know how they groom kids. I figure one of the men on our list lured her from the house and used her as a pawn in his deadly game of chess with us."

Kane nodded in agreement. "Yeah, it was checkmate on the last game but he hasn't finished playing yet. I figure he's just resetting the board."

CHAPTER TWENTY-TWO

Wednesday

Amanda Braxton lay in bed looking at the full moon spreading its light across her bedroom. She had wonderful memories of her grandma's stories of fairies dancing in the moonlight. When she'd told her friend Lucy, she'd laughed at her but Amanda didn't care. She believed in fairies and it would be her secret, her and Grandma's. Sleep came easily as she had no fear of seeing her grandma's ghost – Grandma told her she would watch over her and if she wanted to stand at the foot of the bed, she didn't mind.

The familiar sound of her music box woke her and she peered at the bedside clock. It was two in the morning. Moonlight no longer shone across her floor – the moon had made its path across the sky and would be over the roof by now – but she could see quite clearly. She rolled over to look at her music box. It stood closed on her nightstand, but the tinkling melody surrounded her. She sat up, intrigued to find the source of the music, then slid out of bed and went to the window.

A shiver of excitement made her gasp at the sight of her grandma standing in the trees opposite the house. Wearing her pink dress and cardigan, just like in the photograph, and at her feet she could see fairies. Was she dreaming or had Grandma really come by to show her the stories about fairies were true? She pinched her arm hard and it hurt. *I am awake.* Without a second thought, she pulled on her dressing gown, pushed her feet into her slippers and, taking her house key, left her room, closing the door behind her.

Amanda had memorized the security code for the front door and her dad had instructed her how to disable the sensor lights during the day and turn the system on and off when visitors arrived. If she disabled the lights and CCTV cameras, the house alarm would reset five minutes from when she left the house. She could use her key to get back inside and as long as she input the code and reset everything, no one would ever know she'd gone out to see her grandma.

She looked through the glass in the front door and Grandma was waiting patiently for her. She punched in the code, disabled the lights and CCTV cameras, then opened the door and peered into the moonlight, but she could no longer see Grandma standing in the trees. Disappointment flooded over her as she moved onto the porch, closed the door behind her and searched the trees. She kept her voice low. "Grandma, where are you?"

A flash of movement caught her attention and she bolted down the steps and ran into the trees. Small bushes snagged at her dressing gown and low branches seemed to reach out to grab her hair. A figure came out of the darkness behind her and she huffed a sigh of relief and turned. "Grandma?"

Someone crashed into her with such force that the air rushed from her lungs. Amanda staggered over the uneven ground, trying to remain upright. The next moment a large smelly cloth clamped over her face, covering her mouth and nose, then an arm like steel closed around her, crushing her ribs. She couldn't breathe. Panic gripped her, she thrashed around, kicking, but the cloth against her face held tight and she sucked in a strange taste. Her stomach rolled and her limbs became weak and useless. A strange sleepiness engulfed her and she opened her eyes wide, fighting to stay awake, but the forest seemed to melt around her. A voice, low and husky, came close to her ear. Warm breath brushed her cheek.

"No, honey, it's the Big Bad Wolf."

CHAPTER TWENTY-THREE

Heavy-hearted, Jenna slid out of Kane's truck and made her way into the medical examiner's office. There could be nothing worse than witnessing an autopsy of a young girl and Wolfe had saved her from the more gruesome aspects by offering her a run-down of his findings. Having both Wolfe and Webber as part-time deputies, she covered the legal aspect of having an officer to witness the post. She used her card to access the morgue and glanced over one shoulder, to see Kane's rigid expression. "I figure this is the worst part of our job."

"Yeah, it's not something I generally look forward to." Kane moved through the door. "I've been wondering all night what Wolfe has found. He seemed confused and that's not like him at all."

Jenna inhaled the familiar smell only a morgue carried and wrinkled her nose in disgust. As she pushed through the double doors leading to the examination room, a near freezing chill hit her face. She smiled at Wolfe, sitting beside Webber and his daughter Emily, chatting about his findings as if they were discussing last night's movie. "Morning. What have you got for me?"

"More than I bargained for, I'm afraid." Wolfe rose to his feet and indicated to Webber to bring out Lindy Rosen's body. "As I mentioned, the body temperature I took at the scene didn't add up to the series of events we figured happened to Lindy. Since doing her autopsy, I've a completely different timeline."

Intrigued, Jenna turned to look down at Lindy's body. Her skin was deathly white and Wolfe had made a number of incisions around her throat plus the usual Y-shaped one down her chest. She had prepared for this visit and pushed away the part of her that grieved this girl, allowing her professional side to take over. She needed to see Lindy through Wolfe's eyes and use the information to catch her killer. "Okay. So what was so unusual about this case?"

"The one very pertinent fact is that Lindy died no more than one hour after her parents found her missing." Wolfe took the iPad Emily handed him and held it out to Jenna. "When I took her temperature at the scene, it was too low for her time of death to have been in the last hour or two before we located her and when I loaded her into the van, I noticed the rigor wasn't consistent with the assumed time of death."

"So you're saying he kidnapped her, filmed her and murdered her before he sent Jenna the video?" Kane's brow furrowed. "So what time do you believe she died?"

"At least six hours before you found her. Likely, he killed her within three hours of her abduction." Wolfe pulled on latex gloves and rolled Lindy's body onto its side. "See the apparent bruising on her buttocks, shoulder blades and forearms? That isn't bruising. The cause is when a body lies in the same position for some hours and blood engorges the tissues. It starts quite slowly after about two hours but from the dark color of the hypostasis, Lindy was lying on her back for approximately six hours after death occurred."

"She was last seen around midnight Sunday and we found her at five thirty on Monday afternoon." Jenna pulled out her cellphone and scanned the files. "What a sick SOB, playing a game with me when he'd already murdered her." She glanced up at Wolfe. "Cause of death?"

"Asphyxiation caused by strangulation. All the signs are there." Wolfe met her gaze. "He strangled her from behind using the cord we found with the body. I found no indication of sexual assault."

"Didn't you find any trace evidence at all?" Kane stared at Wolfe's iPad. "That's unusual in itself."

"No DNA but Lindy has a story to tell. The events leading to her death are reasonably clear." Wolfe covered the body and indicated to small red patches on Lindy's cheek. "There's a handprint on her face and the insides of her nostrils are inflamed, as if she inhaled a substance. I'm waiting on the results of blood tests to confirm but I figure he used diethyl ether or chloroform to subdue her, maybe mixed with another substance, perhaps cocaine." He placed his hand over the marks to demonstrate the position of the handprint. "I believe he was straddling her at the time and if you see here, where her teeth have pierced her bottom lip, I would say he used a considerable amount of force."

"Any other scratches or defense wounds?" Kane walked to the end of the gurney and examined Lindy's feet. "Her feet are dirty. Why did she walk out the house without wearing slippers?"

"This worries me as well. She has no scrapes or head injuries to indicate she ran away and was hunted down then subdued. No defense wounds, DNA under her nails, nothing. The dirt on her feet could have come from beneath the bench outside the old schoolhouse. I sent a swab for testing but I would imagine it will only give a local result."

The scene filled Jenna's mind. She lifted her chin and stared at Wolfe. "If the killer was in her room, we're looking at this all wrong. Somehow he gained access to the house, made it to her bedroom, pinned her on the bed and knocked her out with chloroform or similar then carried her out the house."

"How did he get inside?" Kane covered Lindy's feet with the sheet. "Mr. Rosen set the alarm around six and if he snuck into the house and hid beforehand, he would have had to know the code to turn off the alarm when he left."

Jenna shook her head. "This happened to me, remember? Someone followed me inside once, hid in a cupboard and watched me use my code. I was alone, but the Rosens have their daughters running all over – it wouldn't have been easy for him to slip into their house unnoticed."

"I figure they would need to know the layout of the house." Webber moved to Jenna's side. "They'd have to find a safe place to hide and wait until the family went to bed."

Jenna glanced up at Kane. "That would cut down the suspects to men who've had access to the house over the last few weeks."

"Maybe not." Emily's fingers moved swiftly over her computer's keyboard. "The ranches on the new building project are all constructed by the same company. I noticed the blueprints displayed in the window of the real estate broker and they're all available online too." She pointed to the screen. "Look, they're using homes already built in the area as examples and each has a floorplan."

Deflated, Jenna sighed. "Dammit, I thought we'd halved our list of possible suspects." She moved her attention back to Wolfe. "Anything of use on her laptop or cellphone?"

"No, just the usual." Wolfe sighed. "Her diary held nothing of real interest. She had a crush on a boy at school and hoped he'd ask her to the Spring Festival dance, is all."

"Okay, send me your final report when possible." Jenna removed her gloves and dropped them into the garbage. "We'll head back to the office. Rowley is hunting down people to corroborate alibis. I'll be interested to see what he's discovered." She cleared her throat. "The Rosens will want to know when you're through with Lindy's examination."

"I won't be releasing the body today. I'll call them and explain." Wolfe nodded at Webber, who wheeled the gurney away, then turned back to Jenna. "This is an unusual case. Why did he kill her? I can't figure out a motive. In most kidnap cases the motive is money, rape and murder or to keep a sex slave. Lindy died by strangulation but her killer follows no pattern I've seen before. It's too clean for a first kill and a novice would leave trace evidence behind. In my opinion this man has killed before and often."

"Oh, yeah." Kane's gaze followed the gurney. "This killer is well organized, he's planning every move and for some crazy reason is involving Jenna in his madness. It's as if he's playing a game with her, as if he wants to be caught."

Jenna pushed both hands through her hair. Why did killers focus on her? This hadn't been the first time a killer had targeted her. "Why me? If he wants to be caught why not give himself up and confess?"

"You represent the law and giving himself up would be an anticlimax – he craves the limelight." Kane met her gaze. "I'm with Wolfe on this. We could be dealing with a killer who's murdered before and gotten away with it so many times he's bored. He wants to crow about his kills and be famous as the sadistic Shadow Man, so he's using you to gain notoriety. If this is the profile of our killer, Lindy was collateral damage, to get our attention. Taking us out with a bomb makes him a hero in jail. He knows his killing spree won't last forever and wants to go out in a blaze of glory."

CHAPTER TWENTY-FOUR

Jenna lifted her face to the cool breeze and inhaled the fresh pine and wood-smoke fragrance coming on the breeze. It was good to be outside in the fresh air and she leaned on Kane's truck and absorbed the beauty of the green forest and snowcapped mountains to clear the gruesome images of Lindy Rosen from her mind. Who had lured her to her death and how the hell was she going to find her killer? She'd been coming up against brick walls, with a few suspicious men on her list but not suspicious enough to pull them in for questioning, let alone make an arrest.

Her cellphone vibrated in her pocket and a wave of dread caught her unawares. She stared at the caller ID. Relieved to see Maggie's name displayed, she sighed. "Morning, Maggie, what's up?"

"We've another girl gone missin'. Amanda Braxton, fifteen, lives not one mile away from the Rosens' ranch."

Jenna's heart sank. "Send me the address and details; we'll head out there now. Tell Rowley to contact search and rescue, I want them on standby." She disconnected and looked at Kane. "We haven't hunted down a viable suspect for Lindy's killer yet and it looks like the Shadow Man's hit again."

"Another kidnapping?" Kane climbed into his vehicle and leaned over the back seat to pat Duke on the head. "Where this time?" He started the engine.

Jenna's phone chimed a message and she entered the coordinates into the GPS. "About a mile away. Amanda Braxton, fifteen, lives with her mother and older brother. Last seen around ten last night. Her mom figured she'd slept in and sent her brother to check on her around nine this morning and her room was empty."

"If this is the Shadow Man, he's escalating faster than I expected." Kane glanced at the GPS screen, then swung the car around and headed for Stanton Road. "We've a major problem with him because he's playing a game with us in his mind. From the autopsy results, we know Lindy Rosen was dead before he sent you the video of her in the cellar. We never had a chance of finding her alive; the entire thing was a stunt."

Jenna grimaced. "So what's his angle?"

"I'm not sure. Maybe he gets off on watching us trying to save a life when he knows his victim is already dead." Kane shrugged. "Or he's giving himself plenty of time to stage the final scene."

Allowing his conclusions to sink in, Jenna stared at him. Light streamed through the forest in bands, hitting Kane and making him look like a flickering old movie, his movements broken and disjointed. The image looked surreal and Jenna blinked a few times to keep her mind on track. "Uh-huh, so what significance do the murders have to him? This guy doesn't display the brutality we usually see in a psychopath's MO. There's no rape and Lindy was killed by a nice neat strangulation." She glanced into the forest. Thousands of green pines flashed by, mixed with small splashes of color from the abundant wildflowers. She turned back to him. "If Amanda is his second victim and he tries the same stunt again, I have my own theory about him."

"Okay." Kane's mouth twitched down at the corners. "Why don't I like where this is heading?"

Deep in her own thoughts, Jenna frowned at his worried expression. "I'm pretty sure you've come to the same conclusion, Kane, it's written all over your face." She cleared her throat and kept her expression bland, but deep inside, the notion that she'd become the target of a deranged lunatic again scared the hell out of her. "He's only killing to get my attention, to draw me into his perverted game. His trigger is women in authority and he needs power over them. Once he has them following his orders, he plans to kill them in a gruesome way – that's why he set the IED, he wanted to create carnage and would've likely been somewhere close filming the aftermath."

"Let's hope not." Kane slowed to take a left, then after a few yards drove through wrought-iron gates and into a long driveway.

Glacial Heights sure lived up to its reputation for being one of the most beautiful suburbs in Black Rock Falls. Building the new hospital wing and the extension of the college campus had brought an influx of prosperity to the small town. Highly skilled professionals had arrived and built spectacular houses north of town, and in the south where the land was plentiful and cheap, industrial plants producing everything from heavy machinery to barbed wire had blossomed.

She admired the layout of the ranch. The owners had left half in its natural state. Tall pines lined a substantial driveway winding through a wooded area and opening up to a landscaped mirage surrounding the ranch house. Seasonal flowers spilled over flowerbeds in a kaleidoscope of color and a yellow spring rose climbed a trellis beside the front porch. The Braxtons had spared no expense to make their dream home.

She glanced back at Kane. "Right now, I feel like I have a target on my back."

"Then I'll make sure you're never alone, Jenna, until we catch this guy. You'll need to wear your vest when we're on patrol." Kane gave her a long look. "Although, I can't see what motive he has to specifically target you. There's plenty of other female authority figures in town. I've seen people go to extreme lengths to get revenge but with every case you've solved in Black Rock Falls, the perpetrators are either dead or in jail." He shrugged. "Unless he's gotten himself a problem with all women in authority – and if so why kill a teenage girl to lure you? He would've had the opportunity to shoot you a thousand times in the last few weeks, on the ranch or walking down Main Street." He shook his head. "This one is a mystery on so many fronts. For instance, how did he lure Lindy from the house?"

"I wish I knew." Jenna folded her arms across her chest. This time she was going by her gut instinct and nothing he could say would change her slant on things. "Think about it, Kane. If he just shot me, it wouldn't be a game, would it? I mean, for someone who lives for the thrill of dominating women in authority, killing me like that would be too clean. He wants to see me cut up bad. He wants to make a statement to show the world he's a tough guy or something." She shrugged. "I guess if Amanda's case fits the same MO, you'll agree with my take on the Shadow Man?"

"Don't for one minute believe I'm dismissing your conclusions, Jenna, 'cause I'm not." Kane flicked her a concerned glance. "I figured we're discussing theories is all."

Relieved, Jenna nodded. "Okay, sure. It's good to discuss different angles on cases, or we'd never solve any at all."

"Yeah, sometimes we need to step outside the box. Crimes are like people, some appear similar but really they're different." He sighed and pulled to a halt outside the house. "One thing's for sure, the Rosen case killer doesn't follow any particular pattern of behavior. There're way too many variables to fit Shadow Man into any known category. We need more evidence."

"True, but I don't want to find out he's strangled more girls just to prove a point." Jenna reached for the door handle. "Let's hope this is a simple runaway."

A woman ran out the door and down the steps to meet them. Dark hair tied back and wearing a sweater and blue jeans, she was in her late thirties. Jenna climbed out the SUV and went to meet her. "Mrs. Braxton?"

"Oh, dear Lord, my Mandy has gone missing." Tears streamed down her cheeks. "I've called everyone I know and no one has seen her. Her cellphone is on her nightstand and none of her clothes are gone; it's as if she up and walked out the door wearing her PJs, dressing gown and slippers."

Jenna exchanged a look with Kane. Without issuing an order, he slid into action, walked some distance away and pulled out his cellphone to call Wolfe. Soon the ME, Webber and hopefully Atohi Blackhawk would be on scene. She touched Mrs. Braxton's arm. "Can we go inside?"

"Sure, the 911 operator said I wasn't to touch anything in her room but I already searched her cupboard and pulled open her drawers to see if she'd taken any of her clothes." Mrs. Braxton led the way inside the house. "You see, we had an argument last night. Mandy wanted to go to the Spring Festival dance with a boy who works in town but he's nineteen and I grounded her for insisting on seeing him." She led the way into the family room and stood in front of the open fire, wringing her hands. "I figured she'd run off with him."

"No, Ma, I told you, Matt's not like that, he's a decent guy." A young man walked into the room. Tall and good-looking with dark hair and eyes. Jenna put him around seventeen. "He's a couple of years older than me but we're friends and she wouldn't have been alone with him. You're overreacting as usual."

Jenna glared at him. "And you are?"

"I'm Amanda's brother, Luke." Luke lifted his chin toward his mom. "Mom still thinks she's a baby and calls her Mandy."

"What's Matt's last name?" Jenna took out her notebook and pen. "Have you contacted him to see if Amanda is with him?"

"As if." Luke snorted. "His name is Matthew Miller, he's a mechanic at Miller's Garage in town; his old man owns the gas station." He shrugged. "Matt only agreed to double-date with me as a favor. My girl's Amanda's best friend and they insisted on going to the dance together. Mom's making out like it's a big deal. It's one lousy dance and I'd be with her all night. Matt wasn't even planning on giving her a ride home."

Jenna made a note of Matthew Miller's name and looked from one to the other in dismay. "I'll need your girlfriend's name. Have you contacted her about Amanda?"

"Sure, her name is Lucy Mackintosh, I called her first and she hasn't seen her since they met at Aunt Betty's yesterday." Matt scratched his cheek. "She said they chatted on the phone last night and my sister wasn't planning to run away or nothing. She told Lucy she was going to sleep."

"But she's gone." Mrs. Braxton burst into tears and grasped Jenna's arm tight. "You gotta find her."

Trying not to wince at the nails digging through her jacket, Jenna led her to a sofa. "We'll have search parties out looking for her directly." She sat beside the distraught woman. "Deputy Kane has already set things in motion and we'll have help out here very soon."

"Ma'am." Kane walked into the room. "The team are on their way, ETA fifteen minutes. I told Walters to drop the McLeod case for now and come straight here. He's bringing the recording equipment."

Jenna looked up at him. "Roger that. Will you go take a look at Amanda's room? I'm sure Luke will show you the way." She glanced over at Luke. The young man snapped to attention and ushered Kane into the hallway.

Jenna cleared her throat. She hated this part of the job, interviewing the family of a missing child and having to ask delicate questions seemed an intrusion into their grief. She drew a deep breath, the questions sat on a list in her memory. The First 24 Hours list, she'd memorized so long ago it had become almost a mantra and she'd hoped to never use it twice in one week. It was the critical time span required to find a missing person, particularly a child, alive. In fact, only twenty-five percent of abducted children survived the first three hours and seventy-five percent of those who'd survived died by the hands of their abductor within the 24-hour timespan. After that period, the chances of finding a child alive diminished considerably and after seventy-two hours, the chances became negligible. If Amanda had been under twelve years old, an FBI team would be on their way by now but as teenagers were prone to run away after an argument, the FBI deemed her disappearance a local matter.

"When did you last see Amanda?"

"About nine last night." Mrs. Braxton dabbed at her eyes with a balled-up tissue. "I told her to get off her cellphone and go to sleep."

A chill ran down Jenna's spine. Amanda had been missing for twelve hours. *She could already be dead.* She made a note of the time. "We'd like to examine her cellphone to check who she's been calling, if that's okay?"

"Yes, I have it here. It's not locked." Mrs. Braxton pulled a pink-covered smartphone out her pocket and handed it to her. "She never goes anywhere without it. Why did she leave it behind?"

"At this stage, I'm not sure." Jenna scrolled down the list of messages then the log of incoming and outgoing calls. No one had contacted Amanda after the call from her friend Lucy and she didn't find a single message or call from Matthew Miller. She pocketed the cellphone and turned her attention back to Mrs. Braxton. "When did you notice her missing?"

"Nine this morning, I sent Luke up to wake her." Mrs. Braxton let out a small sob. "I ran upstairs and felt her bed to see if it was still warm but it was cold. We ran around everywhere looking for her, and then I came inside and called her friends. When no one had seen her I called 911."

"You did the right thing." Jenna patted the woman's arm. "Can you remember what she was wearing the last time you saw her?"

"Yes, her PJs are yellow with small white roses on them and her dressing gown is pink with a lace trim around the collar, bright pink buttons and pockets." Mrs. Braxton stared into space then drew a shuddering breath. "Her slippers are pink, furry with solid soles."

"Do you have a recent photograph of her?" Jenna made rapid notes. She had to get all the information she could as fast as possible to put out a media release and get a search team out looking for Amanda.

"Yes, on the mantelpiece." Mrs. Braxton pointed to a picture of a pretty girl with long flowing blonde hair, freckles and an upturned nose.

Jenna got up and used the camera on her cellphone to make a copy. "Thank you. I'll be making a statement to the media about Amanda. The townsfolk often call in with helpful information." She explained about setting up a command post in town and the deputies who'd arrive in plain clothes and unmarked cars to monitor all calls. She thought for a moment and had to ask the question: "Has Amanda had any nightmares lately?"

"No, she dreams about her grandma standing at the end of her bed. She figures she's watching over her." Mrs. Braxton's eyes welled with fresh tears. "If she was, she's not doing a very good job, is she?"

At that moment, Kane came back into the room. "Have you touched anything at all in Amanda's bedroom, Mrs. Braxton? Picked up anything from the floor or tidied the room?"

"No, I opened the cupboard and looked in the drawers to see if she'd taken any clothes but everything is there." Mrs. Braxton blinked up at Kane. "Did you find anything?"

"No." Kane gave her an apologetic look and turned to Jenna. "No sign of a struggle."

"Okay." Jenna looked back at Mrs. Braxton. "Do you have a security system?"

"We do." Mrs. Braxton shook her head. "This is why this is so strange. It was on this morning. If someone kidnapped my daughter, I doubt her abductor would've reset the system to activate the alarm. I figure she went out to see that Miller boy."

"I called him, Mom." Luke stood in front of the fire. "He hasn't seen her and said he'd never meet a fifteen-year-old in the middle of the night, he isn't crazy."

"What company did you use to install your alarm system?" Kane's forehead creased into a frown.

"Silent Alarms." Mrs. Braxton shrugged. "All the houses in this area use the same company. When I purchased the house, the realtor recommended them."

Jenna frowned. "Who else has been in or around the house?"

"Let me see." Mrs. Braxton looked suddenly confused. "The Green Thumb Landscaping Service, and Mr. Packer drops by to fix anything I need fixing. They've all been very professional and reliable. My quilting club members speak highly of them too."

With the coincidences piling up, a wave of morbid apprehension crept over Jenna. "Have these men had contact with Amanda at all over the last month or so?"

"Why, yes, I believe so." Mrs. Braxton sniffed. "The gardening service comes once a week and of course they would have met her. Mr. Packer came by to fix the window in the kitchen. It had gotten stuck over winter."

"And Silent Alarms?" Kane gave her an enquiring look. "Have any of their technicians spoken with Amanda?"

"I don't know for sure. They would've seen her, I guess, but they worked outside. I had sensor floodlights installed and the CCTV camera. It was a deal they advertised last month." Mrs. Braxton lifted her red-rimmed eyes to Jenna. "When Mandy went missing, I hit the panic button and they called within a few seconds. The man was very nice, he said the CCTV cameras hadn't been activated overnight and no intruders had entered our property."

It was like déjà vu. Jenna couldn't believe what Mrs. Braxton was saying. Two of their prime suspects had been in contact with Amanda and both girls had left a secure environment with CCTV cameras as if they'd been ghosts. One she might believe, but two was way past coincidence. Cold fingers tickled the back of her neck in a gruesome warning, and she forced her expression to remain calm and in control, but inside turmoil raged. If she received a message from an unknown number right now, she wasn't sure what she would do. She gathered her thoughts. "You did the right thing checking in with the security company. Could you make a list of anyone at all you know who met Amanda recently? Not just friends, anyone at all you can think of, and I need a run-down of her movements over the last weeks." She handed Mrs. Braxton her notebook.

"Sure, Luke will help me." Mrs. Braxton straightened in her seat. "Anything to find Mandy."

"Wolfe and Walters are here." Kane turned and headed out the door.

Jenna stood. "Shane Wolfe is our medical examiner and our forensics expert. He and his assistant Deputy Webber will need access to Amanda's room and her laptop." She turned as they entered the room. "Deputy Walters will remain here and set up a recording device to your landline in case anyone contacts you about Amanda."

"Do you think someone has kidnapped her?" Mrs. Braxton looked horrified.

Jenna gave her a comforting squeeze. "We're covering every angle, Mrs. Braxton."

After updating Wolfe and collecting a large evidence bag from his kit, she turned to Mrs. Braxton. "I'm going with Kane and Atohi Blackhawk to search the grounds for any trace of Amanda. We've a bloodhound tracker dog with us as well. Do you have anything she's worn lately we can use to give him her scent?"

"Yes, I have her jeans in the laundry basket. I'll go get them for you." Mrs. Braxton got up and took a few unsteady steps toward the doorway.

Jenna followed her to the laundry room and handed her the evidence bag. "If you could place them in here, please?" She took the bag. "Thank you." She glanced at Luke, who was hovering in the hallway. "Why don't you make your mother a cup of coffee?"

With the bag tucked under one arm, Jenna made her way outside to meet the others. She glanced up at Kane. "I'm guessing the Shadow Man has struck again."

CHAPTER TWENTY-FIVE

The heady perfume from the flowers each side of the porch washed over Jenna but the delightful scent didn't remove the awful sensation that it was already too late to save Amanda. As she walked down the steps beside Kane, a blast of cold wind rustled through the trees and seeped into her clothes, giving her goosebumps. The blue sky that had greeted her earlier had turned an angry gray as storm clouds rolled over the mountains. She shivered, then, zipping up her jacket, walked across the driveway to greet Blackhawk. "Thanks for coming out again, Atohi. I really appreciate your expertise in tracking."

"I will always be here when you need me, Jenna." Blackhawk indicated with his thumb over one shoulder to Duke. The dog's head hung out the SUV's window and he was whining and giving the odd discontented bark. "Although, you have your own tracker right there."

"Yeah, but he can't exactly tell us what he's seeing. I'll go get him." Kane hustled over to his truck to collect Duke and returned with the crime scene kit.

"That's because you don't listen to him, Dave." Blackhawk shook his head. "Dogs are not as complicated as people." He turned to Jenna. "Wolfe mentioned we've another teenager who up and walked out of her home at night. Is it the same as last time?"

Jenna nodded and stared into the dense wooded area bordering the driveway. "I'm not sure but it appears this one locked up before she left. I can't imagine a kidnapper taking the time to reset the alarm – but hey, this is Black Rock Falls, anything is possible." She turned to Kane. "Ready?"

"I sure am. Open the bag for him to take a sniff." Kane led the dog to Jenna's side.

Jenna looked over at Atohi. "If it's the Shadow Man again, he'd have bundled her into his vehicle. We found no evidence he chased Lindy outside – in fact we found zip." Jenna bent and opened the evidence bag for Duke to sniff.

"Seek." Kane unclipped Duke's leash. "Seek, Duke. Find the girl. That's right."

The dog ran around in circles for some moments with his nose to the ground, and then headed for a path leading into the woodland. Jenna stared after him in disbelief. "I can't imagine a young girl would wander in there at night voluntarily. It looks creepy enough in daylight."

As Duke bounded down a narrow trail, birds lifted from the branches and flew into the air with discontented squawks. Jenna stood to one side to allow Kane and Atohi to go ahead of her; they could translate Duke's whines and behavior far better than she could and by bringing up the rear, she would catch anything they'd missed.

Shrubs and vines had spilled over the pathway, giving the impression no one used it very often. Bushes and low pine branches seemed to reach out and grab at Jenna's clothes. It would have been much worse for Amanda last night. The sensation must have been like ghostly hands dragging her into a dark abyss. Jenna quickened her pace. Ahead, Kane's head moved from side to side as he scanned the area in all directions. Atohi followed close behind Duke, his attention not on the dog but on the ground. Jenna moved slowly over the uneven path, negotiating exposed tree roots, then stopped mid-step when Atohi held up one hand.

"I have something." He paused and looked over one shoulder. "Here." He indicated to a strand of pink thread caught on the lower branches of a Douglas fir. "See? And strands of hair here on the ninebark." He pointed to a shrub at the base of the tree. "Do you want me to keep following Duke, Jenna?"

"Sure." Jenna pulled on gloves, and then used her cellphone camera to take photographs before removing the evidence and waiting for Kane to mark the site with flags. "What do you figure could lure a teenager here in the middle of the night?"

"Search me. It looks as if she pushed her way through the bushes. Maybe she was following someone? But there's no evidence of another person coming this way." Kane placed the flags, and then straightened. "Did you ask her mother if a flashlight had gone missing from the house?"

Jenna shook her head. "No, but I will."

At the sound of Duke's loud bark, they both turned and stared into the distance, but the winding trail had hidden Atohi and Duke from view. Ahead, the twisted dark branches lining each side of the trail, combined with the rumble of thunder overhead, painted a scene from a horror movie. Dread dropped over Jenna like a shroud and she swallowed hard. Memories of murder victims found in forests rushed to the front of her mind and she gripped Kane's forearm. "Duke's found something. I sure hope it's not a body."

"Nah." Kane picked up the bag and headed along the dim path. "We'd have smelled a corpse by now unless he chopped her up and placed her in garbage bags."

Jenna snorted. "Well that makes me feel a whole lot better."

They'd wound their way another fifteen yards into the darkening woods when Duke came bounding back and sat at Kane's feet. Jenna looked up at Kane in dismay. "What does that mean?"

"The trail must have gone cold just ahead." Kane patted Duke on the head. "Stay." He glanced at Jenna. "She must have come this far then vanished."

Jenna smothered a chuckle. "Next you'll be saying she was abducted by aliens."

"Hold up." Atohi came out of the gloom. "You'll need a flashlight. The trail leaves this switchback in a few yards and goes into a clearing. I found signs of a struggle and a partial boot-mark in the mud. You'll need Wolfe to take a look at it soon – I smell rain."

Jenna unclipped the flashlight from her belt. "Later, show me what you've found. Don't worry, we'll take some pics and make a cast of the footprint before it starts raining." She turned on the flashlight and followed Atohi into a small clearing.

"The ground here is disturbed, dirt kicked up." Atohi pointed to a patch of long grass. "See, here it's as if someone plucked at the grass, as if they'd gotten bored waiting for her to arrive."

Jenna peered at the ground. "Shame he didn't chew on it and spit it out, we'd have his DNA."

"The branches are broken over here as well." Kane moved his flashlight over the trees, then down onto the ground. "It's too rocky here for any footprints." He sighed. "More hair here on the branches. She put up a good fight."

"Okay, photograph it, mark and bag it." Jenna turned to Atohi. "Show me the footprint and I'll make a cast."

"I'd say he rendered her unconscious and carried her to his vehicle." Kane marked then photographed each piece of evidence, then plucked fibers from the branches, bagged them and labeled each one. "That's why Duke couldn't track her from here."

"Makes sense." Jenna took photographs of the print. It was a heel of a boot for sure, with a distinctive circle in the center. "At last, one single shred of evidence. Check all the trees and shrubs; the kidnapper must have snagged his clothes or hair too."

"Roger that." Kane handed her the casting kit from his bag and went to work meticulously checking every square inch of the area.

Jenna finished making the casts as the first big splashes of rain bounced off the branches and splattered onto the forest floor. The small amount of remaining light vanished, plunging them into total darkness. The smell of rain and damp vegetation closed in around her. Zigzag lightning flashed across the sky, illuminating them all for a split second, then the ground beneath her boots shook as if angry that someone had taken another girl against her will.

The sky opened up and rain poured down in sheets, slicing through the trees and forming little rivers around her feet. Squirrels bounded across the ground then scampered up trees to take shelter. The sky alternated between day and night with each flash of lightning. Jenna pulled up the hood of her jacket then gathered up the evidence bags. She hated storms and wanted to get out from under the trees as fast as possible. "We can't do any more here. Let's get back to the house and see if Wolfe has found any clues."

"Roger that." Kane waved at Atohi. "You coming?"

"Yeah, shame about the rain, it's washed away the evidence." Atohi followed behind them. "Just as well you took a cast of that print, Jenna."

"Yeah, it looks unusual with that circle in the heel." Jenna glanced down at the bag in her hand. "We should be able to determine the brand by that mark; it may be the breakthrough we've been looking for at last." She turned into the switchback and stared at the place they'd left Duke. "Now Duke's missing."

"He'll be hiding under my truck." Kane smiled at her. "He's obedient right up to the first clap of thunder, and then it's every dog for itself. He trembles with fear; it makes me wonder what happened in his past to make him so scared."

"Ah, I remember what happened. As you know, we raised Duke on the res. He was washed away in a storm as a pup." Atohi shrugged. "My cousin came close to drowning saving him from the falls." He glanced at Kane. "Dogs have long memories, but he won't leave your side if you're injured and gunshots don't bother him."

"That's good to hear, about the not leaving me if I'm injured, I mean." Kane grimaced. "Not good about him near drowning. No wonder he hates having a bath."

"Most dogs hate having a bath." Atohi smiled. "Jenna, do you want me to stow the evidence bags in Wolfe's van?"

The wind howled and the rain came down so hard Jenna could hardly hear him. She turned and handed him the bags. "Yeah, thanks."

"I'll wait in the van, no need for us all to go dirtying up Mrs. Braxton's house." Atohi jogged out the woods and into the storm.

As the rain pelted down, Jenna dashed to the front porch and Mrs. Braxton ushered them all into the mudroom and handed them towels. "We believe Amanda went into the woods to meet someone. My deputy has already put out a BOLO on her and I'll speak to the media as soon as I get back to town." She steeled herself for the next part of the conversation. "We found signs of a struggle in the woods and, at this stage, we believe Amanda was kidnapped."

"Oh, sweet Jesus no." Mrs. Braxton collapsed against the wall. "Who would kidnap her?"

Jenna frowned. "We aim to find out. Have you completed the list? Once we trace her movements and speak to her friends, we might find a clue to who took her. In the meantime, we'll have every available person out searching for her."

"I have the list." Luke emerged from the hallway and thrust the notebook at Jenna. "I included everyone else I could think of as well. Lucy is her best friend and she hangs with her, then there's a boy at school, Peter English, who was pestering her for a date. He'd gotten out of hand, like a stalker, so I talked to him a couple of weeks ago to warn him off and he hasn't bothered her since."

Mind reeling at the idea of a younger suspect, Jenna glanced over the list. "Okay, we'll hunt down these people and see what they have to say. In the meantime, I'll have a deputy with you around the clock to monitor the phone in case anyone calls with demands. I'll be arranging for plain-clothed deputies from Blackwater to come here, as my team will be involved in the search for your daughter. I'll make sure Deputy Walters keeps you up to date."

She gave Mrs. Braxton's arm a squeeze. "Rest assured I'll do everything in my power to find Amanda."

"Thanks." Mrs. Braxton leaned into her son's embrace. "I need to lie down."

"Good idea. We'll be in touch as soon as we know anything." Jenna watched her climb the stairs then turned as Wolfe came down the hallway with Webber close behind. "Find anything?"

"No." Wolfe held up a few evidence bags. "I've collected fibers, and have her laptop and cellphone. I'll need time to do some tests and scan her media files."

"We found a partial footprint and hairs and fibers." Jenna waved a hand toward the front door. "Atohi put them in your van."

"Okay." Wolfe indicated with his chin to Webber. "I have Emily to assist me if you need Webber. With Rowley running the command post, it only leaves you and Kane to chase down clues."

Jenna nodded. "Yeah, thanks, Webber would be a great help."

"There're signs of a struggle." Kane moved closer and lowered his voice. "We've taken photos of the scene."

"Good, get them to me ASAP." Wolfe rubbed his chin and his fingers rasped against the blond stubble. "I've collected DNA samples from the family and I figure I've solved the mystery of the reset alarm." He headed for the front door. "See here." He pointed to the control panel beside the front door. "The CCTV and lights are on a different circuit and are turned off manually. Normally the lights would come on when someone approaches the house but the alarm doesn't activate until two minutes after someone opens the doors or windows. It gives the owners time to come inside and put in the correct code. The same applies to when they leave but the delay is five minutes. Amanda had her own key and it's not in the house, so we have to assume she deactivated the floodlights and CCTV cameras because she didn't want anyone to know she'd sneaked out, then reset the alarm when she left because she planned to return to the house."

Jenna nodded. "So it looks like she knew her kidnapper?"

"Yeah." Wolfe's mouth formed a thin line. "It sure does."

"I hope this is the end of this stupid game now." Jenna balled her hands on her hips and grimaced. "I'm over getting sick to my stomach every time a message sounds on my cellphone."

CHAPTER TWENTY-SIX

It never ceased to amaze Kane how fast the local media got wind of a story. As he turned his truck into Main Street, he couldn't miss the live news TV satellite truck parked opposite the sheriff's office or the crowd of people milling around on the sidewalk like vultures hungry for a tidbit of information. He pulled in at the curb outside Aunt Betty's Café and turned to Jenna. "Do you want a few minutes before you face the media?"

"What did you say?" Jenna looked at him, as if oblivious to the crowd and the commotion. She'd spent the entire trip on her cellphone, organizing the team for the next stage of the investigation.

Kane indicated with his chin to the other end of town. "It's a media frenzy down there. I suggest we slip into Aunt Betty's to write a statement – unless you want to do one on the fly?"

"No, I'll need to be careful what I say or they'll twist my words. I'll need to freshen up a bit as well. I wonder if Susie has a comb I could use?" She glanced out the window. "No one around, let's go." She slipped from the vehicle and jogged into the café.

Kane followed behind. Duke snored on the back seat. He would be fine inside the truck until they returned. He made his way to the counter, glad to see Susie Hartwig serving a customer. "The sheriff's usual and I'll have turkey on rye." He smiled at her. "The sheriff needs to speak to the press and we've been searching the woods for a missing girl. Do you have a comb she could borrow?"

"Don't you worry now. I'll have her fixed up in no time." Susie turned and called out the order, then came around the counter. "I'll go speak to her. The food will be along directly." She bustled off in Jenna's direction.

Before he reached the table, Jenna and Susie had disappeared into the ladies' restroom. The food arrived and Kane stared at the passageway. He'd finished his sandwich and was halfway through his second cup of coffee by the time Jenna returned to the table. He cast an appreciative gaze over her. She had beautiful skin and rarely wore more than a hint of makeup; when he took her to dinner, she usually added a fine line around her eyes and a dab of perfume. Susie had covered the bruises on her face and although the scrapes were still evident, he doubted anyone would notice them. Her hair shone like a raven's wing and her eyes had transformed into hypnotic pools of dark blue – She. Looked. Spectacular. His jaw dropped and he forced himself to look away and act natural.

"Dang, do I look that bad?" Jenna's cheeks colored. "I told her to go easy on the makeup. The light in the bathroom is so dim, I couldn't see properly, I hoped I'd look okay."

Kane pushed the bagel and cream cheese toward her. "You look amazing. I can't see any of the bruises. Eat and we'll work on a statement." He pulled out his notebook and pen.

She didn't reply but when he lifted his gaze away from his notes, she gave him a warm smile. After their distressing morning and previous horrendous days, it took him by surprise. "Okay, what do you want to say to the press?"

"That's the nicest thing you've ever said to me." Jenna's attention never left his face. "So you *do* have a soft side, hidden under all that macho."

Kane chuckled. It was good to see he'd amused her. "I'm a pussycat but don't tell Duke, he'd disown me." He reached for his coffee.

"Sure, it will be our little secret." Jenna took a bite of her bagel and sighed. "Okay, back to work. We'll keep the media statement short and refuse to take questions. How about I just mention we're searching for a missing girl, give them her description and photograph, then ask people to call in if they've seen her?"

Kane made a few notes. "Yeah, but we know she's been kidnapped and searching for her is probably a waste of time if this is the same man and he has her holed up somewhere. If you leave it as 'missing', we'll have search parties combing the area. I'm worried they might stumble into another booby trap." He tapped the pen on the table. "Maybe you should rephrase the statement by saying you'd like residents to be on the lookout for Amanda, who may be traveling with a male companion in or around Black Rock Falls. Maybe ask for volunteers to man the crime hotline like before?"

"Yeah, I'll set up a command station at the office and Maggie will pull in as many people as she can to take calls. I'll leave Rowley in charge and that will leave us free to chase down the suspects. First on the list is Mathew Miller." She pushed the last piece of bagel into her mouth and washed it down with coffee. "Let's do it."

As they arrived at the sheriff's office a swarm of people surrounded Kane's truck. He gave his siren a couple of blasts and the majority jumped back, startled. He pulled into his parking space and glanced at Jenna. "Wait here. I'll come around to your side and keep these idiots away from you."

"I'm sure they'll leave me be." Jenna went to push open the door and the crowd of reporters stepped forward as one. She glanced back at him. "Okay, do your stuff."

Kane rounded the hood, glaring at the excited faces, and waited for Jenna to step from the He raised his voice and gave them his best "back the hell off" stare. "If you want a statement, stand back or Sheriff Alton is going inside."

The crowd fell quiet and an attractive blonde wearing a tailored suit, stilettoes and makeup applied with a trowel appeared at the front, followed by a man carrying a camera on one shoulder.

"Joanne Daly, *Live Now News*." She offered Jenna a smile. "Sheriff Alton, do we have another killer in Black Rock Falls?"

"I have already issued a statement regarding Lindy Rosen. I'm here to speak to you about Amanda Braxton." Jenna spoke loudly and clearly. "Amanda left her home sometime after midnight last night and was last seen in the company of an unknown male. If anyone has seen Amanda—" Jenna held up the girl's photograph "—please call the crime hotline number. I'll issue a further statement when more information comes to hand."

A barrage of questions followed and reporters surged forward sticking recording devices in their faces, but Jenna's face had turned to stone.

"I don't have any answers for you at this time." She glanced up at Kane. "I'm done here."

Kane nodded. "I'll grab Duke." He opened the back door, unclipped the dog's restraint and moved close to Jenna. He waved a hand at the persistent reporters. "Back off or I'll arrest you for obstruction."

The people opened up a path and they hustled into the sheriff's office.

"My, oh, my." Maggie gave them a huge grin from behind the front counter. "Seems like we have a couple of celebrities in our midst. Does this mean I get a pay rise?"

"I figure we should all get one since the population of Black Rock Falls has doubled since I took over as sheriff." Jenna ran her hand along the counter. "Anything come in on the BOLO?"

"Not a thing and search and rescue found zip, but I have somethin' that may be pertinent to the Lindy Rosen case." Maggie turned to Julie Wolfe, who sat beside her. "Julie will explain what's been going on at school."

"Okay, Julie, come into my office. Kane, grab Rowley – he'll want to be in on this." Jenna strode into her office.

Kane turned to look at Julie. "Did something happen to you at school?"

"Not me." Julie blushed scarlet. "It's something I heard." She gave him a small smile and followed Jenna.

"Ooookay." Kane stared after them, then whistled to get Rowley's attention and pointed to Jenna's office.

"What's happened?" Rowley came swiftly to his side.

Kane shrugged. "I don't have the details; it's something Julie heard at school. Do you need help setting up the command center for the Braxton case?"

"Nah, I've organized the Blackwater deputies to take over in shifts at the house and all the hotline calls will come through to here. Maggie's organized a team and they'll be here shortly."

Kane listened with interest as Julie told Jenna about the number of girls at school having nightmares about men in their rooms. When Julie left the office, he leaned back in his chair. "What do you figure that's all about?"

"I'm not sure." Jenna mimicked his stance. "Mass hysteria, maybe?"

Kane rubbed the back of his neck. "Possible, especially as in all the cases Julie mentioned, the parents searched the girls' bedroom and found no trace of anyone but they weren't kidnapped."

"Until you get to Lindy Rosen." Rowley's expression was serious. "She saw someone in her room, and then someone abducted and murdered her."

"I'd be more concerned if Amanda had said she'd seen a man in her room as well." Jenna sighed. "Seeing her grandma after she died isn't at all unusual. I used to see my folks everywhere, in the street, lining up in stores. I figured it was part of the grieving process."

"I've never seen any of my dead relatives at the foot of my bed." Rowley looked horrified. "Don't want to either."

Kane cleared his throat. "Mass hysteria or, in Amanda's case, maybe wishful thinking – but the victims seeing two different apparitions doesn't link the cases together. What does is the fact they both opened the door to a stranger and walked out into a cold night, for no apparent reason."

"There has to be another link. We'll need to speak to everyone in her group of friends, and the boy Luke mentioned. If he's been stalking her he might have seen someone else hanging around her." Jenna picked up the phone. "Maggie, could you send Julie back in please?" She waited for the girl to arrive. "The group of girls you mentioned, you said Lindy was one of them – are you friends with them as well?"

"Yeah, sort of, but they're always hanging around the jocks and never stop talking about Mason. I prefer to go to the library than chase after sweaty gardeners." Julie wrinkled her nose. "They all seem to have a thing about the men who work around the school – not the old ones." She giggled. "The ones around twenty or maybe thirty, I guess."

"Amanda as well?" Jenna smiled at her. "Did she like Mason Lancaster?"

"Him and anything male on two legs." Julie blushed crimson. "Oh, *please* don't tell my dad I told you, he'll make me find new friends and it's taken forever to fit into this school."

Kane turned to her. "We don't have to tell him the information came from you but maybe you should tell him what you know.

Coming forward with this information is a good thing and if this group of girls are heading for trouble, perhaps finding new friends would be a mature thing to do." He smiled at her. "I was an army brat too and I know what you're going through but you've been here for some time now and it will be easier to expand your circle of friends."

"Well, Sara is in the group too and she's more like me. She likes art too and we both attend classes in the community hall." Julie smiled. "Other girls from school go there as well. I'll try to get to know them better."

"That sounds like a plan." Jenna nodded. "If you'd give Maggie a list of all the girls who hang around the workers at school and underline any who've had nightmares of men in their rooms, it would be a big help. We'd like to find out if there's a person stalking these girls and we need a place to start."

"Sure." Julie headed for the door, and then looked back at Jenna. "I'll make a list now."

"Great." Jenna nodded. "And ask Maggie to hunt down their addresses ASAP and send them to me."

Kane waited for her to shut the door. "Now we have two girls who chased after Mason Lancaster. I figure we need another talk with him."

"We'll speak to Miller first, then Peter English. They're in town. If Kittredge is working on one of the Glacial Heights ranches, we'll check his whereabouts last night then we'll head out to the school and tackle Lancaster. I want to cover as much ground as possible this afternoon." Jenna's phone rang. "Yeah, put him through." She placed the phone on speaker. "Mr. Wilts, Sheriff Alton. What exactly did you see?"

"I live near Glacial Heights some ways from the Braxton ranch, I'm on the same road and my house is on the bend before Stanton Road. I was out walking my dog 'bout one last night and a big pickup came

out of the dark then turned on the headlights and near blinded me as it went around the corner. It took off as if the devil himself was after it."

"Did you get a plate?" Jenna lifted her pen and pulled her notebook toward her.

"Can't say that I did." Mr. Wilts sighed. *"The lights gave me red spots in my eyes, I couldn't see a darn thing but I know it was a pickup, maybe a Chevy Silverado or similar. Hard to tell the color in the dark but it did have something written on the door."*

"Okay, thank you for your help, Mr. Wilts. If you think of anything else or see the vehicle again, give me a call." She disconnected and met Kane's gaze. "Now we have to match the suspects with the vehicle." She pushed to her feet. "Do you have everything under control here, Rowley?"

"Sure do, ma'am." Rowley stood. "I'll call you the moment anything useful comes in." He left the room.

Kane pushed to his feet. "You know what's eating at me?"

"What?" Jenna slipped into her Kevlar vest, and then shrugged on a jacket.

"I'm sure this is the same perp but he hasn't contacted you with another countdown. Why has he suddenly changed the game?" Kane scratched his cheek. "It's not logical for this stage of his behavior."

"Huh?" Jenna stared at him with an astonished look on her face. "Since when do we consider anything a psychopath does logical?"

Kane zipped up his jacket and shrugged. "*We* don't but he does. In his mind, everything he does is perfectly logical. He'd have a game plan, so why change it when it worked well the first time? He came close to killing us, Jenna."

"Yeah, but he doesn't know who he's dealing with, does he? This means he's playing by my rules now. And I plan to win." Jenna led the way to the door.

CHAPTER TWENTY-SEVEN

It was so cold Amanda's bones ached. Disorientated and teeth chattering, she woke enclosed in darkness. Under her stiff muscles, cold seeped through her clothes from the unrelenting floor. Her cheek pressed against a rough wooden board and her head pounded. A jolt of fear shuddered through her as the memory of a man attacking her slammed into her. Too afraid to move, or brush away the grit digging into her flesh, she opened her eyes wide and scanned the blackness. *Where am I?*

A musty smell with the awful odor of rats surrounded her but pinpricks of light pierced the darkness. Outside it must be daylight; she'd been asleep or unconscious for hours. The stale air reminded her of her uncle's log cabin in Stanton Forest before her mother opened all the windows. She'd often spent weekends there to go fishing with her family and recalled the way the moonlight peeped through the cracks in the shutters – but this was different. The light came through tiny holes in the walls. She listened but no sound of the man or anything else broke the silence. *I'm alone.*

Relieved the man hadn't tied her up she rolled onto her knees and, running her palms over the rough floor in all directions, inched forward. Heart pounding, she shuffled across the filthy floor. A scuttling noise came from close by and a creature ran up her arm and over her back. Rats! She screamed, jumped to her feet and ran blindly, crashing into a wall and falling hard on her backside. Choking back a sob, she staggered to her feet then, arms outstretched, touched the wall.

Under her fingers ancient paint flaked away from horizontal logs. Underfoot the old floor creaked and moved with each step. Sheer panic had her by the throat as she edged her way along the wall. She found the familiar shape of a window but something had obscured the glass and, after feeling all around, she found no catch to open it. She moved on, step by step, deeper into darkness. The next moment, cobwebs tangled around her face and, gasping, she clawed them away. Convinced a spider had crawled into her hair, she shook her head, smacking at her hair and sobbing. *I have to find a door.* She reached out again but something big and scratchy ran over her hand. She gasped, pulling it away, too terrified to move another step.

The next moment a tiny red light high on the wall cut through the darkness like a laser beam. She turned in shivery apprehension to stare at it, mesmerized; then she heard a voice, soft and menacing. It came out of the air around her, bodiless and creepy.

"Do you know the story of this house, Amanda?"

Icy fingers of fear walked up her spine and she swallowed the scream threatening to explode from her mouth. "No, 'cause I don't know where I am."

"I've heard so many stories about this house. The floorboards carry bloodstains of murder victims and nobody comes here anymore, because they believe it's haunted. Even on Halloween, the kids are too chicken to face the evil spirits lurking here. Murders, suicides going back decades and the list is no way near finished yet. Two men tortured then cut a young girl, just like you, to pieces in the root cellar, and a man murdered his wife in this very room. He cut her throat from ear to ear and then hanged himself in the barn. People have heard the creak of the rope as he swings back and forth from the rafters, and seen his shadow on the floor. They say the ghosts of the dead are trapped inside this house, forever."

Swallowing her fear, Amanda kept her head still and moved her eyes to survey the room. The tiny red light had offered a modicum of illumination and she made out a door and another window. She dashed to the door and pulled on the handle but the door didn't move. Desperate to escape, she rammed her shoulder against it. Tears wet her cheeks. *I'm trapped.* "Let me out of here. I want to go home."

"There's no way out and you're never going home." His voice sounded amused. *"This is your home now."*

Shaking with terror, Amanda turned and stared into the light. "I'm not staying here – you can't make me."

"Oh, but I can. Nobody is going to find you, Amanda." Spine-chilling laughter echoed around the room and bounced off the walls. *"I just wanted you to know that when I kill you, you won't be alone."*

CHAPTER TWENTY-EIGHT

Jenna didn't waste time going to the office at Miller's Garage. She ignored the NO CUSTOMERS PAST THIS POINT sign and marched straight into the service bay with Kane at her side. Three young men wearing coveralls and steel-toe boots lifted their heads from under the hoods of vehicles to peer at her. "I'm looking for Matt."

"I'm Matt." A tall, ruggedly handsome young man, not at all like his five-five rotund father, walked toward her, wiping his hands on a rag. "Did Dad send you back here?" His enquiring gaze moved to Kane then back to her.

"No." Jenna led him outside. "I wanted to ask you a few questions."

"Am I in trouble?" Matt wiped the end of his nose with the back of his hand in a nervous gesture.

"Why do you figure you're in trouble?" Kane leaned toward him. "Did you do something last night you need to get off your chest?'

"No! Luke called me about Amanda going missing. I swear I'd nothing to do with that – heck, I only met the girl once or twice." Matt gave Jenna a pleading look. "I'm not interested in her, she's just a kid. I only agreed to go to the dance because Lucy's mother was making noises about her going alone and Luke didn't want Amanda hanging around like a third wheel."

Jenna wrinkled her nose. The idea that Luke had called him to give him the heads-up annoyed her. If he was involved, he'd had time to have gotten his story straight and figured out an alibi for last night. "Do you have anyone to verify your whereabouts last night?"

"I was home with my folks." Matt cleared his throat. "Watched a movie, and then went out to Aunt Betty's for a burger."

"What time was that?" Jenna took out her notebook and made some notes without looking at him. She had no need; Kane would be watching his body language like a hawk. "Do you remember who served you or did you see anyone?"

"It was after the movie, ten-thirty maybe." Matt shuffled his feet, then leaned casually against the wall in a pretense of calm. "I can't remember who served me but I did see Jake Rowley. He was sitting with three people, like on a double date or something."

Jenna looked at him. "Then where did you go?"

"I ate my burger and went home." Matt moved around nervously, avoiding Jenna's eyes. "Is that all? I gotta finish Mrs. Rushton's vehicle or Dad'll have my hide."

"Did you drive into Glacial Heights?" Jenna lifted her pen. "A pickup was seen leaving there around midnight."

"Nope." Matt took a few steps back. "Is that all? I've really gotta get back to work now."

"What vehicle do you drive?" Kane indicated to a silver Chevy Silverado pickup with the Miller's Garage decal on the door. "Is that your truck?'

"Yeah. Why?" A flash of worry crossed Matt's face.

"The GPS in the vehicle or your cellphone will confirm you went straight home after you left Aunt Betty's." Kane indicated over his shoulder with his thumb. "Mind if I call someone out to confirm that?"

"There's no way I'm letting you near my pickup or cellphone – not without a search warrant." Matt scowled. "I know my rights."

Jenna closed her notebook with a snap. "That can be arranged. We've probable cause." She glanced at Kane. "I want his vehicle searched as well. I'll wait here."

"Yes, ma'am." Kane turned away and strode to his truck.

Jenna looked at Matt. "You can go work on Mrs. Rushton's vehicle but don't use your cellphone or leave the garage or I'll arrest you."

"You're crazy." Matt threw his arms up in the air. "This is crap." He walked back to his bay and glared at the other workers. "What're you gawking at? Show's over. Get back to work."

As he stomped back to his bay, Matt walked through a patch of water and Jenna examined his footprints. A shiver of excitement rushed through her. Had she discovered the Shadow Man? The heel had the exact same circle as the one found at the scene of Amanda's abduction. She pulled out her cellphone and snapped a few images, then she heard Matt chuckle. She stared at him. "What's so funny?"

"You, taking photographs of my footprints." Matt waved a hand at the other men in the garage and grinned. "If you're planning on using my footprints as evidence, you'd better include my boys here in the warrant. We all wear the same darn boots, ma'am. My dad supplies them and he buys them from Walmart. I figure most of the tradesmen in town wear the same brand."

The information came as a blow to Jenna. The first clue they'd found was useless and she'd heard nothing from Amanda's abductor. She nodded at Matt. "I'll be sure to check with your father about that."

"See that you do." Matt bent under the hood of the vehicle.

Half an hour later, Wolfe arrived and strolled to her side carrying a laptop. She moved out of earshot of Matt but kept him in view. "Did Kane get the warrant?"

"Yeah, he's waiting on the judge to sign the paperwork." Wolfe met her gaze. "I've compared all the fibers and hair samples you found in the woods with those I collected from Amanda's bedroom and they're a match. There's nothing apart from the heel print and the signs of a struggle to suggest anyone else was there. This guy is good and he must've been covered from head to foot to avoid getting snagged in the bushes." He sighed. "The rain didn't help. I would've liked time to scan the area myself." He glanced at Matt's truck. "Maybe I'll find some trace evidence in there."

"I hope so." Jenna pushed her hands into her pockets. "Any news from Rowley or Walters?"

"Nothing we can use." Wolfe rubbed his chin. "The usual ambiguous sightings but nothing panned out. No calls to the Braxton house, and search and rescue have been sweeping the area since the first report came in and have nothing." He cleared his throat. "They tailed a white pickup with a logo on the door out to the Pittman ranch north of the Triple Z after someone called in a sighting. Webber went with them in the chopper. It was old Mr. Pittman and his wife returning from the store."

A ringtone chimed and Matt held up his cellphone.

"I need to get this, ma'am. It's someone calling the roadside assistance line." Matt stared at her. "The calls come to me when my sister is on lunch."

Jenna nodded. "Sure, but you're not going anywhere. You'll have to send someone else."

She watched as he filled in a form on a clipboard then walked over and handed the information to one of the other mechanics. He had his back to her for a few minutes but she kept him in view. The next moment, she heard Kane's truck heading toward them. He pulled up outside the garage, climbed out and handed her the paperwork. She smiled at him. "Thanks."

With Wolfe and Kane following close behind, Jenna went to Matt and handed him the warrant. "Your cellphone please and the keys to your truck."

"Okay, okay, so I was driving around Glacial Heights last night." Matt gave her a desperate look. "There's no law against going for a drive, is there?"

Jenna held out her hand. "Keys and cellphone."

"There's no law against driving, no." Kane eyeballed him. "But a vehicle matching the description of your pickup was seen leaving the vicinity of Amanda Braxton's abduction. If you've nothing to hide, why didn't you allow us to check your GPS?" He stood over the younger man. "Where is she? Tell us now and it'll save you a whole lot of trouble."

"I wasn't anywhere near Amanda last night." Matt handed Jenna his keys and cellphone, then gave Kane a deadpan look.

"How well do you know Lindy Rosen?" Jenna watched Matt's face pale. "You *do* know her, don't you?"

"I'm not answering any more stupid questions. I want my lawyer." Matt lifted his chin in defiance. "My dad will give you his details."

"Very well." Jenna handed the keys and cellphone to Wolfe. "We'll check for ourselves."

It didn't take long for Wolfe to confirm that Matt had driven to Glacial Heights and stopped a number of times along Stanton Road over a period of two hours before returning home. As Stanton Road bordered Stanton Forest on one side and a number of houses and ranches on the other, Matt had enough time to abduct and hide Amanda. He'd also been in the area at the same time Lindy Rosen went missing and was on Stanton Road near the old schoolhouse in the right timeframe. Jenna read Matt his rights and cuffed him, then turned to Kane. "Go see George Miller and ask him for the lawyer's details."

Moments later, George Miller came storming into the garage, face beet red and eyes blazing. Kane was close behind him and gave Jenna an exasperated look. She turned from assisting Matt into the back of Kane's truck. "Mr. Miller."

"Why are you arresting my boy?" Miller came up close to her, spittle dripping from his chin like an angry bull. "He ain't done nothing wrong."

Jenna placed one hand on her pistol. "Take a step back, Mr. Miller, and I'll explain."

"It had better be good." Miller spat on the ground. "And to think I voted for you in the last election. That's the thanks I get?"

"You voted for a sheriff who'll keep the town safe." Kane towered over the enraged man. "That's what you have. Sheriff Alton doesn't pay out favors for votes – that's corruption. You want that in Black Rock Falls, Mr. Miller?"

"I guess not." Miller lifted both his arms and then dropped them to his sides in a gesture of disbelief. "My boy wouldn't harm anyone. He's under suspicion for the abduction of Amanda Braxton? Look at him – you figure he needs to abduct women?"

Jenna liked George Miller – he'd always treated people right – and arresting his son left a nasty taste in her mouth, but the evidence was there. Circumstantial maybe but right now, it was all she had.

CHAPTER TWENTY-NINE

He pulled a chair up close and examined Amanda's face. The changes in a person's face after near strangulation intrigued him. The broken blood vessels in the eyes and the way the red line around her neck was turning a distinct shade of blue. He enjoyed this part of the game, the fear when she eventually opened her eyes to find him there, watching her and knowing he hadn't quite finished the job.

Her eyelids flickered for the second time and he adjusted the light so she could see him. "Did you enjoy your near-death experience?"

"N-no." Her voice came out in a raspy breathless whisper and her bloodshot eyes lifted to his face. "Why are you doing this to me?"

He leaned closer so they were almost nose-to-nose. "Because I can." He smiled at her. "Tell me what you saw. Did a white light come to snatch you away from life or was there only darkness?"

When she refused to reply, he soared to his feet, tipping back his chair. It clattered to the ground and he savored the way his sudden movement made her tremble again. He walked behind her, trailing his fingers over her shoulders. "I can make this stop but I need an answer."

He gave the cord around her neck a tug, just enough to let her know his intentions. Then he righted his chair and sat down, waiting for the gagging to subside. "Well?"

"You'll kill me if I answer you or not." Amanda had a defiant look in her eyes. "One thing for sure, you'll rot in hell for eternity."

"Don't you figure I'd enjoy discussing my work with like-minded souls?" He chuckled. "What could be better?"

"That's not what I saw." Amanda's puffy lids closed and a small smile curled her lips. "But I'll never tell you."

He often wondered why some of the women gained bravado when they knew the odds were stacked against them. Amanda couldn't win and yet she chose to anger him. Did she want her end to be brutal? As he sat back in his chair and stared at her, his mind conjured the face of Sheriff Alton. He could almost see her sitting tied to the chair before him. Strangulation would be too quick for her. He needed to eliminate the women who wanted to change a man's world into a matriarchal society. The alpha female belonged in comic books or games. When he took the sheriff to his new hideout, he'd make her death slow and enjoy every bloody second.

CHAPTER THIRTY

Kane escorted Matt Miller to the interview room, gave him a cup of coffee and turned on the camera. The CCTV fed into the computer system and anyone on duty could view the live feed. It was a simple method of doing two jobs at once. Of course, they disconnected the feed during prisoner/lawyer interviews. He closed the door and went to the kitchenette, collected two cups of coffee and went to Jenna's office.

"The lawyer's on his way." Jenna took the cup with a smile. "Thanks."

Kane sat opposite her and placed one booted foot on the other knee. "Do you want me here while you deal with him?"

"Yeah, if we get to question Miller, I want your take on his body language. Although, I'm not convinced he's our guy." Jenna raised both eyebrows. "Why, do you have a lead?"

"No, a hunch maybe. I figured I'd go search the areas around where Matt stopped last night and see if I can find out where he took Amanda." Kane frowned. "She could be in the forest, injured or worse."

"Wolfe's heading out there now and I'm keeping the search and rescue going for as long as possible. Amanda's our prime concern right now and I aim to find her." Jenna leaned back in her chair. "When we arrived, Rowley informed me that Blackhawk's team is out with dogs scouring Stanton Forest along all the points where Matt stopped. He made him aware of the dangers of potential booby traps and the people with him are experienced trackers."

"I sure like having Blackhawk around. You thought of making him a deputy?" Kane placed his cup on the desk. "We need more on the team; we're stretched to the limit right now."

"He won't join the team." Jenna pushed hair from her eyes. "We pay him for his time but he doesn't want a badge." She sighed. "I hate sitting here doing nothing – I feel like I'm wasting precious time. Amanda is out there all alone and we're her only hope."

Kane took in her hopeless expression. She'd done everything by the book: organized a search, set up a command station, had deputies at the Braxtons' house monitoring calls and hunting down suspects. "I feel the same but we're doing everything humanly possible to find her. Right now, we'll have to hope Matt has some information to give us or we have the same problem we had with Lindy. If Matt isn't involved in Amanda's abduction, she could be anywhere – even out of the county by now. We know someone carried her from the woods, so we have to assume he rendered her unconscious or someone would've heard her screaming." He scratched the stubble on his chin. "The ranch is about a mile from Stanton Road, so her abductor must have stashed a vehicle close by. He wouldn't risk someone noticing his vehicle if he left it parked alongside the forest. If it was Matt, we know from his GPS where he stopped and if Amanda's anywhere close by Blackhawk's team will find her."

"I hope so." Jenna lifted the lawyer's card George Miller had given her and peered at it. "I haven't met Samuel J. Cross. He's a returned local working out of an office over the bank. Maggie says the townsfolk like him just fine."

Kane rubbed the back of his neck. "I figure he'll have Miller out within the hour. We don't have enough evidence to charge him."

"Yeah, it's circumstantial at best but I'd like the chance to question him some more." Jenna sipped her drink. "If he walks we'll need to dig deeper. Once the lawyer has spoken to Miller, I want to hunt down Amanda's friend, Lucy. She might have something we could use – they're best friends and girls discuss boys, maybe there's more to the friendship between her and Matt than he's leading us to believe."

"Don't forget the stalker friend from school, Peter English." Kane took a long drink of his coffee. "He ticks a few of our boxes as well. With no contact from Amanda's abductor and no sign of her anywhere, I figure we'll have to speak to all the people on our list again and see where they were last night."

"Okay, while we're waiting for Mr. Samuel J. Cross to arrive, might as well make a few calls." Jenna made some notes and handed the list to Kane. "Chase down the whereabouts of Kittredge, Packer and Lancaster. I'll do the rest."

Kane stood and glanced down at the list, then at his watch. "We need more help."

"We need more time." Jenna reached for her phone. "I'm just hoping it's not too late already."

Kane had finished making the calls when Samuel J. Cross strolled into the office announcing himself loud and clear then leaned on the front counter, chatting to Maggie, as if he had all the time in the world. Kane got to his feet and took in the man with his insolent grin, wearing faded jeans, a battered Stetson and cowboy boots. A long blond ponytail curled down his back and his leather jacket appeared to be his only item of clothing less than ten years old. He looked as if he'd come straight from a cattle ranch rather than the office of a defense lawyer. As Kane approached the counter, Cross turned his head toward him, then straightened to about six-two and gave him an assessing look.

"Samuel J. Cross, and you'd be Deputy Dave Kane." Cross stuck out his hand. "Heard a lot about you since I arrived back in town."

"All good I hope?" Kane shook his hand in a firm grip.

"I guess it depends on the client." Cross gave him a brilliant white smile that faded in an instant. "You've Matt Miller in custody. I'd like some time with my client alone."

Kane nodded. "Sure, but can I see some ID?"

"I guess I don't fit into a lawyer stereotype, huh?" Cross handed him a business card, then pulled out a wallet and flipped it open to display his driver's license. "I'm listed with the Montana Association of Criminal Defense Lawyers. You'll find my qualifications hanging on the wall in my office, or give Mayor Petersham a call. He's known my family since I was a kid."

"He's legit." Deputy Walters came to Kane's side. "Good to see you again, Sam. Where you been workin'?"

"Here and there. Nice to see you again, Duke. Can't chat now, I've a client." Cross turned away from the old deputy, pulled a notepad out of a battered briefcase at his feet and scanned it. "Hmm, suspicion of abducting one Amanda Braxton, fifteen." He lifted his gaze to Kane. "Any sightings of the girl?"

Kane shook his head. "Nope."

"Is this all the evidence you have against my client?" Cross waved the notepad. "If so, it's not enough for you to charge him, it's circumstantial and my client doesn't have any priors." He shook his head. "I'll have him released within the hour."

Annoyance rolled over Kane but he stared back at the man's challenging gaze. "Well, we'd like to interview him. He clammed up the moment we mentioned we'd obtained a warrant to track his GPS." He straightened to his full six-five. "Wouldn't it be better to straighten this out now? Or we'll just have to pull him in again for questioning the moment he steps out the door. We've the right to hold him for twenty-four hours for questioning."

"I'm aware of the law." Cross tucked the pad under one arm and picked up his briefcase. "I'll see if Matt is prepared to speak with you. He's already exercised his rights and if he decides to remain silent, that's his prerogative."

Kane almost wanted to laugh. The lawyer's tone and professionalism were the complete opposite of his appearance. He waved a hand in the direction of the interview room. "I'll take you to him in just a moment." He turned to Deputy Walters. "Anything to report?"

"Nope. I'm heading home now. I'm taking another shift at the Braxtons' house later."

"Okay." Kane turned back to Cross. "The interview room is this way." He led the way along the hallway.

Inside the room, Kane switched off the sound to the camera and pointed to a button mounted on the table. "Press the button when you want to leave or if you need assistance. The CCTV is on and we'll be monitoring the feed for your safety. The sound control is here." He pointed to a control on the desk. "As you can see, I've muted the sound."

"Yeah, yeah, I'll work it out." Cross waved him away, and then turned to Matt. "How've they been treating you?"

"Fine." Matt rubbed the end of his nose and flashed Kane a disgruntled look. "I didn't do anything."

Part of Kane wished he could listen in to Miller's excuses but he shut the door and made his way back to Jenna's office. Sometimes circumstantial evidence was enough to convict and what they had on Miller was substantial, with the GPS records proving Matt had visited Glacial Heights during the timeframes of both abductions. He'd like the opportunity to question him about Lindy Rosen as well.

"Ah good, the lawyer's here." Jenna indicated the monitor above her desk and frowned. "He's a strange one. Did you check his creds?"

Kane handed her the business card. "The card and license match and Walters vouched for him." He took a seat. "Walters is off duty now and will relieve the Blackwater deputies at the Braxton house later. It's all quiet there."

"I wish we'd get a break in either of the cases." Jenna let out a long sigh. "It's all circumstantial or supposition. I feel like I'm swimming upstream, in the rapids."

"I don't figure Sam Cross will take long with Matt." Kane pulled out his notebook. "I've a list of where our potential suspects are working. They're all in the same general area, so depending how long it takes interviewing English and Lucy we'll be able to speak to them today."

"Lucy is at home, not far from the Braxton ranch. And English lives on Maple Drive." Jenna glanced up at the monitor, then back at Kane. "Do you think Matt's involved?"

The evidence had been live streaming through Kane's mind since they'd left Miller's Garage. "It could be a coincidence he was in the area when both girls went missing but he does have friends in the general area. The use of explosives is worrying me. I couldn't find squat to link him."

"He could've gotten that via YouTube." Jenna blew her bangs from her forehead. "Remember what Josh told us – most of the terrorists planting IEDs get their info via the web."

The phone on Jenna's desk rang and she gave Kane a hopeful look and picked up the receiver.

"Sheriff Alton." She lifted her gaze to Kane. "What do you have for me, Wolfe?" She gave him an update, and then put the phone on speaker. "Kane's here. We're waiting on the lawyer to finish speaking with Miller."

"I don't have any good news. Blackhawk's found no clues yet. Nothing I collected from Miller's pickup matches either of the victims and he

hasn't cleaned the vehicle recently. I've the results of Lindy Rosen's blood tests. Her abductor subdued her with diethyl ether. He used a considerable quantity, which makes me believe he wore protection of some kind over his face. I'm waiting on DNA results and Emily is here to run the office. I have some spare time – do you want me to go 'n' pick up Noah McLeod?" Wolfe cleared his throat. *"He's admitted to dealing with a child under the age of sixteen and could be involved in the current cases. Sometimes a perp will admit to a lesser charge so we overlook them in an investigation – or he could be some crazy just trying to get famous."*

"Yeah, go right ahead. McLeod's on our list of persons of interest but we haven't gotten to him yet. It's chaotic here at the moment and we've been hunting down suspects who've had direct contact with the victims in the last week or so." Jenna exchanged a worried look with Kane. "You're right, he could be involved."

"He's confessed to committing a crime in the presence of two deputies, and we don't need an arrest warrant. I'll speak to the girl and see if she confirms his story but whatever she says about him, I'll search his house then bring him in." Wolfe took a deep breath. *"I figure it's best to leave no stone unturned. Look at the facts, Jenna – he knows both girls and has admitted to being a pedophile. He could be the Shadow Man."*

CHAPTER THIRTY-ONE

Overwhelmed with the immense pressure of the job, Jenna replaced the receiver and stood. She stared at the whiteboard for long moments, and then paced up and down the room. She checked her cellphone again. *Why isn't he contacting me?* Time was ticking by and she had a fifteen-year-old girl in mortal danger. The man she had in custody would likely walk and she needed more evidence. She could feel Kane's gaze following her and returned to her desk. She snatched up the phone. "Anything to report, Rowley?"

"Nothing yet, ma'am."

"Okay, we might be chasing smoke here, but I want you to go down the list of girls Julie gave me." Jenna pushed a hand through her hair. "Concentrate on the ones who've had nightmares about seeing a man in their room. Get me their details and contact their parents and ask if it's okay to interview them." Exhausted, she sighed. "I've no idea when this will be, so if it's okay we'll call them and make a time."

"I'm on it, ma'am."

After disconnecting, Jenna stared at the whiteboard again then continued to pace, allowing the information to filter through her mind. There had to be a clue, something to tie the two cases together. No one was perfect – people made mistakes – but so far this killer hadn't faltered. Another strange twist was the fact he didn't seem to follow a pattern. Yeah, he kidnapped girls, but the cases were different enough to make her believe the second could be a copycat. No video file had arrived, no time limit had been set… and she'd kept those pieces of evidence from the media. She stared at Kane. "Do you think this is a copycat?"

"It's too early to tell yet." Kane frowned. "There's a small connection – both girls had dreams about people in their rooms. I figure if it's the same guy, then the next victim will be another one of them. It's as if he's conditioning them somehow."

The idea of something so crazy happening seemed ridiculous. Jenna raised both eyebrows. "You don't mean mind control?"

"Hypnotism maybe, then he uses a trigger word to get the girls to leave the house." Kane shrugged. "I've been thinking on it too but like I said, it's too early to tell."

"That's a cop out and you know it." Jenna leaned on the desk and stared at him. "Not everyone is a serial killer; people do murder one or two people and then stop. You're the profiler – if it's the same person, why hasn't he contacted me yet? What's his endgame?"

"If Miller is our man, he's tied up at the moment and if it's a copycat, he won't know the play." Kane stretched out his legs and looked up at her. "If Miller's not our guy and the Shadow Man's watching the office or the news, which I'd do if I was planning my next move, he'd know we've a man in custody." He shrugged. "Why would he show his hand when he could be on the run and home free if you charge Miller?"

Jenna snorted. "You're sure full of metaphors today, Dave, but not many solutions."

"From where I'm sitting you already have a sound plan of action." Kane got to his feet. "We speak to Miller. If he walks we hunt down Amanda's best friend and the stalker, and then shake down the other persons of interest to see what falls out." He walked around the desk and placed one arm around her shoulder. "You've people out searching for Amanda, there's nothing else we can do." He gave her a little squeeze. "If it's not Miller, we continue to investigate and wait for the Shadow Man's next move. I'm convinced we're still in his perverted game."

A buzzer sounded and Jenna looked up at the monitor. Cross had finished speaking to his client and now she had an opportunity to ask the questions burning in her mind. She turned away from Kane. "Okay, I'm taking the lead in this interview. You watch Miller and see if you can get a take on him. My gut tells me he's hiding something. Lawyers don't come cheap and for him to clam up like he did, he had a reason."

"Roger that."

Jenna swiped her card through the reader outside the interview room and stepped inside with Kane close behind. She took in the cowboy standing before her. "I'm Sheriff Alton, Mr. Cross. Is your client prepared to answer a few questions pertaining to the abduction of Amanda Braxton and murder of Lindy Rosen?"

"I'll allow questioning to clear my client of suspicion." Cross moved to the other side of the desk and took a seat beside Matt Miller.

Jenna sat down and unmuted the sound on the CCTV camera, then pressed the record button. She gave the date and time of the interview and who was present. "Mr. Miller, do you know Amanda Braxton?"

"Yeah, I already told you I know her. Her brother Luke introduced me to her at Aunt Betty's Café. She's a friend of his girlfriend, Lucy." Matt sighed. "Why do we have to go over this again?"

Jenna noted his aggravation. "I want it on the record, Mr. Miller. Do you know or have you ever met Lindy Rosen?"

"Nope." Miller glanced at his lawyer. "Never met her."

"Are you sure? She's a friend of Amanda and Lucy." Jenna pushed a photograph across the table. "Take a look. Do you remember her now?"

"Answer the question." Cross glanced at Miller. "Have you seen her around town?"

"Nope." Miller shook his head. "She's a kid, why would I even look her way?"

Jenna left the photograph on the table and stared at Miller. "We've collected the data from the GPS in your vehicle and cellphone. We've been able to track your movements over the last few days. We know you were in the vicinity when Lindy Rosen and Amanda Braxton went missing. Further to that, we know you stopped near the old schoolhouse on Station Road and visited the Triple Z Bar the same day we discovered Lindy Rosen's body."

As they hadn't given out where they'd found Lindy's body to the media, only the killer would know the location. Jenna observed Miller's body language but he kept the same defiant posture. "Well, did you have a reason to be in those locations at that time?"

"You don't have to answer those questions, Matt." Cross leaned on the table and eyeballed Jenna. "I figure if I did a survey and asked how many people used Stanton Road over the same timeframe on the same days, I'd have a list as long as my arm – it's the main highway out of town – and just how many people frequent the Triple Z? It's always standin' room only when I drop by." He leaned back in his chair. "Come to think of it, I was there on Monday night. I drove on Stanton Road and right past Glacial Heights like at least twenty or more others during the evenin'. Am I a suspect too?"

Irritated by Cross's wide grin, she pushed on. "He was in the area and wears the same boots as the footprint we found at the scene of Amanda's abduction. He knows her and could have arranged to meet her last night." She took a deep breath. "She's out there somewhere alone and frightened." She turned her attention to Matt. "Tell me where she is and stop playing games."

"Hold on a minute, Sheriff. Don't go harassing my client." Cross held up a hand as if stopping traffic. "If you want to charge my client go ahead, but the DA will agree with me. You've no case against him. As I've explained, any number of people use that road. Just about half the tradesman in town, in fact all over America, wear the same brand steel-toe boots. You have no DNA, no hair or fibers; you found no trace evidence in his vehicle. The families of both girls in your investigation exposed them to a number of different tradesmen over the same period. I know for a fact most of the families in Glacial Heights use the same companies on a regular basis. Just the gardening service alone employs a ton of different casual workers." He glanced over at Kane as if waiting for him to back him up. "Surely, if Matt kidnapped Amanda or Lindy Rosen, you would've found evidence in his pickup? The ME's statement states clearly that his vehicle hadn't been cleaned." He turned his attention back to Jenna. "Matt has a clean record and a wholesome reputation, goes to church on Sundays. You'll never get the charge to stick, let alone convince a jury he's a killer."

"The judge agreed with me." Jenna jutted out her chin in defiance but inside her heart sank. Of course, he was right. She was grabbing at straws and they both knew it. "He considered we'd probable cause for a search warrant."

"Okay, okay. I would agree with you on that point but you've zip to charge my client, Sheriff." Cross raised both eyebrows. "Why don't you call the DA and lay it out for him? I know he'll say you'll be wasting the court's time. You've provided insufficient factual evidence and there's no case to answer."

Defeated, Jenna closed the interview. She looked at Miller and caught the way his mouth tipped up in a cocky grin and his eyes flashed in amusement as if he'd won this round. "Okay, you can go. Deputy Kane will return your property to you before you leave." She waited for Kane to escort Miller out, and then headed for the door when Cross caught up to her. She turned and looked at him. "Was there anything else?"

"We've gotten off to a rocky start." Cross flashed a white smile and held out his hand. "No hard feelings?"

Jenna shook his hand and took in his honest expression. "None whatsoever. We all have a job to do, Mr. Cross."

"Call me Sam." Cross hadn't let go of her hand. "Not often I cross swords with such a beautiful sheriff." He lowered his voice to a sexy drawl. "Maybe we could have dinner sometime?"

Memories of the last lawyer she'd been involved with flashed into her mind. James Stone had become a huge problem and this scruffy cowboy didn't come close to her ideal man. *Be tactful. Remember what happened last time.* She pulled her hand away and smiled. "Thank you so much but I'm in a relationship."

"Lucky guy." Cross stepped away but remained jovial. "If you ever change your mind." He handed her his card. "My private number is on the back."

Not in a million years. "Sure." Jenna slid her card through the scanner and pulled open the door, and then watched as Cross sauntered out.

On the way back to her office, she stopped to speak with Rowley. "Are you good?"

"Yeah, everything is under control. The team are taking calls but nothing has come in we can use. A few people have seen Amanda at Aunt Betty's but I called Susie Hartwig – she knows her and she hasn't seen her today. She'll call me direct if she does. The search is progressing with no leads whatsoever. It's as if she's vanished into thin air."

Jenna nodded. "Okay, good work. If the media call, tell them we have no updates and to repeat this morning's interview." She noted the candy bar wrappers in his bin. "And eat some real food – it's going to be a long shift. Order in for yourself and the team and put it on the department's account. Tell the deputies at the Braxtons' house to do the same."

"Yes, ma'am."

She grabbed two coffees to go and emptied the box of chocolate chip cookies into a bag for Kane. She pulled on her Kevlar vest and shrugged into her coat, then took her weapon out of the desk drawer and slid it into the holster. Kane's dog sauntered into the room and she smiled when he looked up at her with big sad eyes. "You coming with us or do you want to stay with Maggie?"

"I figure we take him with us." Kane came into the room, carrying his vest and jacket. "He might pick up a scent on one of the suspects."

"Sure." She gave Kane a sideways look. "What, no comment on Miller?"

"Nah, but I figure he's hiding something." Kane slid his vest over his head. "We should keep a close eye on him."

"Yeah, we will." She handed him a cup and then the cookies. "Cross was unexpected." She raised both eyebrows.

"Yeah, I've a feeling he's going to be a thorn in our sides." Kane frowned. "He's smarter than he looks." He studied her face. "Oh boy – he hit on you, didn't he?"

Jenna smiled at him. "How did you guess?"

"Ah-huh." Kane slipped one arm around her and pulled her against him. "Your cheeks are a little pink. Do I have to challenge him to a duel at daybreak?"

"No!" She looked up at him. "I told him I'm in a relationship." She reluctantly moved away and frowned. "Forget him. Amanda is still missing and she's our priority at the moment."

"Breaking the stress for a few seconds doesn't mean we don't care." Kane touched her cheek and gazed at her with compassion, then dropped his hand. "So who's next on the list?"

"First we go speak to Lucy."

CHAPTER THIRTY-TWO

They arrived at Glacial Heights at three. It was six hours since Amanda's mother had reported her missing. On the way, Jenna called the Braxtons' house to speak with the deputies and contacted Blackhawk. With no valid sightings of Amanda from anyone via the hotline or search and rescue, and nothing from Blackhawk's team, the chances of finding Amanda alive were looking slim. As they turned into the driveway of the Mackintoshes' ranch, she scanned the property. The same architect had designed all the ranch houses she'd visited of late, so, apart from the land surrounding the houses, they all had much the same footprint. They pulled up beside a Green Thumb pickup parked in the driveway. If she found Paul Kittredge working today, she'd speak to him as well.

She'd called ahead to make sure Lucy was at home, and contacted Peter English's mother and arranged to speak with him. It helped that both sets of parents had cooperated. As they pulled up at the front of the house, a teenage girl appeared at the door. Jenna climbed out of Kane's truck and made her way up the front steps. "Are you Lucy?"

"Yeah, that's me." Lucy turned around. "Mom, the cops are here." She turned back and waved them inside. "First door on the left."

Jenna stepped inside the warm house with its scent of woodsmoke and pine. She glanced around at the neat home and then walked through the door into a family room. On a sofa sat a rotund woman, knitting needles in hand and a basket of wool at her feet. "Mrs. Mackintosh?"

"Take a seat." Mrs. Mackintosh eyed them both suspiciously. "Now what do you want with Lucy?"

Jenna introduced herself and Kane, then took out her notebook and pen. "I'm sure you're aware that Amanda Braxton went missing this morning. We're talking to her friends to gather any information that might help us find her." She glanced at Lucy. "Do you mind if we ask Lucy a few questions?"

"Go right ahead."

Jenna nodded. "When did you last see Amanda?"

"At Aunt Betty's yesterday around lunchtime. I can't believe she's missing." Lucy's eyes filled with tears. "Do you think she's dead, like Lindy?"

Jenna shook her head. "No, and we have hundreds of people out searching for her, so I hope we'll find her soon. This is why we need as much information as possible."

"I guess you'll want to know what we talked about." Lucy wiped her eyes on a tissue, and then bunched it in her hand. "Well, nightmares and boys mostly."

Jenna nodded. "Did she mention anything about seeing a man in her room?"

"No, she sees her grandma." Lucy pulled a face. "She likes seeing her grandma's ghost."

"Tell me about the other girls at school who've had nightmares." Jenna kept her face neutral but Kane's conclusions about mind control and hypnotism ran through her mind. "Are they in the same group of friends or classes at school? Can you think of anything special that connects them all?"

"Yeah, we're all friends from school." Lucy thought for a moment. "I made fun of Lindy and the others because the nightmares started after we joined the drama club. We're doing *Macbeth* and I figured it spooked them."

Jenna made a note to dig deeper. "Have you had any nightmares?"

"Nope, I sleep right through." Lucy frowned. "Amanda is sensible and her mother watches her like a hawk. There's no way she would've just walked out into the dark. I know her – she wouldn't do something like that."

Jenna needed answers. "What about the boy she planned to go to the dance with, Matt Miller. Would she have left the house to see him?"

"Matt? No... well, maybe. She did mention they talked about going fishing." Lucy's eyes widened. "Matt's dad has a weekender in the forest, on the river. Luke told me they go fishing there sometimes."

Jenna turned to look at Kane. "Pass that info on to Rowley. Tell him to get someone up there yesterday."

"Sure." Kane got up and headed for the door.

"What can you tell me about Peter English?" Jenna watched the girl's expression. "Luke mentioned he had to speak to him about Amanda."

"That creep." Lucy wiped her nose savagely. "Amanda told me she heard someone in the bushes along her driveway. It was probably him stalking her." She blinked a few times. "Lindy said that too."

Jenna leaned forward in her chair. "Said what?"

"They both thought someone was watching them when they got off the school bus and walked home." Lucy gave a little sob. "Amanda figured it was a bear."

"Then why would she risk walking into the woods at night?" Jenna examined the girl's expression. "Wouldn't they have told their parents?"

"How do I know?" Lucy sniffed. "I can't figure why either of them would leave the house at night."

"Getting back to Peter English." Jenna glanced at her notes. "Did he bother her at school?"

"He hung around." Lucy grimaced. "He kept asking her out and she kept refusing. Luke told him to stay away or Matt would pay him a visit."

Jenna frowned. "Luke threatened him?"

"Yeah, and he didn't bother her again."

"Was there any other boy either girl was seeing or interested in?" Jenna made a few notes. "Anyone else at all?"

"They like Mason, the football player who takes care of the grounds at school." Lucy blushed. "But he's a grown man."

"Just one more thing." Jenna offered her a smile. "Who's the teacher in charge of the drama club and what days do you go there?"

"Two, Miss Dryden and Mr. Ambrose. Tuesdays and Thursdays last class, then after school for an hour. We're meeting at the school this afternoon as well. If you want to talk to the other girls, they'll be there."

"Okay." Jenna folded her notebook and stood. "Thank you, Lucy." She handed Mrs. Mackintosh one of her cards. "If Lucy remembers anything else important, please call me."

"I'll do that, Sheriff." Mrs. Mackintosh took the card.

"Thanks." Jenna headed for the door.

Outside, Kane was leaning against his truck, cellphone pressed to one ear, Duke at his feet. The Green Thumb Landscaping Service pickup was missing. She waited for him to disconnect. "Dammit, the gardening service has left."

"They were leaving as I came out." Kane pushed his phone into his top pocket.

Jenna stared down the empty driveway. "Did you get on to Rowley?"

"Yeah, he hunted down the location but there's nowhere for a chopper to land in the area. Blackhawk and one of his friends are on horseback and they're riding to the cabin now." Kane opened the door to his truck and helped Duke into the back seat. "What did I miss?"

Jenna gave him a run-down of the interview. "Although both girls were infatuated with two of our persons of interest I'd like a chat with Peter English. Not that I figure he has the charm to lure teenage girls from their rooms at night." She sighed. "If the girls are being hypnotized, how come Lucy isn't affected and Amanda had a different dream?"

"Hmm, that's because hypnotism doesn't work on everyone." Kane met her gaze. "Plus mass hypnotism is difficult – but not impossible."

"We'll need to speak to those girls. They've a meeting at the school this afternoon. I'll call Maggie later and see if she's gotten their parents' permission. I want to find out if they're having the same dream. If so, then someone could be hypnotizing them." Jenna frowned. "How do you tell if someone's affected?"

"You can't."

As Jenna had missed the opportunity to speak to Paul Kittredge again, she made a quick call to Green Thumb's head office in town. The manager directed them to a house close to where Peter English lived. Kittredge would be working there for the rest of the week. They arrived at the Englishs' home a short time later. The interview with Peter was interesting but Jenna didn't consider him a suspect. He'd been home both nights of the abductions and posed no threat. The teenager admitted to pestering Amanda at school and following her home one time, but after his talk with Kane, Jenna was convinced Peter's days of stalking girls were over.

With Peter struck off her list, they drove to a nearby home where Jenna spoke to the owner before they made their way to the back of the property. She spotted Paul Kittredge leaning against a tree smoking and led the way across a manicured lawn. "Mr. Kittredge, we'd like a word with you."

"Sheriff, why you goin' to all the trouble of comin' to see me again?" Kittredge gave her a slow smile. "You don't need no excuse. Just sashay down to the Triple Z any night of the week and I'll buy you a drink." He chuckled. "Wear something sexy." He dropped his smoke and crushed it into the lawn with his boot.

Jenna could almost sense Kane moving closer and caught a flash of doubt in Kittredge's eyes. She could deal with him and leaned closer. As the smell of stale sweat and cigarette smoke curled up her nostrils, she lowered her voice to just above a whisper. "Mr. Kittredge, you're a person of interest in the murder of Lindy Rosen. Your alibi for the night she disappeared doesn't hold water." When he leaned down way too close to listen to her, she gave him her best official sheriff's glare. "I suggest you answer my questions. I don't need an excuse to haul you downtown and hold you for questioning for twenty-four hours. During that time, Deputy Kane is well within his rights to question you for eight hours straight."

"I'm sure we'll find plenty to talk about." Kane's eyes flashed with menace.

Jenna stepped back but kept her attention locked on Kittredge. "Do you know Amanda Braxton out of Glacial Heights?"

"Uh-huh." Kittredge narrowed his gaze. "She went missing this morning. I heard it on the radio."

"That's her." Jenna pulled out her notebook and scanned her notes. "You work at the Braxton ranch. Have you spoken to Amanda?"

"Yeah, a few times." Kittredge pulled out a pack of cigarettes, pulled one out with his teeth then held it unlit between his fingers. "She was real cut up when her grandma died."

"How often did you speak to her?"

"She'd hunt us down." Kittredge gave her a lazy smile. "Some days she'd sit on the grass and watch me work. Nice kid."

Nice enough to kidnap? This man hadn't convinced Jenna of his innocence, but with no evidence against him, she'd have to let it slide. "Do you have anyone who can vouch for your whereabouts last night?"

"Same as before." Kittredge settled his shoulders against the tree. "In the Triple Z as always. I eat and sleep there." His mouth curved into a smile. "I bed my women there."

Impatient to get to the other suspects, Jenna lifted her chin. "Give me the name of one person you spoke to last night."

"The barman, and I met a biker chick. She had a tattoo of a snake on one thigh, dark hair. Her name might have been Deidra or something close." Kittredge wet his lips. "She was in my room when I left this morning."

Jenna made a note in her book. "What do you drive?"

"The Green Thumb pickup right now. My own vehicle needs a repair. It's out back of the Triple Z. He shrugged. "It's a red GMC truck."

"What's wrong with it?" Kane moved closer.

"I don't have the spare cash to have it hauled down to Miller's to find out." Kittredge shrugged. "Don't need it no how when I've the company's vehicle to drive."

Jenna closed her notebook. "Very well, thank you for your time."

"I'll leave the invitation open if you want that drink, Sheriff." Kittredge chuckled. "I'll be finishing up here soon and you know where to find me."

Jenna ignored him and hustled to the truck. *In your dreams.*

CHAPTER THIRTY-THREE

Riled by Kittredge's disrespect for Jenna, Kane left rubber on the driveway as he pointed his truck toward Stanton Road and headed for the high school. It had taken one heck of a lot of willpower not to grab Kittredge by the scruff of his neck and shake him. He'd admired the way Jenna handled the jerk but standing by and saying nothing stuck in his craw. It came down to two things: his upbringing and his time in the marines; both had instilled in him respect for and the need to protect women. Old-fashioned to some, but inside he was an old-fashioned guy and when men disrespected Jenna, it made his blood boil. He turned onto the highway and accelerated. His temper dissipated slightly as the roar of the powerful engine filled the cabin.

"Do you know you've a tell when you're angry?" Jenna's voice seemed to cut through his wall of mad.

Kane didn't take his eyes off the road. He'd engaged lights and sirens because he needed to drive hard to clear his mind. Aware it was a juvenile outlet to his temper, he slowed down some. "And what is it?"

"The nerve in your cheek twitches." Jenna cleared her throat. "But the driving like a man possessed is new."

"I don't enjoy men disrespecting women is all." Kane flicked her a glance.

Jenna chuckled. "I felt your eyes boring into my back like laser beams, so I could only imagine the look you were giving him. I know you respect women and I like that but I'm glad you stopped calling me 'ma'am'; it made me feel like your grandma."

Kane laughed and the anger slipped away like rain down a gutter. "Okay, talk to me about Lancaster. He's the football player all the teenage girls are goo-goo-eyed over, right?"

"Yeah, and his alibi about being at his girlfriend's until six in the morning of the day Lindy Rosen went missing is a lie. We need to ask him where he was in the missing hours and find out his whereabouts last night. Maybe with a little persuasion, he'll let us take a look at his vehicle."

"Yeah, it would be good to find some evidence to link one of our suspects to the crime. Everything we've gotten so far is circumstantial." Kane turned onto the road leading to the school. It was strange seeing the place without the usual groups of people milling around. "It's like a ghost town. When do the kids finish spring break?"

"They go back Monday." Jenna was flipping through her notes. "It's not always deserted. A few of the clubs hold meetings here during vacations and then there's summer school. The drama club is here this afternoon and I know the prom committee has meetings here as well. They've teachers who volunteer to supervise and the janitor opens a room for them to use."

Kane rubbed his chin. "I hope they have someone to fill in for McLeod." He pulled into a staff parking lot beside a white pickup.

"I guess we're going to find out soon enough." Jenna's mouth turned down as she slid from the seat. "I hope Lancaster isn't going to be a jerk. I've had enough of his type for one day."

"Yeah, me too." Kane opened the door and Duke jumped down, wagging his tail.

They headed for the janitor's office and found an athletic guy who looked in his thirties, tipped back in a chair. Thick arms, bronzed from long hours of working outside, crossed his chest. A battered

Stetson covered his eyes and his dirty boots rested on the desk. From the snoring, he was sound asleep. Kane slammed his fist on the desk and watched with some amusement as the man woke with a start and gawked at him, wide-eyed. "Sorry to disturb your siesta but we need to speak to the janitor."

"Ah... why?" The man gathered himself, dropped his feet from the desk and slowly looked up at Jenna. "Afternoon, Sheriff." He stared down at Duke. "That's a fine-looking dog you have there."

"And you are?" Jenna stared at him and wrinkled her nose.

"Mason Lancaster, acting janitor." He smirked at Kane. "A deputy dropped by and hauled McLeod out of here. Big guy, looks like Thor – one of your men, Sheriff?"

"Yeah." Jenna pulled out her notebook. "You're just the man we're looking for. We need you to answer a few questions."

"Then take a seat." Lancaster waved them to chairs in front of his desk. "But I already gave Deputy Rowley all the information on my whereabouts Sunday night."

Kane leaned forward in his chair. "We've a statement from Miss Pike stating when she woke at one, you'd already left. Where were you between the hours of ten and seven, when you started work?"

"I couldn't sleep and she'd run out of beer, so I drove around some, then went home and fell asleep." Lancaster raised an eyebrow at him. "I didn't check to see what time it was but the alarm woke me at six and I came to work."

"And last night?" Jenna lifted her chin. "Where were you between the hours of nine and six this morning?"

"Last night?" Lancaster rubbed his chin. "I had a few beers and watched TV, then went to bed."

"Can anyone verify that?" Jenna's dark hair fell over her eyes as she made a few notes.

"Nope." Lancaster frowned. "After the grilling by your deputies Angela isn't speaking to me right now, and my other girlfriends were busy."

"That's too bad." Kane shrugged. "What do you drive?"

"A white Silverado. It's parked out front." Lancaster sat up straighter. "Why?"

Kane smiled. "Nice truck. Mind if we take a look at it?"

"Sure." Lancaster pushed himself up to his feet. "You won't find no drugs, I don't do that shit."

They followed Lancaster to his vehicle and Kane noted Duke's lack of response to the man. If Lancaster had been involved in either of the kidnappings, he would've expected some sort of reaction – although, if he'd covered himself from head to toe in some type of suit, maybe not.

After taking in the state of the man, with his dirty nails and unkempt appearance, it surprised Kane to find the vehicle immaculate. Lancaster opened the door and Kane pulled on gloves and searched inside. From the fresh aroma, the entire interior, seats and carpets had been professionally cleaned and within the last few hours. He verified the time by the date stamp on the sales receipt Lancaster had left in the console. *How convenient.* "Just had it cleaned, huh?" He waved the receipt. "Can I keep this?"

"Sure. I'd just gotten back before the cops hauled McLeod away. Had a call from the principal ten minutes later. He told me to lock up after the drama club has finished."

"The drama club is still here?" Jenna exchanged a knowing look with Kane. "Can you take us there? I'd like to speak with them as well."

"Sure." Lancaster locked his pickup and sauntered toward the building.

When Duke flopped onto the ground as if the short walk had worn him out. Kane hung back; he wanted to speak to Jenna. "He's hiding something. Why else do you figure he's gotten his car cleaned?"

"Suspicions, hell yeah, but again we've no solid evidence… unless…" Jenna's eyes lit up. "Give me that receipt. Maybe the cleaner hasn't emptied their vacuum yet. We might find some evidence."

Kane shook his head. "It wouldn't hold up in court. They'd have cleaned any number of cars before his and since. His lawyer will have the evidence dismissed."

"Okay." Jenna let out a long sigh. She glanced at her watch. "The chances of finding Amanda alive are getting slimmer by the second and we've found nothing. No sightings, no word from her abductor. Not one shred of evidence to find Amanda or lead us to Lindy's killer. I'm just chasing my tail. I hope the girls in the drama club can give us a lead."

Kane shook his head. "It's never too late, Jenna, and the team are working their butts off searching for Amanda right now."

His cellphone buzzed and he glanced at Jenna. "It's Blackhawk." Ahead he could see Lancaster hovering outside a classroom. "Do you want me to take this and catch up with you?"

"Yeah. I'll call Maggie about the drama club girls." Jenna turned and hurried away, cellphone pressed to her ear.

Kane took the call. "Did you find the cabin?"

"Yeah, it was right where Lucy said. No one's been here for months. We're heading back to join the search now. Apart from a few tire marks consistent with Miller stopping along the side of the forest we've found nothing. I figure he parked and walked to one of the houses. There're a hundred or so in walking distance. I called Rowley and asked him to hunt down any of Miller's friends in the area. We checked out three addresses and his friends were cooperative, allowed us to do a walk-through even

though we're not deputies. We checked them real good too. Root cellars, attics, the whole nine yards."

"We've lucked out all day as well." Kane sucked in a breath and let it out slowly. "We had to let him go. We didn't have enough evidence to charge him." He cleared his throat. "He pulled in a real smart lawyer, Samuel J. Cross."

"I know Sam. Honest as the day is long." Blackhawk chuckled. *"Hard to believe he came back here. He studied at Harvard and became a partner in a law firm in New York."*

"You don't say." Kane shook his head in disbelief. "He looks like a hobo."

"He's a cowboy born and raised. A non-conformist. I'd say the New York lifestyle was too fast for him. Old man Cross couldn't understand where Sam's brains came from and figured he'd been swapped at birth."

Kane glanced down the hallway to see Jenna walking into a room. Lancaster was heading back his way. "I gotta go. It'll be dark soon. You might as well call it a day."

"Sure but someone close by is doing this, I feel it in my bones."

Kane nodded. "Yeah, I feel the same way. Thanks for your help."

"Any time." Blackhawk disconnected.

When Lancaster strolled up to him, Kane looked him up and down. "Had any experience with explosives?"

"Nope." Lancaster smiled. "Not much call for them in my line of work." He tipped his hat and kept walking.

CHAPTER THIRTY-FOUR

Kane slipped into the classroom and all eyes turned to him. Jenna sat in the middle of a group of teenage girls. Two teachers he assumed were Miss Dryden and Mr. Ambrose stood to one side, and a few boys were there too, listening with interest. From the conversation, the girls involved all had similar dreams. A shadowy figure appeared in the corner of their room and sometimes they could hear a whisper. When their parents searched the room and outside the home, they found no trace of an intruder.

Outside stimuli often generated dreams and a hypnotist could utilize them as a preset trigger. He walked closer to the group. "May I ask a question, Sheriff?"

"Go right ahead." Jenna turned to look over her shoulder at him.

"The girls who've had bad dreams raise your hands." Kane looked at the six of them and smiled. "How many of you leave your drapes open at night?"

Their hands all remained high in the air. *Interesting.* All the girls had outside stimuli to trigger their dreams. He turned his attention to the remaining three girls. "How about you? Do any of you sleep with the drapes open?"

No hands raised.

"Okay, thanks, girls."

As Jenna continued to chat to the girls, he allowed the information to drift through his mind. He'd found a key to link the girls together. His attention moved to the teachers, wondering if either of them was involved. The problem was all the staff would've undergone vigorous background checks to be able to work with children, so he dismissed them but took note of their names to run a background check anyway. He let the case of Lindy Rosen filter through his mind again. They hadn't considered the fact the killer could be a woman. He'd discuss the notion with Jenna on the way back to the office. He headed over to the teachers with Duke at his heels. He figured it wouldn't hurt to have the dog sniff them; but again Duke didn't react and just rolled on his back to allow them to rub his belly.

He smiled at the teachers. "I hear you're doing *Macbeth* this year. Great play. I saw it at Stratford-upon-Avon in England many years ago."

"We don't mention the title during the rehearsals or anytime during the performance of the play. It's said to be bad luck." Miss Dryden, a petite, dark-haired woman in her late twenties, looked distraught. "We've two of our students involved in the play missing already."

Kane shrugged. "If you believe naming the play aloud caused their abductions then I'd suggest you forget performing it again." He scrutinized their unconcerned reactions. "Did the same thing happen the last time this play was performed here?"

"I've no idea – that was before our time." Mr. Ambrose, middle-aged and balding, glared at the group of boys, who were snorting with amusement. "I moved to Black Rock Falls about two years ago." He indicated to Miss Dryden. "Miss Dryden joined the team this year."

Kane turned his attention on the boys. "I see you find it amusing Lindy Rosen was murdered and Amanda is missing. Why is that?"

The boys sobered at once. Two of them went sheet-white. Kane looked down at one of them. "Well?"

"We don't figure it's funny about Lindy and Amanda." The boy straightened, trying to be tough. "It's the stupid curse about the play and the girls believing in ghosts. We figure it's funny is all… ah, sir."

"Okay." Kane handed them all his cards. "If you hear or see anything unusual, never mind how trivial, call me. We need to find Amanda and stop this happening again."

Out of the corner of his eye, he caught sight of Jenna staring at him. He turned to her. "Are you ready to go, ma'am?"

"Yeah." Jenna turned to the teachers. "Thank you for your time." She led the way to the door. Outside in the parking lot, she looked up at him. "Why did you ask about drapes?"

Kane unlocked his truck and lifted Duke into the back seat, then climbed behind the wheel. "It's a link between the girls who had nightmares." He started the engine and swung the car around to head back to the office. "I'd like to know if Lindy and Amanda slept with the drapes open."

"Why?" Jenna clicked in her seatbelt and turned to look at him.

"Both the Rosens' and Braxtons' houses have trees opposite the girls' bedrooms." Kane accelerated along Stanton Road. "Either the shadows from the trees are triggering the dreams or, if you want to go with a hypnotist's trigger, he could use the shadows from the trees hitting the windows." He glanced at her. "Say he conditioned them to believe they see the man – first he tests it to see if it works, then perhaps he ups the ante and adds something like, 'when the shadows cross your bed on a full moon' or, 'walk downstairs and out into the dark' – or maybe the sunshine. Something that isn't frightening."

"Okay, we'll look into that idea, as crazy as it sounds." Jenna reached for her to-go cup of coffee, sipped, and then pulled a face. "Yuk, cold coffee, and I'm starving but we can't waste time stopping to eat. Wolfe will be at the office with McLeod."

Kane shrugged. "Rowley would have ordered a mountain of food from Aunt Betty's." He glanced at her. "Another thing – we're focusing on a male killer. What if it's a woman these girls know and trust? They'd open the door for her. Even take a ride with her."

"Dang." Jenna hand-palmed her forehead. "You're right. We've never considered a woman killer." She stared at him. "But who would do such a thing?"

Kane slowed as they drove into town. "I have no idea but the majority of kid-killers know the family."

"That's a chilling thought."

It was dark by the time they walked into the sheriff's department. Rowley was at the front counter talking on the phone. It was obvious from his conversation that he was winding up the search for the night. Kane took in his haggard appearance and waited for him to disconnect. "Any news?"

"Not a whisper." Rowley looked at Jenna. "I've sent the search teams home, ma'am. Webber is talking to a local man who thought he saw Amanda in the park about an hour ago. Wolfe is in your office with the DA and Sam Cross."

"The DA?" Jenna's brow crinkled into a frown. "Here?"

"Yes, ma'am." Rowley cleared his throat. "We've been busy and Wolfe took over the McLeod case, called Sam Cross back in and the DA arrived about ten minutes ago. I was just about to call you with an update."

"That's fine." Jenna glanced around. "Where's Maggie?"

"She's making another pot of coffee. I ordered in and Susie just delivered some fresh sandwiches." Rowley smiled. "I made sure there was a bagel and cream cheese."

"You're a lifesaver." Jenna gave him a brilliant smile, then, pulling off her jacket, headed toward her office.

Kane watched her go then shrugged out of his jacket, pulled off his Kevlar vest and followed her. The men had gathered around the desk. When Jenna walked in, they got to their feet.

He noticed Jenna's twitch of disapproval and dropped into a seat beside Wolfe.

"Okay, what's happening in the McLeod case? I gather that's why you're all here?" Jenna leaned back in her chair.

"I spoke to Jocelyn Smythe and she informed me McLeod has been making advances toward her for some time." Wolfe cracked his knuckles. "McLeod admits to stalking her and grabbing her at a party and kissing her. I brought him in, called his lawyer, Sam Cross, and notified the DA. I did a sweep of the house and found a few interesting files on his computer. I've handed the evidence to the DA."

"Long story short, Sheriff." The DA, Bradley Cutler, smiled at her. "I've cut a deal with Mr. Cross and his client. A cruiser will be arriving shortly to escort Mr. McLeod to the county jail. I'll take it from here; he's no longer your concern."

"Then, will you leave?" Jenna gave them a dismissive wave. "I've a missing girl to find."

Kane waited for them to go and waved Maggie inside. She carried a tray of coffee and takeout packets then set them on the table. He smiled to himself as Jenna tucked into the coffee and bagel. He turned to Wolfe. "That was fast work."

"Easy when they admit to committing a crime." Wolfe looked over at Jenna. "Do you need me anymore? It's getting late and I've left Emily at my office."

"No. Thank you for helping, Shane. I really appreciate it." Jenna smiled at him. "That's one person off our suspects list."

"You should try and get some rest, Jenna." Wolfe pushed to his feet. "There's nothing more you can do today."

Kane nodded his agreement. "I'll have the hotline transferred to your cellphone in case anything comes in. You'll be the first to know."

"Okay." Jenna stifled a yawn. "I'll bring the files up to date then we'll head off home."

Kane waited for Wolfe to close the door, and then looked at her. "You've no intention of leaving yet, have you?'

"Nope." Jenna turned to her computer. "Not until I've run down a list of any suspicious females in town."

Kane pushed to his feet and nodded. "I'm on it." He picked up his coffee and a packet of sandwiches and headed for the door. It was going to be a long night.

CHAPTER THIRTY-FIVE

Thursday

The buzz of the alarm hadn't dragged Jenna from dreaming about surfing in Hawaii but the high-pitched whistle Kane used for Duke did. She dragged herself from the sun and sandy beach and cranked open one eye.

"Morning. It's six-thirty, I've turned out the horses and breakfast will be ready in about fifteen minutes." Kane placed a steaming cup of coffee on the bedside table and smiled down at her. "Your clothes are fresh out the drier. They're on the back of the chair." He pushed a hand through his hair, still damp from the shower. "I figured after last night's marathon, we'd skip our workout this morning."

Jenna pushed her hair from her eyes and eased up onto the pillows. She'd happily forgo their usual morning workout together. After working late and with the awful feeling she could be the Shadow Man's target, she'd spent the night in Kane's spare room. She'd taken the offer of one of his T-shirts to sleep in and tossed all her clothes into his washing machine before falling into bed exhausted. When she stayed at his cottage, he refused to allow her to lift a finger. She glanced over at the chair to find her clothes neatly folded with military precision. This and coffee, with breakfast on the way – he'd be any woman's dream come true. "You know, Dave, if you keep this up I won't want to go home."

"That's the general idea." He sat on the end of the bed and his expression became serious. "There were no calls on the hotline overnight. What's your plans for today?"

"Rowley will've restarted the search at daybreak. I can trust him to organize that side of things." Jenna reached for the cup and sniffed the rich aroma. "I guess as we don't have any leads for a possible woman suspect, we'll have to run down our second list of contacts. Sean Packer and Charles Anderson worked for both families. They're on the list as persons of interest, and in contact with both girls at one time." She sipped her coffee, and then looked at Kane over the rim of her cup. "Unless we get a sighting or contact from Amanda's abductor, we've little to go on."

"With both cases tied to the same list of suspects, we've no chance of hunting down who killed Lindy Rosen either." Kane rubbed his freshly shaved chin. "I hope the bomb squad will contact us today with their findings. I'd like to know what they discovered – as in, what explosive he used. We might be able to trace the person responsible from that." He frowned. "I've been giving it a lot of thought, trying to remember the sequence of events. The delay on the IED between the explosions was longer than usual, which makes me wonder how experienced the Shadow Man is in making bombs."

Jenna straightened and looked at him with interest. "How so?"

"It's usual in an IED to use a tripwire or a cellphone to initiate a small explosion and this in turn triggers a second more devastating explosion." He met her gaze. "There were two massive explosions and from the extent of the damage, it was overkill."

Jenna shuddered at the memory of the explosion hurling her into the air before crashing to the ground. "What are the options?"

"C4, dynamite, or the easy-to-obtain fertilizer type, aka the Oklahoma Bomber." Kane shrugged. "All of the above cause a ton load of devastation." He cleared his throat. "C4 and dynamite could be stolen from a mine. ANFO – it's an industrial explosive and is likely available locally as well."

Jenna finished her coffee and placed the cup on the bedside table. "Didn't Packer work for the mines at one time?"

"Nope, that was Anderson." Kane pushed to his feet. "Packer was in the army, and we know he has knowledge of explosives, but he denied it, if you remember?"

"Yeah, I recall." Jenna eased to the edge of the bed. "Both these men could've tried to kill us but I'm not sure about their connection to either of the girls. They completed their jobs and left, unlike Kittredge, who acts like a sleaze, and Lancaster, who admits to Rowley he had them 'hanging around him like butterflies'." She snorted. "Did you catch the stink coming from him? He sure ain't no flower." She dragged her hands through her hair. "They should be our prime suspects but the other two sure need a second look and I'm not discounting Miller either." She glanced at her watch. "It's getting late."

"Okay. I'll go start breakfast." Kane looked down at her. "Got everything you need?"

Jenna smiled at him. "Yes, you keep my favorite toiletries in the bathroom. I'll be good to go in ten."

As Jenna placed her plates in the dishwasher, the message signal sounded on her cellphone and she slid it out her pocket. Her stomach cramped at the caller ID. Private number. *Oh no, not another video from the Shadow Man.* She turned to Kane. "It's a message from a private number." She opened the message and found no text, just a video file.

"Let's hope he wants to deal this time." Kane moved to her side and peered at the screen. "Open it."

With trembling fingers, Jenna opened the file and stared in horror at the image of Amanda captured by an infrared camera. She was frantically trying to escape from a room and screaming in terror. From the way she clawed at the walls, tripped and fell countless times, it was obvious the girl was in complete darkness. Her tear-stained cheeks and frantic pleas churned Jenna's stomach. Then came the disjointed whispers from a voice so evil, her hand shook so hard Kane had to take the cellphone from her. She wanted to cover her ears and look away but bit down hard on her lip and listened in horror as the Shadow Man taunted Amanda. He told her the chilling history of the house to terrify her and by the time he'd finished, Amanda was hugging her knees in the corner and rocking back and forth.

When the clip ended, she stared at the screen, her mind in denial and heart racing. Slowly, she lifted her gaze to see Kane's face, which was ashen. "She's already dead, isn't she?"

Kane didn't reply but walked away, then replayed the attachment over and over again. She went to him and touched his arm. "What is it?"

"I remember Rowley telling me the same story." He looked at her. His face had turned to expressionless stone. "So do you. I know where she is. It's the Old Mitcham Ranch."

"Then let's go." Jenna headed for the family room and grabbed her vest and jacket from a peg by the door.

"Wait! The clues are way too obvious." Kane followed her. "I figure he's luring us into a trap."

"We don't have any choice, Dave. There's a chance Amanda might be alive." Jenna grabbed her cellphone from his hand. "I'll call it in, you drive."

"I'll leave Duke." Kane pulled extra ammo clips from a locked drawer in a cabinet and slid them toward her. "He's safer here."

Jenna called Maggie, then contacted Wolfe and brought him up to date. She pulled on her Kevlar vest and shrugged into her coat.

As they ran for Kane's truck, she turned to him. "Wolfe is on the way with Webber and they'll be loaded for bear."

"Wolfe is hands-on with explosives as well. He'll watch our backs." Kane backed out the garage and accelerated toward the gate.

The large metal gates they'd installed for extra security after the melt slid open as they approached. The beast's back tires dug into the road as Kane turned left and, engine roaring like a mad bull, headed to the Old Mitcham Ranch.

Jenna dug her fingers into the leather seat as the green landscape flashed by in a blur. The SUV accelerated to frightening speeds, bumping over or swerving to miss the potholes on the uneven road, pitted by last winter's snowfall, but Kane drove the vehicle with confidence. It was as if the beast was an extension of himself. He reacted to obstacles in his path with the kind of instinct and split-second timing she could only dream about having. "Where do you figure he has her?"

"It looked like one of the rooms in the house to me." Kane negotiated a hairpin bend then slammed his foot back on the gas, throwing Jenna back in her seat. "I sure as hell don't want to go back into the root cellar – the image of the last time is tattooed on my brain."

The memory of the butchered young woman they'd found in that same cellar some time ago crashed into her head like a bad dream. She'd never forgotten the expression in the young woman's eyes, even after being prepared for the horror waiting inside. It had been her first experience of the Old Mitcham Ranch's curse. Earlier, Kane had ventured down the steps alone, deep into the pitch-black cellar, to discover a horrific scene. The impact of finding a mutilated murder victim who resembled his sister must have been hard on him. He'd said nothing at the time but the expression on his face now spoke volumes. Jenna squeezed his arm. "Me either, but we might not have a choice."

As they flew up the narrow road, Jenna considered the best way to approach the situation. She preferred to lead an investigation, but she had a tactical expert sitting beside her and right now, she needed his expertise. "How do you figure we should play this?"

"We'll drive past the gate and park up a ways, and then enter from round back. He'll be expecting us to drive right in." Kane flicked her a glance. "Tell Wolfe to come in quiet and do the same. I don't want them advertising we're on scene. We'll use our com packs to communicate; we'll need to use stealth, and no running into danger. We're no help to Amanda if we're dead."

Jenna nodded. "Roger that." She called Wolfe again and relayed the message.

"Another thing." Kane had slowed the vehicle to a normal speed and cruised past the Old Mitcham Ranch, hardly making a sound. "This killer has set a tripwire before, so if he is playing a game, he'll change it up a bit this time. IEDs can be anywhere. In war zones, they often place them in drink cans, so if a soldier kicks it out of the way it blows up. Then there are pipe bombs – remember explosive devices can be concealed in just about anything, so look for something that doesn't fit in." Kane pulled to a stop in a clump of trees about a hundred yards from the house. "And look out for tripwires and booby traps. Look all around up and down – this guy could be capable of anything."

CHAPTER THIRTY-SIX

As Kane slid from his truck and pulled out the sniper rifle from the back seat, he stared through the trees, surveying the area. The Old Mitcham Ranch loomed in the distance. Opposite a craggy hill that nature had pushed from the earth in a prehistoric earthquake, and flanked by decaying outbuildings, it resembled the set of a horror movie. The dilapidated house leaned to one side with grass growing in the gutters and peeling paint. It was anything but charming. Its tales of murder and suicide had once made it a creepy hangout for teenagers on Halloween, but not a soul had set one foot inside since the murder of a young woman a couple of years ago.

The string of gruesome murders had been his first case after arriving in town and it wasn't one he'd forget in a hurry. Settling into a new profession in a sleepy backwoods town had seemed ideal, but he'd soon realized Black Rock Falls held secrets deeper than the Grand Canyon. He had to admit that becoming a deputy after being first a sniper in the marines and then a special agent assigned to serve and protect POTUS had been more than a simple life adjustment. The moment he'd laid eyes on Jenna, he'd been compelled to make a complete turnaround.

She'd proved to be a sheriff with guts. Confronted with a fit, beautiful woman who he'd assumed was about twenty-five had brought out the protective side of him – and was the last thing Jenna wanted. She disliked him being overprotective, as if being prepared to take a bullet for her was a bad thing. Just as well he'd realized from the get-go that he could protect her just fine as long as she didn't catch him doing it.

Now he found himself in a dilemma. A crazy was on the loose and, not content to kidnap and strangle teenage girls, he also wanted to play a cat and mouse game with Jenna. His gut told him the Shadow Man had Jenna in his sights and whether she liked it or not, it was his job to protect her. He sighed. *I'll deal with the consequences later.*

He scanned the immediate area, looking for a suitable way to the back of the house, and motioned her forward. "See the animal trail weaving through the trees? We'll need to keep well away from it. He'd expect us to come in that way if we approached from the back, so we should use the perimeter trees instead. The shadows will be cover for us." He pulled off her buff-colored Stetson and chucked it into his truck. "He'll see you coming a mile away in a light-colored hat like that."

"Sure, I get it, keep to the shadows, look for traps… now check your earpiece." Jenna pressed the button on her mic. "Can you hear me?"

Kane nodded. "Loud and clear." He slipped his weapon from the holster. "Take it slow."

"Roger that. This place gives me the creeps, so stay close." Jenna moved off ahead of him.

Underfoot, last fall's leaves crunched and twigs cracked with each step. The aroma of leaf mold hung heavy in the air as Kane's boots sank into the muddy soil. He surveyed the area, searching ahead, above and below for any signs of a trap. The edge of the small wooded area was still damp from the winter melt and a bitter wind rustled through the pines. Ahead Jenna moved like a cat, weaving through the trees, stopping to check ahead then slinking forward again, hardly more than a shadow. When they reached the edge of the woods and the back wall of the old ranch house came into view, she stopped and glanced back at him. He held up a hand for her to wait and hustled to her side. "It hasn't changed since we came by last time."

"If we find any footprints in the dust, it's likely they're Rowley's and Webber's." Jenna turned to him. "This place was on Rowley's list when we searched for Lindy. He found nothing inside the house and he cleared the root cellar in the barn as well. We should be good to go."

"Wait." Kane touched her arm. "The killer's been here since Rowley's visit; I recognized the room from the video clip and the story he told Amanda. He wanted us to come here. It's all part of his plan."

"Then we change the play." Jenna slipped her weapon back into the holster. "I can't make out any disturbance in the long grass or bushes on this side of the house, which makes me think he hasn't set a trap on this side." She held up a hand to silence him before he had the chance to speak. "Yeah, I'm aware he could shoot me through one of the windows but then he'd be trapped in the house with you to deal with, wouldn't he? Any local would think twice before trying to take you on alone."

Kane shrugged. "If he's a local, maybe, but I figure he's been killing for some time. He's reached the limit of his thrill factor and needs more, so he's playing a game with us. It ups the ante."

"I say we belly-crawl over to the house and take a closer look." Jenna glanced up at him. "Unless you have a better idea?"

Kane shook his head. "Giving him the high ground if he's inside the house isn't a tactic I'd use."

"I figure you're overthinking this, Kane." Jenna's eyes flashed. "Amanda could be inside and we're playing tactics. I say we do the unexpected and walk straight up to the front of the house and take a look."

"No way." He shook his head. "If I wanted to kill someone, I'd set a pressure plate near the entrance or set up a shotgun to blow a hole in anyone who opens the door."

"Yeah, but he's not you, and he doesn't have your training." Jenna lifted her chin. "One thing's for sure, we can't just stand here all damn day."

"We don't know what he's capable of doing." Kane took a firm hold of her arm. "Jenna, listen to me. After advertising where he's keeping Amanda, I doubt he's hanging around for us to arrest him. I figure he's already moved her someplace – but he could be close by, watching." He holstered his weapon, then took a pair of binoculars from a pocket and leaned against a tree. "As I recall, the kitchen is at the back and there's a hallway leading to a family room with bedrooms off the side. I'd say one of the bedrooms has had its windows painted out to create a holding place for Amanda." He peered through the lenses and did a slow recon of the entire area. "It's dark inside. In fact, I can't see a darn thing." He pushed the binoculars back into his pocket. "There should be some light from the windows. I didn't see any tripwires or anything suspicious, unless he's set a pressure plate somewhere."

"You saying we could be blown up walking in the house, or do you figure he's rigged the entire house as a bomb?" Jenna's face paled.

Kane moved in front of her. "If there's an IED planted anywhere on the property, we have to assume it was laid in the last twenty-four hours, so the signs should be fresh. We know Rowley checked out the place and he didn't trip anything. I'll go first. Follow in my footsteps and don't step anywhere else, okay?"

"Yeah, got it." Jenna holstered her weapon. "You look for booby traps and I'll watch the windows for any movement."

Kane had mapped out a path. Going through the long undisturbed grass would be the safest; it wasn't likely anyone would risk throwing an explosive device from any of the windows. He moved swiftly, checking ahead before continuing to the side of the house. He could hear Jenna breathing close behind as she slipped into the space behind him against the gray wooden wall. He glanced over one shoulder at her. "Okay, so far so good."

He took latex gloves from his pocket and pulled them on, then edged his way to the back steps that he knew led to a mudroom with a pantry. He crouched to examine the steps, bending low to look under them and all around. Only dusty cobwebs waved in the breeze, and a few dead moths. "Keep right away from the door. He could have rigged a shotgun to fire when we touch the doorknob."

"Roger that." Jenna moved some distance away, keeping her back to the house and looking in all directions.

With memories of similar disastrous situations during his tour of Afghanistan lingering like a warning in the recesses of his mind, Kane pressed his back to the wall then, heart pounding, took a deep breath and reached for the doorknob. The old wooden door stuck tight, the frame warped from years of neglect. *Dammit.* He turned the rusty knob again and pulled hard. With a creak of wood and rusty metal, the door inched open. A rush of stale air leaked out and he heard a rustling from inside. He turkey-peeked around the door, relieved to find that no gun sat cocked and ready to blow him away. It was pitch black inside and the rustling came again, making his gut clench. He used his boot to push the door open, then turned to Jenna and whispered into his mic. "I hear something inside, it could be rats. It's too dark to make out. Can you see the window from your position?"

"It looks like it's been painted over." Jenna retraced her steps back to his side. "Why would anyone do that?"

Kane shrugged and kept his voice just above a whisper too. "So no one would know someone was living here or holding a girl against her will." He indicated toward the mudroom. "Let's take a look inside." He pulled out his weapon and then taking a flashlight from his belt held it against his Glock. He aimed the beam inside then climbed the old wooden steps. The light picked out details of the kitchen. The floor was, surprisingly, free of the thick coating of dust that he'd encountered there a couple of years earlier. An overturned garbage bin had spilled its contents over the floor. Red eyes peered back at him and a large rat scampered away into the darkness. "Someone's been staying here. The kitchen is clear apart from the rats." He moved the light around the room then eased down the hallway.

"Two bedrooms and the family room is at the end of the hall." Jenna slipped in behind him. "We'll be sitting ducks if he's in there."

Kane touched his ear. "The floorboards creak. If he moves, we'll hear him – but the rats are moving around, so it's unlikely that he's in here. They took off as soon as they saw me."

The first door hung open at a strange angle. One of the top hinges had rusted through. Kane shone his flashlight inside but only dust greeted him. "Clear." He moved to the next door. A new padlock hung open on an improvised lock. He glanced at Jenna. "Stay here. That's the room he used, so if he's planted a device it will likely be in there."

He could only just make out Jenna's nod of consent in the dim light. Under his boots, the floorboards groaned with each step as he moved past the closed door to check the family room. An old sofa sat before the fireplace and someone had used the grate recently. "Clear."

"She could be inside." Jenna's voice sounded desperate. "Amanda, can you hear me? It's Sheriff Alton."

Nothing.

"Amanda, are you in there?"

Nothing.

"Can you see if he's rigged the door?" Jenna's flashlight moved all around the frame. "I can't see any wires."

Kane examined the door but found no sign of tampering. "Same as before – move back into the kitchen and I'll try and open the door."

He waited for her to retreat, and then grasped the handle and the door swung open. Darkness and the smell of pee greeted him. He aimed his flashlight inside and then turned to Jenna and shook his head. "Someone was here but it's empty now. Dammit, we'll have to check the cellar." He holstered his weapon. "If the Shadow Man has used this place Wolfe might be able to pick up some trace evidence."

"I'll get his ETA." Jenna made the call. "They've just parked behind your truck and are on their way."

Kane used his mic. "Wolfe, the back entrance is clear. Follow the tree line and don't use the animal track. We haven't swept the front of the house. We're heading out the back door and over to the barn to check the root cellar."

"Roger that. We'll keep clear of the front of the house."

CHAPTER THIRTY-SEVEN

Jenna followed Kane down the back steps and they crept along the side of the house. The barn doors stood open and a shaft of light picked up the hatch leading to the root cellar. She waited for him to scan the area with his binoculars. "See anything?'

"Nope." Kane turned to look at her. "Let me go first. We'll head for the side of the barn, then take a closer look to make sure it's safe to go inside."

"Okay."

As Kane took off across the rough ground between the house and barn, Wolfe's voice came in her ear.

"We're at the back door. Want us to watch your back before we go inside?"

Jenna turned to see Wolfe standing at the corner of the house. She pressed her mic. "Roger that."

Moments later, Wolfe and Webber jogged to her side. She glanced over at Kane's progress. He'd made the thirty yards to the barn without incident. He scanned the area before waving her toward him. She scanned all directions, and then jogged toward him, but halfway across, Wolfe's voice broke the silence.

"Sniper!" Wolfe was aiming toward the hill and emptying his weapon.

As she turned to look at him, bullets slammed into her back and the impact, like a baseball bat to her ribs, threw her flat on her face. Pain shot through her like a red-hot poker and she gasped for breath.

The ground beneath her wavered slightly and the grass pricked her eyes, then the metallic taste of blood covered her tongue. She turned her head to look at Kane and knew from his expression that it was bad. *Oh, Jesus.*

"*Stay down, Jenna.*" Kane's voice came in her ear. "*Don't move.*"

A part of her wondered why Kane hadn't rushed to her side to say goodbye. His professional mask had slipped firmly into place as he scoped the hillside with his sniper rifle then fired a barrage of shots. She understood the drill. Wolfe was close by with the knowledge to tend her and Kane was providing cover fire. She heard his voice again and wanted to say something, but she couldn't lift her hand to turn on her mic.

"*Webber, fire to the west of the tallest tree on my command.*" Kane sounded calm and in control and somehow it made her feel better. "*Wolfe, you're good to go – on my count, one, two, three.*"

She turned her head to see Webber standing at the corner of the house. He lifted his rifle shoulder-high and the barrage of shots made her ears ring. All around the smell of gunpowder tainted the fresh spring air. The next moment footfalls thundered toward her, and then Wolfe had scooped her up and was running toward the barn. She bit back a cry of pain and stared up at his grim expression. *I'm going to miss you all, especially Kane, Wolfe and the girls.* "How bad?" She didn't recognize her raspy voice. "I think they hit a lung, I taste blood."

Wolfe laid her gently against the wall of the barn. "Let me take a look." He tugged off her coat, and then released the Kevlar vest. A cold hand snuck up her back, pressing her ribs. "Take a deep breath."

Jenna found she could breathe. She spat out the blood in her mouth. "It hurts like a bitch."

"You'll be fine. The vest caught the rounds and you'll be bruised, but nothing's broken." Wolfe touched her face. "Let me see your mouth." He nodded as he peered inside. "Don't worry about the blood. You've bitten your tongue is all, when you fell."

Jenna met his pale gaze and smiled. "Thanks, I figured I was a goner for sure."

"I've got morphine in my field kit." Wolfe got to his feet. "I'll go get it and it wouldn't hurt to strap your ribs and ice them."

Jenna shook her head. "I've got Tylenol in my pocket." She pushed a hand inside her jeans pocket and produced a strip. "I'll get into the hot tub tonight. I'll be fine."

"I'll pull the rounds out the vest, and then you should put it back on. It'll support your back." Wolfe went to work and removed the bullets, then helped her dress. "They're a small caliber; he didn't intend to kill you."

The gunfire stopped and Kane came to crouch by her side, his concerned gaze examining her face. "You okay?" He took her hand and squeezed. His latex glove felt strange against her skin.

Jenna nodded. "Wolfe says I'll be fine. I just had the wind knocked out of me."

"You're lucky you turned your back or the rounds would have hit the weakest part of the vest." Kane smiled at her. "You're one tough lady. I know how much it hurts, Jenna; you'll be black and blue come morning." He glanced up at Wolfe. "How fast can you get her a liquid armor Kevlar vest?"

"A what?" Jenna looked from one man to the other.

"It's experimental technology." Kane looked down at her. "The vest is saturated by a liquid called STF. It remains fluid unless hit by a bullet or a knife, then it hardens." He lifted his attention to Wolfe. "I want one for her, like, yesterday."

"I'll see what I can do." Wolfe straightened and leaned against the barn. "Did you take the SOB down?"

"Nope. I didn't catch a glimpse of him." Kane stood and stared toward the hillside. "Where did you first catch sight of him?"

"I caught a glint at the top of the rocky outcrop, which makes me figure he's not military." Wolfe rubbed his chin. "No fool would use a weapon that reflects, and a sniper would have taken a head shot. I'd say hunter, maybe at best."

"Maybe." Kane stared into the distance. "He must have dropped down the other side out of view. I had a clear shot to the outcrop and couldn't see him." He sighed. "It's pointless chasing after him; there's a dirt road on the other side and he'd be heading for the hills by now."

"Would you like a drink, ma'am?" Webber knelt beside Jenna and handed her a bottle of water. "I always bring a couple of extras with me."

Jenna took it with a smile. "You're a lifesaver. Thank you." She took a couple of pills with a sip, and then glanced up at Kane. "We need to check the root cellar. This might have been a distraction to keep us from finding Amanda." She tried to get to her feet but Kane laid a hand on her shoulder.

"Rest awhile longer. I'll go." He turned to Webber. "Stay with her until I get back."

Jenna shook her head. "I'll be fine. I'm safe here in the shadows and Wolfe needs him to do a forensic sweep of the house." She pulled out her weapon. "And I have this. Go. Amanda may be down there."

"I hope not." Kane grimaced and edged toward the barn door.

Kane slid around the door of the barn and peered into the dim light. Nothing had changed since his last horrendous visit. He pulled out his flashlight and aimed it all around, noticing a wire running from a small hole in the floorboards up a post beside the hayloft and out through a hole in the roof. On closer inspection, it appeared to be the same solar panel set-up they'd found in another old house during the search for Lindy. The Shadow Man had required a power source in the cellar. The idea of finding another dead girl in that godforsaken place curdled Kane's gut. He made his way slowly to the hatch and examined it for wires. Not willing to pull it open and risk detonating an explosive device, he searched around and found an old hay-rake handle to lift the lid. It came open easily and fell back with a clatter onto the floor.

After waiting a beat, he aimed the light down the steps – and grimaced. The treads carried bloodstained footprints in a grisly reminder of the past. He sucked in a deep breath and dropped his mind into combat mode. His heart slowed and his muscles tightened on alert as he edged down the steps. The smell of mildew, damp and rats greeted him with each step into the murky darkness. At the bottom of the steps, he drew his weapon and aimed the flashlight down the muzzle of his gun.

He'd never forgotten his first visit to this hellhole. He gritted his teeth, and then took a quick look around the corner. Ahead, a long red brick passageway led to an open door. His flashlight lingered on the black footprints on the concrete floor, flooding his mind with unwanted memories. After the murder, no one had bothered to remove the blood spilled during the slaughter of a young woman. The victim had resembled his sister and the memory of finding her mutilated body haunted him to this day.

With his pulse pounding slowly in his ears, he moved forward. The darkness closed in around him, suffocating, and so silent he could hear his own breathing. As he edged to the doorway, a cold breeze lifted his hair and made a spider run up a dangling cobweb suspended in the doorframe. He searched all around the doorframe for signs of an explosive device but found nothing. The dusty floor had footprints overlaying the bloody reminders of the past but they likely belonged to Rowley and Webber.

His mind's eye recreated the image of the girl's dead body. The gaping red smile slashed across her throat came to him like a nightmare from hell. He took a beat to gather himself, refusing to allow a memory to unnerve him. Dammit, he'd been in worse situations, seen more horrendous murders than he was prepared to admit. He turned into the cellar and used the flashlight to scan the room. It hadn't changed much. Apart from a chair pushed to one side and a disturbed area of dust in front of an old wooden table, the place was empty. Relieved, he drew a deep breath then stared at the pool of dried blood, no longer red but a black reminder of murder. As he turned the beam, he picked up a wire running to a light bulb suspended from the ceiling. He'd make sure Wolfe knew this was a new addition to the cellar and the same battery set-up as the one they'd found in the other house. "Your knowledge base just keeps on growing, Shadow Man."

He examined the chair, figuring it could be the one in the video where the killer had used to restrain Lindy. Another blast of cool breeze shot down the air vent, sending shivers down his spine. He'd seen enough. He was heading for the door when his flashlight picked up a glint on the dirty floor. He squatted to take a better look and found a silver chain with a bluebird charm attached. He used his cellphone camera to take a few shots, and then examined the chain. It was complete, so the killer hadn't torn it from the girl's neck. He pulled an evidence bag from his pocket and dropped the necklace inside. He frowned. None of the parents of the missing girls had mentioned that their daughters owned a silver chain. *I hope this doesn't mean he's taken another one.*

CHAPTER THIRTY-EIGHT

The moment the deputies moved out of sight, Jenna let out a long painful breath. She'd gripped her trembling hands together to prevent them seeing, but the shock of what happened racked her body with tremors – and it hurt. She'd put on a brave face to put Kane's mind at ease but the pain in her back was significant and it had taken an inner strength she didn't know she possessed to hold back the tears stinging the backs of her eyes. The Shadow Man was a callous coward. She didn't want to imagine the terror he'd inflicted on Lindy before her death and now Amanda was in his clutches. She laid her weapon on the ground beside her, pulled out her cellphone and called Rowley. She updated him, and then listened with interest.

"*Nothing on the search or from the Braxtons. The hotline calls are much the same, nothing of significance. I've spoken to everyone who called but all the leads run dry.*" Rowley sighed. "*We've had a couple of calls – one came from Lucy's mom just before. I wasn't going to bother you with it right now but since someone tried to kill you, I figure it might be important. Lucy recalls Packer and Kittredge having a conversation about shooting out at the range. They chatted about their hunting rifles and made plans to meet there.*" He cleared his throat. "*I followed up and spoke to the manager of the rifle range and both men are more than capable of shooting from the distance you mentioned.*"

Jenna rubbed her forehead. "We had them on the list to interview again. What was the second call?"

"It came in on the 911 line. The Zammits' place backs onto the hillside, where you figure the shooter was standing. Mrs. Zammit said she caught sight of a light-colored pickup truck driving recklessly toward town on the dirt road bordering their property just before. Called in thinking the driver could be drinking and was worried about him speeding through town with all the kids on vacation and all." Rowley took a breath. *"I would have driven out to take a look but I'm alone here, so all I could do was to go outside and watch the flow of traffic. I didn't see anyone speeding but there is a ton load of light-colored pickups in town. Looks like I missed an opportunity to catch the man who shot at you. I'm sorry, ma'am."*

"He couldn't have gotten to town that fast." Hearing a rustling sound close by, Jenna scanned the area. "At least it confirms the pickup was a light color. Keep me updated."

"Sure will, ma'am."

Unsure what the sound was that was getting louder by the second, Jenna disconnected. A large bush a few feet away would offer her more protection. She eased painfully into its shadows and sat panting. The small effort had sapped her strength. Staring all around, she noticed a shadow moving at the other end of the barn. She slipped her Glock into the palm of her hand and aimed, then flicked the mic switch on her com pack. "Kane, I see someone on my side of the barn. I have a clear shot."

"That would be me, Jenna, so hold your fire." Kane's voice sounded less than amused. *"There's no sign of Amanda in the root cellar. I went around back to check on something. Where are you? I can't see you."*

Relieved, Jenna leaned back against the wall. "I'm behind the bush a couple of yards from the barn door."

"Roger that."

Kane seemed to emerge from the shadows like a ghost. He came to her side. Jenna looked up at him. "You vanished then reappeared. I didn't hear you coming."

"That's good; when you spotted me before, I figured I was losing my edge." He crouched down beside her and pushed a strand of hair from her eyes. "You gonna be okay sitting here if I go get the beast?"

Wondering why he was treating her like a casualty, Jenna stared at him. "I'm fine. I'm quite capable of walking back to your truck."

"I'd rather you didn't." Kane gave her a long, searching look. "You're as pale as a ghost and if the sniper is intent on taking you out, we'd need to run to the cover of the house at least."

"What makes you think he's still out there?"

"This." Kane pulled an evidence bag from his pocket and dangled it in front of her nose. "I don't recall any of the victims' parents mentioning their daughters owned a silver chain with a charm like this, do you?"

Jenna swallowed hard. "So if the Shadow Man left it behind on purpose, he'd be waiting for a reaction?"

"Oh, yeah. He's been careful to cover his tracks – this isn't an oversight." Kane's mouth turned down. "I'm hoping he's not abducted another victim."

"Dammit, we haven't found a trace of Amanda and if he's taken another girl already, he's escalating faster than anyone we've dealt with before. I've stretched our resources to the limit and since the FBI figure we can handle this on our own, I'll have to start deputizing some of the local volunteers to assist. The problem is everyone's exhausted from searching already." Dismayed, Jenna shook her head. "I'm done here. Wolfe doesn't need our help, so we'd better get our butts into action and chase down the other suspects on our list."

"Not so fast." Kane rested one large hand on her shoulder "Jenna, I've been hit wearing a vest and it's similar to being shot, just without the blood. I know Wolfe figures you're okay but you should let the paramedics examine you and maybe have an X-ray."

As if I have time. She stared up at him. "Not until we find Amanda."

"At least ice the injury or you'll be no good to anyone." Kane cleared his throat. "You know I'm right, Jenna."

"Dave, I know my body." Jenna shook her head. "Nothing's cracked or broken. I'm sure you know the feeling and yeah, it hurts, but I'll be fine. I don't need to go see the paramedics. I'll get some ice on it when I get back to the office."

Wanting to prove a point, Jenna tried to push to her feet and a wave of agony seared up her spine. She bit back a moan and decided leaning against the wall was a better option. "Okay, go get the truck."

"I'll drop the necklace in to Wolfe on the way. I won't be long." Kane moved his concerned gaze over her. "Drink the water. I've a bunch of instant cold packs in my field kit you can use."

Jenna smiled up at him. "Yes, Doctor."

After Kane insisted on carrying her to the front passenger seat of his truck, Jenna had reached her pain threshold and his offer of cold packs suddenly seemed like a good idea. Her teeth chattered as he slid them up her back, setting them over the T-shirt she wore next to her skin. "Oh, this is wonderful. Why haven't I tried this form of torture before?"

"Trust me, it will help." Kane pulled down her clothes and fixed her seatbelt, then wrapped a blanket around her. He shut the door then headed around the hood of the vehicle.

Her phone signaled a message and she met Kane's gaze as he slid behind the wheel. "I'm getting jittery the moment I hear the message tone. I figure they're all from the Shadow Man." She pulled the cellphone from her pocket.

"If it's from him, he's different to any psychopath I've profiled before." Kane frowned. "He's changing his gameplay so rapidly it's difficult pinning a profile to him."

Staring at the caller ID, she lifted her gaze to Kane and swallowed a rush of fear. In trepidation, she opened the message and groaned. "It's from him."

Don't imagine you're lucky to be alive. If I'd wanted to kill you, I'd have aimed for your head.
You'll need to step up your game, Sheriff. You're making it too easy for me and I figured with your reputation, you'd be an opponent worthy of my skills.
But you're not.

Bile rushed up the back of Jenna's throat. Kane had been right – the Shadow Man had her in his sights and Lindy and Amanda were his means to get to her. He would consider the girls collateral damage, with no meaning or worth to him as a killer. She reached for a bottle of water and sipped. The cold fluid unclogged the lump in her throat. "It seems to me your profile of him is fitting just fine. This animal goes way past monster – he is a twisted SOB." She stared at Kane. "How are we going to catch him before he kills Amanda?"

"By not rushing into one of his traps." Kane met her gaze. "He's had the advantage from the get-go and is using his communications to direct our moves. While we're checking out his red herrings he's making his next move."

Jenna winced at the reality of the situation. "Okay, okay. Then we go back to basics to beat him by following kidnapping procedure and hunting down persons of interest."

Her message tone chimed again and the cellphone slipped from her hands. It took an effort to pick it up again and look at the screen. "Oh, my God. He's sent another message with attachments." She held the phone so Kane could view the screen.

Now look what you've made me do, Sheriff.
That's 2–zip to me.
Maybe I'll kill you next time – or maybe I won't.
How many sweet innocent girls will I have to kill before you stop me?

Anger at this smug remark tightened Jenna's stomach. "He's killed Amanda and now he's blaming me? What makes a person so evil?"

"He's using the guilt trip method by placing the blame of his actions on you, Jenna." Kane shook his head slowly. "He's obtained some basic skills in psychoanalyzing, which would make me believe he's received therapy along the way or studied it at some point." He cleared his throat. "Open the image files."

Steeling herself, Jenna bit down hard on her bottom lip and opened the files. The first picture was of a person wrapped in a blood-red shawl. The shawl partially covered the face like a hood. The second was of the face. It was Amanda Braxton and her sightless eyes stared at the camera as if surprised, but her lips carried the blueish hue of death.

"It's Amanda. Can you make out where she's at?" Jenna enlarged the image and handed the cellphone to Kane. "Is that the bench outside the library in town?" Sick to the stomach, she stared at him. "Surely someone would have noticed a dead body – look, I can see people close by." She chewed on her bottom lip. "Unless it's been superimposed on the background."

"I don't think so, the shadows look authentic. Her mom didn't mention anything about a red shawl." Kane frowned. "We have a CCTV feed on that corner. I'll bring it up on my phone." He accessed the app, and then turned toward her, a puzzled expression on his face. "The cameras are down. The error report states the cameras from Main Street through to Mill Road went offline at five this morning."

"How the hell did he manage to disable the CCTV system when it runs from our office?" Jenna stared at him in disbelief. "That's impossible."

"They're not wireless." Kane scratched his cheek. "Cut the main feed and the entire section goes down. It wouldn't take an expert." He unclipped his seatbelt. "I'll go and bring Wolfe up to date."

"No." Jenna gripped his arm and winced at the pain the small move produced. "I'll call him on the way to town but first I'll send Rowley to secure the scene. If the Shadow Man has planted an explosive device like last time, he'll need to clear the area."

"Roger that." Kane started the engine and they roared down the driveway and out the gate.

Jenna made the calls and notified Wolfe first, then contacted Rowley. "You'll have to get Maggie to drive my cruiser to one end of Mill Road and block it – the keys are on my desk. She can leave the keys with you and walk back to the office. Use your cruiser to block the other end. Don't approach the body. Use your loudspeaker to clear the people out the area."

"Roger that." Rowley sucked in a deep breath. *"Do you want me to check for any life signs?"*

"No, don't go near her." Jenna swallowed the bile crawling up the back of her throat. "The killer could have rigged the area with a bomb. Wait until we get there. Kane has experience in explosives and Wolfe will be on scene soon." She disconnected and looked at Kane. "What's the chances she's alive?"

"From the photograph, I'd say she's been dead for hours."

As Kane took the turn back to the highway leading to Main Street his deadly expression sent a shiver down her spine.

CHAPTER THIRTY-NINE

Concerned about Jenna's ashen face and trembling hands, Kane bit back the impulse to call the paramedics and have them meet them in town. He'd known Jenna long enough to know she'd see this case to the bitter end even if it killed her. He concentrated on driving, all the while figuring a way to insist she'd remain inside his truck when they arrived. As he wound the vehicle through the traffic, he turned to her. "Do you mind if I check the scene for explosive devices? We don't have time to wait for the bomb squad."

"Looking at the image, people have been walking past the body all morning." Jenna turned her gaze on him. "Okay, go take a look at the scene, but I figure if he didn't plant an IED, he's probably rigged the corpse – so be alert." She let out a long sigh. "I'll contact Walters and ask him to inform Amanda's mother. I don't want her to find out about this on the news."

Relieved she'd decided to remain in the truck, Kane looked at her. "What about the search parties?"

"I'll tell Rowley to bring everyone in." Jenna sighed. "They'll be exhausted." She lifted her cellphone. "Then the media will expect an update. I just hope the killer doesn't decide to kill me live on TV."

"Then we take that option off the table. I'll handle the media." Kane used the siren to move the crowd gathering like crows waiting to feed on roadkill, then drove onto the sidewalk, placing his truck between the wall of the library and Rowley's cruiser. If the Shadow Man had a mind to take another shot at Jenna, it would be practically impossible to hit her with the truck in that position. He slid from the seat and pulled a pair of latex gloves from his pocket. He walked to Rowley's side. "I want these people at least one hundred yards from the scene. Tell them to move back and to leave room for emergency vehicles."

As Rowley got on the loudspeaker, Kane used his binoculars to get a close-up look at the immediate area surrounding Amanda's body. The red shawl covered her well and could easily be concealing a vest of explosives or a bloody corpse. He turned and watched the crowd move away. People with eager expressions hovered in store doorways as if they believed the flimsy façades would protect them from a blast. The situation was perilous and although he hadn't spotted a tripwire near the body, the killer had a shit load of options if he'd planned an explosion. His attention moved over the crowd. Most of them were filming on cellphones, holding them high to capture his every move. Any one of them could be the killer, just waiting for him to make his move before he triggered a concealed bomb using a cellphone. He'd no protection other than his Kevlar vest but that would have to do. The bomb squad was hours away in Helena. He'd need to rely on his years of training in explosives and handle the situation alone.

He'd need a cool head and a steady hand. He drew a few deep breaths. His pounding heart slowed and a self-induced calm came over him. He'd used this relaxation method many times before. A pounding heart and anxiety had no place in the world of a sniper or anyone dealing with explosives. With his breathing controlled and body relaxed, he moved forward step by step across the blacktop to the sidewalk. The traffic noise had ceased and the crowd behind him fell deathly silent as if every one of them was holding their breath waiting for something to happen.

Once he'd reached the sidewalk, he performed a visual scan of the body and surrounds. Amanda sat with her hands resting in her lap, leaning to one side and slightly hunched. The slumped position could be a good sign – a vest filled with explosives would act like a corset and make a body sit more erect. He crouched, bending low to search beneath the bench, and found no trace of a device. Standing, he edged closer and the familiar stench of rotting flesh drifted toward him. It wasn't rank yet, but decomposition had set in with a vengeance.

Enforcing his need to remain calm, he kept his breathing slow and even. He moved closer and tried without luck to peer through the loosely knitted shawl. Aware that at any moment a blast could rocket him into eternity, he removed the telescopic baton from his belt. Behind him, he heard a collective intake of breath from the watching crowd as he extended the weapon and slipped the end under the edge of the shawl. Moving in delicate stages, he held his breath and eased the material away.

When the body didn't explode into a million pieces, he groaned with relief. Apart from the distinctive red shawl, Amanda appeared to be wearing the same clothes as when she'd walked out of her house. Her dressing gown was dirty and covered in cobwebs and leaves. It hung open to reveal intact nightclothes. A wave of sadness swept over him and he steeled himself to bend and peer at her young face. The tragic eyes stared into oblivion, no longer clear but fixed and misty. The whites showed signs of hemorrhaging. He could clearly see her neck and discovered distinct signs of trauma.

Straightening, he searched the bench, moving all around and behind it, and then scanned the surrounding area. He examined a nearby trashcan, carefully checking the items inside, and then turned to see Jenna's pale face watching him over the roof of his truck. He waved at her. "All clear, Sheriff."

To his surprise, the crowd applauded and the chatter resumed in a wave of unintelligible noise. People pushed forward and Rowley's voice boomed out over the loudspeaker.

"This is a crime scene. Have some respect, folks." Rowley waited a beat but the crowd edged closer. "I'll be arresting anyone moving forward. Now go about your business and allow the ME in here to do his job."

Moments later, Wolfe's van jumped the sidewalk and stopped in front of the bench. Kane went to greet him, and the rush of adrenaline from searching for a bomb mixed with the despair of finding another dead teenage girl rolled over him, making his heart thunder in his chest. He rubbed the end of his nose. "She doesn't smell so good. I figure he killed her sometime last night."

"Some corpses smell within seconds of dying, some are covered in excrement." Wolfe snapped on his gloves, and then fitted his mask. "Decomposition depends on a variety of factors, so don't jump to conclusions just yet. Give me time to take her temperature and perform an autopsy." He tipped his head to one side. "Webber can assist me. I'd recommend you take Jenna back to the office ASAP – she doesn't look so good. She might be going into shock. You'll need to keep an eye on her."

Kane closed his baton and nodded. "I'll do my best."

CHAPTER FORTY

Sara Nelson had come to his attention a few days earlier and it was as if fate had placed her before him as an offering. How convenient that she left town at the same time as him each day. She'd spent her time with friends then taken the same bus home every day and he'd followed at a distance. When the bus slowed to a stop on Stanton Road, Sara Nelson stepped off. The bus blew out a puff of diesel fumes, and then continued on its way. The smoke dissipated in the light breeze until only the fresh scent of pine needles and wildflowers filled his truck. He scanned the area and smiled to himself. He'd dreamed of this opportunity and planned it a hundred times in his head. The spaced-out houses seemed deserted, not a soul lingering outside to enjoy the spring sunshine. He drove past her, and then stopped some ways ahead.

He grabbed a pulley from his toolbox but everything else he might need he'd already pushed into the pockets of his coveralls, including a small bottle of diethyl ether. After slinging a thick coil of rope over one shoulder, he jogged across the blacktop and stood staring into the trees. It never ceased to amaze him just how gullible a teenager could be and how easily he could bend them to his will. They'd all be aware the Shadow Man lurked in the area, but just as he'd imagined, he heard the sound of her footsteps as she crossed Stanton Road.

He pretended he hadn't heard her following him and moved into the cover of the trees, dropping the rope into a clump of bushes. He kept his attention fixed on the green canopy and moved forward into the dense forest with careful steps, making sure to stay on the thick coating of pine needles underfoot.

"What are you looking at?" Sara caught up to him and tugged at his arm. "What's up there?"

He turned and gave her his best, worried expression. "Crows. I saw an eagle go down close by. Crows always seem to find anything injured or dying. I wanted to find it before they kill it."

"I'll help you look." Sara shielded her eyes with one hand and peered into the forest. "How far in?"

"Some ways." He frowned at her. Acting concerned for injured wildlife made him appear safe. "Maybe you should head home. Your parents will be worried."

"They're both at work and won't be home until after six." Sara gave him a sunny smile. "I've nothing else to do."

"If you're sure? Maybe you should give them a call."

"I don't have to check in with them." She frowned. "I'm not a kid."

"I can see that." He smiled back. "You look so darn pretty with the sun coming through the trees on your hair. Can I get a photo of you?" He pulled out his burner cellphone.

"Sure." Sara blushed, her cheeks rosy and eyes dancing with pleasure. "Shall I pose?"

He shook his head. "Nah, just stand there." He took the shot, and then showed her. "I'll always remember you just like this."

"Look, I see some crows." She turned away and headed deeper into the forest, then turned to look back at him. "Are you coming?"

"Yeah. Just a minute, I dropped something." He went back to collect the rope and slung it over one shoulder.

It took only a few strides to reach her. Images of women who'd made his life a misery came at him front and center. Anger came in a rush and it only had one cure. He needed to see terror in Sara's eyes. He moved so close to her, strands of her long hair brushed his cheek. He took a breath, inhaling the sweet scent of her. The fear fix was all he'd gotten from the other girls, but Sara was special. She'd take care of all his needs. "Have you heard of the Shadow Man?"

"Yeah, it's all over the news." Sara picked her way along a narrow trail. "They figure he killed Lindy and now Amanda is missing."

"He killed her too." He'd gotten so close, he bumped into her when she stopped and turned to face him.

"How do you know that?" Sara stared into his eyes and a flicker of doubt crossed her face.

"Because I'm the Shadow Man. Nice to meet you, Sara."

CHAPTER FORTY-ONE

Walters and one of the Blackwater deputies met Jenna as she slid painfully from Kane's truck. They joined Kane and formed a cordon around her as she climbed the steps into the sheriff's department. Once inside, she went straight to her office and found Agent Josh Martin staring at the whiteboard. "I could have used you in the field, Agent Martin. We've been run off our feet today." She eased her aching body into her chair and waved her deputies into the room.

"I'm sorry, we've been dealing with a child abduction case in Deep Valley and that takes priority." Martin leaned against the wall and folded his arms across his chest. "You've had two murders, so we can't even class the perp as a serial killer. It's a local issue. But I'll hang around and help until I'm called out on another case."

Jenna didn't feel like pleading with the man to stay and assist them. "Okay, thanks. I'll appreciate any assistance you can give me." She stared at her notes and gathered her thoughts. "Walters, will you head out to Rowley's position and secure the crime scene until Wolfe has finished and send Rowley back here?"

"Yes, ma'am." Walters pushed his hat onto his gray head and ambled out the door.

Jenna glanced up at the Blackwater deputy. "Deputy Smithers, thanks for your assistance at the Braxtons' but I'll need you here for a couple more days if that's okay? I'll clear it with the Blackwater sheriff." She didn't wait for his reply. "I'd like you to go pick up Sean Packer and Mason Lancaster and bring them in for questioning."

She turned her attention to the whiteboard. "You'll need to contact Packer's employer and find out where he's working today; Lancaster should be at the high school. The details on both men are in my daybook." She slid the book across the desk to him.

"Sure thing." Smithers, a middle-aged deputy with a sunny smile, took out his notebook and copied down the details.

"What about Kittredge and Anderson?" Agent Martin stared at the whiteboard.

Jenna nodded. "Yeah, they'll be coming in as well. We spoke to Kittredge yesterday. We haven't had time to get out to the Triple Z Bar to check out his alibi yet, but he's using the same ambiguous excuse he gave us last time. He's working out at Glacial Heights this week." She looked up at Martin. "Do you mind riding along with Smithers?"

"Sure." Martin raised an eyebrow, and then turned to Smithers. "When you have the info, come get me and we'll take my vehicle." He led the way out the door.

"And me?' Kane slid one hip onto the edge of the desk. "Kitteridge? He doesn't have an alibi for last night."

Jenna nodded. "Yeah, and bring in Anderson as well, but wait for Rowley to return and go in his cruiser. It's the better option for bringing in suspects." She stared at the whiteboard. "I figure it has to be one of those four men but I have a niggling feeling about Miller. He's the only one of the five men we can put at the scene of Lindy's abduction. I'll dig a little deeper into their backgrounds and see if any of them have had problems with women in authority."

"It might not be in their records." Kane rubbed his chin. "Trauma bad enough to impact a personality to the extent of releasing psychopathic behavior usually happens during childhood, so I'd be looking for a foster kid, broken family or a kid brought up by a female relative."

Jenna rubbed her aching back. "Yeah, think outside the box, got it."

A knock on the door brought Maggie, carrying coffee and sandwiches. Jenna smiled at her. "Thank you so much, Maggie, but I don't figure I could eat right now."

"Then try." Maggie placed the food on the desk. "You can't work these long hours on an empty stomach without consequences, and you being shot and all."

"Thanks, Maggie, you're an angel. I'm starving." Kane gave Jenna a shrug, grabbed the coffee and a packet of sandwiches then headed for the door. He turned to Jenna. "I'll eat while I'm chasing down the whereabouts of the suspects."

Jenna stared after him, and then noticed Maggie's satisfied expression. "Nothing interferes with Kane's appetite; he'll eat after attending an autopsy." She sighed. "I'm not feeling hungry right now but keep the coffee coming. I've a lot of grunt work to do."

"I've two fresh pots on now." Maggie smiled. "The hotline volunteers are still taking calls." She narrowed her brown gaze. "The media will be crawlin' all over town soon. You want to speak to them or do I tell them 'no comment'?"

Jenna pushed the hair from her eyes and leaned back in her chair. "Kane will deal with them later. When they call tell them they'll have to wait until we prepare a statement." She palmed her forehead. "Oh, I almost forgot. Can you get someone out to repair the CCTV cameras? They're out from the library back to Main Street. If you give Wolfe a call he'll give you the name of someone."

"Okay." Maggie walked out the door and closed it softly behind her.

Jenna closed both hands around a cup of coffee and stared into the steaming brew. Her back hurt so bad it was an effort to sit in the chair, let alone lead a murder investigation. A soft knock came on the door. "Yes, come in." She smiled at Emily's worried expression. "Hi Em, what's up?"

"What's up, she says, as if some crazy man hadn't just shot her." Emily's eyes widened in disbelief. "Dad said you're lucky you took the rounds in the vest." She held up a hand. "Before you come up with an excuse, I've come by to rub some of this into your back." She held up a small box between thumb and finger and wiggled it. "Dad says it will help with the pain and the bruising and it lasts around twelve hours."

Jenna shook her head. "I'll be fine."

"Dad told me you'd refuse and I was to persist." Emily turned and locked the door. "I'm helping you, Jenna, if you like it or not."

Jenna looked at her determined expression. "Sure. It hurts like hell and I can't drug myself into oblivion. Tell your dad thanks."

She allowed Emily to help her undress, then clenched her teeth and waited for the pain. To her surprise, the cream worked swiftly, easing the throbbing in her ribs. "That's powerful stuff you have there."

"Yeah, Dad said he used it in the field." Emily finished and used some wipes to clean her hands. "Any idea who did this to you?" She helped Jenna dress.

Jenna eased back into her chair. "I have my suspicions but no evidence to back them up."

"Why do you figure this maniac is targeting you? It's not another rejected boyfriend, is it?" Emily squeezed her arm. "I'm always here if you need to talk, you know, woman to woman."

"No, it's nothing like that. Kane believes it's a man with a problem with women in authority." Jenna rubbed her temples. "The back is much better, thank you. Now if I could get rid of the headache I'd be good as new."

"Well, if you need me, I'll drop by again." Emily smiled at her. "Just give me a call." She headed for the door. "Same goes if Julie is a nuisance, I'll come and take her over to Dad's office."

Jenna smiled. "She's doing just fine."

"Okay." Emily unlocked the door. "Catch you later."

Jenna sighed as the door clicked shut, and stared at the murder books on her desk containing the case files. The thumping in her head didn't help her sift through the fragments of information swirling through her mind. The items left behind at the scenes were crucial pieces of evidence. Why hadn't Lindy or Amanda's parents mentioned them before? A silver necklace would be significant if one of the girls wore it regularly, and surely someone would notice a shawl of that size and color missing. She'd need to show both items to the parents of the murdered girls as soon as Wolfe sent the photographs. She frowned and sipped her coffee. If the items didn't belong to either of the victims – then what?

A sinking feeling rolled over her as the implications set in. She'd been left with a "what if" and she'd solved many crimes with a "what if". Could the shawl and necklace be trophies from the murderer's previous kills? She allowed the disturbing possibility to percolate into her mind. Both Kane and Wolfe figured the Shadow Man had killed before. Had the killer left behind a few subtle clues to indicate just how many people he'd killed – and gotten away with? Perhaps he believed his kills hadn't received enough recognition and no one feared him, so he'd play a game with her – and if he won, killing a sheriff and a ton load of teenagers would be all over the news and he'd be famous. If he craved publicity, she sure wouldn't feed his ego by mentioning his alias. She'd insist the press stop calling him "Shadow Man" and the reason why. *Who is he?* Jenna sipped her coffee and stared into space. Panic gripped her stomach. Somehow, she had to fit the pieces together and find the killer before he struck again, but without solid evidence it was like trying to build a house from dry sand.

CHAPTER FORTY-TWO

He moved through the crowd listening to the gasps of horror, seeing the terror on some of the people's faces and the unhidden morbid fascination on others. Parents moved their children far away from the spectacle he'd provided for the town's entertainment. The quiet conversations from small groups of townsfolk amused him – as if a raised voice might upset the dead! A mark of respect, others might say, but they all stood around gawking at the dead girl – surely averting their eyes would be more respectful?

As he made his way to his truck, people passing by looked at him and raised their eyebrows or shook their heads as if to draw him into a conversation. He offered them no response – what could he say? "Hey, I see you're admiring my work."

Soon the flowers would arrive and teddy bears with notes of regret pinned to their chests would cover the bench where he'd left Amanda. Did they really believe she'd appreciate the gifts, or did they make a show of leaving them to impress their friends? No doubt they'd light candles too, and leave them to drip wax over the sidewalk. People would gather for a nighttime vigil to show an outpouring of grief, even if they hadn't known Amanda, as if praying would suddenly bring her back to life or prevent another girl dying.

No amount of praying will stop me. No cop is smart enough to outwit me. Many have tried and all have failed.

He couldn't understand why women wailed on each other's shoulders. All crying did was make them look unattractive. Crying never solved anything – in fact seeing them make those funny faces made him laugh. Most of them cried – the girls he'd killed – but at least the last thing they'd seen before the spark of life had faded from their eyes had been his smile.

CHAPTER FORTY-THREE

It had taken some time to track down Anderson as he moved from job to job, but with Rowley's help, Kane delivered him and Kittredge to the interview rooms, then went to the kitchenette to pour himself a coffee. He leaned against the counter and listened to Rowley.

"You're the profiler and I figure after listening to you, I'm starting to understand how different psychopaths are to normal people." Rowley held up a hand. "Yeah, I know not every psychopath becomes a killer and they can have multiple mental disorders, but one thing I've noticed, they don't stick out in a crowd."

Kane sipped his coffee. "That's the problem. Most of them could easily be a best friend or the nice man next door, who's dismembering people in his cellar." He indicated with his thumb to the interview rooms. "Take Kittredge and Anderson. Both men agreed to come in for questioning and they chatted like old friends on the way here." He shrugged. "Either of them could be our man because the charm of a psychopath is why so many are never caught. They slip under the radar so easily."

"I'm not so sure about Kittredge." Rowley poured coffee from the jug into a cup. "He's got a smart mouth but figures his remarks are funny when they're actually sexist and crude. Some women obviously think he's attractive, though. He's overconfident and self-assured and reminds me of Ted Bundy."

"Yeah, his lack of empathy places him on the list." Kane put down his coffee and opened a jar containing Jenna's chocolate chip cookies.

"We pulled in Packer because he's the quiet one, the likeable guy. Everyone he's worked for trusts him inside their houses. Pedophiles like to get close to children, and he makes a point of getting to know the kids in the houses where he works. The only problem I have is Lindy's killer didn't sexually assault her, which possibly leaves him without a motive – although we don't know exactly what happened to Lindy. Packer could be the type that prefers to take pictures to show his friends. They come in many types. Any one of them or none of them could be Shadow Man."

"Why do you figure they kill?" Rowley helped himself to a cookie.

"A few years ago, I interviewed a man who'd dismembered his victims while they were alive." Kane's head filled with the man's confident attitude, his need to be one of the boys. "I asked him why he tortured the women."

"What did he say?" Rowley raised one eyebrow.

Kane frowned. "He said he'd never killed a woman who hadn't deserved it." He met Rowley's gaze. "This is the kind of personality we're dealing with. No remorse, no real motive for killing, but I'm guessing he's using Jenna as an excuse for killing the girls."

"How so?"

"I figure he's reliving something in his past." Kane dunked his cookie in his coffee, and then popped it into his mouth. "A woman did something so bad to him as a kid, it warped his mind. I figure he's not getting any satisfaction from killing the girls. He wants to kill Jenna because she's a person in authority and he's using the girls as bait." He cleared his throat. "I didn't mention it before but out at the Old Mitcham Ranch, someone didn't just shoot at Jenna, they put two rounds in her back. Her vest caught it but she's pretty banged up."

"Oh, Jesus help us." The color had drained from Rowley's face. "We can't protect her twenty-four hours a day. Holy cow, you know how stubborn she is. She'll want to take him down no matter how much danger she's in."

Kane straightened. He'd expected Rowley's reaction and kept the information from him until they'd secured the suspects. "Wolfe took a look at her and figures she's bruised, and Walters and the deputy from Blackwater know what happened. I needed help getting her into the office, so we closed in around her." He sipped his coffee and watched Rowley's expression go from shocked to mad. "There's another thing you need to know. The killer is messaging Jenna – he told her he didn't intend to kill her yet. I figure he wants her to play a game with him first."

"Oh, this just gets better by the second." Rowley pushed a hand through his hair, making it stick up in all directions. "You can't keep the suspects here indefinitely unless we charge them with something. How do you intend to keep her safe?"

Kane had already given this some thought. "After we've interviewed them, I'm hoping we'll have enough to charge one of them. If not I'll take her home then you can release them. The ranch is safe; no one can get in there."

"That's fine for today but what about tomorrow?" Rowley gulped down his coffee. "He could be anywhere at any time."

"I'll have another vest for her by then – it's a new design – and I've a helmet coming for her as well." Kane rinsed his cup in the sink and placed it on the rack. "I won't leave her side for a second until we catch this animal."

"Good." Rowley placed his cup in the sink. "When are you going to start the interviews?"

Kane grimaced. "As soon as I've spoken to the media, then with any luck they'll leave us alone." He indicated with his chin toward Jenna's office. "First we check in with the boss."

He hustled to Jenna's office and tapped on the door. "Anderson and Kittredge are in the interview rooms."

"Good." Jenna lifted her pale face. He could see dark circles under her eyes. "Shut the door, will you, Rowley?"

Kane dropped into a seat. "What's up?"

"Wolfe sent me the images of the chain and the shawl." Jenna swallowed. "I contacted the parents of the victims and asked if they belonged to their daughters. The answer was in the negative." She met his gaze. "Wolfe's examined both items and found human blood on both of them. He's running tests now."

Kane groaned. "They're trophies from previous kills."

"Yeah, that's the same conclusion I had." Jenna leaned back in her seat, grabbed her ribs and moaned in pain. "Dammit!" She took a couple of breaths, and then lifted her chin as if defying him to say anything. "I've asked Agent Martin to search the databases for crimes with similar items missing and he is using the computer in the control room. He already sent the images to his head office for assistance."

Kane leaned forward. "Jenna, you'll work better if you have something for the pain. There's codeine in the first aid kit."

"Okay, okay. I'll take something. I guess I'll need to appear normal for the interviews." Jenna gave him a determined look. "If it's one of the men we've hauled in for questioning, I don't want him figuring he's winning." She pushed a piece of paper across the desk to him. "Don't go searching for pain meds for me. Rowley can find me something. I want you to deal with the press before they start invading my office. I've written a statement. If they want any more info, it's 'no comment'. If they insist on knowing about the men we brought in for questioning, you'll have to tell them we don't have any suspects yet. As none of them were brought in in handcuffs, they'll believe you."

Kane nodded. "I'm sure they will."

"What do you have for me, ma'am?" Rowley leaned forward.

"Run the office while we're interviewing the suspects." Jenna glanced down at her notes. "Give Wolfe a call and ask him when Amanda's parents can view the body." She cleared her throat. "He'll probably prefer to speak to her parents personally, so ask him to notify us when he's obtained a positive ID. I need to know the possible cause of death ASAP, before I interview the suspects – even if it's not conclusive, an approximation will do."

"Yes, ma'am." A worried look crossed Rowley's face. "I figure I'll go chase up those pain meds first." He got up and headed for the door.

Kane scanned the press statement. It was concise and easy to memorize. He placed the document back on her desk. "Have you had time to dig up anything new on the potential suspects?"

"Not yet." Jenna reached for her coffee. "I'll take the meds then spend some time going over their files. I'm in no hurry to interview them. They can cool their heels for a time until I'm ready." She took a sip, grimaced and placed the cup on the desk. "I'm so used to go-cups keeping the coffee hot. Lately, by the time I get around to drinking coffee it's cold."

"I'll get you a refill as soon as I've dealt with the press." Kane straightened. "What's your plan for the interviews?"

"I figured I'll go in alone and have you outside observing through the window." Her lips twitched up at the corners. "I don't want them to believe they've scared me, and you'll be outside decoding their body language."

No way. Before Kane could object, a sharp knock came on the door. It opened slowly. Agent Martin stood in the doorway.

"I've some information on the items found at the scene." Martin stepped inside, closing the door behind him. "Both items are listed as missing from the bodies of two women murdered last year. Christine Pullman and Joy Coran. The strange thing is, the women were both out of different counties and there's been no connection between the murders until now."

Mind reeling from the information, Kane cleared his throat. "Time of year the same?"

"Yeah." Martin frowned. "How did you figure that out?"

Kane shrugged. "The distance between the crime scenes suggests the killer moves around, so he's either a truck driver and it's a coincidence, but most likely he likes to spend his vacations on killing sprees."

"What age are the victims?" Jenna stared at Martin.

"Thirty-five and forty-one." Martin frowned. "I've downloaded the case files into the current murder book."

"Do they resemble me?" Jenna turned to her computer as if unconcerned.

"No, they're both different." Martin raised an eyebrow at Kane. "Where's this heading?"

Kane explained. "What were their occupations?"

"A psychiatrist and a social worker. They tick the boxes." Jenna looked at Kane and sighed. "My day is just getting better by the second."

CHAPTER FORTY-FOUR

After watching Kane's live press conference through the window, Jenna waited for him to return, and then made her way to the interview room. She sat down opposite Paul Kittredge and placed a legal pad, folder and pen on the table. Although both she and Kane had revisited the files of the four men, they'd found nothing to add. It would take her skill as an interviewer to pry some more details from the potential suspects. She stared at the man leaning back nonchalantly in the seat opposite her. "I just have a few more questions."

"Wanting to see me three times in one week, isn't that somethin'?" He glanced at his watch. "Can't be more than twelve hours since we last spoke. Did you miss me?" He grinned.

"And I'll keep hauling you in until I've gotten the answers I need." Jenna took the remote control from a drawer in the desk. "Do you have an objection to me taping the interview, Mr. Kittredge?"

"Nope." He leaned forward and stared into her eyes. "Want a little somethin' to drool over later, Sheriff?"

Ignoring him, she pressed the record button on the remote and stated her name, then asked Kittredge to do the same. "I appreciate you coming in. You're not under arrest but if you'd like an attorney present for this interview, you're within your rights to do so."

"I know my rights." Kittredge smiled at her. "I don't have anything to hide from you, Sheriff. Ask your questions so I can get back to work."

Jenna stared at her notes. Dear Lord, the smell of stale beer, cigarettes and sweat reeked out of him. She figured he hadn't bathed or changed his clothes in a week or so. Deciding to start with a few general questions, she picked up her pen. "How long have you worked for the Green Thumb Landscaping Service?"

"Since I came out of jail." Kittredge stretched. "I completed a landscaping course in prison."

"I see." Jenna made notes as if every word he said was important. "You live at the Triple Z. Didn't you have a family to go to when you came out of jail?"

"Nope." Kittredge moved around in his seat. "My ma died young and I never knew my daddy."

Jenna frowned. "That must have been hard. How old were you?"

"Why all the questions, you plannin' on askin' me to marry you?" He chuckled.

Not in this life. Jenna cleared her throat. "We've already established you know Lindy Rosen and Amanda Braxton. As you're probably aware, both girls have died."

"I didn't kill them." He barked out a laugh. "I prefer my girls breathin'." He gave her a long hard stare. "You know darn well I used to like them young, but six years of therapy cured me of that inclination. Now my interest lies in a more mature woman."

"Ah, I see." Jenna smiled at him. "So you'd have no objection to giving us permission to search your room and truck?" She wrote a few lines on a statement pad and pushed it across the table to him with a pen. "So we can prove your innocence?"

"Sure, why not." Kittredge signed and slid the notepad and pen back to her. "Can I go now?"

Agent Martin had supplied graphic crime-scene images of the two murdered women who'd owned the shawl and necklace. She pulled them from the folder and laid them on the table. "Do you know these women? Christine Pullman and Joy Coran?"

The expression on Kittredge's face changed in a split second. His eyes had changed to dark and dangerous the moment he lifted them from the gruesome pictures.

"There's no way I'm taking the rap for the murder of those girls or these women." Kittredge flew to his feet in a rage. "I want a lawyer." He pointed a finger at Jenna. "You women cops are all the same. Ugly bitch. I'd rather sleep with a rattlesnake."

Fighting back the fear, Jenna stood her ground. "Sit down, Mr. Kittredge, or you'll be spending time in the cells until we contact your lawyer."

"Don't tell me what to do." Kittredge picked up his chair and hurled it at the wall a few feet from her.

The chair clattered to the ground and the next moment the door opened and Kane walked in with a bored expression. "Do you want me to book him for threatening an officer of the law, ma'am?" He moved toward Kittredge. "It's all on tape and I've been right outside the door."

Jenna swallowed the lump in her throat. Normally she'd have gotten to her feet and faced him but her injury prevented her from defending herself. She didn't look at either of them. "Yeah, and lock him up." She raised her attention slowly to Kittredge. "I'll allow you to cool down, and then we'll see about that lawyer."

When Kane grabbed his arm and removed him from the room, Jenna sucked in a deep painful breath. She hadn't expected such a violent reaction and it had made her realize how close she'd come to becoming a victim. In her condition, even with Kane outside the door, Kittredge could have snapped her neck in a second.

When Kane returned she looked up at him. "Thanks."

"Thanks, huh?" Kane's eyes blazed. "It takes me more than a few seconds to swipe my card, have the system recognize me then open the damn door. He could have killed you."

Jenna pushed slowly to her feet. "I wasn't expecting him to go crazy. He changed personality in a split second." She swallowed the bile rushing up the back of her throat. "The Shadow Man wouldn't act like that, would he?"

"It depends if that show of anger was real or an act." Kane leaned against the door. "If the killer believes he can outsmart you and has some knowledge of psychopathic behavior, acting like this would be out of character. For them it's charm and deny. He could be playing the game, so we don't rule him out just yet."

"I hadn't planned to." Jenna used her card to open the door and stepped into the hallway just as Rowley turned the corner. "Looking for me?"

"Yeah." Rowley glanced down at his notebook. "A call came in from Mr. Wilts, the old guy who called before, lives out near Glacial Heights? He was out walking his dog again around twelve-thirty last night and had another sighting of a light-colored pickup leaving Glacial Heights. It was a full moon and he insists the decal on the door was for Miller's Garage."

"We know Matthew Miller was in the area when Lindy Rosen disappeared and he drives a Miller's Garage truck." Jenna sighed. "With Sam Cross as his lawyer, he'll accuse us of harassment, so we tread easy with him this time. Give him a courtesy call and let him know we plan to question Miller again." She tapped her pen against her bottom lip and thought for a few seconds. "Call his father and tell him we want Matt to come in for questioning. Tell him we've a witness who places him in the vicinity of Glacial Heights last night." She cleared her throat. "Make it clear – he comes in or we arrest him on suspicion of double homicide."

"Yes, ma'am." Rowley nodded. "Agent Martin called and they have the suspects in custody."

"Okay, thanks." She turned to Kane. "I guess next up is Anderson?" She flicked through her files. "Let me see… ah yeah. He worked out of Colorado in the mines some years ago and could've had experience with explosives. He's had contact with both girls and installed the security systems at both residences."

"He doesn't have any priors." Kane shrugged. "But maybe he hasn't been caught yet. He knows his way around electronics and disabling the CCTV cameras in town wouldn't have been a problem. If you recall, he asked about suspects in the Lindy Rosen case. I figured that was strange at the time." He frowned down at her. "Are you going to object to me coming in this time?"

"Nope." Jenna took the few painful steps to the next interview room and swiped her card. When Kane pushed open the heavy door for her, she straightened her aching spine and went into the room. "Mr. Anderson, thank you for coming in." She explained the situation and switched on the recorder. After giving the details of who was in the room, she flicked through her files. "I hear your art class is very popular. Did Amanda Braxton attend the classes?"

"Amanda?" Anderson frowned. "No, I don't think she's very interested in art. She often sat in the window reading. Quiet girl, didn't have much to say."

"When did you last see her?" Jenna looked down at her notes to give him the impression she had a list of questions.

"I don't remember, maybe in town." He shrugged. "There are kids everywhere during spring break. I noticed Julie Wolfe helping behind the counter. She's young to be handling criminal types." He smiled. "Now there's a talented young artist. I hope she's not going to end up as a deputy. She should be studying art."

Jenna wrinkled her nose. It seemed every man she interviewed oozed unpleasant odors. Anderson smelled like dirty socks. She looked up from her notes. "We're not here to discuss Julie, Mr. Anderson. I'm already aware she attends your art class." She sighed. "When you worked out of Colorado in the mines, did you handle explosives?"

"Yeah, I've laid a few charges in my time." Anderson had a bored expression. "Where's this leading, Sheriff?"

"These are just routine questions." Jenna offered him a small smile. "You'll have noticed the CCTV system around town. What would you consider in your expert opinion would be the best way to disable it?"

"That would depend it if is wireless or hard-wired. I haven't had occasion to get up close and personal with it." Anderson leaned back in his chair. "For both the best way is to remove the power source. So cut the wires or remove the battery. If the camera is too high to inspect, and you don't want to destroy it, then a laser pointer would disable the optics for a time."

"How long?" Jenna scribbled on the notepad as if very interested in every word he uttered.

"That would depend on the set-up. Some cameras have filters, so not so long, and those with infrared would be undetermined."

"Can you account for your movements last night and early this morning?" Jenna looked up at him. "Between the hours of eleven and six."

"Yeah, I was working." He scratched his cheek. "I told you before I work the graveyard shift on Sunday and Wednesday nights. It's good money and there's not much to do. I was at head office from midnight until six this morning, had breakfast at Aunt Betty's, went home and slept until midday, went to work at one. I had a job to finish over at Glacial Heights." He glared at Kane. "Until Deputy Kane arrived."

"Okay." Jenna removed the images of Christine Pullman and Joy Coran from the folder and slid them across the table to him. "Do you recognize these women?"

She watched him closely as he swallowed with his Adam's apple bobbing up and down.

"I'm not sure." Anderson leaned back in his chair. "It's hard to tell with all the blood and all."

"They're Christine Pullman and Joy Coran."

"I'm not familiar with their names, no." Anderson lifted his attention back to her. "Are they out of Black Rock Falls? I didn't hear anything about them on the news."

"No."

"So why drag me away from work?" Anderson rolled his eyes. "You're wasting my time."

Jenna cleared her throat. "We've two murdered girls in the morgue, Mr. Anderson. I'm sure if they were your daughters you'd want me to interview everyone who'd met them. The deaths of the other victims form part of our investigation into the Rosen and Braxton cases." She placed her pen on the table and looked him straight in the eye. "You've worked at both the ranches and installed a so-called foolproof security system and yet someone abducted both girls from their beds. How do you account for that, Mr. Anderson?"

"Human error, I guess. The systems we install are state-of-the-art." He opened his arms wide. "But they only protect a property if they're activated. I've personally inspected both systems and they're working just fine."

"Tell me about the codes. Do you give the owner a code?"

"Sure do, we use a basic code, 1-2-3-4, on all the systems for us to make sure it's operating." Anderson gave a bark of a laugh. "Before you ask, no, I don't have a little book with all their codes. I always give them a complete run-down of the system and leave instructions. I insist they reset the codes immediately I've gone."

Jenna exchanged a look with Kane and he shrugged. She turned back to Anderson. "Where did you live growing up?"

"My family came from Butte." He smiled at her. "You know they hold tours of a nineteenth-century brothel?"

"Ah no, I'll be sure to remember if I'm ever by that way." Jenna blinked at him, trying to keep her mind on track. "Do you have any objections to one of my deputies searching your home and vehicle?"

"Why?" Anderson frowned. "Am I a suspect?"

"We're just eliminating everyone who came in contact with both girls." Jenna inclined her head. "It would save time if you agree, Mr. Anderson, or you'll have to remain here until a judge gives us a warrant – and we do have probable cause. You drive a similar vehicle to the one seen both nights the girls went missing, we've yet to establish your alibi and—"

"Yeah, I know, because I worked inside both houses and spoke to both girls?" Anderson towered his fingers and thought for a moment, then shrugged. "Sure. I want this over."

"Thank you for your assistance. I'll leave you a statement form to complete giving us permission to search your vehicle and home. Once the search is completed, I'll arrange a ride home for you." She pushed to her feet and bit back a groan of discomfort. "Can you get the door, Kane?"

"Yes, ma'am."

Outside in the hallway she handed him her notebook and gripped her back. "What do you think?"

"I'm glad you pushed him to allow us to do a search but I doubt we'll find anything. If he's the killer, he's way too smart to leave any evidence." Kane scratched his cheek. "He's very confident, so either he's a good liar or has a solid alibi for both murders."

Jenna sighed. "Call his workplace and check out his alibi. If they corroborate his story, and we find zip at his home, we'll have to cut him loose."

"It won't be today." Kane frowned and glanced at his watch. "We'll have to do the searches in the morning but they're going to walk unless we find some evidence."

Jenna nodded in agreement. "Okay, I'll call a lawyer for Kittredge then update the case files and leave you to chase up Anderson's alibi. You might as well call the Triple Z and see if the barman knows the woman Kittredge said he spent time with on Wednesday night." She glanced down the hallway. "When we're done, we'll speak to Lancaster and Packer."

"I'll interview them if you need to take a break." Kane touched her face. "You're so pale. I wish you'd let the paramedics take a look at you."

Jenna leaned into his hand. "Thanks, but if one of them is intent on killing innocent girls to get to me, I want to look the SOB straight in the eye."

CHAPTER FORTY-FIVE

As Jenna disconnected from a call to Sam Cross, she looked up, to see Rowley waiting in the doorway. "How did you go with George Miller?"

"He's bringing Matt in now but he insisted on having his attorney present." Rowley frowned. "I've been calling Cross for a while now but the line's busy."

"Don't worry." Jenna rubbed her temples. "He's coming here to represent Kittredge, so he's going to be a busy man this afternoon."

"Wolfe called with a message. The unofficial cause of death in the Amanda Braxton case was a broken neck." Rowley rolled his eyes. "He insisted I emphasize the word 'unofficial' and said his opinion is from a visual examination only and wouldn't hold up in court, but he did say the killer inflicted the injury in a typical military combat move."

"That's interesting." Jenna moved her attention to the whiteboard. "Packer was dishonorably discharged from the army and has already lied about his knowledge of explosives." She pulled up his file on the computer and went through it again. "Ah, and he was raised in a variety of foster homes. He ran away a number of times then ended up joining the army. The reason for his discharge isn't listed." She glanced up at Rowley. "He's moved around the state but has lived here for the last four years."

"So he fits Kane's profile." Rowley rubbed the back of his neck and frowned. "He's worked for me – refitted my kitchen last fall. He seemed like a nice guy."

Jenna looked up at him. "Since I've been living in Black Rock Falls, I haven't met a psychopathic killer I haven't liked." She shrugged. "Think about all the murdering SOBs we've caught, Rowley. I wouldn't have picked them out in a line-up of men likely to commit robbery, let alone labeled them as sadistic killers. So right now, even the nice guys are in my sights."

"So I see." Rowley nodded. "If you don't need me for anything else, I'll head back to the front counter now, ma'am."

"Sure. Thanks for your help." A knock on the door drew her attention away from Rowley. Kane waited outside the door and Smithers and Martin chatted in the hallway behind him. Jenna waved him inside. "What's up?"

"Smithers is awaiting orders and Martin's heading back to his office." Kane tipped his head toward the men in the hallway. "The Millers have arrived and they're not happy."

In an attempt to keep her mind running in chronological order, Jenna pushed both hands through her hair and took a few deep breaths. "Okay, will you thank Martin for his assistance and ask Smithers to escort the Millers to an interview room, and then wait at the counter until Sam Cross arrives? Tell him to take Cross to see Kittredge first, then show him where we're holding the Millers when he's done."

Kane gave her a nod and turned back to the hallway. Jenna glanced at the clock on her office wall. The afternoon was slipping away fast and she so wanted this day to be over but it was getting longer by the minute. She heaved a sigh – with at least two, maybe three interviews to conduct she'd be lucky to get home tonight.

"I've spoken to the barman at the Triple Z." Kane walked back into the room and dropped into a chair. "Same as before, he recalls seeing Kittredge there with a woman but he's always with some woman or another so days run into each other. He's going to ask around for a woman fitting the description Kittredge gave us and if he finds her he'll give us a call." He rubbed the darkening stubble on his chin. "I called Silent Alarms and Anderson's alibi checks out. According to his boss, he did work both Sunday and Wednesday nights. Unless someone triggers an alarm, all he has to do all night is watch TV."

Jenna sighed. "Then I guess if we search his property and come up empty we'll have to cut him loose?"

"Yeah, we don't have an option. We've no evidence to implicate him at all." Kane drummed his fingers on the arm of the chair. "Ready to interview Packer?"

"Yeah, but before we go, I've some interesting information." Jenna explained Wolfe's preliminary conclusion of Amanda's cause of death.

"Okay." Kane got to his feet. "That places Packer firmly in the ballpark."

"So it would seem." Jenna pushed to her feet smothering a groan and trying to ignore the pain in her back. "Let's see what Mr. Packer has to say for himself."

To Jenna's surprise, when they entered the interview room, Sean Packer stood and greeted them with a smile. She explained the need to record the interview and his rights. As soon as Packer had agreed to answer the questions, she looked him in the eye. "I understand you had a rough childhood? Being moved around in foster care must have been hell."

"It was better than being locked in a home for orphans." Packer's smile had faded at her first question. "It was like being in jail. They treated us less than animals." He shook his head. "I figured it would be good to be in foster care but I ended up with a bunch of kids and a couple who spent all their money on booze. I was glad to join the army."

"That's awful. I'm glad they don't have that system in Black Rock Falls. The foster families here are very well supervised." Jenna frowned to give the impression she sympathized with him. "I gather the army didn't go so well either?"

"It did for a time." Packer shrugged. "They taught me a wide variety of skills I wouldn't have achieved alone. I can earn a living because of the army."

"I see." Jenna made a few notes. "So why did they dishonorably discharge you?"

"I went into the army to survive, not to be killed in some godforsaken country." Packer leaned back in his chair and eyed her with curiosity. "I took non-combat jobs but when the time came, I refused to be deployed."

A grunt came from Kane beside her and she could almost feel his wave of disgust. She exchanged a look with him and his mouth turned down. She turned back to Packer. "I see."

"I'm not a coward." Packer's eyes blazed with anger. "I figured it was a good excuse to leave." He cleared his throat. "People shouting orders all the time and telling me what to do. I'd had enough."

Jenna leaned back in her chair. "Can you account for your whereabouts on Wednesday night?"

"I was at home with my wife, Aileen." Packer sighed. "Same as the last time you asked me. My wife told me how a deputy had arrived on the doorstep and made her sign a statement. When he goes by again, she'll say the same thing. You're wasting your time."

"Okay, Mr. Packer." Jenna tried to gauge what he was thinking. "We're aware the army trained you in the use of explosives. Why did you deny this the last time we spoke to you?"

"Basic training, maybe." Packer sighed. "I don't recall."

"So you'd know your way around a variety of weapons. Do you hunt?" Jenna raised an eyebrow. "Or do you prefer the range?"

"Yeah, I hunt. Elk or deer and I own a number of weapons." Packer gave her a stubborn stare. "Like most of the men who live here. I often go to the practice range. It's the responsible thing to do."

"Sure is." Jenna slid the photographs of Christine Pullman and Joy Coran out of the folder. "Do you know these women?"

"Are they dead?" Packer lifted his expressionless gaze to her. "Nope, can't say that I do."

Jenna pushed a little harder. "Do you have any child pornography at home?"

"No!" Packer reeled back in his chair. "Why would you ask me that?"

"So you'd have no objection to handing over your computer or media devices for inspection and allowing a search of your home and vehicle?" Jenna kept her gaze fixed on his face. "Well, Mr. Packer? Or do we need a search warrant?"

"I guess not. I've got nothing to hide." Packer glared at her with contempt. "I can't believe you'd figure I was involved in hurting those girls." He pointed at her. "You're a sly one, make like we're going to have a chat and you come on like a police prosecutor."

"You're within your rights to have an attorney present at any time." Jenna waited a couple of beats. "No?" She took a statement book out of the file and gave it to Packer with a pen. "Please write a statement to say we have permission to search your premises and vehicle, and then sign it." She shrugged. "It's up to you, Mr. Packer. Think about it – if you come up clean, you'll be able to leave with your head held high. Nobody is aware of why you're here."

"Just how long is this going to take?" Packer picked up the pen, wrote a statement and sighed.

"You'll have to remain here until we search your premises." Jenna collected her files. "If all is as you say, we'll have no reason to detain you for more than twenty-four hours."

"I'm allowed to make a phone call." Packer glared at her. "I need to tell my wife."

"You haven't been charged, Mr. Packer." Jenna got to her feet. "You're being held for questioning. I'll have Maggie contact Aileen and tell her you're here."

Outside in the hallway, Jenna leaned against the wall and looked up at Kane. "There's something creepy about him. I can't put my finger on it."

"He ticks the boxes." Kane stared at the door. "He's been in the army, so is capable of breaking a person's neck quietly in a few seconds, and has admitted to some expertise with a rifle. He's made friends with the kids in the families where he worked, so the girls would trust him, and he knows how to use explosives. As a handyman, he'll have skills we're not aware of – but on the downside, he does have an alibi for both nights and no apparent motive."

"Wives lie and he could easily have a motive." Jenna glanced down at her notes. "What if he suffered abuse by a woman authority figure as a child in foster care? It's something we'll need to check. Maybe his wife would know?" She glanced at Packer through the one-way glass. "We'll ask Wolfe to come with us when we search his home. Lock him up for tonight. We'll deal with him in the morning."

CHAPTER FORTY-SIX

"Sheriff Alton."

Jenna pushed away from the wall as the lawyer Sam Cross brushed past Rowley on his way out of interview room three, with George Miller on his heels. "Are you looking for me, Mr. Cross?"

"Yes, I am." Cross glanced both ways, and then lowered his voice. "May we speak privately?"

"I've four interview rooms and currently they're all occupied." Jenna glanced at George Miller, who refused to meet her gaze. "Unless you want to come to my office?"

"We can speak in front of my client." Cross and Miller stood to one side to allow Jenna to pass. She nodded at Rowley standing at the door. "I can take it from here, Rowley. We're going to have visitors in the cells tonight. Call the Blackwater sheriff's department and see if they can spare a few deputies to take over from Walters at six."

"Yes, ma'am." Rowley turned and headed back to the main office.

They crowded into the interview room and Jenna sat down. "What do you want to discuss?"

"I'm aware you've a witness who places my client in the vicinity of Amanda Braxton's disappearance?"

Jenna nodded. "Yes, we do."

"Then we want to cut a deal." Cross sat down beside Matt Miller and placed one cowboy boot on his opposite knee, then leaned back in his seat. "Full immunity for Matt and the witnesses necessary to clear my client."

"Full immunity from what?" Jenna shook her head. "If this is a trick to get your client off a murder charge, you're crazy."

"A minor offense is all." Cross waved a hand in the air as if he was swatting a fly. "Problem is I'll have trouble getting them to step up to the plate if they figure they'll be incriminating themselves." He shrugged. "If you'll agree not to charge my client with a minor offense, we'll give you the reason why Matt was in the location of the missing girls, but if you want proof, we'll need to cut a deal with the DA."

How bad could it be? Jenna would be happy to eliminate a suspect. She sighed. "Okay, what did you do, Matt?"

"He's not saying a word." Cross stared at Jenna and his eyes twinkled. "Matt was delivering grass to his friends. He obtains it from a dealer and they split the cost is all. His friends will verify his whereabouts on Sunday and Wednesday nights and give you the approximate times, if they all get immunity."

"And an assurance he won't deal drugs again?"

"Sure." Cross smiled at her. "He wants a quiet life."

Jenna turned to Kane. "I figure we call the DA."

"Yeah, but you won't get him here this afternoon, he'll be in court." Kane glanced at his watch. "Maybe first thing in the morning?"

"Okay." Jenna turned back to Cross. "Matt will have to stay here until we arrange a meet with the DA. Maybe in the morning."

"I don't want to stay here overnight." Matt rose to his feet. "I've admitted why I was in Stanton Road."

"It's just one night and they'll feed you well." Cross placed a hand on Matt's shoulder. "It will all be over soon."

Jenna got up to leave. "We'll make the arrangements and call you with the details." She glanced at Matt. "Wait here and Rowley will take you to the cells." She followed Kane out the door with Cross and George Miller close behind.

"Thanks for your consideration, Jenna." Cross gave her a brilliant smile. "We should have dinner sometime?"

Jenna laughed. "A sheriff and a defense attorney. Been there and done that. Trust me, it wouldn't turn out well, but thanks anyway." She turned away and followed Kane to the next interview room.

She noticed the way Kane looked at her and smiled at him. "It's nice to have an ego-stroke sometimes."

"Ah-huh." Kane gave her a slow smile. "I'll have to remember that."

As much as she loved the attention Kane gave her off duty, when they were on the job it made it difficult to keep her head straight. *After what I've been through today, a cuddle would be just fine.* Her face grew hot at the thought and she cleared her throat. "Lancaster is next."

CHAPTER FORTY-SEVEN

He stared at the clock hanging on the wall. It was a familiar, generic round clock, metal, eight inches across with a clear glass front. The face had the usual twelve numerals in black and seconds marked off in sections with hands to match. A red second hand ticked away the seconds, sixty seconds to one minute, sixty minutes to one hour. The rhyme sat in his head like an earwig as he watched time slip away. He had nowhere else to go right now and he liked to watch the clock. Tick tock, tick tock.

The sound calmed him and put everything in his mind firmly into place. Up to now, he'd planned a schedule, each move carefully timed – but he'd added another twist to the game with Sara. Meeting her had been different and he'd decided on impulse to kill her there. The forest had turned out to be a perfect place to kill and he'd consumed her fear. If only the sheriff had wandered into his trap instead.

Tick tock, tick tock. His eyes followed the red hand, moving past the number nine and on to ten. It was almost hypnotic. Clocks were amazing inventions; they measured an illusion that only existed in a person's mind. An invention by man to measure a creation of man.

From a young age, he'd enjoyed discovering how things worked. Books or the internet filled in the information he lacked but the workings of the mind confused him. He'd once wanted to ask someone, a shrink maybe, why his grandma's image appeared over the faces of the women he killed, and then the moment he killed Lindy, everything had changed.

It had just been Lindy's big scared eyes looking up at him as he tightened the rope around her neck, not his grandma's angry glare. Killing the girls had been different – exciting – and watching their fear of him had seeped into him like a drug. Maybe he could slay his demons for good by killing the sheriff and winning the game. After all, the thrill of abducting and killing a teenage girl was so much better.

The first time he'd laid eyes on the sheriff, ordering men around like she was all that, he'd seen his grandma's eyes flashing with anger and cursing him, telling him he was useless and would amount to nothing. For a long time, he'd figured she'd been right because as a kid, all the women he'd met treated him like a bug they wanted to squash under their feet.

But he wasn't a little boy anymore.

One by one, he'd made them apologize and then delivered his sentence. He'd expected one day someone would put a stop to his revenge and he'd grown bored waiting for the fun to begin. The chase he expected had never occurred and the notoriety of murdering twenty-seven women had not rated a mention – then he'd strangled Lindy. His life had changed in that dark root cellar and the Shadow Man had risen, feared and respected. Now one woman stood in the way of redemption – Sheriff Jenna Alton. He had to win the game and destroy the final vision of his grandma then he'd be free. *Lady, you're so gonna die.*

CHAPTER FORTY-EIGHT

Exhausted, Jenna waited for Kane to open the door to the interview room, and then walked inside. She recognized the muscular man sprawled in the chair with his feet on the table and cowboy hat tipped down over his eyes and cleared her throat. "Mr. Lancaster."

"That would be me." Lancaster tipped up the rim of his hat and looked at her. "Afternoon, Sheriff, nice to see you again, ma'am." He dropped his boots from the table and sat up in his chair.

Jenna took in the man before her, handsome with a sexy smile – no wonder the young girls chased after him. She explained the situation and his rights and, when he agreed, turned on the recorder. "The last time we spoke, you mentioned knowing Lindy Rosen. Have you met Amanda Braxton?"

"The other girl that went missin'?" Lancaster's forehead creased into a frown. "Yeah, she was one of the girls who hung around me at the school, just the same as Lindy. Is that why I'm here? You figure I'd something to do with abducting those girls?"

If that was a proclamation of innocence, it sure looked genuine. Jenna ignored his question, opened the file and slipped out the crime scene photographs Agent Martin had given her of the two murdered women. "What about Christine Pullman and Joy Coran?" She placed the images in front of him. "Take a good look. Do you recognize them?"

"Jesus." Lancaster stared at the images, and then lifted his gaze slowly to her. "You're prankin' me, right?" He stared into the camera. "Okay, you got me." He turned his attention back to Jenna. "This isn't funny – those women look all beat up and they're making me sick to my stomach."

"They're dead. Beaten to death." Kane's expression turned to disgust as he leaned forward in his seat. "Do we look like we're joking? Do you figure the sheriff has time to prank you with the murders of two teenage girls to solve?"

"Hey, man." Lancaster held up both hands as if to ward him off. "I can't kill a snake, let alone a woman, and those girls were just kids. Just because they follow me around don't mean I killed them. Heck, they didn't cause that much trouble and it's kinda nice being someone's hero."

"We just find it strange when a girl goes missing and you choose that morning to have your truck professionally cleaned." Kane glared at him. "Then you can't prove your whereabouts on the nights someone abducted them."

"Listen, I get my truck cleaned same time every week." Lancaster cleared his throat. "If you check out the envelope that's with my stuff the deputy took you'll find my bank statement. It shows I pay for car detailing every week, same time." He shrugged. "I'm seeing a woman who works there. She's married and I spent the night Amanda went missing with her. That's why I said I was alone; she's in a bad situation." He looked at Jenna. "Check it out but don't let her husband know. He's abusive and she's planning on leaving him."

"I'll keep her statement confidential." Jenna exchanged a glance with Kane. "Give me her name and number." She took down the details. "Okay, wait here. Kane, with me."

Outside in the hallway, she made the call, then disconnected and looked at Kane. "Yeah, she covered for him and is on the way to give us a statement."

Jenna went inside the room. "Okay, Mr. Lancaster. I'll take a look at your bank statement and when your mystery friend drops by to make a statement, you'll be able to leave. Thank you for your time. I'll arrange a ride back to work for you."

"Thank you." Lancaster looked up at Jenna and anger flashed in his eyes. "So you have a human side after all."

Jenna ignored his sudden change of demeanor and went into the hallway. She pulled shut the door to the interview room and went to Kane's side. "Give me something. We've three possible killers in custody and have to narrow it down."

"I'll need to look over the interview tapes." Kane rested his thumbs in his belt and stood feet apart, taking up almost the width of the passageway. "I'm not discounting the school janitor, McLeod, either; he's the only one with a solid motive."

Jenna shook her head. "I don't think it's him but we'll know for sure the moment the Shadow Man makes his next move. Go over what you have on the other three and see if you can narrow it down."

The tone of Jenna's cellphone announced a message. She glanced up at Kane, not wanting to interrupt his line of thought. "I'd better take a look, it might be from Wolfe."

She opened the message file and stared in disbelief at the private number, then lifted her gaze to him. "It's from the Shadow Man – and there's an attachment."

CHAPTER FORTY-NINE

Heart thumping, Jenna opened the message and held the screen between them for Kane to read.

You're not so hot on playing games are you, Sheriff?
Let me make it easy on you.
Here's the girl I'm going to kill next.
Pretty isn't she?
You have one hour and then I'm coming for you.
Won't that be fun?
Tick tock. Tick tock.

Sick to the stomach, Jenna opened the attachment and stared at the girl in the photograph. She looked happy and excited, standing in front of a backdrop of pine trees. She turned to Kane. "I know the men in custody were searched before they entered the interview rooms and none of them have cellphones." She chewed on her bottom lip. "Will you grab Rowley and strip-search them all? I'll show this picture to Julie, she might know her."

"She looks familiar. I'm sure she's one of the girls we spoke to at the drama club." Kane stared at the image, his face grim. "He could already have her holed up somewhere."

Stomach cramping with worry, Jenna stared at the picture in dismay. "I made a list of the girls in the club. I'll contact the parents and send the photo to all of them. Someone will recognize her." She looked at Kane. "At last he's made a mistake. We need to find that damn phone."

"I'm on it." Kane hustled down the hallway and into the main office. "Rowley, with me."

Jenna ran to the front counter, dropped her files and notebook on the desk then held up her cellphone. "Hey, Julie. I could really use your help. Do you know this girl?"

Wolfe's daughter lifted her startled gaze to her and hurried to the counter.

"She's from school, I'm not sure of her name." Julie frowned at the screen of Jenna's cellphone. "Lucy would know. I can get her number for you." She pulled her cellphone from her pocket and scrolled down the screen, then gave Jenna the details. "Has something happened to her?"

In full panic mode, Jenna thumbed in the number. "Nothing yet, I hope."

She waited for what seemed like an eternity for Lucy to pick up. "Lucy, this is Sheriff Alton."

"Er… yes. Do you want to speak to my mom?"

Trying to keep the concern from her voice, Jenna sucked in a breath. "I've an image of a girl from your school. I need to know her name and contact details. Can you help me please?"

"Sure. Has she done something wrong?"

"No. I just need to find her. I'll send it through and call you back." Jenna disconnected, sent the text, waited a long minute and then called her back. "Do you know her, Lucy?"

"You didn't need to hang up. I can receive texts and talk at the same time. I'll show you how to do it if you like?"

Jenna pushed down the rush of anxiety and tried to remain calm. She didn't want to frighten Lucy. "That's very kind of you but I need to know the name of the girl."

"It's Sara Nelson. She lives out at 209 Stanton Road, Glacial Heights. I have her number if you want it?"

Jenna balanced the cellphone under her chin and scribbled the details in her notebook. "Do you have her landline number as well?"

"Ah, yeah, but if you need to talk to her parents they won't be home for ages yet, like after six. They work at the hospital. Her mom's a nurse and her dad's a surgeon."

If the Shadow Man had already abducted Sara, the girl had no one to report her missing.

"Okay, thank you, Lucy." Jenna disconnected, and then took in Julie's sheet-white face. It was as if she'd read her mind. She forced her mouth into a smile. "Thanks for your help, Julie, I'll see if I can contact her."

After picking up her paperwork, Jenna walked as casually as possible back to her office, and then thumbed in Sara's number. The call went to voicemail and she left a message asking Sara to contact her. Next, she tried the home phone and got the machine. She called the hospital and, after waiting what seemed like an eternity, finally reached Sara's father. She explained the situation. "I need you to call her friends, in case she's with one of them. If you find her, call me – and if you don't, call me. This may be a copycat, or a hoax, but we need to make sure she's okay."

"I'll go get my wife, we'll call everyone we know then get back to you." Dr. Nelson sounded strained. *"Please keep me informed. I'll give you my cell number."* He rattled off the number.

Jenna took down the details then disconnected. She heard footsteps in the hallway and stared at the open door. If her deputies found a cellphone, missed in the pat down, they'd have their killer. The next moment, Kane and Rowley came into the room. She looked at their stone-faced expressions and knew they'd found nothing. "So you're telling me the killer is still out there somewhere?"

"It sure looks that way." Kane balled his fists on his hips.

Stymied, Jenna leaned heavily against her desk. Tired, sore and exhausted. She sat down slowly in her chair. "He needed a cellphone to send the message."

"Not necessarily." Wolfe walked into the room with Webber close behind. "Some cellphones have text scheduling. He could've set it then made sure he'd gotten an alibi for that time." He gave Kane a knowing look, then handed him a new Kevlar jacket and a helmet. "Or it could be a copycat."

Jenna heaved a sigh seeing him and the new super-vest he'd managed to obtain for her with amazing speed. "The killer didn't know we'd planned to haul him in for questioning, did he? And we've not informed the media about the messages."

"No but I'd bet he had a neat alibi set up for this afternoon." Wolfe leaned one shoulder against the wall. "The first question you ask a suspect is their whereabouts at the time of the incident."

"Yeah, problem is all of the potential suspects we're found so far were at work with a ton load of witnesses." Jenna pushed a hand through her hair in frustration. "But if he's kidnapped Sara and stashed her somewhere, he can't kill her if he's one of our suspects."

"Unless he's rigged up a way to kill her using a timer, and with explosives that's not difficult." Kane's eyes flashed with anger. "If we split up, we could search their homes now. One of them could have her holed up in his cellar." He rubbed the back of his neck. "Their keys are in the property room and we've gotten their written permission to do a search." He leaned on the table and looked at her. "We can't risk you going out alone, Jenna, not until we've solid evidence against this maniac, so leave the searching to us, okay?"

"Sure. I'd be useless trying to do a search right now." She glanced at her watch. Ten precious minutes had already passed. "Go get the keys. Rowley, make sure everyone has the correct addresses." She waved everyone out her office.

"I'll call Blackhawk." Wolfe turned back and frowned down at her. "He's in town with one of his friends. You'll be able to deputize them if everything goes to hell."

"Yeah, thanks." Jenna removed her Glock from the desk drawer and slid it into the holster. "The Blackwater deputies aren't due until six but I still have Walters."

"Yeah, but I'm with Kane on this, maybe we have the suspect locked up and maybe we don't. If the Shadow Man is as smart as we figure, he'll be out there watching us and know you're alone. With his track record, he could be capable of anything. You'll need backup." Wolfe pulled out his cell. "I'll call Blackhawk now." He headed out the office.

Jenna's ringtone chimed and she stared at the caller ID, relieved it was Dr. Miller. "Sheriff Alton. Have you had any luck tracking down Sara?"

"No, she met her friend in town earlier and she waited with her until she caught the bus home. I'm at home now and she's not here." Dr. Miller's voice broke. *"Dear God, someone has abducted our baby girl."*

CHAPTER FIFTY

The wind had picked up and the branches of the tree outside Jenna's office window scratched against the pane. The back of her neck prickled as unease crawled over her. If they'd made a mistake, the Shadow Man could be outside watching her and be aiming his rifle at her head right this moment. She swallowed hard and rolled her office chair to one side of the desk, then stood and pressed her aching back against the wall. Taking small steps, she eased her way to the side of the window.

A dark shape appeared in the doorway and she instinctively pulled her weapon and aimed at it, holding the pistol in both hands.

"Hey, it's only me, Jenna." Atohi Blackhawk lifted both hands and froze on the spot. "Shane called me, said you might need some company. He said to bring Joe along. He's talking to Maggie." He tipped his head to one side and regarded her with interest. "Something spook you?"

Relieved to see a friendly face, Jenna holstered her weapon and took a few breaths to slow her racing heart. "Yeah, I heard a noise outside the window and was taking a look when you suddenly appeared at the door."

"I'll close the blinds." He walked to the window and pulled the cord and the metal blinds shut tight. "Maybe you should have closed these earlier with a lunatic in town taking shots at you." He turned to face her. "I bet it hurts like hell. No wonder a noise spooked you."

In an effort to appear unruffled and in complete control of her sanity, Jenna sat down in her chair. "It does hurt but I'm coping just fine. Thanks for caring." She looked at him. "Don't worry about me; we've a missing girl to locate."

"Wolfe asked me to remind you to take pain meds." Blackhawk frowned. "You're as white as a ghost – maybe you need some now."

Slightly annoyed, she stared at her daybook. "No need for concern. Emily's been by and rubbed a pain reliever into my back. I'll be as good as new in the morning."

Her cellphone buzzed a message and she stared at it, unable to prevent the rush of anxiety. *I'm acting like an idiot and letting the Shadow Man win. It could be any number of people texting me.* She snatched up the cellphone and stared at the message ID, then dropped it on the desk. *Oh dear God it's him again.*

"Jenna, what's wrong?" Blackhawk had crossed the floor in seconds. "Is it the Shadow Man again?"

Suspicion crawled through her bones, twisting her gut. She stared at him and one hand crept to the handle of her weapon. "How do *you* know about the messages?"

"Shane's kept me in the loop." Blackhawk frowned. "He figured it was best if you needed to deputize me." He gave her a quizzical stare. "You can trust me, Jenna. You know that, right?"

Although she doubted Wolfe would keep anyone but the members of their team "in the loop" she examined his expression, trying to find a tell or something to give her a clue to his intent, and found nothing. "No offense but I'm not sure who to trust anymore." Jenna swallowed the bile creeping up the back of her throat. "It's been a crazy few days and I'm exhausted."

"None taken. You should be suspicious of everyone." Blackhawk backed away, looking concerned. "I know Shane and Dave both did background checks on me the first day we met." He barked a laugh. "Your deputies are very protective of your inner circle."

"Yeah, that's because we had a leak in the office a couple of years ago and it cost lives." Jenna stared back at the cellphone but was reluctant to open the message in front of him.

"Jenna, I'm here as your backup. If you've gotten a message from the Shadow Man, you need to deal with it. As you said before, a girl's life is at stake. I'm calling Kane to put your mind at ease. I'll put the phone on speaker." He made the call. "Hey, man, I never figured Jenna would draw down on me but she had her Glock aimed at my head when I arrived. She's listening in. Can you tell her I'm cleared for the Shadow Man case?"

Kane's voice came through loud and clear.

"Sure, yeah, Wolfe filled him in. He's good people, Jenna."

Fearful that a man who could appear as a ghost in a girl's bedroom then vanish without a trace might be able to fake a simple phone call, Jenna considered her options as she chewed on her bottom lip. She needed to ask Kane a question and one which only they'd know the answer. "Do you mind confirming ID? You once told me the name of the love of your life. Who was that?"

"That was Annie. You sure you're okay, Jenna?" Kane sounded confused. *"Why don't you open the text now and read it to me. We might have time to save Sara."*

"Sure, give me a second." Heart pounding, she picked up her cellphone and opened the message. *What's your next move, Shadow Man?*

As if trapped in a void of disbelief, she stared at the words. It was as if he'd been watching her.

I know it hasn't been an hour since my last message but I never stick to the rules and now seemed like a perfect time to call.
Sara's alive but won't be for long.

*How fast can you move, Sheriff, now you've taken a couple of rounds
in the back?*

*Are you afraid? I'm getting closer, Sheriff – or should I call you Jenna?
You won't be quick enough to stop me.*

I'm so going to enjoy this one.

Tick tock, tick tock.

"Jenna, what does the message say?"

Kane's voice jolted her back to reality and, holding the cellphone
in trembling fingers, she relayed the message.

*"He's not given you a clue, there has to be more. He's a gamer, he has
to give a clue or it's no longer a game, it's just a threat."* Kane cleared
his throat. *"Is there another message?"*

As if on cue, her cellphone buzzed again and a video file arrived.
"There's a file attached. I'm opening it now."

Blackhawk moved around the desk to stand beside her as the video
file played. Knowing Kane would want exact details Jenna wanted
desperately to drop into her professional persona and tried to slow
her heartrate. It wasn't about her, or some lunatic chasing her, it was
about saving Sara Nelson. On the screen, Sara sat on a boulder in
the forest, a rope around her neck tied like a hangman's noose. Her
mouth was covered and her head hung down. As she breathed, the
hair falling over her face moved.

Jenna relayed the information to Kane. "I'll send you a copy."

"I know that place." Blackhawk took the cellphone from her
and replayed the file repeatedly. "It's close to the swimming hole in
Stanton Forest, the one near Stanton Road."

Jenna stared at him. "That's a narrow trail. We'll need horses if
we plan to get there in a hurry."

"Our dirt bikes are right outside." Blackhawk picked up his
cellphone. "Kane, we're heading out now."

Jenna got slowly to her feet. "Not without me, you're not." She lifted the new Kevlar vest and shrugged into it, then pulled on the helmet. "Kane, what's your status?"

"I found nothing in Anderson's truck. I'm in his house now. There's no cellar. The place looks clean. I'll grab his laptop and head in your direction. I'm not far from that location."

Jenna could hear Kane's boots clattering over a wooden floor. "Bring everyone up to date. I'm leaving now."

"Roger that. Stay safe, Jenna." He disconnected.

After giving Maggie a rushed update, she moved swiftly out the door and down the steps to meet Blackhawk and Joe astride their dirt bikes. She eyed Blackhawk's blue and white machine with concern, then bit down hard on her cheek to take her mind off the pain in her back and swung her leg over the seat. She settled in snug behind him, found the footrests and hung on tight. The motorcycles roared and they headed down Main Street.

The suspension on the bike was surprisingly good but the vibration was like a baseball bat to the spine. Jenna rested her head on Blackhawk's wide back, inhaling the scent of his leather jacket as the houses flashed by. As the men pushed the speed to the bikes' limit, the forest became a band of green. Then all at once they slowed and Blackhawk turned off the highway and followed Joe down a narrow trail deep into the forest.

Bushes and low branches seemed to reach out to grab her at every hairpin bend and switchback. As they traveled deeper into the tall pines, the temperature dropped and frigid air buffeted her cheeks. The dirt bike stopped and she could hear Blackhawk's voice over the engine. "We've found her."

Jenna peered over Blackhawk's shoulder to see Sara in a clearing a short distance away. The girl appeared to be alive. She slipped from the bike. "She looks okay, thank God, we're in time."

Ahead, Joe leapt from his bike and ran toward Sara.

"Stop, wait for us, you idiot." Blackhawk turned off his engine, slid from his seat and cupped his mouth. "Joe. Stop! It could be a trap."

A groaning sound came from the trees, and then a loud crack sent birds flying high in the air. In a twang like an arrow leaving a bow, a spear shot through the air. The sharpened wooden stake thumped into Joe's shoulder, flinging him to the forest floor. A split second later, Sara flew high into the trees then dropped with a sickening snap to hang by her neck, feet twitching. From the angle of her head, Jenna could see it was too late for Sara. Her stomach cramped and she turned towards the bushes and vomited.

"Jesus." Blackhawk pulled a hunting knife from his belt. "Stay here, I'll cut her down." He took off, moving in a careful wide arc around the clearing. "Joe, if you can hear me, stay down."

He moved fast, leaping over bushes, but Jenna could see his head moving in all directions searching for another trap. He'd reached Sara moments later, and was sawing at the rope to release her. With one hand on the cord, securing Sara, he attempted to lower her slowly but the rope slid through his hands and she tumbled to the forest floor in a nauseating thud.

Jenna wiped her mouth and scanned the area, searching for tripwires, then retraced Joe's steps. A length of fishing line lay across the dirt track. Taking careful steps, she inched her way to Joe's side. He was out cold but alive. Apart from the wicked stake sticking through his shoulder, he had an egg on his head. Jenna checked him, pressing two fingers on his jugular and relieved to feel his pulse under her fingers. She reached for her cellphone and called the paramedics, explaining the situation and the danger involved. Next, she called Kane. "It's all gone to hell. Sara's dead and Joe has a stake through one shoulder, paramedics are on their way."

"I'm making my way to you now." Kane's voice was reassuring. *"The others are close behind. No one found anything at the homes and we've taken all their computer equipment."*

"Roger that." Jenna turned to see Blackhawk returning. "I'll send Blackhawk to give you a ride." She heard Kane's sharp intake of breath. "I'll be fine."

"Stay on the line with Kane and I'll move Joe into the cover of the trees." Blackhawk dragged his unconscious friend into the bushes, and then turned to her. "Stay here."

Jenna crawled into a secluded area and Blackhawk ran back to his dirt bike. As the noise of the engine disappeared in the distance, the forest closed in around her. She'd never felt so alone and pressed the cellphone to her ear. "Dave."

"I'm here."

In all the years Jenna had been in law enforcement, she'd never given up, not once – but seeing Sara die in front of her had shaken her to the core. She wanted to scream, cry out in frustration, hit something, but she was too damn tired. After checking Joe again, she propped her sore and battered body against a tree and let out a long sigh in desperation. "He's winning."

CHAPTER FIFTY-ONE

The sun had long set by the time Kane had gotten Jenna back to his truck. The streetlights along Stanton Road were a welcome sight as they drove out of the dark forest. He'd taken the lead, with Rowley doubling with Blackhawk. They'd managed to process the crime scene in good time but removing the injured man and Sara's body had taken longer than expected. The narrow trail was barely wide enough for the gurneys and they'd needed to use the headlights on the dirt bikes to illuminate the way for Wolfe and the paramedics. With Joe safely on his way to the hospital, awake and insisting he'd be fine, he'd waited until Sara's body was in Wolfe's van before helping Jenna into his truck; she was pale and likely in shock. "I'll just be a minute, I've gotta help load Joe's bike into the back of Rowley's pickup then we can go home."

"I'll be okay." Jenna buckled her seatbelt. "I figured you'd be more worried about Duke. He'll be howling the place down by now."

Kane smiled at her. With all that was going on, she was worried about his dog. "He'll be fast asleep by now. He uses the dog flap to go out to do his business and I filled his food and water feeders before I left home."

After heaving the dirt bike into the back of Rowley's pickup and securing it, he gave Rowley a slap on the back and turned to walk back to his truck. "See you in the morning." He waved at Blackhawk. "Thanks for your help, Atohi."

"Before you go." Wolfe pulled him to one side and lowered his voice to a whisper. "This murder is different. From the brief examination at the scene, I figure Sara was sexually assaulted. I've found nothing similar in either of the other victims. If we add the other inconsistences, we could be dealing with a copycat. If not, and this is the work of the same killer, he's becoming a sadist."

Kane stared at Wolfe under the dim streetlight and growled in frustration. "You telling me there're two killers in town? Because as sure as hell, we already have one locked up."

"You have the autopsy reports of both girls on file. I'll do this one directly and send it through. If I find conclusive evidence it's the same killer, I'll call you." Wolfe sighed and stared at his van. "I'll need a positive ID but from the images he sent, it's Sara Nelson. I'll have Webber prepare her for a viewing and go see the parents." He glanced back at Kane's truck. "You need to get Jenna home. Everything else can wait until morning."

Kane walked with him back to Wolfe's van. "Sure, I'll call Walters. He can give our suspects the good news they'll be spending the night in the cells." He cleared his throat. "Sam Cross is representing them and he's a no-show until the morning. Last I heard he was chasing down the DA for a deal for Matt Miller."

"I'll call you later." Wolfe waved at Webber to join him and climbed into the van.

Kane's truck was the last vehicle remaining on the dimly lit street. An owl hooted and his attention moved to the dark forest. It changed at night, as if the day shift had gone home and the night stalkers taken over. The wind rustled the pine needles, making the trees seem to move in a wave as if they dared anyone to step into their midst. A shiver lifted goosebumps on his flesh and he hustled back to his truck.

By the time Kane pulled up outside Jenna's house, she'd fallen asleep. Her breathing was deep and even. He touched her face and called her name but she didn't wake. He slid from behind the wheel and heard an excited bark as Duke shot out of the dark to greet him. "I figured you'd be asleep by now." He scratched the dog on the head. "Be quiet now."

He jogged up the front steps, used the code to open the front door and disabled the alarm. He went back to his truck and opened the passenger-side door. "Jenna, we're home."

When she didn't stir, he unbuckled her seatbelt, carried her into the house and laid her down on her bed. After removing her weapon and boots, he covered her with a blanket and then slipped silently from the house. He had steaks in the refrigerator and the fixings for dinner. The thought made his belly growl in anticipation. After placing the potatoes in the oven, he headed for the shower.

Later, as he cooked, his mind centered on the case. He'd processed the crime scene with Wolfe and found a number of similarities in the method of killing. Maybe not in the crime scene itself but Sara's death had added a different dimension to the killer. Deployed on a number of missions during active duty, he'd witnessed the ingenuity of man's ability to kill or maim, but the way the killer had mixed it up was pure genius. The Shadow Man had a number of skills not common to most men – skills like his own. In fact, if he'd chosen the criminal path, breaking into houses or killing would've been a walk in the park – he doubted anyone would've been able to catch him or come close to discovering his identity. So who did he have locked up with those skills? He ran possibilities through his mind. Neither Packer nor Anderson had shown any anger toward Jenna but the jury was still out on Kittredge. His cellphone ringtone told him Jenna was awake. "Hey, how are you feeling?"

"Sore but I'll live." He heard a splash of water. *"I'm in the hot tub. I won't stay long."* She sighed. *"We need to discuss the case and I really need to eat something. I can't take pain meds on an empty stomach. Can you drive into town and grab some takeout from Aunt Betty's?"*

Kane checked the food in the oven and went to the counter to toss the salad. "No need, I'll have dinner ready soon. Just need to toss the steaks into the pan."

"One of these days I'm going to wake up and find out you're just a dream." Jenna yawned. *"I'll be there in ten."*

CHAPTER FIFTY-TWO

After finishing her meal, Jenna sipped her glass of juice and listened with interest to Kane's insight into the case. "So you wouldn't consider Wolfe's theory that Sara's murder was a copycat?"

"Nope, its planning and execution—" Kane frowned. "Sorry that's a bad choice of words, but the way the Shadow Man is changing up the game all the time is consistent in a way. Think about it – if you're playing a video game, you'd face a variety of challenges and in each one, you have the chance to lose a life. I figure he's doing the same thing. He doesn't want to kill you, just knock you down for a time, but then you'll be back to play the next level."

Incredulous, Jenna stared at him. "Just how many lives will I have?"

"I figure until he grows tired of playing with you. We know he's started to enjoy killing the girls." Kane got up from the table to collect the plates. "Wolfe believes Sara suffered sexual abuse."

Horrified, Jenna sucked in a breath. "So he's no longer killing them to get to me, he's killing them for fun?" She drained her glass. "Well, he won't be having any fun tonight, will he?"

"I just hope we'll have enough evidence to hold the suspects until we discover which one of them is the Shadow Man." Kane shrugged. "We'll have a problem with Sam Cross. He'll likely put a case to the DA to have them released in the morning."

Suddenly exhausted, Jenna rubbed her temples and looked at him. "Surely if he figures one of them is guilty and another girl's life is at risk, he won't, will he?"

"From what I can make of Cross, he follows the letter of the law." Kane filled two cups from the coffee maker and gave one to Jenna. "Innocent until proven guilty and right now we're skating on thin ice with the way we conducted the interviews."

Jenna poured cream into her coffee. "How so?"

"Oh come on, Jenna, you coerced all of them into giving you permission to search their homes and vehicles. One look at those tapes and Cross will be screaming foul." Kane sat down and added sugar to his cup. "Then we held them overnight, after we'd conducted the searches and found zip." He frowned. "They'll walk free the moment he speaks to them."

Jenna opened her mouth to insist she followed the book when Kane's cellphone chimed. It was Wolfe and he put him on speaker.

"I've conducted an autopsy on Sara Nelson." Wolfe's voice came through the speaker in his usual professional calmness. *"It's not good."*

Jenna stared at the cellphone, willing it to give her some evidence she could use against the Shadow Man. "I don't need a blow-by-blow tonight, Wolfe, just give me an outline. I'll read your report later."

"Sure but with these cases, Kane should take a look at the bodies of Amanda and Sara before they're released to the families."

"Okay." Kane exchanged a puzzled look with Jenna. "Why me?"

"Because you're trained to kill." Wolfe sounded exhausted. *"I've examined the necks in the three victims and they're all too neat, if that's the correct word, for someone who* hasn't *been trained to kill. I had reservations when I examined Lindy Rosen – her injuries are consistent with her attacker coming from behind but, after careful consideration, I'm convinced he looped the tourniquet around her neck then turned his back on her and bent to lift her with the cord over one shoulder. I've seen the move. It's effective and uses less strength."*

"Yeah, but the tourniquet usually slides up under the chin, so it cuts higher than, say, by using the cord as a garrote." Kane turned his cup in his hands. "Did you find evidence of that type of injury?"

"*Yeah, the injuries were consistent. Then we go to the second victim, Amanda Braxton. She had her neck broken in a chokehold. Clean, easy and effective. The classic chokehold is taught in basic training by the police as a restraining method; the twist is added in the military as an effective and silent way to kill.*" Wolfe cleared his throat. "*So we've two victims, with no apparent motive to kill them. Although a psychopath doesn't need a reason to kill, it's as if he kidnapped and murdered these girls to prove a point. I found nothing, no trace evidence. The buttons on their clothes had their fingerprints on them. He scared them, we know that from the video files, but apart from that, he killed them without the usual raging violence and discarded them like trash. The brutality, agreed, was in the strangulation but what he aimed at Jenna was far worse.*" He sighed. "*Until he killed Sara Nelson.*"

Jenna sipped her coffee, listening with interest. "So what's changed? He set up a slingshot to kill anyone trying to save her. In my opinion, she died by virtually the same method."

"*I'll agree to some point, Jenna. Yes, ultimately, they all died from neck trauma but he raped Sara. Her clothes were torn as if he ripped them open, then he dressed her before he set her on the boulder. I don't believe she was fully conscious when it happened.*"

"Strangulation is personal." Kane frowned. "Up close, feeling the life leave the body – and it's not a quick death. Yet he depersonalized it by using different techniques."

"*Why rape an unconscious girl?*" Wolfe's agitation was obvious. "*In my understanding, rape is a punishment and from what we've seen, this killer feeds on fear. What do you make of this, Kane?*"

"I figure he's changed direction from revenge against women in authority to enjoying scaring young women. The killing was to hide his identity so he could continue the game, but now he's discovered a new thrill. Scaring the victims is feeding his ego – he now has control and the ultimate domination of a woman is rape. The kill is a form of disposal. It means nothing to him."

The memory of Sara's neck breaking as she shot into the air had replayed in Jenna's mind so many times, making a constant flow of bile rush up the back of her throat. She stared at Kane across the table. "I gather the spear-throwing slingshot is something you're familiar with, Kane?"

"Yeah, but it's not necessarily military." Kane met her gaze. "I've seen it used to kill game. They bend and tie down a sapling, so when released it springs back with force. To release it you attach a slipknot to a tripwire. Once tripped the tree propels the attached arrow or small spear into the target. It's a method used since the Stone Age." He frowned, staring down into his cup. "The killer wanted to enhance the shock value by hanging Sara in front of you. He used the same principle to construct a snare to hoist Sara into the air, and then used the same tripwire to trigger both of them. He planned the whole thing. I found a pulley tangled in the rope."

Jenna rubbed her temples. "So how the hell did he subdue the girl then drag her and a long rope deep into the forest without anyone seeing or hearing him?" She lifted her gaze to Kane. "It was hard enough getting out of the forest alone over that narrow track."

"He could've had a weapon and made her walk to her death. I know how he subdued her long enough to collect the things he needed. I found a pair of panties stuffed in her mouth soaked in diethyl ether. She would've been close to death by the time you found her and certainly not capable at any time of being able to call for help. The panties didn't belong to her, or any of the other girls. I figure they're from another kill." He cleared his throat. *"Agent Martin asked to be kept in the loop and he's offered to help. I'll text him the images."*

Jenna nodded as if Wolfe was in the room. "Thanks. If this is a previous kill, forget the teenagers and tell Martin to narrow down the search by using the same parameters of the killer's previous victims – ages and occupation. I figure he's showing me what he's capable of doing if he catches me."

CHAPTER FIFTY-THREE

Friday

Jenna's week was on a downward slide. She arrived at the office to find the media crammed into the waiting area and Maggie doing her best to keep order. To make things worse, Rowley had arrived early as usual and was on a callout to a traffic accident. The Blackwater deputies had left after spending the night watching the suspects and Walters had called in sick. With Kane clearing the way, Jenna slipped behind the counter and glared at the microphones waving in front of her. "We found the body of missing teenager Sara Nelson yesterday afternoon. As of this moment investigations into the killer of Sara Nelson, Lindy Rosen and Amanda Braxton are ongoing. When I have an update, I'll contact you through the normal channels. Now will you leave so I can find their killer?" She turned and, with Kane at her back, walked into her office to come face to face with Sam Cross, looking like he'd just walked off a dude ranch. *What next?* "Mr. Cross, I was just about to call you."

"No need. Maggie informed me I'd gained three new clients." Cross gripped the back of the chair and stared at her. "Have you charged my clients?"

Jenna sat at her desk and looked up at him. "Only Kittredge. He came in for questioning and decided to throw a chair at me."

"Okay, and what about the others? You've had them locked up overnight for what reason?"

"We believe they could be involved in three homicides." Jenna got up, went to the file cabinet and pulled out the murder books. "All the men we detained waived their rights but we also obtained signed agreements to search their property. As is their right under the law, they decided they wanted representation the moment they hit the cells. We haven't spoken to them since. As I'm sure you're aware, we've a killer on the loose, and these men are of interest. I'd be putting the community at risk if I'd released them before we'd searched their properties. This was explained to them during the interview and they didn't object."

"Ah-huh, so no coercion on your part? I'll require copies of any statements they signed and I want to view the interview tapes." Cross waved a hand absently toward the whiteboard. "You're gonna have to come up with a better case than that load of baloney if you're planning on keeping them here." He glanced at Kane, and then moved his attention back to her. "Not having an alibi overnight if you live alone gives me reasonable doubt. And we've already established the truck seen in the vicinity of two of the three abductions belonged to Miller, so the fact all of these men drive pickups is irrelevant." He shook his head. "See, Jenna, I've created reasonable doubt already. You don't have a case on any of them."

Angry with him treating her like a student who hadn't completed her assignment, Jenna cleared her throat. "Have you taken into account the girls at school are attracted to him? It wouldn't take much to convince them to go with him willingly. He knows all the victims and has no alibi for the nights they went missing, then he conveniently has his car detailed the morning after – it's a little more than circumstantial, Mr. Cross."

"Then let's look at what you have on Charles Anderson." Cross pointed at the whiteboard. "Sure, he's gotten a knowledge of explosives from working in Colorado, but we've a mining industry right here in Black Rock Falls. Any one of a hundred men could've set the IED. Add up the facts – Anderson has no priors and he passed a substantial background check by Silent Alarms and the local council to work with kids in his art classes in town." He raised both arms, and then dropped them to his waist in a display of frustration. "Why the hell is he here? You've nothing to hold him."

Jenna bristled. "Why don't you go and look at the interview tapes? All of them had the opportunity to do the crimes. They're here for questioning until we prove otherwise."

"I'll see pigs fly first." Cross straightened and glared at her. "The time to hold them for questioning is running out and unless you charge them, they'll be walking out with me. The courts decide guilt or innocence, not POTUS or the sheriff of Black Rock Falls. The DA is arriving at nine to strike a deal with Mr. Miller. I'll be speaking to my clients this morning and when I'm done, I'll be asking the DA to take a long look at how you run this office. I can't figure out why you found it necessary to detain my clients overnight."

"I'm not arguing with you, Mr. Cross, I'm just doing my job." It was like dealing with a yapping dog. No explanation Jenna offered would be good enough. She lifted her gaze to Kane. "Would you take Mr. Cross down to interview room one and go get Miller? I'll escort the DA down when he arrives."

"Yes, ma'am." Kane opened the door and waved Cross through. "Through the office, take a right at the passageway, first door on the left." He looked back at her and rolled his eyes to the ceiling. "Then do you want me to go and examine Wolfe's autopsy findings?"

"Yeah." Jenna leaned back in her seat. "I hope he finds one tiny shred of trace evidence to match a suspect. It would come in real useful right now." She frowned. "Although with Cross as their lawyer, we'll have no chance of collecting a DNA sample from them."

"Yeah, we do." Kane smiled at her. "They had breakfast delivered from Aunt Betty's earlier and the garbage hasn't been collected from the cells yet. I'll bag and tag them all and take them to Wolfe."

Jenna heaved a sigh of relief. "Trust you to have the answer." She looked up at him. "Hurry back."

She had a thousand things to do and needed to prioritize. The last thing she wanted was Cross making life difficult. She took out her notebook and flipped through the pages. There had to be something she'd missed and she'd never convince the DA until she'd made a solid case against one of them. To do this she'd need to eliminate them one by one. She needed a prime suspect and the more she considered the facts, the more she worried about allowing Mason Lancaster to walk. His married girlfriend had signed a statement confirming his whereabouts, and his bank statement had checked out, giving her no reason to suspect him – and yet the niggling feeling in her gut told her otherwise. The teenage girls' magnetic attraction toward him worried her. The nice-guy psychopathic classification fit him like a glove. *He's the person no one would expect. If he moved around with the football team before his injury, he could've been killing all over – but why would he want to hurt me?*

Her landline rang and Jenna lifted the receiver. "Sheriff Alton."

"Hi Jenna, it's Josh Martin. I've had a hit on the evidence found at the crime scenes. The panties from the Sara Nelson case belonged to a police officer, Clare Dumas, out of Helena. She was raped and beaten to death three years ago visiting Yellowstone National Park."

Jenna stared at the whiteboard. "Any suspects?"

"None found and there was a report of a white truck in the area at the time with interstate plates, but from what state remains a mystery." Martin sighed. *"There are similarities in the MO between the three older victims. The killer covers his tracks as none of the women lived in the same county, no trace evidence left on scene. It has to be the*

Shadow Man, Jenna. How else could he have gotten the trophies from the murdered women?"

"Unless these freaks trade between themselves." Jenna stabbed her pen into her notebook. "Problem is, our killer doesn't appear to be collecting trophies."

"That's because he doesn't consider them worthy of remembering." Agent Martin cleared his throat. *"If I find anything else on this case or the others I'll let you know."*

"Thanks." Jenna replaced the receiver in the cradle and leaned back in her chair, thinking through their conversation. *If the Shadow Man didn't consider Lindy and Amanda worthy enough to take a trophy, what about Sara?*

She made a call to Wolfe and gave him the information she'd received from Agent Martin. "Go through every item taken from Sara's body. See if he's taken a trophy – as she was raped, I figure she meant something to him."

CHAPTER FIFTY-FOUR

Kane swallowed two antibiotic capsules with a mouthful of coffee and tossed the empty bottle into the trash outside the ME's building. He'd been too busy to make a follow-up appointment with his doctor for the splinters received in the explosion, but like magic, a prescription had appeared on his desk with a curt note from Wolfe insisting he take them until finished. With the murders and attempts on Jenna's life over the last few days, the last thing on his mind was a few splinters. The responsibility for Jenna looking like she'd gone ten rounds with a heavyweight boxer weighed heavy on his shoulders – heck, if he'd allowed the same thing to happen to POTUS he'd have been fired.

The moment he stepped into the cool, white outer office of the medical examiner's office, the awful realization that he'd come to view the slaughtered remains of three young women pushed all other thoughts from his head. At the counter seeing the sunny smile of Julie, Wolfe's middle daughter, surprised him. "What are you doing here? I figured you'd decided to join the sheriff's department."

"Don't be silly." Julie giggled and her cheeks pinked. "I'll be heading to med school after I graduate."

He smiled back. "A fine profession. And we need another doctor in town."

"Oh, if I do decide on med school, I'd be interested in pediatrics. I like kids." Julie beamed at him. "Dad says I should follow my dreams."

"Yeah, never lose sight of that, will you?" Kane looked over her shoulder to see her sister Emily following a gurney pushed by Webber into a side room. "Busy day?"

"Car wreck. Deputy Rowley came by before and spoke to Dad. Em and Webber went out to process the scene and pick up the victims." Julie shrugged. "That's all I know. Hey, now Em is back, can I get a ride back to the sheriff's department?"

"Sure." The door to the morgue whooshed open and Wolfe strode out and beckoned him. Kane waited for Julie to buzz him through the door, and then walked down to meet him. "What have we got?" He took the surgical gloves and mask Wolfe handed him then put them on.

"Jenna called before. She figures Sara may hold some value to the killer as she was the only rape victim." Wolfe walked over to a body draped in a white sheet. "I called her mom and she confirmed Sara was wearing a pair of small blue sapphire and gold earrings the day she disappeared. She never took them off." He pulled back the sheet and frowned down at the face of Sara Nelson. "She's not wearing her earrings."

The air inside the room was like walking into a freezer and the young face was pale with a gray tinge, the lips had turned to lines of dark blue. Kane stopped the rush of emotional rage simmering beneath the surface and reached for his professional side. Viewing the bodies of murder victims had a purpose and if he wanted to arrest the person who killed them, he needed to listen to the story they'd tell him – and they all told a story. "They're so small they could be concealed anywhere. When we searched the suspects' homes and vehicles, our main priority was finding evidence of a missing girl or child porn." Kane couldn't take his eyes away from Sara's face. He gently pushed the hair away from one ear and then the other. "He didn't tear them from her ears."

"Exactly, which means he didn't want us to notice they're missing." Wolfe lifted the sheet to uncover the arms, showing utmost respect for the victim. "No defensive wounds, not even a broken nail." He uncovered her legs. "No bruising on her thighs but there's evidence of rape. This wasn't consensual sex by any means but the killer was meticulous – he left nothing behind, no trace evidence, not one hair, which is difficult unless he's removed his body hair. We have seen that before in rapists." He covered her again, and then went back to her head. "At first, I believed this contusion on her temple came from the fall when Blackhawk cut her down, but after speaking with him, he insists she fell on the opposite side, in the same position as in the crime scene photographs. She wasn't moved post-mortem."

Kane pulled the light down and closely examined the mark. He glanced up at Wolfe. "That mark has to be bruising from his knuckles. He punched her in the temple and raped her. This one is up close and personal, not like the others."

"Yeah, a short sharp jab to knock her out then used the ether to keep her subdued." Wolfe covered Sara and turned his attention back to Kane. "He raped her, and then set the scene. Before he left, he gave her enough ether to kill her but she didn't die. I found a fragment of cotton in her hair. It could be from work gloves but I'll need more time to narrow down what brand."

Kane grimaced. "Yeah, and if you do, no doubt all our suspects own work gloves and they're the same as the darn boots – everyone wears the same cheap brand."

"No doubt." Wolfe moved to the next gurney. "Lindy Rosen. See the ligature marks on her neck, how they grazed her chin?"

"Yeah, I've seen that injury before; he hung her over his shoulder." Kane shook his head. "She was disposable."

"This one will interest you." Wolfe moved on to Amanda Braxton. "Killed from behind in a move to snap her neck. Clean and quick."

Kane nodded in agreement. "Yeah, again not as personal as when the killer uses his hands to strangle. In those cases they make the victim suffer; it takes some time to strangle a person." He pulled off his gloves with a snap that sounded loud in the stark room. "He used the first two girls to get Jenna out on her own, but now he's got a taste for killing teenagers. He craves watching their fear but dominates them by raping them." He frowned. "This is an incredible turnaround. Not many killers change MO mid-stride. He's getting the upper hand in his macabre game. If we can't find him soon and his compulsion has changed, he could be miles away by now and we'll never find him."

CHAPTER FIFTY-FIVE

By the time Kane arrived in Jenna's office just after two with takeout from Aunt Betty's Café, she wanted to scream. Sam Cross had found grounds to have all of the suspects released. He'd even accused her of provoking Kittredge to such an extent that he threw the chair out of frustration; then he'd raved on about the interviews until she wanted to pull her hair out by the roots. She leaned back in her chair and stared up at Kane. "Am I glad to see you. Shut the door."

"You look like you need this." Kane placed a to-go cup of coffee in front of her, and then arranged the packages of food on the desk. "Bad morning?"

Jenna sipped the coffee then sighed as the rich hot brew spilled over her tongue. "Oh yeah. The DA did a deal with Matt Miller and he's walked – along with the other potential suspects. I was told to back off until I had something better than circumstantial evidence." She threw one arm up in the air. "Now what?"

"They're still suspects." Kane opened a bag and pulled out a large wedge of apple pie. "If we remove Miller from the equation, we have at least three men with ample opportunity and they were all in the vicinity where the girls went missing."

"Yeah, you're preaching to the converted, Dave, but I didn't win any brownie points from the DA. I figure if he had it his way, he'd have me fired." Jenna opened a bag containing her usual bagel and cream cheese. Tucked inside was a bar of chocolate. She lifted her gaze to him. "You knew?"

"Nope, but I guessed Cross would give you a hard time." Kane smiled at her. "I figure chocolate fixes most things." He attacked the pie with a plastic fork. "Cross might be a brilliant lawyer but you had the notion that Sara Nelson's murder was special to the Shadow Man. Her earrings are missing, Jenna. He kept a trophy."

Excited and filled with a burst of energy, Jenna stared at him. "But none of you found anything unusual at the suspects' homes. No secret hoard of trophies."

"One is married and they've all had recent involvement with women. It's normal to see a few female items left in a single guy's home." Kane took a sip of his coffee. "Most serial killers have a shrine of one kind or another and keep the trophies together, then there's the ones who give them to women they're close to, so they can relive the kill just by seeing the other woman wearing the object."

A tingle of revulsion skittered up Jenna's spine. "But they don't kill their friends, do they? So how do they draw the line?"

"I wish I knew." Kane frowned. "One study says they don't have empathy and yet they must have some feelings. There're some who don't make friends and then there's the man with his wife and six kids who murders prostitutes on the way home from work, washes up and sits down to eat dinner with his family." He shrugged. "Go figure. One thing's for sure, they don't think the way we do and trying to make logical sense of criminal psychopathic behavior is a waste of time."

Jenna considered his words and chewed her food. "You're trained to kill and do it without a second thought. You're not a psychopath and yet I've seen you turn off your emotions as if you have a switch."

"I never killed without a second thought, Jenna." Kane narrowed his gaze at her. "I received my orders, knew the target was a threat to our country, but I never for one moment failed to recognize I was taking a life." He took another drink. "Snipers for special missions are put through vigorous psych training. We get one chance, maybe a window of a few minutes, to hit the target then escape out the country. Imagine how history would've changed and how many millions of lives would've been saved if someone like me had taken out the key instigators of the world wars?" He shrugged. "I've no regrets, I was doing my job." He met her gaze. "Emotions, fear, anxiety have no place in a sniper's world, so we learn to turn them off and drop into a special place where it's ultimate calm. I know you've received the same type of training. I just had to be able to drop into my peaceful zone and endure waterboarding at the same time."

Unable to control the burst of laughter, Jenna covered her mouth and took in his astonished expression. "They really did that to you?"

"Ah-huh." Kane's mouth twitched at the corners. "It wasn't funny at the time."

"I didn't figure it would be." Jenna turned her attention to the whiteboard. "What if we look at the nightmare angle again?"

"Sara was in the drama club." Kane placed his to-go cup on the table and turned to look at the whiteboard. "We did extensive checks on all the teachers these girls shared and they all came up squeaky clean. It's not a teacher. The only people they all met was Mason Lancaster and the three tradesmen who worked at their homes. We've already cleared Lancaster, so he's out the equation." He let out a long sigh. "Problem is, the killer's changing his MO and escalating at an extraordinary rate. I figure I've seen this before and it's disturbing."

Jenna turned to look at him. "How so?"

"Remember Ted Bundy? Good-looking, smooth talker, hung around campuses with a sling on one arm and pretended to have trouble opening his car door to get a girl to help him. Or he'd pretend to be someone in authority to get their trust. He'd kidnap and murder his victims and do things that would make your skin crawl. He never touched his close female friend then one day he went berserk, broke into a sorority house and bludgeoned girls to death with a hunk of wood." He sighed. "Like I said before, they're not normal and we can't outthink them because there's no logical steps to take. In his mind, he's involved in an elaborate game with you, so we'll have to wait until he makes his next move – *if* he has another move. For all we know, he could be over playing games with you. He's changed his MO and might've found a different thrill to satisfy his urges."

"You think? When the DA told me to release the suspects, I wanted to place a tracker on each of their vehicles but when I made the request, he told me I'd have as much chance of getting that approved as waking up as Tinker Bell in the morning." Jenna pushed a hand through her hair, tucking it behind one ear. "Then he told me we can't watch them around the clock because Cross made it quite clear he's just waiting for a chance to make a complaint about police harassment." She sighed. "The name Shadow Man fits this killer well – he's like catching smoke and I've no idea what he's going to do next."

"I do." Kane's mouth turned down. "He's not finished killing yet."

CHAPTER FIFTY-SIX

Stymied, Jenna spent the next couple of hours with Kane going through the murder books, checking and rechecking every angle in each case. She called the mothers of Lindy and Amanda and asked them to recheck their daughters' belongings to make sure nothing was missing. She sent Rowley out to visit each of the homes of the other girls from the drama club to check on the homes' security and offer their parents a warning to be aware the killer was still on the loose.

Jenna glanced up from the files. "Anything?"

"Nope." Kane lifted his gaze from the murder book. "None of them had anything illegal on their computers either. We have zip." He sighed. "Maybe we should—"

The door opened and Wolfe barreled inside, his eyes wild. "I can't find Julie."

"I gave her a ride back here around two." Kane pushed to his feet and went to Wolfe's side. "Have you asked Maggie?"

"Yeah, I called about an hour ago and she said Julie's been going down to the stalls outside the town hall around two each day to buy candy. She hasn't returned yet." Wolfe's large hands clenched and unclenched. "I closed my office and I've been searching with Emily and Webber – we can't find her and her cell has dropped out." His face drained of color. "I can't get an accurate fix on her. Her last location is here. If someone's using a GPS jammer to block the signal, her tracker won't work either. Dammit! No one outside our team knows about the trackers."

"I figure she hasn't been able to activate it yet." Jenna picked up the phone. "Maggie, get a BOLO out on Julie and contact the media. I want her found. Do you remember what she was wearing?"

"Oh, my Lord, yes, I remember." The line went dead.

Heart racing with terror for Julie, Jenna took a beat then moved around her desk. "Kane, coordinate a grid search of town. Is there anywhere she might go? The library?"

"I looked there but she knows the rules – she wouldn't just wander off without telling someone first. Maggie told me she's usually gone about fifteen minutes." Wolfe turned to Kane, his face distraught. "We're wasting our time searching for her in town. I figure the Shadow Man's taken her and we need to know which one of the creeps you dragged in for questioning has taken her."

"Then we'll split up and find the suspects." Jenna walked past the deputies and leaned out the door. "Rowley, grab Walters and head out to the school and see if you can get eyes on Lancaster. He could be in the janitor's office."

"Yes, ma'am, but you've cleared him." Rowley hustled to the office door. "What's happened?"

Jenna lowered her voice. "Julie's gone missing and he could be involved. Get going now."

She turned back into her office to find Wolfe and Kane on their cellphones getting information on the whereabouts of Anderson and Packer. She grabbed her phone to call the Green Thumb Landscaping Service office and soon had Kittredge's location. "Kittredge is at Glacial Heights."

"So is Anderson." Kane looked at her. "Get your vest on, we'll hunt down both of them at the same time."

"Packer is working in the same area too." Wolfe stared into the distance as if thinking. "I just had a thought. One of Julie's paintings is in an exhibition at the town hall. They're holding an art competition and announcing the winner tomorrow. She might have gone inside to take a look at the display." He dashed a hand through his hair. "There's plenty of places inside for someone to grab her and it has a basement."

Fingers shaking from seeing the men's deep concern, Jenna fumbled into her vest, and then pulled her coat over the top. "Then we start there. Use the com packs, we'll need to keep in touch." She headed for the door.

The next moment, Emily and Webber dashed through the front door. Jenna pulled them to one side. "Has anyone seen her?"

"Not since she purchased candy and a drink from a stall outside the town hall." Webber rubbed the back of his neck. "The woman working on the stall said she didn't notice where she went afterward."

"Webber, with me." Wolfe headed toward the door. "Emily, stay here. Don't set a foot outside until I return. Call home and tell Mrs. Mills to make sure your sister remains inside the house." He hurried out the door with Webber on his heels.

Jenna caught the door and ran down the steps. As they climbed into his truck, she glanced up at Kane. "Drive round back of the town hall. If anyone took her from there, they would've gotten her out of one of the fire exits."

"Roger that." Kane hit the gas, reversing out of the parking space, horn blaring. "She's probably in the town hall and lost track of time. If someone attacked her, she'd have hit her tracker. She's smart and I don't figure she'd walk into danger."

Jenna swallowed hard, trying to release the fear clutching at her throat. "What if the Shadow Man carries a GPS jammer?"

"Let's hope not." Kane had slowed and was rolling his truck slowly into the parking lot behind the town hall. He buzzed down his window and looked outside, then hit the mic on his com pack. "Wolfe, I'm out back. You need to see this." He pulled the truck to a halt.

Jenna turned in her seat. "What is it?"

"Evidence. I'll need to take a closer look." Kane slid out the vehicle, then walked some distance away and crouched down.

Jenna leapt from the seat and ran around the hood to see what Kane had found. Moments later Wolfe came thundering through one of the exits with Webber close behind. She arrived beside Kane and stared down at a spilled bag of candy. "Oh, Jesus, that's her favorite candy."

"Don't touch anything." Wolfe was beside him, pulling on gloves. "Look over there." He pointed to an empty paper cup rolling back and forward in the wind. "The contents spilled in an arc, as if she was surprised from behind and swung around, dropping the candy and cup." He collected the bag and cup and dropped them into an evidence bag, then turned his furious gaze on Jenna. "We need to find this SOB now." He glanced at his watch. "She's been missing for almost two hours and it will be dark in less than three."

Jenna forced her voice not to tremble but she had to follow protocol. "Go home and wait for me to call you. You can't be involved in the investigation, Shane."

"Oh no, Jenna. I'm so gonna be involved. That's my baby out there all alone with a maniac. Not you or Kane can stop me searching for her and if that SOB has hurt her, I'm gonna tear him apart with my bare hands." He turned to Kane. "You'll have to shoot me before I'll stand down." He swung around to Jenna. "We're wasting time. I'm gonna find Packer. It has to be him." He headed back into the town hall.

Jenna turned and stared at Kane. "Let's go."

"You drive." Kane started back to his truck. "I have the suspects' cellphone numbers and I'll try and get a fix on them. If he's using a jammer, we won't be able to track his cell."

"That's illegal." Jenna climbed behind the wheel, started the engine and headed the beast out of the parking lot.

"So is kidnapping."

CHAPTER FIFTY-SEVEN

Jenna took the entrance to the ranch where Kittredge was working and pulled up beside a Green Thumb Landscaping truck. "That might be his truck. I've no idea how many of the men working here have one."

"The GPS on his cellphone is blocked." Kane glanced up at her. "Anderson and Packer are in Glacial Heights. I guess after we hauled him in for questioning, Kittredge might have disabled the feature on his phone. Big Brother is watching and all that."

As she opened the door, Jenna's cellphone chimed in her pocket. "It's Rowley."

"Lancaster isn't here. I've spoken to the guys replacing some of the seats in the football field stands. They said he gave them orders then left."

"Dammit." Jenna looked at Kane and shook her head. "Okay, go check his residence. If he isn't there, head back to the office and wait for orders. If anything comes in on the BOLO, call me."

"Roger that."

"Can I help you, Sheriff?" A woman, late twenties, with a mass of curly brown hair, wearing jeans and a leather jacket, walked out of the trees and headed toward her.

Jenna turned and smiled at her. "Yes, I noticed you've the Green Thumb Landscaping Service here today. Would you happen to know if Paul Kittredge's team is here?"

"Paul, yeah, he's working on the other side of these trees." She waved a hand behind her. "I'm having the clearing made into a secret garden for my girls."

Stomach tightening at the thought of Kittredge working near kids, she forced a smile. "Has he been here all day?"

"All day?" The woman frowned. "Yeah, apart from leaving around two to pick up some turf."

The hairs on the back of Jenna's neck prickled. "When did he get back?"

"Just before the men unloaded the turf into wheelbarrows and took it down the path."

"Ah, good." Jenna fixed the smile to her face. "Do you mind if we have a word with him?"

"Go right ahead." The woman walked past them and hurried up the front steps to her house.

"Hold up, Jenna." Kane indicated to Kittredge's truck with his thumb. "Windows are open. I'll take a look inside." He pulled on gloves and raised one eyebrow. "If this is a problem, just look away. I won't take long."

Unease filled Jenna as she stared down the pathway in the direction the woman had come. Kittredge could be the Shadow Man. Her earbud crackled. It was Wolfe and she pressed her mic. "Rowley is chasing down Lancaster. He was a no-show at work. Have you found Packer?"

"Packer's not our man, he's been working here since seven this morning, and he hasn't left the premises. He brings his lunch pail from home."

She brought him up to date with Kittredge. "He's a possible but there's a ton load of places between here and town he could've stashed Julie."

"I want someone watching Kittredge." Wolfe's voice had dropped to a growl. *"He'll have to go back to her. Has he sent any messages?"*

"Not yet." Jenna heard the gravel crunch behind her as Kane moved to her side. "I'll get Rowley to sit down the road in his pickup, he'll follow him."

"Too risky. Can you get near his vehicle?"

Jenna could see Kane was listening through his earbud. "Yeah, and we can get inside, the window's open."

"Kane, activate your tracker and hide it inside the cab. Do it now and I'll see if he's using a GPS jammer in his vehicle."

"Roger that." Kane jogged back to the vehicle.

Jenna watched as he unclipped his tracker button and pushed it under the driver's seat of Kittredge's vehicle, then closed the door without a sound and gave her a nod. She pressed her mic. "It's done."

"It's working fine." Wolfe sounded stressed to the max. *"We're going to do a drive-by of Anderson's house. I'll ask the neighbors if he's been home anytime today. I doubt Kittredge would risk taking Julie to his room at the Triple Z."*

"Roger that." Jenna looked at Kane. "Let's go. You drive." She turned to the truck when she heard a familiar voice.

"I'm gonna have to get me one of those orders of protection against you, Sheriff." Kittredge stood, hands on hips, eyeing her with disgust. "It's not been more than a few hours and here you are in my face again." He waved his cellphone at her. "I figure I'll give Sam Cross a call."

Jenna spun around to glare at him. "Go crawl back into your hole, Kittredge. I wouldn't waste a second of my time on you." She climbed into Kane's truck and looked at his astonished expression. "Drive."

"Where to?" Kane headed down the long tree-lined driveway.

"The Rosens'. Anderson is back there working today, installing panic buttons." She gave Kane a sideways glance. "I'm not sure I'd be happy having Anderson back after what happened to Lindy."

"He wasn't charged, so he's innocent until proven guilty. I figured it was Kittredge until Lancaster went missing. We might be wasting our time here." Kane accelerated along the winding road, made a left then drove the two hundred yards to the Rosens' ornate gate. "That's new."

As they slowed to pass a group of men using a post-hole digger, Jenna looked back at Kane. "I figure that's an electric fence going up. No doubt they'll have a camera fitted on the gate later."

Jenna's cellphone rang. It was Rowley. "Did you locate Lancaster?"

"Nope. I asked the neighbors, they haven't seen him. It looks like he's left."

Jenna bit her bottom lip. "Okay, check at the car detailers and Aunt Betty's, see if anyone's seen him."

"Roger that." Rowley disconnected.

She looked at Kane. "I hope we didn't let the killer go free."

"So do I." Kane grimaced.

When they reached the Rosens' home, Anderson's truck was nowhere in sight. "This doesn't look good." She slipped out of the passenger seat and hurried up the front steps.

Jenna knocked on the front door. Mrs. Rosen, looking pale and shattered, opened the door and stared at them blankly.

"Yes? Have you found the animal who murdered Lindy?"

"No, I'm sorry, not yet." Jenna swallowed hard. She could see the woman's pain. "Do you mind if I ask you a question?"

"More questions? You had me going through Lindy's things again and now you want more information? Why aren't you out searching for her killer?"

"We're doing everything possible but we still need your help." Jenna looked into the woman's red-rimmed eyes. "This is why we're here. Can you tell me if any of the technicians from Silent Alarms have been by today?"

"They have. A couple of them stopped by and Charlie has been here since around midday, I guess. He's been back and forth all afternoon."

Jenna exchanged a long look with Kane. "Can you be more specific?"

"He went into town to buy lunch and pick up some parts. Came back around three and then left about a half-hour ago." Mrs. Rosen blinked as if trying to understand. "Why? He isn't a suspect, is he?"

Jenna shook her head. She hated lying to the woman but if Anderson was involved, she might be placing her in danger. "We don't have any suspects but we're keeping track of people who knew Lindy."

"I've nothing else to tell you." Mrs. Rosen shut the door in Jenna's face.

"Poor woman." Kane turned to leave and indicated to the driveway. "Well, I'll be darned."

Jenna spun around as Charlie Anderson's pickup pulled up beside Kane's truck. She lowered her voice to just above a whisper. "Now what? Can you sneak my tracker into his pickup?" She pulled it from her buttonhole and passed it to him.

"That's the plan." Kane smiled at her. "Distract him, and I'll drop it somewhere. Leave your mic on so I'll hear what he's saying." He headed back to his truck.

"Done." Jenna lingered at the bottom of the steps, pretending to look at her notes.

"Well, fancy seeing you here, Sheriff." Anderson climbed out his pickup, carrying a cardboard carton. "Checking up on me?"

The challenging way he looked at her sent a shiver down her back. "No, Mr. Anderson that would be police harassment. I came by to speak to Mrs. Rosen." She noticed Kane emerging from around his truck and offered Anderson a smile. "I see you're beefing up the security around here."

"Can't get too much security. Maybe you should call out Silent Alarms to secure your ranch. Out there in the middle of nowhere, you'd need a reliable alarm system." Anderson's gaze moved over her face. "We don't want you going missing in the middle of the night, now, do we?"

A cold sweat beaded on her flesh as she took in his satisfied smile. It was as if he was taunting her. "I'll be sure to look into it." She noticed Kane edging toward Anderson's truck and pressed on. "How long does it take to install a complete system?"

"It depends what level of security you need." Anderson inclined his head. "Are you all alone out there?"

Jenna frowned, waiting a beat as if considering his question to delay him a little longer. "Yeah, I live alone so I guess I'll need the works."

"No dogs?" Anderson lowered his voice. "I figured you and Deputy Kane lived together. I see you heading off home with him most nights."

Most nights? Has he been watching me? "No dogs and Kane has his own place." She could see Kane in her periphery, sliding behind the wheel of his own truck. "I'll give Silent Alarms a call on Monday and get a quote."

"Mention my name. It's good for a discount. Look, I've gotta go." He winked at her. "Mrs. Rosen expects me to have this installed before I leave for the day." He headed up the front steps and knocked on the door.

Shaken, Jenna headed to Kane's truck and climbed into the passenger seat. "Is he using a GPS jammer?"

"Nope." Kane was staring at an app on his cellphone.

Jenna moved her attention away from the screen and back to the house. "He's been watching us."

"Yeah, I heard." Kane's mouth turned down and he shook his head. "Creepy guy but that doesn't make him a killer."

Unease crept over her as she glanced back at the house. "I guess not but I'm suspicious of everyone right now."

"Why Anderson? He didn't threaten you." Kane frowned at her. "I figured that was the salesman in him. Maybe he tried to make you uneasy so you'd buy something."

"Oh, I don't know, something's not right about him." Jenna's cellphone buzzed a message. She glanced down at the caller ID and panic shot through her at the sight of a private number.

Heart pounding, she stared at the house as the door opened and Anderson slipped inside. It couldn't be him; too many pieces would have to fall into place. For instance, if he was the killer, how did he know she'd be at the Rosens' at that precise moment to schedule a call? Then again, if he'd made sure to be in plain sight of Mrs. Rosen at the time the message went through, she'd make the perfect alibi for him. It all came down to reasonable doubt. Did he have access to a burner cellphone with call scheduling? If they couldn't prove it and Mrs. Rosen didn't witness him using a cellphone at that time, the DA wouldn't issue an arrest warrant because the moment he went up against Cross in court, that simple fact would be used to cast reasonable doubt on his guilt. She had three dead girls, Julie was missing and their suspect list had shrunk away to nothing. She wanted to break down and cry but she bit back a sob and turned to look at Kane. "It's another message from the Shadow Man."

Unable to stop shaking, she opened the message. "It has an attachment."

"Show me." Kane leaned his head toward her. "Message first."

Now you've made me mad and when I get mad, I get even.
You've broken the rules, so now there are no rules.
Maybe this one will count more. You have an attachment to her, don't you?
We'll meet real soon, Jenna. I'm so going to enjoy watching you die.
The oxygen lasts 3 hours.
Tick tock, tick tock.

Terror gripped Jenna as she opened the video file attachment. She couldn't breathe. "Oh, my God, he's buried Julie alive."

CHAPTER FIFTY-EIGHT

So cold. Icy tendrils seeped through Julie's clothes and her teeth chattered. A strange damp smell surrounded her as she tried to drag herself awake. Her head throbbed and her tongue stuck to the roof of her mouth. Dazed and disorientated, she forced her heavy eyelids to open. Darkness surrounded her, in deep shadows. The memory of a strong arm around her and the smelly rag pressed to her face slammed into her. She tried to sit and struck her head. *Where am I?* With trembling fingers, she found rough boards surrounded her and panic tightened her chest making it hard to breathe. *I'm inside a wooden box.*

She lifted her legs and tried to kick at the lid. Dust spilled into her eyes but the lid didn't move. Terrified, she searched the front of her shirt, found her teddy bear brooch and pressed it hard. Her dad would come and find her. Sobbing, she counted, knowing it would take a few minutes before the tracker alerted him. His voice seemed to drift inside her head. So many times, he'd repeated the instructions since her sister Emily had come close to being murdered.

"*Stay calm, use the tracker. Count to two hundred then give me as many details as possible. If you know the person who has you, speak their name. If you know where you are, tell me. I can hear a whisper but if it's too dangerous, say nothing. I'll come find you.*"

He'd want details. She stretched her arms out both ways, then above her, trying to estimate the size of the box. She found a thin plastic pipe and could feel air blowing through the end. Why had the man supplied her with air if he wanted her dead? She shuffled down and her feet touched the end of the box. Something hung down from the lid. When she touched it with her shoe, the glow from the screen of a cellphone filled the small interior. The small light stilled her sobbing. "D-Daddy, c-can you hear me? I'm locked inside a box."

CHAPTER FIFTY-NINE

Wolfe's cellphone screamed out the emergency ringtone he'd assigned to his daughters' trackers. He slammed on the brakes, sliding his SUV to a shuddering halt at the side of Stanton Road. Grabbing up the cellphone, he activated the app and heaved in a deep breath at the sign of a red beep coming from the other side of town. He placed the cellphone in the holder on the dash and slammed his foot on the gas, then turned to Webber. "Contact Kane, tell him Julie has activated her tracker, she's out near Gold-mine Road." He pulled out his earbud. "I need to listen in case she contacts me."

"Roger that." Webber made the call then turned to him. "The Shadow Man just contacted the sheriff. He's buried Julie alive. Says you have three hours before the oxygen runs out."

Wolfe slid his medical examiner's SUV around a sharp right turn and accelerated until the engine screamed in protest. "I'm heading for the search and rescue headquarters. It will be dark soon and we'll need a chopper with a thermal imaging camera. Tell Kane and Jenna to meet me in Stanton Road. I'll pick them up there. Then call search and rescue. Tell them to ready the chopper, police emergency."

His heart thumped so hard he thought it might burst through his ribs at the sound of Julie's sobs. He wanted to comfort her and tell her he would be there soon, but using a two-way com in the tracker would alert the Shadow Man to the tracker's existence. "Talk to me, Julie, tell me everything you know."

As if she'd heard him, her wavering voice, broken with sobs, came through the speaker.

"I figure I'm underground because if I push on the lid dust comes down. A man, I didn't see him but he wasn't as big as you. He was medium-sized. He grabbed me from behind and put something over my face. It smelled strange and made my face feel cold. I woke up just before. The box is not small like a coffin but square. I can stretch out. I found a cellphone at the end of the box. It lit up when I kicked it. I'll try and reach it." Julie was breathing heavily. *"I'm trying to get my shoes off. I'll try and snag it with my toes."*

Wolfe gripped the steering wheel and, with lights flashing and siren blaring, weaved his way through the traffic heading into town. He could hear Julie panting and wished she'd stop moving and conserve oxygen. He turned to Webber. "As soon as we get there, grab the rifles and spare ammo. We're going in packing for bear. If the SOB is anywhere close by, I'm taking him down."

"Yes, sir."

"Daddy." Julie sounded exhausted. *"I have the cellphone, it was recording a video. I turned that off."* She let out a distressed sob. *"I can't remember your number."*

Wolfe turned into the parking lot of the Fire and Rescue. He grabbed up his cellphone, wishing she could hear him. "Dial 911. Come on, Julie. Dial 911." He shot a desperate glance at Webber. "Call Rowley, tell him to patch the call through to Jenna if Julie calls."

"Roger that." Webber slid from the vehicle and made the call.

Wolfe fitted his earbud. "Jenna, Julie has found a cellphone. I figure the Shadow Man used it to send you the video. I'll need to keep my cellphone for the tracker so if she calls 911, Rowley will patch her through to you. Tell her to lie still and try not to talk much unless she hears a chopper. She needs to conserve oxygen." He climbed out the door and took the rifle Webber handed him.

"Roger that. We're waiting on Stanton Road south of Glacial Heights. The road is wider here."

As they jogged to the chopper, buffeted by the wind from the spinning blades, the pilot slipped from the seat and waved them forward. Wolfe gave him a nod and climbed inside, dropping his rifle on the back seat. Webber was just standing there staring at him. He wanted to grab him by his shirtfront and drag him inside. "What are you waiting for?"

"Do you have a license to fly that thing?" Webber's face had drained of color.

Wolfe pulled on the headset and stared at him. "Yeah, I flew a MEDIVAC in the marines and I'm leaving in two seconds."

"Okay." Webber climbed into the back and stowed the rifles under the seat.

The chopper lifted into the air, drowning out anything Julie was saying, but it didn't matter if Wolfe could hear her or not, her terrified sobs would remain in his head forever. He had to find her. Then he'd make it his business to get up and personal with the Shadow Man.

CHAPTER SIXTY

Kane pulled his duffel out the back of his truck, assembled his rifle and slung it over one shoulder, then walked to Jenna's side. "He won't have an exact lock on her signal and if she's too deep we won't pick up thermal imaging." He sighed. "If he's set any IEDs we'll have difficulty spotting them in the dark. He's thought this one through and made it as difficult as possible. I figure he's had these murders planned for some time and all he needed was the girls to make it work."

When Jenna's cellphone buzzed, she gave a triumphant squeal. "It's Rowley. He's patching her through now."

Kane pressed his mic. "Wolfe, Jenna is speaking to Julie now."

"Thank God. I'm close. You should be able to hear me by now."

The sound of chopper blades cutting through the air came in a whoosh of air swirling the tops of the pines in Stanton Forest. Moments later, Kane and Jenna ran toward the chopper and jumped inside. Kane strapped in beside Wolfe and fitted his headphones. "If she's buried we may have trouble picking up a reading. More so if she's cold." He glanced at Wolfe's chiseled expression. "We don't know how long she's been down there."

"We've narrowed it down to two suspects: Kittredge and Anderson. So far neither of them have moved, so it has to be someone else. Someone has slipped under the radar. Think about it – we know a number of men worked on the security systems around Glacial Heights and if Anderson has come up clean it has to be one of them." Wolfe lifted the chopper high above the trees and headed out to the mines. "I've figured out how he lured the girls from the house." Wolfe's eyes narrowed to slits. "He used a wireless projector."

Unable to follow, Kane stared at him. "What do you mean, you know how he did it?"

"All this talk of girls having nightmares about a man in their room." Wolfe shook his head. "I should have thought of it before." He glanced at Kane. "He hid a projector in the floodlights outside the girls' windows and projected an image into their bedrooms to make it look like a ghost." He sighed. "I'll dismantle the systems myself and check, but I know I'm right. The parents searched the girls' rooms each time and found nothing. By the fifth or so time they wouldn't search as diligently, I figure he was already in Lindy's room."

"Why alert the parents by scaring the girls in the first place?" Kane frowned. "Seems to me they'd be wide awake."

"You obviously never had kids." Wolfe gave him a condescending stare. "Trust me, after being woken five nights in a row, they'd sleep like the dead and would more than likely ignore their daughter."

Kane let this process through his mind. "How'd he get past the security system?"

"Really?" Wolfe gave a bark of disbelief. "How would you bypass a security system? I'm sure you've done it a thousand times."

"Yeah, but I have a device." Kane swallowed hard. "He couldn't have one, they're only supplied to the military."

"How do you figure a technician resets a system when a customer forgets their code?" Wolfe snorted in disgust. "I've been such an idiot. I figure he wouldn't have the same device as yours but he'd have a way of remotely rebooting the system. Once inside, he'd use an override code. Any of the security guards would have access to all the homes in Glacial Heights, so why single out Anderson?"

"Anderson was the last person to work on the system but I have to admit, his record is spotless and he has an alibi for both nights. He was in custody when we found out about Sara. Any of the security guards working for the same company would have access to the homes in Glacial Heights protected by Silent Alarms." Kane cleared his throat. "Who the hell did we miss?"

Wolfe glanced at the beep on his cellphone. "We're close now. See anything? I'll drop lower."

Kane watched the screen on the thermal imaging camera. He could see animals bounding away, frightened by the chopper noise – then he picked up a small glow. "There, on Goldmine Road, two hundred yards straight ahead." He zoomed in with the camera. "She's in an old mine shaft." He turned to look at Wolfe. "Use the spotlight to scan the area. We could be walking into a trap."

As Wolfe flew the chopper back and forth in a grid pattern, Jenna and Webber stared out the windows, searching for any signs of disturbance. If the Shadow Man had rigged a trap in this desolate spot, it would have to be an IED. Kane pressed his com and spoke to everyone. "Listen up. This man is experienced in killing – watch your step, don't wander off, and stay together. Don't step on any disturbed ground. Don't move anything and look for tripwires."

When Wolfe landed the chopper, they all slid out, collected their weapons and moved slowly toward the mine entrance, using their flashlights to scan the ground. Kane could hear Wolfe speaking to his daughter, telling her they were close by and needed to be quiet for a few moments so they could search the area. In the twilight, the grasslands appeared gray and stark. Silence surrounded them and even the cold breeze rustling through the long grass seemed magnified to Kane's heightened senses. With the time ticking by, Kane dropped into his zone. He needed to use every one of his talents to keep them safe. They moved like a line of ants, stepping in each other's footprints toward the mine entrance. Kane held up his hand to stop and secured the entrance. A few feet inside the mine, he made out a large packing crate, covered with a thin layer of dirt and leaves. He waved Wolfe forward. "She'll be in there."

"I'm here, Julie." Wolfe spoke into the cellphone, and then stared at Kane. "See any traps?"

"It looks okay but we don't know what's under the lid." Kane took the cellphone from Wolfe. "Julie, use the light on the phone to look around. Can you see any wires or canisters inside the box?"

"N-no." Julie's voice was almost a whisper. "Just a tube with air coming out."

"Yeah, I can see the oxygen cylinder. Hold tight, we're getting you out now." Kane handed the phone back to Wolfe and used his flashlight to search every inch of the surrounds. "We're good to go."

Kane dropped down into the hole with Wolfe close behind. A vibration under his feet was the only warning. He grabbed Wolfe's arm and dragged him to one side as the world went to hell. A plume of dirt shot into the air as an explosion rocked the silence. As earth and rocks slid down the hillside above them, Kane raised his voice over the rumbling. "Flip the locks. We have to get her out before we're buried alive."

They heaved open the lid as soil, rocks and debris poured over them like a gravel waterfall. Kane used one shoulder to wedge open the crate as Wolfe reached inside. "Hurry, man, she's barely conscious."

"It's okay." Wolfe scooped Julie into his arms "I've got you." He pulled her lolling head tight against his chest.

Kane ducked a shower of boulders, and then dropped the lid. "Go, go, go!" He shoved Wolfe hard in the back, pushing him up the side of the shaft.

He blinked through dust and saw Webber grab Wolfe and pull him to safety. More rumbling, then a ripping sound filled the tunnel. He scrambled up the rock face then strong hands grabbed his arms and wrenched him the rest of the way.

"Run." Webber's voice seemed a mile away.

Kane ran blindly, eyes filled with dust.

"Kane, it's okay, we're out of danger." Jenna was beside him. She pulled on his arm. "Stop and I'll get the dirt out your eyes." She brushed at his head. "Sit down."

Cold water splashed down his face and he blinked as Jenna's face came into focus. "Thanks." He took the bottle of water from her and took a long drink. "Is Julie okay?"

"She looks shattered but she's wide awake now." Jenna's voice had lowered to just above a whisper then she raised it to speak to Wolfe. "Wolfe, is she okay?"

"Yeah, I think so." Wolfe looked into Julie's eyes. "Did he hurt you?" He dropped Julie to her feet, and then cupped her tear-stained face in one large hand.

"Apart from d-drugging me and b-burying me alive?" Julie gave him an incredulous look and coughed. "No, he didn't r-rape me or anything. I'm fine, D-Dad, but I'm so c-cold and thirsty."

"You're a survivor and I'm proud of you for being so strong." Wolfe ripped off his jacket, wrapped it around her, and then pulled her close again. He stared over her head at Kane, his eyes wild. "No one gets away with hurting my girls. Now we turn the tables on him. This time we're going to lure *him* into a trap."

"How so?" Jenna moved to his side and offered Julie a bottle of water.

"We don't let anyone know we've found Julie. So far he's covered his tracks and left no evidence." Wolfe's face was a mask of controlled rage. "Everything we have is circumstantial at best. We'll need to make him reveal himself by using his own technology against him." He turned to Kane and his lips curled in a sadistic smile. "This SOB didn't figure on me joining the game."

CHAPTER SIXTY-ONE

He'd decided not to go home and be alone. Having no alibi was, after all, a trap for the inexperienced. He had all the creature comforts in Aunt Betty's Café and he'd linger here for as long as it took to make sure they remembered him. He'd ordered a thick steak with all the trimmings and set himself down with a good view of the TV. It amused him to watch the local law enforcement running around chasing their tails, but he didn't have to step onto the sidewalk to find out what was happening. The media were all over his murders and reported every move the sheriff made. The sexy newsreader called him the Shadow Man and it fitted him well. The darkness and shadowy places always made the killing so much better. The fear in his victims' eyes when they realized he'd planned to kill them and the soft moans as they gasped their last breath regenerated him. It was as if their life force filled him with energy. *It must be what happiness feels like.*

A breaking-news banner flashed on the screen, catching his attention. He stared at the TV with interest. *Have they found Julie?*

The blonde newsreader was waving a microphone in front of the sheriff's face. The sheriff looked dusty and had dark circles under her eyes.

"Sheriff Alton, you look dead on your feet. Can you give me an update on the Shadow Man Case?"

"The Shadow Man is a name you've used." Alton frowned. "The name romanticizes the seriousness of the crimes of an ignorant coward who believes killing young girls is a game."

Unperturbed, the interviewer pressed on. "We understand Julie Wolfe has gone missing. What are you doing to find her?"

"We've had volunteers assisting us all afternoon. The search and rescue helicopter is out, plus we've ground teams in action." Alton stared into the camera. "We've deputies from other towns on their way to assist and with their help we'll be working around the clock in teams to keep the command post open. The search will not stop because it's dark, nor will the investigation into this brutal killer."

"Have you stepped up the investigation since the medical examiner's daughter became a victim?" The interviewer's eyes flashed as if in private triumph. "It looks like all hands on deck right now."

"We've been following the same procedure since Lindy Rosen went missing." Alton waved a deputy forward. "As I said, as none of us have gotten a break since Monday, we need help. My team will be splitting up and working in shifts with the other deputies." She motioned to the deputy. "This is Deputy Kane and his team will be taking over now. I'll be back around ten to relieve him, and so on." She cleared her throat. "You can be assured a Black Rock Falls deputy will be on duty all night directing the search for Julie and leading the investigation to catch the murderer of Lindy, Amanda and Sara."

As the interview wound up, his anger simmered just below the surface. *She called me a coward.* He cut a slice of bloody steak, pushed it between his lips and chewed slowly. There was nothing cowardly in walking into a house and taking a girl from her bed with her parents sleeping in the next room, or abducting one off the street where anyone could've seen him. Like most women of her type, the sheriff figured she was above men. Heck, he'd given her a chance and if she'd found Julie, he might've walked away. Maybe he could've waited a few months, acting the innocent, and then started up again in another town, but now she'd gone and made it personal. He stared at the image of Sheriff Alton on the TV screen. *Oh, I'm so going to enjoy killing you.*

CHAPTER SIXTY-TWO

Jenna waited in her office until four deputies from Blackwater arrived. Not long after, Kane and Wolfe left the sheriff's department, roaring through town with lights flashing and sirens blaring. She glanced at her watch; Walters had recovered and would arrive in a few minutes and she could leave. She leaned back in her seat. In the time since they'd rescued Julie, Wolfe had taken his daughter to the ER for an examination. She'd come through her ordeal amazingly unscathed but Jenna had first-hand experience of how easily PTSD could creep up on a person. No doubt, Wolfe would be keeping a close eye on her.

"Evening, Sheriff." Walters' gray head poked around her office door. "Glad to see young Julie home safe and well."

Jenna pushed to her feet. She'd been ready to leave for the last hour. "So am I but don't tell anyone, will you? Thanks for coming in on such short notice."

"No worries, ma'am." Walters moved to one side to allow her to pass. "Like me to walk you out to your vehicle?"

Jenna shook her head. "I figure I'll be safe enough with a news crew parked outside. I'll be back soon." She hurried out the door, ignored the questions from the press and slid into her cruiser.

The drive home seemed darker and more ominous than usual and her heart pounded in her chest as she drove through the gate into her ranch. Coming home alone with a lunatic on the loose wasn't her idea of fun. The security system recognized the device in her vehicle and by the time she reached the house the place was flooded with light. She slid out from behind the wheel when she heard a sound. Spinning around, weapon drawn, she aimed in the direction of Kane's cottage. A dark flash bounded out of the shadows and an excited yelp broke the silence. Jenna laughed as Duke almost knocked her over. He jumped around her, his backside wagging and tail whipping the air. She holstered her weapon, then bent and scratched his ears. "Is this your happy dance?" She straightened and headed for the steps. "You should be asleep by now. Come on, I'll find you a snack." *Well, Kane hasn't been here. He'd have locked him in the cottage.*

Once inside, she reactivated the alarm, removed her coat and weapon belt, and then placed her Glock on the nightstand in her room. She glanced down at the ring containing her spare tracker resting beside her weapon and slid it on before heading into the kitchen. She filled Duke's bowl although Kane had a doggy feeder in the cottage and Duke never went without. After filling the coffee maker, she headed for the shower but couldn't push the idea from her mind that a killer could be watching the house. Sure, Wolfe had grandiose plans to catch the killer and get evidence against him in one sting but keeping her out of the loop was unforgivable. Kane's insistence that she trust him and act natural wasn't helping her nerves either. She flipped the lock on the bathroom door and took a shower.

Dressed in a bathrobe and slippers, she headed back to the kitchen. "Where are you, Duke?"

She heard a whine, then loud barking. It was coming from behind the laundry door. She frowned. How had Duke gotten stuck in there? She took a few steps toward the door – and caught sight of a movement in her periphery.

"Nice to see you again, Sheriff."

Every hair on her body stood to attention as she spun around and took in the grinning face of Charlie Anderson. *I knew it was you.*

Dressed in coveralls with a woolen cap pulled down over his hair, her attention shifted to the pistol gripped in his gloved palm. She clasped her hands before her and pressed the stone in the ring to activate the tracker and one-way connection to Kane's cellphone. "Mr. Anderson, why are you pointing a weapon at me?"

"Because tonight is a good time for you to die." He glanced at the laundry door. "But I'll put a bullet in the mutt first if you don't shut him up."

Jenna glanced toward the door then raised her voice. "Lie down, Duke. Lie down." The barking eased to a whine and she could see the dog's nose pushed hard against the crack at the bottom of the door.

"You told me you didn't own a dog." Anderson waved the gun at her but his index finger was above the trigger.

Jenna buttoned the front of her bathrobe to the neck and tightened the cord around her waist. "He belongs to Kane." She frowned. "How did you get past my security?"

"It was a little more complicated than I'd imagined but no security system is safe." He shrugged. "Didn't I tell you to upgrade?"

How did he breach a military-installed system? "I didn't have time to arrange an upgrade this afternoon and now it's too late." Jenna sighed. "Why do you want to kill me so bad, Mr. Anderson – or should I call you Charlie?"

"Man, you're the dumbest women I've ever met." Anderson shook his head, his face holding an incredulous expression. "You spend your days ordering men around and can't figure out a simple game. Hell, woman, I gave you enough clues."

As Kane's insistence to trust him filtered through the shock of knowing she'd been right about Anderson, she didn't break eye contact and shifted her position to place the kitchen table between them. Not that a table could prevent instant death if he decided to fire at close range, but after seeing images of the other women he'd killed, a bullet would be way too fast to satisfy his needs. She shrugged nonchalantly. "What game are you talking about?"

"The game where I gave you a certain time to find a girl before I killed her." Anderson narrowed his gaze at her. "Come on now, I know you figured out it was me but you couldn't prove it, could you? Now here you are, alone with me, and all your men are out searching for Julie. When you go missing they'll say, 'How did he abduct the sheriff, he left no evidence.' He chuckled. "I had it all planned. They'll never find your body."

Trying to recall everything Kane had mentioned in his profile of the Shadow Man, Jenna pushed down her rising terror. Allowing Anderson to see her fear would give him a high and he'd escalate. *Agree with him and praise him.* She nodded and tried to keep her bottom lip from trembling. "Yeah, you sure outsmarted me. I guess you're behind the nightmares the girls are having in Glacial Heights. Is that how you lured Lindy and Amanda out of their homes?"

"I didn't lure Lindy out of her home. I projected a holographic image of the Grim Reaper into her bedroom, same as the others. Over time, the parents grew weary of their kids' complaints and stopped checking their rooms. You should have been there. I hid in the shadows and when Lindy ran out to call her dad, I slipped behind the drapes. He was so pissed he didn't as much as look my way. I heard his door shut then sedated Lindy and carried her outside." He grinned. "You know the rest, I sent you the pictures."

Jenna feigned interest. "You're good. How did you slip away from work without anyone noticing? The manager checked the footage and confirmed you were there all night both times."

"I created a film of me in the office and fed it through the machine in a loop." Anderson snapped his fingers. "Just like that, I had everyone fooled."

Hoping Kane would come crashing through the door anytime soon, Jenna steeled herself and tried to portray an image of a woman resigned to her fate. "I'd have never figured that out but Amanda was different to the others – she didn't have nightmares, she welcomed the ghost of her grandma."

"She was easy, I snapped a copy of her grandma's photo in the family room and Amanda followed the projected image out the bedroom. I swiveled the projector and placed the hologram at the edge of the woods on the path. She walked straight to me, it was pure genius."

"So was the IED. You almost killed me." Jenna moved so her back was against the counter, the bubbling coffee pot within reach. "That takes skill setting up and you did it in a few hours."

"I had that baby set up for days." Anderson chuckled. "All I had to do was dump the body, and then attach the tripwire." He dropped the hand holding the weapon to his side as if his bragging had overtaken his common sense. "The tree and spear took longer. I took one hell of a chance there using a pulley but I did take it from a packet I'd purchased at Walmart. I bet Sara sailed right up there. Did you hear her neck break?"

A wave of nausea rushed over Jenna at the memory and she swallowed hard. "Yeah, it was quite... er, spectacular." She glanced at her ring, hoping Kane was getting all the proof they needed to arrest this animal, and then looked back at him. "Why did you leave the shawl and other items belonging to Christine Pullman and Joy Coran? Did you kill them as well?"

"Oh, boy – really? They're nothing. I've another twenty-five bodies out there." Anderson moved closer and placed his gun on the table, leaned on both hands and stared at her. "I wanted to show you who you're dealing with and make the game of catching me more exciting – but you failed miserably. You're a failure, a useless piece of shit." He snorted. "Those girls were a distraction, is all, but I still couldn't get to you. I mean, what normal woman has a deputy living in their yard?" He gave her a long look. "Frightened yet? No? Well, you soon will be." He pulled zip-ties out of his pocket and dangled them in front of her. "Turn around."

"I don't think so." Heart thumping, Jenna tried to keep her eyes on Anderson as Kane, and Wolfe slid silently into the room behind him.

She glanced down at Anderson's gun. Did her deputies know he had a weapon? On a rush of adrenaline, she grabbed the coffee pot and swung it at Anderson's face, spilling the coffee in a steaming stream. When he screamed and turned away, Wolfe hit him with a right cross that dropped him to the floor. Jenna snatched up the weapon, dropped out the clip and tossed it into the sink.

"Get up, you sack of shit." Kane grabbed Anderson by the shirtfront and lifted him to his feet as if he weighed nothing and shoved him against the wall. "You have the right to remain silent." He continued to read him his rights. "Do you understand your rights, Mr. Anderson?"

"Yeah. Oh God, it hurts so bad. I'm burned, call 911." Tears from a swelling black eye spilled down Anderson's red cheeks. "You have a duty of care."

Jenna shrugged. "Yeah, I'll be sure to get to that, later."

"Dammit." Wolfe walked to Jenna's refrigerator, pulled an ice bag from the freezer and shoved it at him. "Duty of care satisfied and that's more kindness than you offered your victims." He turned to Jenna. "Maybe we should forget taking him in and bury him alive. No one would know."

Jenna smiled at Anderson's terrified expression. "I'd love to but I figure he's going to be buried in prison." She bent to look into Anderson's eyes. "Game over."

EPILOGUE

Saturday

"Hey, sleepyhead." Kane's voice penetrated Jenna's dreams. She dragged herself away from the sun-drenched beach and sparkling ocean to open her eyes. The aroma of freshly brewed coffee curled around her nose and she looked up at Kane's smiling face. He was dressed casual in blue jeans and a black sweater. "I figured you wouldn't want to sleep through the visit to the art show."

Jenna pushed her hair from her eyes. It had taken hours to process Anderson, have him formally charged, do the paperwork then have him shipped off to the county jail. She'd fallen into bed around 4 a.m. "What time is it?"

"Almost noon." Kane placed two cups of coffee on the bedside table and sat on the edge of her bed. "I've removed all the recording devices from the house. We'd set them up in just about every room."

"So I didn't need my tracker?" Jenna sat up and reached for her cup. "You should've told me."

"Nah, it was better you didn't know. For a while there you believed you were alone and it showed." Kane shook his head at her. "You should've cleared the rooms when you arrived home. You knew Anderson was out to get you. He could've been inside already."

Jenna sipped the hot brew, and then shook her head. "No need, I had Duke with me." She stroked the head of the bloodhound, who was resting his chin close to her hand. The dog hadn't left her side all night.

"Yeah, he nearly gave the game away. If you'd looked before you took a shower, you'd have found us hiding in the spare bedroom. I knew you'd use the tracker, so I turned off my cellphone." He chuckled. "We could see Anderson heading down the driveway and I had to sneak out and lock Duke in the laundry. It was closer than you think."

Jenna smiled at him and squeezed his arm. "I knew you wouldn't put me in danger but when he came in with a weapon aimed at my head, I did have second thoughts." She bit her bottom lip. "How did he get through my security? The front and back doors don't even use keys anymore. Without the code, there's no way he should've been able to get inside."

"Wolfe." Kane shrugged. "He disconnected a few things but they're up and running again now. We had to make Anderson believe he'd won, so we made it easier for him to walk right in."

Jenna shuddered. "I wonder if they'll ever find the other twenty-five women he claims to have murdered."

"That will depend if he talks." Kane finished his coffee and stood. "But I doubt the DA will cut a deal with him. We've enough on tape to put him away. He'll never be free." He glanced down at her. "I'll make a few sandwiches. We'll have to hurry if you plan to see the end of the judging."

Jenna threw back the blankets. "Yeah, I promised Julie we'd be there." She dashed into the shower.

The number of townsfolk who came up to Jenna and shook her hand in gratitude for placing herself in danger to catch a serial killer surprised her, but she was even more so when Mayor Petersham stood up in front of the entire crowd and thanked her and her deputies. Seeing Wolfe and his three daughters chatting to Agent Martin, she eased through the crowd to join them. She squeezed Julie's arm. "Are you excited?"

"I don't expect to win a ribbon." Julie smiled. "It's wonderful just having my work in the town hall gallery." She pointed to three landscapes some ways down from hers. "Those are Mr. Anderson's. I'm surprised they allowed him to compete considering he tried to kill me."

Jenna stared at the pictures, then grabbed Kane's arm and dragged him closer. "That place is familiar and yet it doesn't resemble Black Rock Falls."

"I recognize it as well, especially the broken windmill." Kane moved closer, then turned and beckoned Wolfe. "We recognize this place, do you?"

"Yeah." Wolfe pulled out his cellphone and scanned his files. "Look, it's from the crime scene photographs of Christine Pullman." He moved to the next picture. "This is where he murdered Joy Coran."

Jenna noticed a long hair curled in the paint in the right-hand corner of each canvas. Shocked by the implications, she swallowed hard, and then lowered her voice to just above a whisper. "Shane, look here." She pointed. "Is that a hair?"

"It sure looks like it and from what I can see they're different colors." He leaned closer. "There's a red flower on each of these three paintings and they resemble dried blood but I'd need to test it to be sure."

Astonished, Jenna eased her way to Agent Martin's side and explained. "He has pictures all over his walls. If he used the paintings as reminders of where he murdered or buried his victims and left blood and hair on each one, you'll be able to tie him to all of them."

"Wolfe will be able to check if that's human blood in minutes." Martin frowned. "That's all I need to haul all the pictures into the FBI forensic labs."

She didn't need to ask Wolfe; he'd already dashed to his vehicle to collect a testing kit. They all stood waiting for him to complete the test. "Well?"

"It's human blood." Wolfe held up a test tube. "It's overlaid on dry oil paint, so we'll be able to collect viable DNA." He squeezed Jenna's shoulder. "If these match the missing women, you've just solved about twenty-five crimes."

"I'll confiscate these paintings now and have a forensics team out at Anderson's home within the hour." Agent Martin shook Jenna's hand. "You can leave this to me now, Jenna, and take some downtime."

Jenna grinned at him. "I think I might just do that."

An announcement came over the loudspeakers.

"Ladies and gentlemen and fine young people of Black Rock Falls, the committee has made a decision. Second runner-up goes to Julie Wolfe for her picture titled Brutal Winter.*"*

The whoops and hollering that echoed around the hall as Julie mounted the stage to collect her ribbon continued on, drowning out the names of the other winners. Jenna reached for Kane's hand and they linked fingers. She smiled up at him. "That's our town. Perfect one day—"

"Crazy as hell the next." Kane squeezed her fingers. "I wouldn't have it any other way."

A LETTER FROM D.K. HOOD

Dear Reader,

I am delighted you chose my novel and joined me in the exciting world of Kane and Alton in *Whisper in the Night*.

If you enjoyed *Whisper in the Night*, and would like to find out about all of my latest releases, you can sign up at the following link. Your email address will never be shared and you can unsubscribe at any time.

www.bookouture.com/dk-hood

Writing this story has been a thrilling adventure for me. Pushing Kane and Alton to their limits and the limits of my imagination was exciting and kept me awake into the early hours. I love forensic science and crime investigation, so enjoyed researching every aspect of the crime scenes.

I really love hearing from readers because when I write, I want you to follow every aspect of the story – so please get in touch on my Facebook page or Twitter or through my website.

Thank you so much for your support.
D.K. Hood

@DKHood_Author

dkhoodauthor

www.dkhood.com

dkhood-author.blogspot.com.au

ACKNOWLEDGEMENTS

Many thanks to all the wonderful readers who took the time to post great reviews of my books and to those amazing people who hosted me on their blogs. I'd like to add a huge THANK YOU to the Bookouture team, who make writing books a pleasure.

Made in the USA
Monee, IL
24 August 2020